Godwine Kingmaker

Part One of

The Last Great Saxon Earls

Mercedes Rochelle

Godwine Kingmaker

Part One of
The Last Great Saxon Earls

Mercedes Rochelle

Winchester, UK
Washington, USA

First published by Top Hat Books, 2015
Top Hat Books is an imprint of John Hunt Publishing Ltd., Laurel House, Station Approach, Alresford, Hants, SO24 9JH, UK
office1@jhpbooks.net
www.johnhuntpublishing.com

For distributor details and how to order please visit the 'Ordering' section on our website.

ISBN: 978 1 78279 801 9
Library of Congress Control Number: 2014949209

A CIP catalogue record for this book is available from the British Library.

Design: Stuart Davies

Printed in the USA by Edwards Brothers Malloy

1

Disentangling a squirming lamb and nudging it from the woods, a tall sturdy youth stood up, hands on hips, and stretched his back. Suddenly he froze, turning his head at the sound of rustling leaves. For a moment he didn't see anything and he looked at the tree-tops, noting the stillness of the branches. He cocked his head and listened once more before shrugging his shoulders and taking a step. Then he stopped, letting out his breath in a long, wondering aah.

Pushing his way out from the trees, an obviously confused Dane stumbled into the clearing, easily recognized by his forked beard and heavy braids. The man's brawny arms were naked but for heavy gold bands, though his chest was covered with a coat of chain maille. He wore a conical-shaped helm with a long nose-piece. A broadsword was gripped in one hand, poised to strike.

The other's first inclination was to stay hidden. The stranger hadn't noticed him as yet; however, he seemed to be looking with interest at the herd. That was too much. Deciding to take his chances rather than lose a sheep, the youth stepped forward, startling the Dane.

Turning with the agility of a wild animal, the warrior crouched, sword upraised. He eyed the other for only a moment before standing again, and slapping his weapon into its sheath.

"Well, it appears that you and I are alone in this accursed forest," he said familiarly in the Saxon tongue, "and I can see that you are unarmed. My name is Ulf, and I have managed to have gotten myself lost. What be your name, lad?"

The other looked at him curiously. In these days of turmoil, the sight of a Dane was not an uncommon one. But the Saxons tended to keep their distance from these unwelcome visitors, and the herdsman had rarely seen one close up. And yet, though the Danes were cursed as the enemy of England, this man didn't seem to be all that terrible. Indeed, his blue eyes sparkled, and his round cheeks, ruddy above a thick, yellow mustache, bespoke a genial acquaintance with his native ale.

Trusting to his own impulses, the young man held out a hand. "My name is Godwine, son of Wulfnoth."

The Dane grasped his hand with a crushing grip, nearly making the shepherd grimace. But Godwine prided himself on never showing pain.

"Well, Godwine son of Wulfnoth. As I said, I have been trying to find my way out of these woods since yesterday eve. I am quite turned around. I will make it worth your while if you would show me how to get back to my ships, which lie in the Severn River."

Disturbed, Godwine turned his back to the man, sending his dogs after the sheep. "Do you come from the battle at Sherstone?" he asked finally.

His companion raised his eyebrows in surprise, but said nothing.

"I suppose you got lost chasing Saxons from the battle-field," Godwine added bitterly.

This one was no laggard; Ulf decided to be honest with him. "If you want to know the truth," he said, trying to look as sincere as possible, "I am not sure who won that battle. Your countrymen are fierce fighters, when inspired by your Edmund Ironside..."

"Our King," the shepherd said, his tone demanding respect.

"I am not one to argue that point," Ulf demurred. "Come, while you show me the way, I will tell you about it..."

Godwine did not move. "You must be mad, asking help from a Saxon."

The Dane hesitated, losing some of his assurance. The young man looked hard at him with sharp brown eyes, and his perfectly straight teeth were clenched. His arms were crossed, exposing sinewy muscles. Then, suddenly inspired, Ulf pulled a gold ring from his finger, holding it out. "Here, lad. It is yours for the asking."

Relaxing, Godwine took the ring. It was beautifully worked, intricately wound with curling serpents. Seeing that the ring was of great value, Godwine stopped to think of the powerful position this man might hold with the Danes. Perhaps he was an important chieftain, commander of many men. One could go far in his favor.

And what was Godwine's alternative? Although his father was Thegn of Sussex, his reputation had been tainted several years ago by an accusation that destroyed his command of the King's fleet. Wulfnoth was disgraced—wrongfully he said, mouthing the name Eadric Streona as the author of all his woes. But it made no difference. Perhaps this was his one opportunity to turn things around.

All these thoughts went through Godwine's head in seconds, while he looked from the ring to the waiting Dane. Then, nodding, he gave the band back to Ulf.

"No. I will not take your ring. But I will try to bring you back to your ships, and you can reward me however you see fit."

Turning, he started to move his herd, motioning for his companion to follow. "But the way is long and difficult," he said, whistling to the dogs. "And the woods are full of Saxons, who would do great harm to you, and to me as your guide. We must return to my house and await the darkness so we can travel in secrecy."

Ulf followed willingly, trusting the good sense and decision of his guide. Not that he had a lot of choices.

Godwine did not live far away; he led the Dane to a modest thatched-roof house, perched on a hill above a considerable barnyard. The youth herded the sheep back into their pen, and motioned for Ulf accompany him to the house.

An older man was standing at the door, whose smoldering face resembled Godwine's too much to doubt his identity. One glance at his son's companion was enough, however, to change his expression from irritability to curiosity. He turned inside without a word, pulling a chair from under the table as he passed, and nodding at his wife to go into the other room.

Ulf didn't seem to notice any discomfort on the part of his host. He pulled out the chair from the head of the table, graciously thanked Wulfnoth for a large mug of ale, and contented himself with the company of the sheep-dogs, while Godwine followed his father outside.

Wulfnoth was a reasonable man. "I did not expect to see you until nightfall," was all he said.

Godwine turned a look toward the house. "I met this man in the forest. He needs a guide back to his ships."

The older man stroked his chin, his sharp eyes narrowing. "An enemy, all alone and at your mercy. And you decided to help him."

Stumped for a moment, Godwine's smile came to his rescue. "What an opportunity, father. He has the look of a leader. With luck, maybe he will take me into his service."

Wulfnoth sighed. Godwine was his son in more ways than one. Unbeknownst to Godwine, he, too, briefly served the Danes when it served his purpose. But that was many years ago…actually, not that many years. Nonetheless, in this time of change, the lad had learned on his own how to take advantage of his opportunities.

Even so, it was unusual to welcome a Dane into his house.

"I had great plans for you...but I did not quite expect it to turn out this way." He put an arm around his son's shoulders. "You know what this means. You must go with him now. There is no turning back. If anyone were to discover that you aided a Dane..."

"I know. But father, they conquered this country once. It will not take much for them to conquer it again. And then, I will be on the right side."

Wulfnoth smiled sadly at his son. "Is it the right side because it's the winning side?"

But Godwine was already pulling away from him, anxious to join his new friend. "Father, I have seen what it means to lose. When you are defeated, it does not matter what is right or wrong."

Confounded, Wulfnoth let him go, turning aside to check on the animals. He needed a moment to recover himself. Was Godwine right? He didn't like being on the wrong side of the law, no matter how justified his actions were. And with that cursed Eadric Streona turning up at every opportunity, he had no way to improve his situation.

Filling the water trough, Wulfnoth decided to follow his son's lead. What else could he do? If he were to destroy Godwine's chances now, he might only make matters worse.

And Godwine was right: the Danes were very likely to take over the country again. It was a mere three years ago—in 1013—that Swegn Forkbeard conquered all of England. Only Swegn's untimely death a few months later gave the Saxons the opportunity to overturn the Danish advantage. They recalled Aethelred to the throne, even though he was the one who had abandoned England in the first place

Yes, it was easy to blame their troubles on old Aethelred, who some called *un-read*—no counsel—because of his habit of making all the wrong decisions. His policy of paying tribute money to the Danes was utterly self-defeating. They would leave, loaded with English silver, then come back the next year for more.

When Aethelred finally died, only a few months ago, his son Edmund Ironside was left with a kingdom little larger than London. His resources were severely limited; there was no money in the treasury after the shambles of his father's reign.

And now he had to deal with a new invasion of Danes, led by Swegn's son, the fierce Canute. It was a wonder that Edmund withstood the Danes at all. But he kept coming back, somehow finding a new army, somehow finding the energy to attack this Canute, whose very name made a Saxon tremble.

There was no doubt that Canute had a claim to the throne, as far as it went. His father had been King of England; the Danish half of England had already elected him king before the Saxon half recalled Aethelred. The Saxons had hoped that on Aethelred's return Canute would then go away and leave them alone. After all, he had Denmark to keep him occupied.

Foolish hope indeed, as the Saxons learned.

For in taking this step, they didn't reckon on Canute's determination. He went away all right, so furious that he mutilated his father's 200 hostages, cutting off their hands, ears, and noses. But he left only to gain reinforcements from his native Denmark, and re-invade England with a vengeance.

Wulfnoth shivered, hanging his bucket on a nail. This was not the kind of man one looked forward to calling King. And his son Godwine had chosen to serve him.

"I tell you, Godwine," Ulf was saying, as Wulfnoth entered the house. "Sherstone was one of the damnedest battles I ever fought." He turned around, nodding a greeting. "Fine ale you have, I will say. Could you spare another mug full?"

Wulfnoth went to his cask, filling a pitcher. Then he told his wife Godgifu to make enough food for four.

Waiting until his mug was refilled, Ulf continued, as Wulfnoth joined them. "For two days we fought, shedding the blood of many good men. The ravens had no lack of food, I tell you. My Lord Canute had the men of Wiltshire and Somerset on his side..." Wulfnoth nodded; he wasn't the only Wiltshire man to have served the Danes.

"The first day, there was no telling who had the upper hand," the other continued, after taking a deep draught, "but in the forenoon of the second day, your Edmund gathered a great deal of strength, and forced his way right up to Canute. Amazing man," he added, wiping his mouth, "the kind of warrior about whom legends are made."

Wulfnoth nodded, pouring more ale. Despite himself, he was

beginning to like this Ulf. It was always a good man who appreciated his enemy's qualities.

"And Canute?" asked Godwine.

"Ah, lad, sometimes I think he leads a charmed life. He was mounted, and Edmund's blow was so fierce, that it cleaved his shield in two, and went right through his horse's neck. I know. I was there. If my boys had not been so quick to rush forward, Canute might be feasting in Valhalla right now."

Godwine shot his father a knowing look.

"As it was," Ulf went on, "your Edmund killed many of my men, though they succeeded in pushing him back. But I could see that more reinforcements were coming to his aid. Things might have gone badly for us, but..."

He turned a clear eye on the boy, unaffected by alcohol. "It was Eadric Streona who turned the battle."

Wulfnoth dropped the jug and it fell over on the table; luckily it was almost empty. Godwine jumped up and pulled off his shirt, sopping up the remaining ale while pretending not to notice his father's reaction. "Whose side was he fighting on this time?" he asked bitterly.

"Ah, I see that you know what I am talking about. I tell you, Godwine, there never lived a fouler creature in the guise of a man. He has done your country more harm than all the Northmen put together."

The Dane leaned forward. "He fought for Canute. At just that moment in the battle, Eadric cut off the head of some man, whose face resembled Edmund's and held it up to the English, shouting, 'Fly, ye men of Dorset and Devon! Fly, and save yourselves. Here is your Edmund's head.'"

Godwine and his father stared at each other. This was news, indeed.

"Yes, it was mad for your countrymen to heed him, knowing that he fought on the other side. But men do not reason well when their blood is flowing from their veins, and at any moment death may come to claim them. The Saxons took one look at that gory head, and all the fight went out of them. They simply panicked, lad, and wanted to run away as fast as possible."

Even Ulf seemed saddened. "Well, your Edmund had his head about him yet, and he tore his helmet off and shouted at his men to look, he was alive, it was all a trick. Seeing the dastard Eadric, he took aim with a spear and nearly pierced the traitor through. But Eadric was quick, and the spear missed, running through two men who were next to him.

"Too bad for you that the spear missed its mark. We would all be better off without that man. Although Canute cannot do without his treachery, he despises the sight of him."

He paused for a satisfied belch and tried to refill his mug, shrugging his shoulders when he found the jug empty.

"As I was saying, Edmund did his best to rally his men, but it was too late. They were fleeing as fast as they could, throwing their weapons on the ground and scattering in every direction. I and my men pursued a portion of them into the forest, but I became separated from the rest, and spent the night searching for a way back. But I fear I must have gotten more and more lost. That is when I met you, Godwine...a most fortunate accident."

That said, Ulf paused while Godwine's mother placed some food in front of him. He grabbed a chicken leg and took a big bite. Ulf hadn't eaten for some time.

His listeners were silent, but only for a few moments. Shaking off his distress at the plight of his fellow Saxons, Godwine joined him. He had made his decision; there was no turning back.

After the sun had gone down, Ulf and his new young friend made ready to leave. While Godwine was busy saddling two of Wulfnoth's best horses, his father took the Dane aside with a heavy face.

"We place into your trust our only son. I am sure you understand that he can no longer stay here. If any of our neighbors discover that he has aided you..." Wulfnoth seemed to falter, but he recovered himself. "Let us say, his safety would be in doubt. If you have any influence with Canute, perhaps you can place him into the royal household."

Ulf looked at his host with sympathy. "Wulfnoth, you have no need to worry. I give you my word. Your boy shows great promise...I see many noble qualities in his bearing. Besides…" His face broke into a wide grin. "I did not tell you before, but I am a Jarl, and wield much influence among my people."

Wulfnoth stepped back a pace, and looked at his wife. A Jarl, same as an Earl in England. He had dared not hope for so much.

"And," added Ulf, "I married Canute's sister." He was about to say more when Godwine came up, leading the horses. The Dane immediately mounted, moving out of earshot.

Left alone with his parents, Godwine suddenly felt uncomfortable. Beneath all his bravado, he was still an inexperienced eighteen year-old who had never left home before.

His mother, ordered to stay in the back of the house, did not know what was happening, aside from the indications that her son was leaving. Shaking off her husband's restraining hand, she threw herself into Godwine's arms, crying and begging him to stay.

"Hush, woman," Wulfnoth said, more sharply than he intended. "This is none of your business."

Not used to disobeying her husband, Godgifu stilled her objections, but clung to her son, sobbing. Godwine raised his eyes imploringly, and Wulfnoth moved forward, taking his wife into his arms. He held out his right hand.

"Remember all the things I have told you, son," he said softly, "and you should not go wrong."

Blinking back the tears, Godwine clasped his father's hand. Then, before Wulfnoth knew it, he was on his horse, riding in a circle for one last look, before joining his companion.

Their hoof beats seemed to last forever in the quiet night air. "Godspeed," said Wulfnoth softly, although his son could no longer hear him.

2

The Dane and the Saxon started off at a good pace, maintaining a companionable silence until they were safely at the edge of the forest. Godwine drew rein then, turning in his saddle to take one last look at the land he knew so well.

"Yes, lad, remember it now," Ulf said quietly, "because when you return, you will be a different man, and all this will have changed for you."

Godwine glanced at this man who had so suddenly come into his life. Although probably anxious to be on his way back to safety, Ulf showed surprising patience with one whom he must consider a boy. A rush of gratitude flowed through Godwine, which suddenly changed into elation.

Finally he was free, to venture into that capricious world out there, and he felt totally prepared to face whatever was waiting for him. Kicking his horse, the youth surged forward, saying, "What are we waiting for?"

He felt a little ashamed at the jovial tone of his voice, when he should be sorry about leaving his family. But Ulf didn't seem to notice. He was following right behind, as though prepared for Godwine's abrupt start.

Godwine was right about the difficult passage. It took the pair all night to reach the river Severn. The morning light was filtering through the thinning woods when Ulf caught sight of a patch of red. Slapping the boy on the shoulder, the Dane let out a whoop, and kicked his horse into a gallop.

"There is my very own warship," he called back, "just as I left her."

His voice startled the men on watch, but their defensive postures gave way to joy when they recognized their chief. Running forward, they met Ulf halfway, shouting their relief and practically pulling him from his mount.

Godwine followed more slowly, somewhat taken aback by his companion's boisterous welcome. At first, no one seemed to notice him, until Ulf waved him forward, introducing the youth as his guide.

"Treat him like one of us," he said more seriously. "The lad did me a great favor, at much risk to himself. I intend to take him under my wing, and teach him how to become a warrior."

This statement was met with good-natured laughter, as the others turned back to the ship. Tying the horses to a tree, Ulf and Godwine climbed aboard the longship, as the other Danes began to wake up.

The Jarl pulled up a box and sat down for a full breakfast, gesturing for Godwine to take a seat at his side. He listened as his men told him of their situation—that the battle at Sherstone greatly reduced their numbers. Ulf nodded grimly at their losses.

Godwine didn't listen too closely at first; he was all eyes, taking in his new surroundings. The ship was surprisingly shallow, which accounted for the ease with which it could slip into rivers. The sides, gracefully curved from a heavy keel, were made of overlapping planks so thin that Godwine was amazed they didn't crack in the waves; at their thickest they weren't much more than an inch. The ship was painted nearly everywhere above the water line. A tall, intricately carved dragon's head adorned the stem of the boat; its tail made a corresponding curl. Down-river from them, Godwine could spot two more ships.

Tearing his eyes away from the dragon-head, Godwine tried to pay attention. But he found himself staring at the scar that ran down the speaker's face, perilously close to one eye.

"...and so Canute withdrew our men around midnight of the second day, and headed back to London. It is reported that Edmund is pursuing him there."

Ulf nodded, deep in thought.

"Of course," continued the other, "Canute wanted us to

follow as soon as we were able. But we decided to rest another day, in the hopes that you would return."

"I am glad of that," mumbled the Jarl, pulling off a piece of bread for Godwine. "And so the battle was a defeat?"

"I cannot say. We left the Saxons in possession of the field, but their loss was severe.

"Oh, and our old friend Eadric," he added with a grunt, "decided to change sides again, although perhaps it is no more than a ploy to distract that fool Edmund."

Godwine stiffened.

"Forgave him all his treachery, did Edmund, and took him back into favor."

"He will be sorry for that," Ulf said, looking sideways at the Saxon.

Reluctantly, Godwine couldn't help but agree. Big-heartedness seemed to be the King's only fault.

Ulf had heard enough. He strode across the deck, drinking his ale and pausing here and there to playfully kick the men who were still sleeping. They woke instantly, joking with him about his disappearance.

"What was her name?" shouted one.

"She must have been very good, to keep you from your men," cried another, who got a faceful of water for his effort.

"There was no *She* this time, my lads, but my own blindness that got me lost," said Ulf as he sent a man with a message to the next ship. "If you are not too sodden to notice, you will see that a fine young Saxon has joined our ranks. If it were not for him, I would still be wandering that cursed forest. Any one of you gives the boy trouble, you will have to answer to my fist for it."

Godwine leaped to his feet, ready to interpose; he wanted no one to champion him. But his words died in his throat when he saw how the men were taking Ulf's threat. They laughed and guffawed, taking him no more seriously than if he had promised to throw them overboard. Indeed, they seemed unconcerned about the youth. One of the Danes called him over to help take down the tent.

"You take this down to travel?" Godwine asked, regaining his old confidence.

"This tent serves us for sleeping," the other said, as he began to unlash the wool tent cover from the triangular wooden frame spanning the twenty-foot deck. The Dane straightened, handing Godwine one end of the tent cloth.

"We fold it this way, first," he said, demonstrating. "What was your name again?"

"Godwine, son of Wulfnoth. And yours?"

"Eirik. Yes, there you have it. And you want to go a'viking with us?" There was a hint of disdain in the man's voice, though Godwine suspected that he was only a few years older than himself.

"And why not," he said, more in challenge than in truth; this was not his idea of putting his talents to better use.

"Well, it seems to me that you are not trained for such a life." Eirik looked him up and down appraisingly. *Trained he may not be,* the Dane thought, despite himself, *but the Saxon had a body that was firm and strong. The boy was accustomed to hard work.*

Godwine reddened under his scrutiny. "My father fought in our land's defense. He taught me all I needed to know. Although," he added in a lower voice, looking around in embarrassment, "I do not own a weapon."

The Dane threw back his head in a loud laugh, ignoring Godwine's insulted expression. "You are a straightforward fellow. That is good. If a blade is all you lack, we can fix that right away."

Striding to a small pile of weapons in a box, Eirik shuffled through them, until he found a sword he liked. He pulled it out, balanced it in his hand, then unexpectedly threw it, pommel down, at Godwine.

Startled, the Saxon automatically caught the handle.

Eirik grinned. "We collect extras if we see something we like. I think it will suit you well." He turned back to the box and pulled out an axe with a short handle. "Then I'll show you how to use my favorite weapon." Pausing only a second, he threw the axe and it thudded into the tent post, just behind Godwine's head. The Saxon suppressed a shudder, pretending not to notice his close brush with death.

Godwine concentrated on the sword and turned the blade over, admiring the engravings along its center. Eirik had spoken rightly; the sword had a good weight, not too long, nicely balanced, and lent itself to a good, solid cut. Godwine gave a couple of experimental slashes in the air, when he was interrupted by Ulf's hearty laugh.

"Not so fast, lad. I am right behind you."

Embarrassed, the Saxon turned.

"You will have to give your sword a name," the Jarl went on conversationally, "when you have used it a bit. I call mine snake-biter," he added, patting his sheath, "because it strikes with the quickness of a snake.

"Come, I would bring you forward, so you can watch my little fleet come together."

Pushing the sword through his belt, Godwine followed curiously. Ulf seemed to be able to do many things at one time; he gave orders for the two horses to be brought aboard, while inspecting the sail, chattering away as if Godwine had his full attention.

"Don't be laggards, boys," he laughed, as four men struggled with the two frightened horses. Godwine held his breath; never before had the beasts left solid ground.

Ulf grinned. "Do not worry, lad. Those men know exactly what they are doing. We do not like to bring horses aboard, for they crowd us, but we manage when we must. Your mounts are too fine to leave behind."

Sure enough, with a sudden burst and a scramble, the horses

leaped aboard, while the men moved aside for them. Slowly, the animals were coaxed to an open area where the deck planks had been removed to make room for cargo.

Not worried about that minor detail, Ulf turned proudly, sweeping his arm around. "Twenty-five ells long she is," he bragged. "And yet the mast," the Jarl added, pointing to the thick, wooden beam, still couched amidships, "is only twenty ells high. You will see the sail in its full glory soon enough... Are you ready yet, you laggards? I see the other ships moving."

Godwine looked forward, watched their neighbors glide quietly away. He felt a surge of excitement.

The Danes picked up their oars and sat, sixteen on each side. First they stood the oars on end, leaned them away from the boat, then passed their handle to the fellow on the opposite side, who pulled the oar toward himself before fitting the blade into the opposite oarhole and pushing it back. They paused, waiting for everyone to be ready. It was an amazingly fluid motion.

The iron anchor, attached to a rope, was quickly hauled up with strong hands. Then, after a few deliberate pushes with the oars, the ship was grabbed by the current, and moved quickly downstream. One man stood at the rear of the ship, holding a thick steering oar fastened against the right side.

Godwine marveled at the symmetry of the rowers. Together, the oars were raised then lowered into the water, barely slipping below the surface before they came up again, dripping identical streams from each flat blade.

"We row in a river, in the fjords, and in waters of precarious navigation," said Ulf, returning with the rest of his breakfast in hand. "And, of course, when there is no wind. But these are sailing ships, and perform best as such."

Godwine saw nothing wrong with their performance. The movement was so smooth... As if they were a part of the river.

"I tell you," Ulf murmured, his mouth full, "there is no other life than on the sea. With the salty spray in your face, and the cries of the gulls all around you, the mystery of unknown shores to discover, what more does a man need to call himself complete?"

One of the horses snorted. Ulf laid a hand on its neck. "You will come to like it too, my nervous friend, if you do not kick the ship apart first," he laughed.

They were a quarter-mile from the river's mouth, and passed to the sea quickly. As they cleared the last of the overhanging foliage, Godwine let out a gasp. The rest of the fleet was already on the water. "I thought there were only three of us."

Ulf chuckled heartily. "I would be a poor Jarl, only to own three ships. Why, I have three longships that make this one seem small, but they are with Canute right now. No, lad, we merely drop anchor in different tributaries, or in different harbors, so as not to be trapped all together. Twenty ships I have here, and more at home. I tell you, it is a sight to gladden the heart of any sailor."

As if in response to this, the men began cheering at the other vessels, and answering shouts carried across the water.

Godwine could see that all the fleet was painted the same—in red and white swirls—and that many had a dragon prow like their own. The Danes were busy setting a row of shields along both sides; on his own ship, Ulf's men were doing the same, having pulled in their oars.

Without a pause, the Northmen readied the mast. Ulf pointed out a heavy block of oak, fastened to the center of the keel, with a hole to take base of the mast. "We call that the old woman: the keelson. Watch, lad, how easy it all is."

Standing at the stem, some of the men began tugging on a heavy rope attached to a pulley. As the mast slowly stood on end, others made sure that the base was guided directly into its socket. They wedged it all in.

Once vertical, the mast was supported by ropes on both sides. Then the yard was raised with more pulleys and ropes, and the sail was unfurled. Godwine nodded. Ulf was right; it was indeed glorious.

The sail was about twenty-six ells long, which made up for a lack of height in the mast. Red and white striped, it was made out of heavy woolen strips, woven into a rope network that gave it strength.

"That must be heavy," said Godwine.

"Yes, lad, and awkward at times, especially in a storm. There was once a King of Norway, Eystein, who was knocked overboard and drowned by a yard that belonged to another ship; that's how close were they while sailing. That is why we tie it at both ends, as you can see. Now look behind you, Godwine. A sight you never saw before, eh?"

As Ulf's ship took the lead, the rest came behind in a loose triangular formation, their sails unfurled, riding over the waves instead of cutting through them. The bows moved down, looking like they would plunge under the surface, then rose again majestically, undaunted.

As Godwine opened his mouth to say something, a swell broke against the ship, filling his mouth with water. His stomach took a big lurch.

"Alas," commented Ulf, handing the youth a pail, "we do have to bail."

* * *

It was obvious to everyone that Canute was chafing from their inactivity. The fleet had been sitting at anchor for a whole day at the mouth of the Thames rather than at London, where he wanted them to be. As he paced furiously across the deck, the crew gave him a wide berth.

Canute was no more than twenty years old, but the others on the ship, many years his senior, regarded him with caution and even a little fear. They knew they were not dealing with a capricious juvenile; Canute, King of the Danes, was a rigid, dangerous ruler whose very bearing commanded respect. However, his manner bespoke one who had come to power before he had learned the patience that went with wisdom. He was a handsome blond man, of medium height. The only thing that marred his looks was a slight bend to his long, narrow nose, as if it had once been broken.

The young king paused in his pacing for a moment, frowning at the thought of Edmund Ironside, who had broken up his force so effectively. Not for the first time, Canute wondered how that weakling Aethelred could raise such a formidable son. Since he made his bid for England, Edmund had been his constant shadow, always within striking range, nipping, prodding, resisting for weeks now, and showed no sign of tiring. This last incident, Canute had been unable to withstand Edmund's attack without the support of Ulf, and he had retreated downstream, to await the return of his Jarl.

Taking a deep breath, he looked for the hundredth time at the horizon; then he squinted, cursing the sun's glare. Yes, there they were, the long awaited ships. Canute allowed himself a smile, relieved. He was glad his brother-in-law had decided to show up; if Ulf had let him down, things would have gotten ugly...for the both of them. *Lose control of Ulf, and the rest of the Jarls would follow.* This he could not allow to happen. Ever.

Canute resumed his pacing. He was fond of Ulf; of that there was no question. Ten years his senior, Ulf had taught him how to drink, how to wench, even how to fight. Canute couldn't have found a better companion. But, unfortunately, this gave Ulf a certain power over him while he was still a prince, which managed to carry over into his kingship. No matter how hard he tried to fight it, Canute still found himself looking to Ulf for approval—even for guidance. And the Jarl, ever a sharp judge of character, knew this and used his power accordingly. So far, there had been an uneasy truce between them while Canute tested his way through the early months of his reign; but the young king half-expected a confrontation, as soon as Ulf tired of playing the game. At best, Ulf would be unpleasantly surprised. At the worst...

* * *

Godwine was trying to absorb all of his new experiences without betraying himself as an outsider. But as he and Ulf approached Canute's flagship, he gaped at the size of the vessel. The sides were so high that it looked like climbing a castle wall. Quickly, he counted thirty-six oar holes along its length.

Noticing his wonder, Ulf nodded. "She can carry 300 men. They do not get any larger. She's bigger than anything I have."

Godwine thought he detected a note of envy. They climbed a rope ladder to the deck, and Godwine took a good look around before clambering over the gunnel. There was a white silk tent on the deck, before which stood a tall young man, hands on hips. He nodded, frowning, as the pair approached.

"Ulf, you old renegade. I was concerned about you." The corners of Canute's mouth moved upward a bit as Ulf came closer, and Godwine could see that he had trouble keeping a stern tone with the Jarl. Ulf paid little heed to his tone, casually pushing into Canute's tent in search of some ale.

"What happened to you, Ulf?" Canute followed him to the door-flap. "You and your men have been sorely missed these last two days." He spoke crisply, without hesitation.

"Canute, I would introduce my young friend, and rescuer, Godwine." Ulf poked his head from the tent, gesturing to Godwine with a drinking-horn. "If it had not been for him, I might still be wandering those cursed woods near Sherstone."

"Ah, I begin to understand." Canute studied the youth, raising his head slightly. "Tell me, Godwine, what is your father's name?"

"Wulfnoth, Thegn of Sussex," he replied, surprised.

"Wulfnoth, Thegn of Sussex. Very Saxon indeed." Canute looked thoughtful for a moment. "You have taken a great risk, in helping an enemy of your father's."

Godwine's mouth separated and his lips drew back, betraying his intense concentration. The observation was blunt, and it stung a little. Did Canute mean to insult him, or was he trying to be sympathetic? The King's tone was flat, unfathomable. It could go either way. Godwine resolved to be straightforward.

"Frankly, Sire, I do not see the Danes as our enemy. Perhaps England would be best served by putting an end all this useless fighting."

"Yes, yes, you are right," said Canute, but his eyes pierced through Godwine, as if searching to see if his words were genuine. Godwine held his gaze, though he quailed inside; for even he did not know whether he spoke from the heart, or from the head.

After what seemed an interminable time, Canute looked back at Ulf, who was coming out of the tent, satisfied. "I see why you trust the boy. He is outspoken, but not foolish."

Godwine silently let out a breath, relaxing his guard. He had said the right thing.

"Godwine, you are welcome to serve with us. But will you fight on our side, if fight we must, against your own kind?"

The request was as upsetting as it was logical, yet so unexpected that Godwine nearly flinched. There hadn't been time to give this issue any thought; just a few hours ago he was a bored, restless shepherd, and today he was asked to fight his own people. *Could this really be happening?*

Godwine knew what kind of danger he was in. Life meant little to these people. But he suspected that Canute was merely testing him. If he seemed too anxious to cooperate, he might be labeled an assassin. Too guarded, and he could be equally mistrusted. This young king was not one to be lied to; already he could see that. Straightening, Godwine shook his head. "I cannot."

Ulf turned to him, his mouth open. But Canute put a hand on the Jarl's arm.

"He is proud," the King said, his eyes narrowing at the Saxon. "He is young and inexperienced. But not for long, I promise you, Godwine. You will learn that the boundaries blur, between right and necessity.

"It is all right, Ulf. Let the boy stand guard on your ship. Someone must. You will do that, will you not, Godwine?"

Shaken, the youth nodded. He knew how close he had just come to disaster. "Yes, of course."

"Very good. Go now, back to Ulf's ship. I need to speak to him alone."

Godwine bowed, backing away. When Canute turned away, he quickly climbed down, happy to get out of sight. He needed time to consider what kind of man he had come to serve, without facing those scrutinizing eyes. Looking again at the Danish flagship, Godwine shivered. The magnitude of his decision weighed upon him. He had not merely gone over to the enemy camp; he admired the Danish King.

* * *

The next morning Godwine felt like he hadn't slept a wink all night. He discovered that not everyone fit under the tent, and he wasn't used to curling up on a pile of ropes under the stars using an old sailcloth for a blanket. But then, he decided, he preferred not sleeping so close to a bunch of smelly, hairy, snoring strangers anyway.

And then, before he had even fully awakened, the whole lot of them were preparing for battle, and the ship was once again being secreted up a little stream for protection. A second boat followed and was quickly tied down behind theirs. Godwine was watching the preparations when Ulf poked him with a piece of bread.

"Here, lad, take this for now. We will be back in no time, and you can guard the ship while we are gone. And keep a good watch," he warned, swinging his leg over the gunwale. He dropped into the water and the others followed him, leaving Godwine and two others on this boat, and three men to guard the second ship.

The Saxon stood nervously gripping and ungripping the handle of his new sword. The Danes disappeared into the trees and he marveled at how quietly they moved. He didn't want to think about where they were headed and shook his head slowly, pulling his sword out of his belt and placing it on the wooden seat. After five minutes, he sat down beside the sword.

"What am I doing," he asked himself, taking a bite of the bread. It was stale and he threw it to the side. "I could just disappear right now, and they would consider themselves well rid of me." He scooped a handful of water and splashed his face. "I could find my way home and pretend that nothing happened. Who would be the wiser?" *What about the horses?* The whole adventure had lost its allure by now, and Godwine wished himself back home with his sheep. He stood up again, took a few steps, sat on another sea chest, turned around, scratched his neck, then took a look at Eirik.

His companion stood perfectly still at the stern, axe on his shoulder, listening. He didn't waste energy in idle movements and he had a calm about him that Godwine envied. The Saxon watched the other for many minutes before fidgeting again, trying to imagine a scenario where he could just slip away unnoticed. He stood, rested his foot on the chest and picked up his sword, placing the point next to his toe. He practiced moving the point back and forth. He sighed, letting his eyes close for a second, feeling himself breathe. Then he heard a little splash. Was it a fish?

Godwine jerked his head around then suddenly the planks

beneath his feet shifted, as a man tried to pull himself onto the boat, then another, then another. They were not Norsemen! Before he even knew it, Godwine heard rather than saw an axe fly past him and bury itself into the first man's shoulder. The intruder shouted as he fell backwards, but the others kept coming on, and Godwine took a step backward, putting up his sword to block a cut to his head, then he started swinging wildly to protect himself. This wasn't anything like the training the local sheriffs had imposed on the fyrd.

"Slow down," Eirik barked, coming up beside him. The Dane drove his sword through another man and kicked him into the water, then hacked upward at an arm as it was descending toward Godwine's head. The Saxon fell back then scrambled to his feet just in time to plunge his blade into another man who had suddenly appeared behind Eirik, swinging a club. The man crumpled onto the deck, and the fight was suddenly over.

Godwine knelt over his first kill, chest heaving. He heard the remnants of the attackers running into the forest, dragging a wounded companion between them. From the other boat, two arrows were let loose and one hit its mark. There was a shout and a crash, and then he heard the clamor of returning Norsemen, finishing off the survivors.

Eirik knelt beside him. "It's all right now," he said, almost sympathetically. "They were bold fellows." He got up, nudging his attacker with a boot. "Come, let's get rid of him."

Almost mechanically, Godwine helped Eirik pick up the body and heave it off the ship. Then Ulf and the rest of his companions were back among them, tossing some bundles over the sides and calling to Eirik, some laughing and others cursing. Godwine straightened up as Eirik put an arm around his shoulders.

"How did you fare?" the Jarl called from the shore.

"He did fine," Eirik called to Ulf, knowing that Godwine was still shaken. "Bloodied his sword, he did."

Ulf nodded, turning to attend some other business. Then Eirik moved away, slapping Godwine on the back. No one else seemed to pay attention to him.

Godwine looked at his sword, then slowly wiped it on his tunic. It had all happened so fast that he hadn't had time to think.

But as the day progressed, it seemed that his new companions treated him with a little more tolerance than before, and Ulf gave Godwine enough work to keep him from fretting. After all, Canute was waiting for them.

3

The ships in Canute's force numbered over 200 as they converged on the Thames. The mouth of the estuary started wide then tapered quickly at Tilbury, and the ships naturally spaced themselves to accommodate the narrowing river. Canute had anchored at Greenwich, a favorite gathering place for generations, and was waiting for the rest of his ships. Before long, the river looked black with silent shapes, like so many watery dragons come to the surface.

Godwine couldn't suppress a shudder as he studied the fierce ships, with flaming shields lining the gunnels and dragon heads pointing upriver. London had been the target of so many invasions that it was amazing the city survived at all. All along the river, little settlements sheltered fishing boats that bobbed alongside wooden docks, and thatched-roof huts huddled inside the occasional wooden palisade. By the time the Northmen appeared, the inhabitants had fled into the woods, leaving the villages ripe for the picking.

Once enough ships had gathered, the fleet moved forward, amazing in their symmetry. After passing one last hook-shaped turn in the river, they came within sight of London.

A walled town, London was well protected by towers and turrets, and several spearheads could be seen above the wall as the defenders stood on a raised platform. An occasional arrow was released through slits in the wall, but since their bows were mostly used for hunting, the use of archery was half-hearted.

However, the defense of London Bridge was another matter. Blocking their way, the wooden bridge extended from the city walls, over the river and into the town of Southwark on the opposite shore. At the shore, both ends of the bridge were lined with shops and walls, heavily fortified with covered sheds, turrets, and shelters from which to hurl rocks and other missiles gathered for defense. The bridge was built on stone pilings spaced far enough apart for average-sized boats to fit through while two drawbridges accommodated larger ships. These drawbridges, naturally enough, were lowered for defense and today the rough-hewn timber planks were lined with a throng of determined Saxons. Crouched behind shields, boards, and whatever screens they could wedge into place, the Londoners stood ready with stockpiles of projectiles, arrows, and even boiling water to pour on the ships below.

Standing behind the last oarsman on Ulf's warship, Godwine listened to the muttering of the other warriors as they neared the bridge. "This isn't going to be as easy as Canute said," someone behind him grumbled. "If we can set fire to the bridge," another mused aloud, "that would keep them busy." "I don't think we'll get close enough," a third added. Godwine nodded to himself. He wondered what Canute had in mind.

As they neared the bridge, the foremost ships slowed, waiting for others to catch up while still keeping distance between each other. Ulf's dragon ship was so close to Canute's flag ship that Godwine could hear the banners flapping in the wind and see the great chief pacing across the deck. He almost held his breath as he looked up at Canute's vessel, which seemed to loom, sinister and ominous, over their heads.

Half of the oarsmen stayed at their posts while the others pulled shields from the sides of the ships and held them ready with one hand, balancing javelins with the other. Archers strung their bows, and some readied slings. For a few minutes they eyed the Londoners until someone bellowed "Forward" from Canute's warship. The other ships repeated the order and they inched toward the bridge. The men on the ships worked as a team, ready to release their missiles on command. Having lined up across the river, anchors were thrown to hold the ships in place, dragon heads pointed forward. They were close enough to hear the Saxons shouting at them.

Suddenly all hell broke loose. The Danes from the rear lines released their arrows over the heads of the crouching shieldmen, who then stood and threw their javelins all at the same time. The air was filled with the sharp whoosh of wooden shafts. Then the Londoners responded, and the force from above was devastating. Rocks, spears, arrows came hustling down, and first line of men began to fall back. Other fighters took their place, aiming their bows, throwing more javelins, but they were slowly losing their advantage.

It felt like rain coming back from the bridge, then an avalanche. Godwine tried his best to shield Ulf from the projectiles, but the Jarl was striding back and forth, shouting orders and pulling arrows from his armor, throwing them to the side. Luckily, he seemed to have a charmed life.

Then Godwine heard a thunk at his feet, and whirled around just in time to slap the flames that were licking at his tunic. A blazing arrow was quivering out of the deck, then another sunk into the wood next to it. Someone threw a bucket of water at the fire, and most of it splashed onto Ulf. The Dane turned with a curse, then looked toward the bridge as other flaming arrows came rushing toward them.

"Raise anchor," he shouted. "Reverse oars!"

The other ships were doing the same. No one wanted to deal with a ship on fire. What started as a Norse attack on London Bridge ended as an embarrassing retreat. The ships withdrew back to a bend in the river with a large natural bay and a town called Rotherhithe on the south bank. The Viking chiefs jumped from their ships and gathered on the shore, surrounding Canute.

"We've laid siege to London before," Canute was saying as Ulf and Godwine approached. "We must do it again. This is the key to the kingdom." Most of the men grumbled their agreement, though there were a few loud objections.

"You know that Aethelred and Olaf dragged the bridge down, not three years ago," Canute said, reasoning with Earl Thurkill, his most powerful supporter.

"I was there," someone shouted, and a couple of others concurred. "We tied ropes to the bridge piles and rowed with all our might, tearing them down."

"Yes, but look how quickly they rebuilt it, and stronger than ever," someone else objected.

Everybody was arguing and Canute stepped to the side, frustrated. He gazed out over the marsh, crossing his arms over his chest.

Looking south and west, the land below the Thames spread flat as far as the eye could see; great lowlands were covered with vast stretches of marshy water. Immediately below London, the burgh of Southwark was protected from the tidal waters by a Roman dyke. Who else would build a road atop the sturdy hill and continue the line of water defense all along the south shore of the Thames? In fact, one could see many such dykes crisscross Lambeth Marsh, as it was called, which served to keep Southwark out of the flood plain.

Ulf and Godwine approached Canute and stood by his side, following his gaze. A flock of geese passed overhead, making a huge V and squawking to each other. "You know," Godwine mused, "you could almost sail a ship over that marsh."

Canute turned to him, staring hard. "Say that again," he said.

Godwine blinked in surprise. "I was just speculating that it looks like you could sail across it."

Canute set his mouth, looking over the marsh then back toward the ships. "You might have something there," he muttered, more to himself than to Godwine. "I wonder..."

The King strode back to Thurkill and pulled his elbow, pointing to the marsh. The volume of argument rose considerably.

"Now look what you have done, boy," Ulf said, half scolding, half in wonder as he pushed the Saxon toward the rapidly expanding group. By the time they reached the others, it seemed like a decision had been reached.

"Why not," challenged Canute. "It can be done within a couple of days."

Some were shaking their heads, but these were men of action. "Come," Canute gestured, taking a stand on high ground while the others started gathering a work crew. "Look, there. All we need to do is break through the dyke here, and there," he pointed, "and let the river do the rest of the work. We'll pull our ships through the marsh below Southwark and rejoin the Thames on the other side of the bridge."

Already the King was on the move. "We set up camp here and use this as our base," he directed. "Come, Godwine. Let's show them how it's done."

He slapped the Saxon on the shoulder and grabbed two shovels from one of the Danes as they passed by. Since the Northmen came prepared for siege work, they had many of the necessary tools to get started; for the rest, smaller boats had already set off downstream to raid the local towns for food and supplies.

"Come, Ulf," Canute was calling, "Eirik, come. You have a good head for details. Tovi, Bardi, to my side, friends. We have many hours of daylight left." Canute started down the far side of the dyke, pointing to some trees.

The King turned, looking at the others. Godwine glanced quickly at Ulf then clambered down after Canute. He plunged his shovel in to the hill and started throwing dirt over his shoulder. Canute grinned, then started digging next to him. He started to sing, in time with the shovel strokes:

Yet you broke the Bridge of London
Stout-hearted Warrior
You succeeded in conquering the land
Iron swords made headway
Strongly urged to conflict;

Ancient shields were broken,
Battle's fury mounted.[1]

Godwine didn't know the words, but some of the others did, and soon they were lined up, digging for all they were worth and bellowing the words to the song. Before long, they were vying with each other to call out their favorite work songs, as more and more joined the crew and they started making significant progress. Canute stripped down to his hose and braes, and his wiry muscular arms glistened with sweat. Godwine had a hard time keeping up with him.

By dusk, the camp was ready and food was being passed around. The Danes had made significant progress with the dyke. Canute was pacing again and passed a wineskin to Ulf. He shrugged back into his tunic.

"That was a good day's work," he said to no one in particular. "Once we have broken through and let the tidal waters in, it will be slow going but easier than dragging the ships overland." There were murmurs of assent.

"There are already many large pools of water," Ulf agreed. "Perhaps you have the right of it."

And so it proved. By the end of the next day, as the tide came in, the Danes stood on the top of the bank and watched the water seep through the breach they had made. Canute nodded in satisfaction. The tide was inexorable but the flats were vast and it would take a long time to make a big difference.

Godwine scratched the back of his neck. "What a mess. I thought it was marshy before."

Ulf laughed. "By the time we are finished, you will be used to wet feet."

No one seemed particularly concerned about the labor they were facing. They were only going to bring the smaller ships, after all. The largest warships would remain at Rotherhithe.

They decided to let the tide do its work overnight, and the

Danes resolved that another break in the dyke closer to London would be a good idea. A score of smaller boats were loaded with supplies and moved upriver to the next sandy beach. Godwine watched them go then found a new spot on the hill to set up a little tent. He still preferred to sleep on solid ground whenever possible.

The morning broke fine and cool. Godwine poked his head out of his tent and observed his companions as they were already wrestling the first boat. It was a small supply boat and looked a little dwarfed by the surrounding dyke. Not wanting to be left behind, he threw on his clothes and raced down to help them.

One of the Vikings looked up and it was Canute, sweating and grunting with the rest of them. Godwine gladly took a place at a rope and began tugging. For a moment the boat seemed stuck, then it jerked forward and landed comfortably in the shallow water, rocking a bit. Quickly, the men loaded the vessel with tools and left it to drift. The next boat was a little bigger and was loaded with their gear; soon they would have progressed too far to slough back and forth through the muck; it was a good idea to bring all they needed. Godwine packed up his little tent and stowed it in the third boat; the forth would have to be large enough to accommodate a few men for the night. As he went back to the front Godwine saw that each vessel would break off a little more dirt than the previous one and widen the gap as they went along.

As others struggled with the third boat, Canute called for help to see how they could move the first boat along. More hands joined them as the morning progressed; the men were in good spirits and seemed to enjoy their labor.

Since it would be hard to trench the marsh, it looked like pulling the ships across the water would work best. Placing the rope on his shoulder, Godwine bent to the task. At first, the little boat seemed to move easily enough, but it hit a snag and he went down on his knees. The fellow behind him nearly careened into him but caught himself in time.

"First lesson," Godwine grumbled, embarrassed. "I will need to be more buoyant."

"Like the water," the other man laughed. "Don't worry. Soon we will all be soaked."

It was slow going, and as they directed their steps toward Southwark, the water came to their knees in places. The next dyke rose up before them, this one heading due south.

"More shovels," Canute said, stretching his back. He grabbed two and handed one over to Godwine. "Let's put a dent in this thing before we sup."

Godwine fished a water bag from the boat and took a deep draught. He needed a rest but it looked like the others were putting him to shame. Looking behind them he saw that the next boat was being dragged along pretty much the same path they had just crossed. Soon, they too would have to stop and lend a hand at breaking through the next dyke. "It will go quickly, once we get used to it," Canute assured him, reaching for the water bag. He took a drink then handed the bag to the man next to him, then a big grin spread over his face and he took a deep breath:

Oh, It is best for man to be middle-wise,
Not over cunning and clever:
The fairest life is led by those
Who are deft at all they do.

It is best for man to be middle-wise,
Not over cunning and clever:
No man is able to know his future,
So let him sleep in peace.

It is best for man to be middle-wise,
Not over cunning and clever:
The learned man whose lore is deep

Is seldom happy at heart.

Cattle die, kindred die,
Every man is mortal:
But the good name never dies
Of one who has done well.

Cattle die, kindred die,
Every man is mortal:
But I know one thing that never dies,
The glory of the great dead.

The coward believes he will live forever
If he holds back in the battle,
But in old age he shall have no peace
Though spears have spared his limbs.[2]

And back he was to the digging, leading the chorus and laughing, occasionally throwing a shovelful of dirt in someone's direction. Godwine forgot all about his aching back, falling in with the rhythm of the work and shaking his head ruefully. He was enjoying himself despite the fact that they happened to be invading London at the time!

By mid-afternoon, some welcome newcomers were pulling a small raft loaded with food and the Danes took a noisy break, grabbing some bread and cheese and drink and climbing onto the dyke so they could spread out on dry land. Ulf climbed up the hill and passed a wine skin to Godwine.

"There you are, my Saxon friend. I should have known you would be hard at work already." Ulf pulled off his boots, pouring water out of them. "We shall have your marsh crossed in a week. I think it will get easier with every new tide."

Ulf joined the digging party and added his deep voice to their chanting. Godwine didn't know all the words since many of the songs were in Danish, but he was able to absorb the sentiment of these songs, the emotion, the pride and occasional thrill of their verse. This was a side he had never seen of these fierce warriors, and it moved him more than he cared to admit.

The first night many slept on the dyke, though they had a hard time with the mosquitos. Someone had the foresight to bring along some wood and the smoke from a large fire helped keep the nasty insects at bay. They were up before dawn, determined to get as far forward as possible.

As the week progressed, the Danes broke through many places, some high, some slight, and as the tide rose, filling the breaches, the marshes rose too creating a shallow lake. While tugging and pulling and wrestling the ships, the men succeeded in bypassing London Bridge altogether, and after much struggling they met the Thames again at Chelsea. Soon, Canute had spread his army around the walled city and cut it off from outside help.

For two weeks, the Danes attacked London from one angle then another, but the citizens were vigilant and always repulsed the attacks. Canute was losing patience, and the Danish chiefs kept their distance from him. All knew that Edmund Ironside was nearby in Wessex gathering an army, and finally messengers started coming in with reports that the great Saxon king was nearly ready to give battle. The Saxon army had swelled greatly since Sherstone, despite several telling skirmishes, and at first no one was able to understand where Edmund Ironside found new recruits. In time, though, it became clear that all Canute's former Saxon allies had gone over to Edmund.

It was with frustration mixed with relief that the Danish host broke off the siege and headed south to meet the Saxons, leaving half their force to guard the ships.

* * *

Godwine shifted his grip on the sword and took a deep breath. *How many weeks have passed,* he wondered, *since he plunged into this dangerous world?* He had honestly lost track of time, what with constant movement and training and strange customs and endless self-justification.

And now he was faced with his final dilemma: here he was in the battle-lines fighting against his own people. Godwine set his mouth, squinting at the Saxons. It seemed that Canute had spoken true; the boundaries did blur between right and necessity. No matter what his scruples, the Saxons viewed him as an enemy now, and there was no going back.

Unfortunately for Edmund Ironside, Canute knew his movements better than he knew Canute's and the Danes caught up with him in Essex, challenging him to battle while he was still on the move. Frantic, some of the Saxons deserted on the spot, while Edmund hastily lined up the balance of his army and faced the enemy for what was to become the most decisive battle of his short reign.

The Northmen were lined up behind their round shields, presenting a solid bristling front to the enemy. Canute stood in the center, underneath the raven banner of Woden. And above them on the forested ridge, the Saxons chafed in their battle-lines, hesitant to give up their advantageous position atop the hill called Assandun.

In the second rank of the shield wall, Godwine looked to the right, exchanging nods with Eirik, and his tension ebbed a little. Godwine was grateful for his new friend's support; it was Eirik who was teaching him to fight, Eirik who had helped him understand the Viking point of view. Then Godwine glanced to his left, admiring Ulf's confidence. This hardened Dane moved as though his battle-gear was a second skin.

For a long time, neither side did anything. Godwine was daunted by the uncanny silence settling over the Danish host. It was as though every man was making peace with his own god;

but one look at the determined faces of the warriors and Godwine was not sure that peace was their aim. Finally, when it became clear to the Saxons that Canute had no intention of attacking uphill, Edmund gave his orders to advance. Slowly at first, then breaking into a run, the Saxons dashed down the hill at the Danes. They came on with great speed shouting their battle cries, and crashed into the enemy line, pushing them back.

Godwine nearly tripped over the man behind him as he gave way with the rest. His first inclination was to swing wildly with his sword, but he forced himself to remember his drills. Block and cut, block and cut. Feint and cut. The enemy was a blur of colors and noise, but suddenly a face thrust out from the heaving mass. It belonged to a boy little older than himself. Godwine saw fear in the boy's eyes and hesitated. Then he saw something else. He saw his own death reflected there. Grinding his teeth, Godwine brought up his sword with a fierce thrust from below, and the tip slipped underneath the short leather jerkin and into the Saxon's ribs. He just barely saw the boy fall, mouth twisted, when he was shoved back and a shield from nowhere blocked a blow that would have split his skull.

"Steady, lad," Ulf cautioned, as he grabbed Godwine by the arm—for it was he who had just saved Godwine's life.

Gasping for breath, Godwine panted his thanks, but Ulf had already plunged back into battle. Raising his shield, Godwine tried to do the same, but his small reserve of determination had fled. He found himself blocking blows but returning none, except when necessary. Ulf's move had given him an idea; if he didn't directly confront anyone, the battle would just sort of flow past him. This was a perfect solution.

The battle seemed to last forever, when at one point Godwine happened to glance toward Canute's position. To his alarm, the King's standard was wavering, then it suddenly fell.

"Look," he cried, pointing, but the shock had already communicated itself in the ranks. Many of the Danes hesitated, to their own ruin; the Saxons were not loath to take advantage of the situation. Groaning their dismay, bodies began to drop, thinning the ranks. Godwine found himself chopping and hacking automatically, without thought; all seemed lost.

But a new development caused further faltering, this time with the Saxons. Rallying, the Danes cheered each other, for in the space where had flown Canute's banner, now was seen up thrust a large beech branch: a sign that all was well and the King had survived.

Following this, a roar of dismay momentarily brought the attention of everyone around to the west, where nearly a whole rank was in full flight. It was a Saxon rank that had taken to their heels, and the Danes heeded the commands to "Hold". Their chieftains were disciplined enough to refrain from pursuing them; there was a time for chasing and a time for stopping, and the leaders knew best.

"Eadric again," muttered Ulf through clenched teeth. Godwine shuddered at the name, which always came up at a battle's turning point: Eadric, who changed sides as often as some men changed clothes, but who managed to stay on top. True to form, the traitor had taken advantage of the confusion to pull his troops out, making the retreat look like panic. Apparently, all had been pre-arranged.

It was clear who Eadric Streona served this day.

The loss of Eadric's troops had an immediate effect on the battle. Demoralized, confused, the Saxons fought desperately, but without hope. Their triumphant advance deteriorated; their position became defensive instead of offensive.

The Danes rallied. The Saxons refused to acknowledge defeat, doggedly fighting on through the sunset and into the dark, until the moon's setting diminished all available light. Little by little, the Saxons dispersed, until the last survivors fled the field; the Danes knew better than to pursue them on strange ground.

Canute searched out Ulf, his eyes glittering through his grimy face. "We did it this time," he said, betraying no sign of weariness. "I think we broke his strength."

The Jarl shrugged, unconvinced. "Were you hurt at all?"

Canute shook his head. "My standard bearer went down, and my banner trampled underfoot. For a moment, I fell under him, but I was soon on my feet again. My good chieftain Tymme the Zealander was fast in his thinking, and chopped down the beech branch that saved the day."

Ulf nodded. "That was well done. Why do you think Edmund's strength is broken?"

"Already, I have seen the corpses of many nobles and earls on the field. I would venture to guess that Edmund has lost a large number of his more prominent supporters. We shall camp here tonight, and take a tally in the morning. After we give our dead a decent burial, we will chase Edmund Ironside if we have to follow him to the ends of the earth." Turning, the King left without another word.

Jarl Ulf watched him disappear into the night, then he gave Godwine a careful scrutinizing. "You did not fight well. Are you hurt?"

Godwine was glad it was too dark for Ulf to see his blush of shame. "I...I'm not used to murder."

The Dane looked at him in surprise. "Murder? That is not murder. You were in battle; to die in battle is honorable, no matter what side a man is on. To kill an unarmed man...now, that is murder."

Putting his other arm around Godwine's shoulders, the Jarl pulled him away. "Come, let us leave this terrible place. I have had enough of warfare to last me at least a week."

4

Godwine stood quietly near Ulf on his warship, and couldn't help but wonder whether his father would recognize him today. For they were sailing back toward the Severn—back toward Wulfnoth's lands—though he no longer knew whether he would want to return home even if he had a choice. He turned his eyes on the Jarl standing so proudly on his deck, hair blowing behind him, and a surge of affection overcame him for this strange man. At times, it felt like Ulf was his father...sometimes more so than Wulfnoth ever did. Feeling his gaze, the Dane laid a hand on Godwine's shoulder.

"It seems like so long ago," the youth said.

"Yes. You have become a man, Godwine. You are not the same person who led me through these woods."

After the battle of Assandun, Canute was as good as his word and vowed to pursue Edmund to his stronghold at Gloucester. The Danes needed to sail up the Bristol Channel and they wanted to catch King Edmund before he slipped away again. Luckily, they had nature on their side.

The Bristol Channel narrowed into the Severn estuary like a funnel before transforming into the Severn River. Even the ancients knew that at certain times of the month, the tides were so high in these waters that the flow of the Severn was reversed and surged several miles upstream, creating what was known as a tidal bore. This river supported one of the highest waves in the northern world, and Danes had calculated that this day they would have the tides in their favor. They were going to ride the tidal bore all the way to Gloucester.

It was a delicate maneuver, only to be undertaken by the most experienced mariners. "We can't just float along the river like a log," Ulf said to Godwine, pacing the deck and watching the sky and the sea. "We have to wait until the first surge is past then take to the oars, or else our steer-board will be useless. We must move faster than the current, but not overtake it. Look, here it comes."

Godwine could just see it…a small but long lump in the water that slowly became a little wave.

"Now," shouted Ulf to his rowers, who slowly maneuvered the ship away from the shore. "The next ship must count twenty strokes of the oars before following us," he shouted back at Godwine, "so we don't run into each other. Then the next ship, then the next." Ulf leaned forward, grasping the gunnel. The wave was getting taller and the surf was beginning to roar as they suddenly caught the current and shot forward, leading the others in a wild ride down the middle of the river.

Godwine held his breath as the rowers stayed their course, straining to keep the ship steady as the current pushed them along. Before long the leading wave was almost fifteen feet high. Ulf turned to look around as the other ships slowly lined up behind them. The spray splashed against his face and Godwine thought he looked almost like a Norse God as the water flowed through his beard. Then the Jarl grinned ear-to-ear, breaking the spell.

"We will gain several hours," he shouted. "And catch Edmund Ironside completely by surprise."

As they continued further upstream, the tidal bore started to lose momentum until they neared a place where the river split, running around both sides of a long island. Canute's scouts were good; they had led the Danes exactly to Edmund's position. Godwine could see campfire smoke rising from the forest.

The King's ship was right behind Ulf's vessel. As they tied up, Canute motioned for Ulf and the rest to stay aboard; he and a small following disembarked.

"I do not understand," said Godwine. "They act as though they were going to parley."

The Jarl shrugged. He was as puzzled as the rest of them. "I think Canute is trying a different approach."

The small group of Vikings waited on the shore, until a handful of Saxons came out of the trees. Godwine squinted, trying to recognize them, but they were too far away.

"The red-headed man," said Ulf, pointing, "is Eadric. It confounds me that he is still in Edmund's confidence, after his behavior at Assandun. He may be the King's brother-in-law, but there comes a point where that no longer matters."

Godwine frowned, squinting. He wished he was closer.

One of the Saxons stood head and shoulders above the others, and they were treating him with great respect. Godwine turned a questioning glance at Ulf. "Yes, the tall one is your King Edmund," said the Dane, "in case you did not know."

Godwine let out his breath in a slow whistle. The man certainly had presence; he could tell even from such a distance. "I did not know he was so big."

The Dane laughed shortly. "And strong. He can wield an axe better than the best of us."

Edmund stood away from his followers, arms crossed on his chest. He had to look down at Canute, but the Dane did not seem to be bothered by that. For a moment, the two Kings stared at one another; the tension in the air was palpable. Finally, Eadric Streona stepped forward, breaking the silence. His arms moved while he spoke, and he pointed toward the island, as if emphasizing something he was saying. Edmund had his head half-turned toward the speaker, though he never seemed to take his eyes from Canute's face.

Finally, the Saxon King cut the other short by a swift motion of his hand. He turned his back to Eadric and faced Canute squarely, as if waiting for an answer. After a moment's hesitation, the Dane nodded, then turned back to his ship; silently, his companions followed. The Saxons watched them without moving.

"Thor's blood! What just happened?" Ulf slammed his fist

down on the gunnel, betraying his irritation.

Canute wasted no more time. He climbed back onto his ship, directing his oarsmen to push out and turn the vessel, heading back downstream; the rest had no choice but to follow. One by one they quickly tied up along the shore below the island, preparing to settle for the night. But once the preliminaries were done, Ulf lost no time in satisfying his curiosity. "Let us find out what this madness is," he said over his shoulder.

They found Canute pacing his deck. He looked down at Ulf as the pair approached, and for the first time, Godwine saw indecision on the King's face.

"What went on there?" demanded Ulf as he climbed aboard.

Canute frowned. "Eadric Streona came forward, claiming that he was representing Edmund Ironside's remaining Saxon nobles. They no longer want to risk the bloodshed of their people for our dynastic struggle, and insist that we solve our differences in single combat."

Ulf was at a loss. "Whose side is that man on?"

Canute shook his head. "He put me at a disadvantage. Edmund is larger and stronger than myself. And a deadly opponent. I do not want to fight him. But I could not refuse, without seeming a coward." He looked at Godwine without really seeing him. "I do not understand what he is up to," Canute finished.

For a moment, all were silent. Godwine fidgeted. Perhaps it was time he started speaking up. "Eadric did prove himself your ally at Assandun," he said finally, surprised at the assurance of his own voice. "It makes no sense for him to desert you now."

Canute's eyes cleared, and he looked at Godwine with relief, finding a focus. "Of course. You are right. He would not betray me without good reason." He renewed his pacing. "This must mean that he will send me a message tonight, declaring his purposes. Yes. It can only be that. It has to be that."

"You did say that you trust his ingenuity," added Godwine.

"Yes, yes. I did, at that."

Canute seemed to have regained his composure. "Come, Ulf, Godwine. Join me later for some food."

Ulf's face broke into a grin, anticipating the drink that would go along with a king's feast. The best of their plunder was always reserved for their chief.

They had to finish setting up the night's camp first, and by the time they returned, three rabbits were merrily dripping from a skewer into a healthy fire. Ulf and Godwine ate hungrily, and Canute seemed to be in a rare mood, joking and telling stories. *He's trying to forget,* Godwine said to himself, *the formidable task before him.* Only Canute's eyes gave away a preoccupation.

Ulf consumed much more alcohol than the other two, and after a few hours, he laid his head happily upon a log and went noisily to sleep. Canute laughed, pointing at the Jarl.

"He enjoys his drink," he said, reaching behind them for a blanket, "but some day it might be the death of him." He threw the cover over the slumbering Dane. "There. Now he is set for the night."

Canute took a moment fidgeting with the blanket. When he turned back to Godwine, the smile was gone from his face. "However, I am glad for the chance to talk to you. I find you an interesting man, Godwine, and I would know more about you."

Alone with him for the first time, Godwine found Canute's manner different, more personal. It was as if the King had been laid aside, and the man was allowed to come out. His face was even less harsh, although Godwine wondered if that was just the effect of the firelight.

Yet there was no denying the allure of the Dane's manner; Godwine found himself drawn to him like a moth to a flame. Canute's voice was caressing, yet precise. Soft, yet unyielding. Although the man's eyes were piercing, alert, even calculating, he still inspired a certain trust as if scrupulously bound by his own set of rules. One had only to determine what those limits were.

"I do not know what Ulf has already told you about me."

A smile crossed Canute's face, then was gone. "It is no matter. I would rather hear you tell me."

"All right. I am the son of a Saxon Thegn. From my childhood, my father pushed me toward bettering myself; a local monk taught me to read and write. All went well until a few years ago..." He paused, looking hard at Canute. Something had just occurred to him.

The Dane nodded. "I suspected as much. Let me finish your sentence. A few years ago, your father was accused of treason. Do you know the whole story?"

Godwine swallowed hard. This was totally unexpected. "I...um, no, not really."

"Well, I think I can help you. Your father commanded several ships in the Royal fleet, did he not?"

"Yes," Godwine answered in a hushed voice.

"I thought he might be the same man. I know that in 1009, Eadric Streona's brother accused Thegn Wulfnoth of betraying King Aethelred. It is said that because of this Wulfnoth took twenty ships and resorted to piracy."

Godwine was shocked, but things were starting to make sense.

Canute leaned forward, poking the fire with a long stick. "Why do I know this? Because Eadric didn't have any trouble persuading Wulfnoth to join with him in supporting my own father."

There was a long silence. Godwine finally let out his breath. "I see. So he went with the Danes, too."

Canute let out a short laugh. "It seems that both you and I have reason to suspect Eadric and also to be indebted to him. Me, because I need his help with Edmund. And you, because through him, I have occasion to reward your father's son."

Godwine brushed aside a tear, hoping Canute didn't see.

"All because Ulf got lost in the forest," Canute said.

Godwine nodded. At least he was beginning to understand why Canute was so accommodating.

"Do you regret your decision to go with Ulf?" the Dane asked quietly.

"Regret? It seems I was fated to be here..."

"Perhaps you were." Canute paused, looking at Ulf to see if he was still sleeping.

"Godwine..." he said more softly, leaning forward. "It encourages me to know that you are with us. In a way, I see it as a sign. Your loyalty is important, in that you have given it willingly. I hope that eventually others will follow where you have led the way. And save us all a lot of trouble in the future. Whether your people like it or not, I am here to stay."

Godwine was stunned by the enormity of the possibilities. Perhaps, just perhaps, the Danish King needed an emissary between himself and the Saxon people.

Canute sat back, still considering the other's face. "Godwine, I think you are wiser than you know. But I suspect that you do not yet trust your instincts."

The Saxon shifted his legs at that. Canute had spoken more truly than he wanted to admit. "Perhaps. All this is so new to me. But it is a great challenge."

"Good. Stay with Ulf a while. He is a good warrior, and brave."

"He means to bring me to Denmark this winter..."

"Yes. A good idea. Watch, Godwine. Study our ways. Learn from us. I would have you serve me, when you are a bit more comfortable with yourself. I would have you be my friend."

Godwine was won over at this unexpected disclosure. Canute bent forward, putting out a hand. He grasped it willingly.

At that moment, the Dane turned his head at a sound from the forest. He stood noiselessly, waiting. Godwine heard a gruff word from a guard, then a covert answer. Footsteps followed upon this exchange, and a Saxon moved into the firelight, shadowed by his guard.

"Thank you, Bork," said Canute, dismissing his man. "I recognize him."

The Dane faded into the trees.

The newcomer stared for a moment at Godwine, then turned to Canute. "Can I speak in front of him?"

"Go on. He is in my confidence."

Despite himself, Godwine was flattered.

"Eadric sends me to tell you not to worry. It was good that you accepted the challenge. If you win, the Saxons will accept you as their overlord. If Edmund proves too much for you, stop the duel by appealing to his sense of fairness."

"Impossible," spat Canute.

"Oh? Remember who you are dealing with. That is your opinion, not necessarily his."

A bitterness escaped from the messenger that both Canute and Godwine noticed.

"Eadric said," the man went on, recovering himself, "that you might well succeed in convincing him to divide the kingdom between you. The King is tired of this war; more and more he has to rely on untrained serfs. He lost many good men the last battle."

Canute bit his lip, thinking. "Did he say anything else?"

"No. Only for you to think about it. Half a kingdom is better than none."

Ignoring the implicit threat, Canute gave the man a gold coin and sent him on his way. He turned to Godwine.

"What do you think?"

"It is very possible. A man who would be foolish enough to trust such a one as Eadric could be persuaded to accept your proposal." At that moment, Godwine felt more scorn than loyalty toward Edmund.

Canute paced a few minutes, then stopped. "Godwine, I agree

with you. I will go through with it. One cannot fight his own destiny."

It was an uneasy position for Godwine to be in. If things went wrong, Canute might very well blame him. But Godwine was beginning to realize that taking these kinds of chances was the fastest way to gain Canute's confidence. The King was not the sort of man to put much faith in an advisor who always played it safe.

* * *

Early the next morning, Canute was up and ready. Gone was any semblance of hesitation; indeed, he acted like a man who looked forward to the challenge ahead of him.

"Wake up, you old laggard. I need you at my side today." Sliding his chain maille over his head, Canute clumped over to Ulf, nudged him with his foot. The Jarl sat up with a groan, looking around.

"Bring two dozen of your best picked men to go with my hundred, and Godwine, too. That is all we can bring; it seems that the island will not hold the lot of us."

Ulf growled his answer, rubbing his forehead. "I do not like the sound of that. It could be a trap."

"That's not Edmund's way. Still, just in case, let us post guards along the opposite shore; the river can be swum at that point. Though I do not expect any trouble this day. In fact, I anticipate a solution to all our troubles."

Shaking his head, Ulf got up and moved toward his ship, scattering the remains of the previous night's dinner. Canute watched him for a moment, a slight smile on his face, then turned and accepted his helmet from the armor-bearer.

* * *

The isle of Olney was little more than a long sandbank with willow trees growing unsteadily on its shore. The two Kings and their followers disembarked on opposite sides at the same time. They made their way to the center, where an enclosure was quickly roped off.

Godwine was even more impressed by Edmund's great size from close up, and he understood Canute's reluctance to meet him in single combat. The man was intent—nay, grim—and there was no evidence of any softness or weakness about him. Edmund's mouth was set and his black eyes were steady as he scrutinized his antagonist, looking for shortcomings. He motioned with his head for the man beside him to step forward.

Tearing his eyes from Edmund, Godwine assumed he was facing Eadric who walked to the center, acknowledging both opponents with a glance and a nod, as though he ruled the assembly. Godwine was surprised at the man's ugliness; his bulging blue eyes so pale they seemed empty. For just a second Eadric's eyes met with Godwine's, and the Saxon couldn't suppress a shudder; how could such a loathsome creature inspire such confidence?

And then Eadric spoke, clearing up the little mystery. His voice was so melodic that it was a delight just to listen to him. Godwine had heard that Eadric was of common ancestry and had risen in Aethelred's favor by way of his own abilities. *It was no wonder*, he thought to himself. One could get lost in that man's voice.

"We are gathered here," Eadric was saying, "to decide the fate of the kingdom by single combat. Canute claims the crown by right of his father, Swegn Forkbeard." He bowed to the Dane.

"And Edmund Ironside claims the kingship by right of his inheritance from King Aethelred." He bowed to the Saxon. "Both men have good and valid claims; and yet, it stands to reason that the misery wrought on our good country should come to an end. Let God in heaven make the decision for us, and grace the rightful King with a victory this day."

Pleased with this little speech, Eadric moved back, waving for the assembled to give the combatants more room.

Canute and Edmund moved into the center of the clearing, their eyes locked. The Saxon was armored in chain maille like Canute, his choice of weapon broadsword and shield against the Dane's axe and shield.

No one in the crowd made a sound.

The two Kings circled, each looking for an opening, then suddenly they both dashed together, shattering the silence with a deafening crash of steel against wood. Both men had aimed a blow for the head; both easily stopped the blade with their shield.

Canute was transformed by the first encounter. He lost all of his uncertainty when the fighting began. Crouching so that Edmund had a smaller target, Canute began concentrating on the Saxon's timing, and forgot about his overwhelming size.

Edmund followed quickly with a series of well-aimed blows—first high, then low—and pushed forward, trying to overcome his enemy with brute force.

Quickly recognizing Edmund's reliance on his strength, Canute began to weave and duck, cutting in and out of his opponent's range. He struck quickly, more to weaken Edmund and draw blood than to maim him; Canute realized that one solid blow from the Saxon could easily finish him.

The chain links began to burst and fly off Edmund's armor, displaying Canute's skill. Edmund was forced back momentarily and stopped, gasping for breath. The Dane straightened up, seeing his difficulty, and said in a loud voice, "Edmund, you are too short-winded."

Stung, the Saxon jumped forward, responding with a stunning wrap-around blow to Canute's head; the Dane fell to the ground.

"Not too short-winded if I can bring so great a King to his

knees."

Smiling grimly, Edmund stood back for a moment, allowing his opponent to recover; then he moved in again, chopping so heavily at the Dane's shield that huge splinters flew in every direction.

Canute stepped back, then again, and realized that he was not going to hold up much longer. His shield arm was growing numb; frenziedly defending himself, he couldn't return any of the blows.

Then, with a gasp, the Dane was forced again to one knee. "Bravest of youths," he cried out, "why should either of us risk his life for the sake of a crown?"

Edmund stopped his hammering and stood back, waiting for Canute to continue.

"Let us be brothers by adoption," Canute went on, staying on one knee, "and divide the kingdom, governing so that I may rule your affairs, and you mine."

The Saxon looked at Canute with lowering brows; he seemed unconvinced.

"Even the government of Denmark I submit to your disposal."

These last words came out more reluctantly; they cost Canute dear. Edmund knew that. He dropped his shield, passed the sword to his left hand, and gave Canute his right, helping him up.

"I hope he knows what he is doing," Ulf growled to Godwine. "This is more than the rest of us bargained for."

Godwine glanced at Ulf, worried at his tone.

King Edmund ceremoniously held Canute at arm's length, then gave him the kiss of peace; as though they were brothers, the Dane returned his gesture, amid the cheers of the Saxons. Canute's followers were less vociferous in their enthusiasm, but out of regard for their chief, they raised no objection.

Edmund seemed to have come prepared; releasing Canute, he motioned for his scribes to advance, and record all that was to be decided. It seemed that the division was going to take place in that very spot.

"He must want witnesses," Godwine said, nodding, "so that there will be no questions later. It seems that Edmund wants to be rid of our presence at the soonest."

Canute did not react to this hasty gesture, nor did he give any indication that he suffered humiliation from his defeat. His first demands were for the Danish fleet to be paid a certain amount of money, as a matter of course. Edmund agreed without demurring, so habitual was this method of dealing with the Danes. Then, the actual division was decided upon. Edmund was to have all the land south of the Thames: the earldom of Wessex. In addition to this, East Anglia, Essex, and London. Canute was agreeable. "Done. Those last belong to you anyway, even with my troops all over them. Wessex has always been yours."

Canute was to have all of Mercia and Northumbria: a sizable portion of England, if somewhat less populous. It was agreed that each would succeed to the territories of the other in case of death; Edmund's two children were very young, and therefore given little consideration for the moment.

Both Kings appeared content, though Godwine wondered how deep that satisfaction went. But when all was finished and Canute came nearer, an angry glint in his eye gave the Saxon his answer.

However, Ulf didn't seem to notice. "Why did you do that?" the Jarl said angrily. "You should not have included Denmark in the bargain."

Canute turned on him furiously. "What business is it of yours, what I do with my kingdom?"

Ulf stepped back, but he was too committed to stop now. Nor did he want to. "It is very much my business. Do not forget the rest of your Jarls. Without our support, where would you be?"

Canute's face tuned red, but he restrained his temper. He said icily, "I would watch what I say, if I were you."

His manner made Godwine more nervous than if he were to explode in anger. But still Ulf did not heed his wrath. "You had just better watch yourself, Canute. We will have no foreign king telling us what to do."

"You will do as I say!" Canute turned to the field, observing the last of the Saxons. When he looked at Ulf again, his eyes were shuttered, his voice even. "Do not worry, Ulf. What you fear will never happen." Then he spun on his heels and strode off, motioning for his Danes to follow. A couple of the older men held back, waiting to talk to Ulf.

"Do you think that was wise?" Godwine asked in a low voice.

Ulf glanced worriedly at him, and let his breath out in a heavy sigh. "Never mind Canute. He will soon have forgotten our little dispute." Trailing off unconvincingly, he left Godwine and moved toward his friends, checking around to see if he was watched.

It seemed that no one was observing them but Godwine, who looked back as he was leaving; he thought they were huddled a bit too conspiratorially, and he wondered, not for the first time, whether Ulf was completely Canute's man.

* * *

Some time later, Canute came looking for Ulf, all signs of annoyance wiped from his face.

"I have come to you with a request," said the King. "I intend to winter in London, but I need a regent in Denmark. Will you do it for me?" Since everyone knew that Ulf was returning to Denmark, Godwine reasoned that the request was a formality.

Ulf was not as skilled as Canute at hiding his emotions; a look of triumph flickered in his eyes, quickly squelched. "You plan on wintering with your brother Edmund, then," said the Jarl, a touch sarcastically.

The King affected not to notice. "No. Edmund intends to

winter in Oxford, with Eadric. I will keep my housecarls with me, in case anything untoward happens."

Listening from a few feet away, Godwine looked questioningly at Canute. It all seemed very strange, since London was in Edmund's territory. But the Jarl seemed to follow Canute's thought.

"Ahhh," he said mysteriously. "Now I begin to understand. We may pick the bones of London yet."

"Nothing of the sort," retorted Canute, pretending to be shocked. "I just want to be prepared."

Nodding conspiratorially, Ulf said he would stay a week more, then sail back to Denmark. He turned to Godwine. "You still want to come with me, I hope."

Godwine nodded, relieved to get away.

Canute pursued the conversation. "Oh, and by the way. Let Godwine stay with me, until you leave. Now that everything has changed, I need him to demonstrate to the Saxons how well I treat one who has voluntarily accepted my rule."

Ulf was not a jealous man. He grinned broadly at Godwine. "A wonderful idea. Perhaps you can find some better clothes for him as well."

Everyone within hearing burst into laughter. Embarrassed, Godwine looked at his own ripped and dirty tunic. Smiling broadly for a second, Canute strode away with his usual abruptness. Ulf and Godwine gazed after him.

"That man is a mystery to me, lad," the Dane admitted. "I never expected him to summon you at such a time. I cannot explain... But I will tell you this: continue to stand by him, and he will make your fortune. He has taken a rare liking to you, and I am happy for it."

Godwine was about to protest, but Ulf had already guessed his objection. "No, Godwine. I know that you feel loyalty toward me. But I cannot do for you what Canute can. Nor do I intend to stay forever on English soil. I love my native Denmark, and though I also love to go a' Viking, I could never make any other country my home."

* * *

As the ships approached London, it became clear that the news had preceded them. This time, with a groan of timbers under stress and the squeaking of pulleys, the drawbridge lifted and allowed the Viking longships to pass underneath. Canute gripped the railing as they sailed past the wharfs, fluttering with gaily colored pennons waved by laughing and shouting citizens. "See how they humor me," he murmured to Godwine, who stood quietly beside him, dressed in a fine new tunic. "The first sign of trouble, and these cheerful flatterers will all turn into raging devils."

Once past the bridge, they were inside the Roman walls and in the center of the city. The walls were rebuilt two hundred years before by Alfred of Wessex, surnamed by some The Great, who reclaimed the city from ruins and renamed it Lundenburgh. Right in the middle, where the river Walbrook flowed into the Thames, a natural harbor provided the principal quay for loading and unloading diverse goods from around the world. Many narrow streets ran from the markets to the river, and the little wooden overhanging houses competed with each other for road frontage. The quay was called Aethelredes Hythe.

On this day, most of the quay had been cleared of merchant ships, allowing Canute to disembark; a welcoming committee led by a distinguished Ealdorman was on hand, cheering the Danish King as if they had never experienced any disturbance at his hand.

As the crowd parted for them, Godwine noticed that the Londoners took an occasional furtive glance in his direction; he wondered just what they were thinking. There was no denying that he felt self-conscious; in his mind he looked every bit the

Saxon. It was evident that his presence was much wondered about, just as Canute had intended.

Godwine smiled grimly, uncomfortable in his conspicuous position. He would have much rather entered with Ulf and stayed in the background. The Jarl was in the next rank, not in his usual place at Canute's side, as befitting a brother-in-law. But Ulf did not seem affronted by the change; his jovial face looked unconcerned as ever.

The Ealdorman of London led Canute to a large stone palace next to the Thames, with a flagstone courtyard and supported by five auxiliary buildings. The Roman wall towered over the far side of the enclosure, forming its western border. And just north of the palace across a huge courtyard stood the old St. Paul's church that even Godwine knew was at least 500 years old. The big front doors of the church faced the stone palace.

"Aethelred's residence," the Ealdorman said, bowing and gesturing toward the palace, hand outspread. "We welcome you to London."

Canute mounted a short row of stairs and turned, facing the small crowd. His chief jarls placed themselves beside him. Godwine marveled at the proud demeanor of these sturdy Danish chieftains, as several nervous Londoners paid their respects and moved quickly on. Twenty officials, one for each of the city's twenty wards, advanced in a tight group, holding their staff of office and a small bag of gold coins. Canute gestured for Godwine to collect the gifts and the Saxon nodded to each man as he accepted a pigskin bag and passed it on to a waiting page.

After about an hour, Canute beckoned to the Ealdorman and graciously dismissed him. Nothing loth, the few remaining men followed him quickly out the gate and into the city.

"Tovi." Canute spoke quietly, turning his head to the side. His standard bearer leaned toward the King. "We will billet the men throughout the city, but tell them to make sure there is no trouble. I intend to spend the winter as quietly as possible." With a few gestures, the Dane sent most of the followers off to one errand or another. The palace had to be hastily prepared, ships had to be secured, guards needed to be posted.

Canute removed a circlet from his head and handed it to Godwine, running his fingers through his thick hair. "Come, my friends," he said, smiling suddenly. "We earned a look around the city, don't you think?" Nodding at Godwine and Ulf, Canute strolled across the churchyard, followed by ten of his closest Jarls. Godwine wrapped Canute's circlet in his cloak, gripping it tightly. The Londoners gave them wide berth, uncertain as to how they were supposed to act.

The far corner of St. Paul's courtyard passed through a gate into the Cheapside marketplace, which was lined with innumerable stands of goods from all over the world. Many of these foreign merchants ignored the Danish chieftains, hawking their wares to whoever came within shouting distance. Godwine could see that Canute liked this bit of arrogant aloofness, as though kings would come and go, but commerce was forever.

Nonetheless, the little group passed through the marketplace and followed the Roman wall, heading toward Cripplegate and the old Roman fort. They could see the remains of the oldest wall, and the fortified gate to the north which was heavily guarded. Nearby stood an even older palace than the one Canute was settling into. And beside this compound, a Roman amphitheater looked chalky white in the glow from the setting sun.

"So many feet have trod this path," Canute said quietly. "I wonder if we will leave our mark on history." He looked sideways at Godwine, a half-smile on his face. "Why not?" he added, almost a challenge to the others. "Just because we conquer, does this mean we have to live as enemies with our neighbors?" Some of the Jarls shrugged unconcernedly.

"Well, pay attention, friends," he added in a low voice. "I mean to stay. This will be our country, and these will be my people. Before I have finished, England will be a Danish kingdom."

Godwine wondered if it might end up the other way: could Canute end up more Saxon than Danish? Hiding a smile, he kept his thoughts to himself.

* * *

In the two hours they strolled through the city, Canute's staff had performed miracles and his new palace stood ready for its new king. This night, however, Canute chose to dine in seclusion, with only a few close confidants while the court enjoyed a rich feast in the great hall.

Once again Godwine marveled that Canute didn't dismiss him along with the rest, though he really didn't want to leave. He enjoyed Canute's company and he felt stimulated by the man's excellent mind. *Perhaps,* he thought, *the Dane liked him;* that was certainly possible. At any rate, Godwine appreciated all the attention. People were beginning to treat him with respect.

Before the night was over, all had left the chamber except Canute and Godwine. The King had insisted that he tarry, although Canute was so distracted that he barely kept track of the conversation. Giving up, Godwine sat back and enjoyed the quiet. After all, they had a table, a place to sit, a sideboard and a fireplace. It was quite cozy, although Canute didn't seem able to stop his pacing. But suddenly, hearing a brisk knock at the door, the Dane whirled around and opened it himself.

A man slid quickly into the room, his face wrapped with a wool scarf as if against the cold, although the brisk September wind did not yet warrant such a precaution. Once assured that the three of them were alone, the man quickly shed his outer clothing, and Godwine was surprised to see Eadric Streona standing before them, warming his hands at the fire.

There was really no reason he should have been startled; it all made perfect sense. Canute and Eadric had been communicating all along through intermediaries. But if this man had felt compelled to show up in person, there must certainly be some critical development.

"Did you get away all right?" asked Canute.

The other nodded, eyeing Godwine cautiously. "I told him that I had to attend to certain problems within my earldom. He was too exhausted to accompany me." He had yet to look away from Godwine. "Is this the man my messenger told me about?"

Canute offered Eadric a goblet of mulled wine. "Yes. This is Godwine, from Wiltshire. He is in my confidence." Godwine noted that Canute kept his relationship with Wulfnoth quiet.

Eadric nodded, then finally looked at Canute, graciously accepting the wine from him.

"Well then, Godwine, you have made a very good move. The future lies with Canute." His eyes closed for a moment, as if savoring the drink.

"So tell me, has Edmund shown any tendency to break our agreement?" Canute spoke hurriedly, almost nervously.

"He has said very little to me; he is close-mouthed these days." Again, Eadric's eyes closed for a second.

"Do you think he will attempt anything serious?"

Eadric began pacing the room. "For the winter, at least, we are safe. He is exhausted, as I said, and needs rest. He plans to overwinter in Oxford. You have pressed him very hard, my liege." He bowed.

"And in the spring?" Canute made no attempt to hide his impatience.

"Ahhh. That is another thing. Make no mistake: the King is a man to be dealt with. He will bide his time for now, until his country is ready for another confrontation." His eyes narrowing, he paced faster. "But he seems to have much hidden strength."

"I thought you said he was exhausted."

Eadric stopped, his eyes widening in emphasis. "For now. Nonetheless, he considers you as an invader. Do not underestimate him."

"As you seem to have, on occasion. Almost effecting my destruction."

Godwine was amazed. That was odd of Canute to push blame on someone else. But Eadric seemed to take it all in stride.

"Everyone makes mistakes," he said, almost flippantly; but seeing Canute's frown, he changed his tone. "Sire," he added, lowering his voice, "there is another way to deal with him."

Canute put out a hand, warningly. "Stop. I do not want to know."

Closing his eyes for a moment, Eadric considered. "All right. Do I have your countenance?"

"Yes." Canute turned his back on the man in dismissal. It kept him from seeing the quick glimmer of hatred that flashed across Eadric's face.

But Godwine saw it. He poured more wine into his own mug, pretending not to notice. Eadric glanced hard at him, and Godwine boldly held out the pitcher. Shaking his head, the Earl placed his half-full goblet on the table, and moved to put on his outer garments. He turned, arranging his cloak on his shoulders.

"Is there anything else, Sire?"

"No." Canute let Godwine refill his own cup. Then he turned to Eadric with an effort. "Thank you for coming all this way. Yours is a delicate mission, and I am aware of the danger."

Eadric's face visibly softened, and he even allowed himself a smile. "I am sure you will find a way to reward me."

Covering his mouth with the scarf, the man left as quietly as he came. Canute pushed open the shutter an inch, silently watching him glide into the street. Then he spat into the rushes, as if to rid himself of a bad taste. "I despise that man," he grimaced.

"It shows," Godwine said softly.

Canute smiled, almost embarrassed. "It is true, Godwine. I can usually hide it. But this man is so cursed, I hate to be in the same room with him. Too bad he is so efficient. Nonetheless, he is used to such treatment. Most men who know him tend to shun him. Except King Edmund, to his own misfortune. Of course, he's married to Edmund's sister, so I guess he can call him kin."

Shaking his head, Canute sat beside Godwine. "What did you gather from all this?"

The other sighed. "I fear great harm will come to Edmund."

"It is possible." Canute did not take his comment amiss. "The kingdom cannot be divided forever. But what can you say about Eadric, now that you have seen him close up?"

"I would not believe all that he says; I think he has motives all his own. And it seems to me that he closed his eyes whenever he considered a deception."

Canute leaned back against the wall, thinking. "Closed his eyes, you say."

"Yes. I am sure he does not even realize it. Watch him next time, and see if what I say is true."

The King was searching his memory; then he sat up. "By God, you are right. He did that very thing. You are an astute observer, Godwine. That is a rare quality in an advisor."

He turned to Godwine earnestly. "Come back to me in the spring; remain in my service. We are only a couple of years apart, you know. Between the two of us, we make a formidable pair. With a little practice, your talents may even surpass my own."

Godwine was gratified; this was what he wanted all along. Such proof of Canute's trust eased the last lingering doubts about the ethics of his position. Once he firmly established himself, he could begin to push Canute in the proper direction, and persuade him to respect the rights of the Saxon people.

Was he following in his father's footsteps? Would the people call him traitor? How much time needs to pass before a stigma goes away?

5

Godwine took a long look at England's receding shore, relieved to put his country's troubles behind him. Although he knew nothing about their destination, Godwine was sure that any change would be an improvement. It had been a strain to suffer through Canute's early days, during which the King was obliged to make politic, though not always merciful decisions to insure order. He was preparing for the inevitable purge of undesirable chieftains, and Canute and Thurkill spent many hours together consolidating their plans. Godwine was more than relieved to be excluded.

In ten days they reached their destination, sailing through the North Sea, around the mainland of Denmark—called Jutland—to a smaller island named Saarland. Like a long finger, Roskilde Fjord thrust deep into the island, and Ulf's fleet dropped anchor at the narrow end of it, at the settlement of Roskilde.

Godwine jumped into the water, relieved to be off the rolling deck. He watched, bemused, as the children and women began to pour onto the shore, shouting and laughing. For a while the beach was a jumble of color and splashing, until finally small groups began to break apart, as the reunited families made their way home.

But not all of them. Some of the wives looked in vain for husbands they would never see again, lost on the battlefields of faraway Britain. It wasn't until the arrival of the warships that the bereft discovered their sorrow, and it was a miserable day for them, listening sadly to the story of their loved ones' death.

It was Ulf who carried the heavy load on his shoulders; Ulf had a word for every widow, a hug for every orphan. The Jarl was their leader, and they looked to him for solace, for succor. He took his responsibility seriously, spending long hours on the beach, until the last survivor was comforted to the best of his capacity.

When Ulf finally straightened, his eyes met Godwine's; the Saxon had stood all the while at his side, silent, unheeded, supportive. Glad of his presence, the Jarl put an arm around his companion's shoulders and showed him to the settlement, leaning on him slightly.

Before them rose the principal stronghold of Roskilde. It was essentially a circular fortified encampment, with raised earthworks around the circumference, surmounted by a wooden wall. At four points, a gated opening tunneled through the earthworks, from which led a road made of boards. The compound was divided into four quarters; in each quarter, four elliptical-shaped longhouses made a square; each square had a building in its center.

Like spokes on a wheel, a row of longhouses made an arc around the outside of the earthwork wall. Godwine was surprised that the last building was a Christian church.

As they passed the outbuildings, Ulf's step quickened, bringing them through the nearest gate of the palisade. Godwine lagged behind, admiring the stronghold; he had never seen such precision.

Meanwhile, Ulf burst through the doors of his longhouse, shouting for ale. He was greeted with hearty laughter, and Godwine watched at the door while his friend tossed a handful of squealing children into the air, one after another. Then he put them aside and gathered a buxom brunette into his arms, smothering her with kisses until she pushed him laughingly away.

"My Lord," she gasped, "will you not introduce me to this handsome stranger?"

Guffawing, Ulf swept Godwine into the room with a grand gesture. "My wife, I would have you meet Godwine, who saved me from blundering through the everlasting forests of England. Godwine, meet my wife and Canute's sister, Estrid."

Smoothing her hair back, Estrid extended her other hand.

"Excuse our rudeness, Godwine, but I haven't seen my husband for so long, I nearly forgot what he looked like."

Ulf slapped her behind then went off, looking for a flagon. Estrid smiled at him, and then slipped an arm through Godwine's, directing him toward the fire pit.

"Be comfortable, Godwine. I was preparing food for my lord." She paused, looking at him appraisingly. He returned her gaze curiously, for he had never seen a full-blooded Danish woman before.

"You are very beautiful," he said, without even realizing it. Estrid was evidently used to compliments, for she didn't even blush. "You should see Ulf's sister," she began, then turned to one of her children, tugging at her sleeve.

"All right then, little one. You shall have your dinner. Keep Godwine company for now."

The child stood looking uncertainly at the stranger, his lip trembling. Godwine tried a big smile and it seemed to work, because the boy came closer, a thumb in his mouth.

"And what might be your name, lad?"

"Svein," came the answer, spoken around the thumb.

"Are those your brothers and sisters?"

Turning, the child scrutinized the other siblings. "Yes," he said proudly, pushing his chest out. "I take care of them. I am the oldest boy." The wet thumb rested proudly against his chest.

"So you have an elder sister?" Godwine was running out of things to say; he was unused to children.

"Oh yes, that is Hilde, there, helping mother stir. But I don't talk to girls. Only my aunt Gytha," he added proudly, pointing to a tall woman who had just entered the door. Overcoming his shyness, Svein prattled on, but Godwine heard no more.

As he would recall much later, Godwine was stuck momentarily senseless by her perfect beauty. Blonde, shapely like Estrid, Gytha slipped across the room to greet her brother who seemed, to Godwine's amazement, oblivious to her grace. Ulf barely paused in conversation long enough for Gytha to kiss his hairy cheek, yet she took no notice of his rudeness. Moving toward the fire pit, she paused, considering Godwine.

The Saxon could feel the blood rising to his face. For a long moment he squirmed uncomfortably under her gaze, until finally someone called her name and Gytha turned away in answer.

Godwine bent his knees, bringing him eye level with the child who had begun fingering the hilt of his sword. Pulling the sheath from his belt, the Saxon held the handle out to him, making sure not to let go.

"Is your aunt Gytha married?" he said softly, hoping not to be overheard.

"Oh, no. She would never do that. Is this a real warrior's sword?"

"Yes, the very best. Why would she never marry?"

"Aunt Gytha is waiting for me to grow up, so I may marry her myself."

"She told you that?"

"Of course. Can I hold it all by myself?"

Svein was interrupted by a soft, melodic voice, which carried a definite note of authority. "No you may not, and you are perfectly aware that you are too young."

Both Svein and Godwine jumped up guiltily. Smiling sheepishly, Svein let go the hilt and the Saxon replaced the sheath shakily on his belt.

Gytha bent for a kiss. "Now go help your mother, Svein. I will tend to your new friend."

Looking jealously back at the pair, the child went off, dragging his feet.

Godwine looked away from the boy to meet her eyes; Gytha was the same height as himself. Her naturally dark lips were pursed in amusement, her round blue eyes crinkling. It seemed that even the firelight faded beside her, so commanding was her presence.

"Would you sit, My Lord?"

Godwine's legs collapsed, while she sat beside him, not noticing his awkwardness.

"You come with Ulf from England?"

Godwine nodded; his mouth was uncomfortably dry.

"My boorish brother will never remember to introduce us. What might be your name?"

"Godwine, son of Wulfnoth, Thegn of Sussex."

"Oh." Gytha seemed disappointed.

"We met, you see, in the forest. Ulf was lost, and I helped him find his ships."

She nodded, looking at her brother. He could see that she was fast losing interest.

"His men thought he had vanished, you see." Godwine trailed off; he cursed his own faltering words. It was not like him to be so nervous.

"Are you in his service, then?" The words were polite, detached.

"The King's, rather. He has granted me leave to visit Denmark." Godwine hoped that would help.

"Oh."

The pause was maddening. He must say something. "Have you been to England yet?"

Judging from her expression, this wasn't the way to start a conversation.

"No. Forgive me, Godwine. I believe my services are needed."

He would have added something, but she was too fast for him, slipping away without another word. A gentle whiff of musk lingered in the air. Godwine sniffed, feeling perfectly miserable.

Trying to regain his composure, he looked up at the roof, watching the smoke linger before drifting under the eaves at both gables. Then he was distracted by the clamor of several men entering the building, arms around their women, laughing and singing. There was Eirik, along with the rest, waving his greeting; for the moment he was too busy with his young wife to pay attention to Godwine.

Soon, they were setting up tables; evidently dinner was not a small affair. Before long, Ulf was shouting his name, pointing to a seat at the trestle-table, between himself and his sister. Godwine would have preferred a less prominent spot, far away from the girl. But, hoping his natural wit would not fail him again, he determined to make the best of it. The quality of the food made it even easier to forget his troubles; heaping platters of rabbits and bear flowed past, skewered by hungry Danes brandishing daggers. All was washed down with copious draughts of ale, drunk from horns not relinquished until empty.

Gytha ate slowly and carefully, dipping her fingers into a bowl of water and wiping them on a cloth. Her conversation throughout the meal was casual, and she showed no reluctance about talking to him. Godwine took heart from that, and began to tell her about his homeland, the hills and forests that were so different from her flat surroundings. Despite herself, Gytha took an interest, even beginning to ask questions of her own.

But when the meal was over and the servants were clearing the table, she suddenly stood and took her leave. Godwine watched her embrace Estrid; he longed for her to come back, but her aloofness confused him. Hadn't she been interested in what he was saying? Was she merely being polite? Surely she must have detected an undercurrent of encouragement in his words... or had she?

6

The days that followed were filled with activity: unloading the ships, pulling them out of the water, making them ready for winter. Godwine welcomed the exertion; physical labor was something he knew how to deal with.

And, too, while he worked and sweated, he seemed to attract the interest of Gytha in an inexplicable manner. Often and again, Godwine stood to catch a breath, and would find the girl staring at him, though she was quick to look away.

Women were not an uncommon sight on the shore; they were handy with tools, and could manage ropes with the best of their men. Gytha, because of her birth, did not stoop to labor, but was ever on hand with a flask of water or ale.

Once, when offering a wine-skin to Godwine, her hand touched his, making a thrill run through his body. Did she notice? He could not tell. Eirik saw Godwine looking hungrily after her, and gave his friend a rough nudge. "Shame on you," he laughed.

For a second, Godwine's anger flared. Then he realized he was on the verge of making a fool of himself. Gytha was truly beyond him; he had no right to desire her. He smiled impishly. "A man can dream, can't he?"

"Ah, but your dreams are dangerous. A man can get burned, flying so close to the sun. That one is a she-devil when she gets riled. It is wise to stay away from her."

Godwine sighed. He knew Eirik was right.

* * *

After the ships were taken care of, came the hunting. This was everyone's favorite time, and the enthusiasm was contagious. The men rode out with a supply of provisions, bundled up against the already chilling wind. The women stayed behind to ready the smokehouses, for it was important that this meat last throughout the harsh winter.

Ulf and the highest ranking men were mounted, and each carried a spear, a sword at his side and a hunting knife. Godwine followed on foot with the huntsmen and grooms who held their *hundr*, or hounds, on a rope leash with the end wrapped around their wrist. As they were leaving the settlement, the air was filled with horns blaring and dogs barking and men urging the dogs to stay together.

In the fall, the wild boar moved from the fields where they feasted on remnants of the harvest, into the forest, where they gorged themselves on acorns and dug up roots. Now was a good time to hunt the boars in their wallow while they were distracted by their rummaging.

The group of about twenty men and almost as many hounds made good time, following well-worn trails into the forest. After an hour the pack had quieted down and the huntsmen and grooms forged ahead with their best dogs, searching the woods for scat and rubbing marks on the trees. It was a long and arduous process, but eventually one of the hunters indicated that he had located a marshy area with fresh droppings, and the group set up camp nearby.

In the deep of the night, the huntsmen quietly took up their posts near the wallow with their dogs, keeping them quiet. Just as soon as they could see clearly in the early light, the first dogs were slipped from their leash and they moved out of sight. The grooms followed without making a sound, until one of the hounds barked, indicating he found their prey.

Then all hell broke loose. Quick as could be, the other huntsmen loosed the next pack of hounds, keeping a few in reserve. The dogs started to bay in unison, and soon the men could hear growling and snarling. It was tough going and the grooms followed as best as they could, trying to reach the wallow before too many dogs got hurt.

Godwine and the rest broke through and discovered four full-grown boars with three young ones. The hounds found the smaller boars easier prey, and one had already been killed when the huntsmen interfered, moving forward with spears and bows. The younger quarry were soon dispatched. The man at Godwine's side plunged his spear into the shoulder of a full-grown boar, while two dogs leapt on its back and three others came at it from all sides. Meanwhile, the other adult boars charged into the forest, closely followed by the mounted hunters.

All seemed like chaos. The boar was plunging back and forth and trying to get the dogs off its back. Men were thrusting spears into its body then hanging on, taking it down together. The dogs had to be pulled off, and one or two were bleeding from the pig's tusks. Finally, after what seemed forever, the animal collapsed and the men declared themselves satisfied. Godwine could still hear the horn blasts from the other hunters.

They wasted no time cleaning the kill. A fire was soon lit and the grooms put themselves to work splitting the carcass and pulling out the intestines, which were duly cooked and served to the dogs, along with morsels of bread soaked in blood. They were eventually joined by the rest of the party, who carried in the other prizes. It was a good day's work.

* * *

Ulf and the senior huntsmen returned first. Bawdy songs and ballads of conquest echoed throughout the woods, but, following on their heels, Godwine was too distracted to pay much attention. He did not want to admit to himself how much he yearned for a sight of Gytha, but as they neared the settlement, his heart was pounding.

There she was, standing apart from the others at the door to the longhouse. Her mouth slightly parted, she watched the homecoming with a detached contentment, though no one went up to greet her right away. Finally, Ulf put an arm around her shoulders and they went inside together. Godwine stood uncomfortably alone, watching. She had not even deigned to glance at him.

It was going to be a long winter.

* * *

And indeed it was...long and frustrating. Nights were interminable and boring, and daylight ended at an ungodly early hour, leaving the Danes with little else to do but eat and drink and tell endless stories; Godwine learned to share Ulf's penchant for ale.

Gytha began to spend more time in Godwine's company, though he still didn't know whether it was by inclination, or merely because he was a novelty. She was a woman of rare insight and intelligence, and Godwine found himself daily more fascinated with her.

The Saxon soon became a great favorite with the children. Svein initially eyed him suspiciously, jealous of his time spent with Gytha. But the boy's innate curiosity got the better of him, and he was soon following his new friend everywhere, trying to copy his walk, even imitating his speech.

Svein's little brother, Beorn, was just old enough to walk, and Godwine found his blond curls and blue eyes irresistible. The child loved to ride on his back, clinging to his neck and smiling wide enough to split his face.

The little girls, of course, could barely make themselves heard, until they clambered onto aunt Gytha's lap, where they could easily dominate the conversation. Of course, only Godwine and Gytha knew that playing with them was the perfect excuse to avoid a serious discussion. Godwine was relieved at the distraction, since it was daily more difficult to contain his thoughts; he often had to bite back words which he feared would turn against him. He had no delusions about the intensity of her scorn; yet sometimes, he thought she really cared for him. It was impossible to tell.

One night, as Godwine was teaching Eirik how to play chess, Gytha walked into the room. Godwine paused, piece held high, and stared at her. She had changed the style of her hair; normally she wore a circlet, but tonight her hair was loose and flowing. Her dress was tighter, almost clinging. Seeing Godwine's distraction, Eirik turned, following his eye. He made an appreciative grunt.

"She's dressing for you, I suspect," he teased. "Never saw the like." Expecting Godwine to grin, Eirik realized that his friend was rather taking him too seriously. "Godwine," he whispered, leaning over the board. "Watch yourself. Your thoughts are as easy to read as the rune stones on Thror's hill."

Godwine barely paid attention to his friend.

"Don't be a fool, man! That girl is not for you."

Almost as though she heard his words, Gytha made her way directly to the pair. Looking for a moment at the board, she took Godwine's piece and made his move for him. Then she sat on his bench, forcing him to move over. She did all this without looking at him.

The game was ruined. Even Eirik saw that Godwine wasn't concentrating, and the student beat the teacher easily. Making a wry face, Eirik stood up, about to make some comment about not wanting to intrude. But he saw that his words would be lost on the pair.

"Look at them," Eirik said, nudging Ulf on the way out. Ale horn in hand, the Jarl turned, grinning at his sister.

"So Godwine is her next victim, eh?" He took a deep draught.

"Haven't you noticed? Can't you say anything to her, Ulf? He's burying himself."

"Talk to Gytha? I'd as lief talk to my dog; the beast pays more attention. No, stay out of this one, Eirik. She will have her fun, no matter what."

* * *

As winter began to fade into spring, and the Danes started getting restless for the sea, Godwine couldn't restrain himself any longer. He had to know how she felt about him, before it was too late; already it was the middle of March, and he was due to return to England on the first of Ulf's warships.

For many days he gave his decision deep thought, but felt he would go mad if he didn't know something; even the worst rejection was better than his torturing uncertainties. On the eve of their departure, when the men had finished loading their supplies, Godwine went in search of Gytha. He found her in a garden, picking herbs.

She stood, shaking dirt from the hem of her skirt and looking steadily at him. It was clear that Gytha would not be the one to break the silence.

Godwine swallowed, his mouth dry. He knew that this was the wrong time, the wrong approach. But his impatience had control now, and he had no choice but to commit himself and take the consequences.

Gytha seemed uncharacteristically patient, as though she expected such an interview. She even smiled a little. Encouraged, Godwine moved closer, took a hand that rested quietly inside of his own, unresponsive.

"I leave tomorrow," he began, hating himself for sounding so lame. She nodded.

"Gytha, I know I have little to offer, but I will be active in the King's service. I doubt not that I will rise to a position of power."

He paused, not really expecting a response. "I would come back to you, then, and hope that you might view my suit with a more agreeable eye." These were not words of love, but they were all he dared utter.

The edge of Gytha's mouth turned down, and her eyes narrowed.

"Do I hear you right, Godwine? Did you say your suit?" The tone of her voice was cold, but not biting.

"Gytha, do you not realize how much I care for you?"

For a second her eyes lowered, but they snapped back, determined. "I do not see how this enters into our discussion. I am of noble birth; I will marry a noble. There is no other way."

"Unless you so desire. I could talk to Ulf."

She laughed, and the sound struck Godwine like the merriment of fairies: enticing, but fatal. "My brother would be less reasonable than I."

He did not want to believe it, but a stab of unease penetrated his heart. *What if she spoke the truth?*

"Then you will not hear me?"

"I cannot, even if I would."

She tried to pull her hand away, but he did not let go until her scathing look commanded it. Dropping her hand Godwine watched helplessly as she picked up her skirts and walked away.

But he could not let her leave like that.

"Gytha..."

She stopped, her back to him.

"But would you?"

Gytha turned her head, looking him up and down, her lashes lowering seductively. Godwine felt himself stiffening yet again. He held his breath, waiting for an answer.

"I know not."

It was all she would say, and she left him standing there, fists clenched, biting his lip until he tasted blood.

She did not occupy her usual place at the feast. The next morning, she did not come out to see them off.

Godwine boarded Ulf's ship and stood by the mast, searching. He stared at the shore, until Roskilde was a dot in his vision. Ulf came up behind him, and placed a hand on his shoulder.

"I did not realize you loved my land so well." He sounded pleased with himself.

Godwine was about to speak his thoughts, but Gytha's mocking words gave him pause. How much could he rely on his friendship with the great Jarl? He merely contented himself with a nod. He would be back, no matter what she said. And she would find it difficult to refuse him a second time.

7

Ulf had left his small fleet at Greenhithe, downriver from London, and sailed to the city with two ships. They were welcomed by a small Norse guard who seemed to have little else to do besides inspect the merchant ships and collect tariffs. Canute did not keep them waiting and met Ulf's little party in the great hall of the palace.

The Danish King was sincerely happy to see Ulf and Godwine again. He looked fit and confident after the long winter.

"It has been a long and quiet season," he said, giving Godwine a quick pat on the shoulder before straddling a bench. "There has been no trouble here with the population. Of course, things have moved along rather easier since Edmund Ironside's death."

"Death?" Ulf moved in his chair.

"Did you hear nothing of what happened here?" Canute was surprised and a little peeved. "I expected some ship to have visited you before you came."

"There were none. And we came to you directly upon reaching England."

"Then you have missed a great piece of news. Edmund Ironside is dead."

The word dropped into the silence like a pronouncement of doom. Seeing that the servants had paused in their work, Canute impatiently dismissed them. He leaned toward Ulf. "No one seems to know the cause. Perhaps he was exhausted. Perhaps he was ill." He shrugged his shoulders.

"Perhaps he was murdered," whispered Ulf.

"Perhaps. It was none of my doing, no matter what happened."

Godwine wondered; he remembered Eadric's words.

Canute added, "Aethelred's race is a short-lived one. No one seems to question that he did not last out the winter. They know he was worn out from his rigorous campaign."

Ulf was as dubious as Godwine, but Canute shrugged off their objections. "Anyway, you will see for yourselves; England gives me no trouble." He got up and started pacing.

"I intend to divide the country temporarily into four great earldoms: Thurkill, my kinsman, will retain East Anglia; my brother-in-law Eric already governs Northumbria; Eadric still retains Mercia," he paused, "for now. And Wessex I will retain for myself, as it is the most powerful.

"You shall meet them all, Godwine, for I have decided to make you Earl of Kent, which is a shire in my own Wessex."

He paused, a smile on his face. Godwine had sat up, shocked at this unexpected disclosure.

"I...do not think I am worthy of such an honor."

"That is for me to decide. As Earl of Kent, you shall remain by my side; for Kent borders on London. I know you can do it, Godwine. It only remains for me to guide you through the first few months."

As Godwine and Ulf exchanged glances, Canute added, "It is in no way contradictory to my policy. The Saxons will see me raise one of their number to a great rank; they will understand that I bear them no ill will. You, Godwine, will help set the standards for my new government."

The Saxon could do nothing else but place himself on one knee, and swear fealty to his King.

* * *

Canute's housecarls, his personal fighting force, had eventually settled into their own section of London, near Canute's residence, complete with barracks, brothels, and alehouses. It was to one of the latter that Ulf directed Godwine, to celebrate his good fortune.

But the Saxon had something on his mind that was more important than celebrating. With his new status came an elevation in rank that placed him almost on a level with a Jarl. Surely this must bring him closer to wedding the woman of his choice. He tried to drink the ale that Ulf shoved into his hand, but the liquid tasted bitter to him. Godwine was not really thirsty; it was time to screw up his courage now, before his companion was too far gone in drink.

"Ulf," he said earnestly, putting a hand on the Jarl's arm. Jesting with an old acquaintance, it was a moment before Ulf gave Godwine his full attention.

"Eh? What is it?"

"Ulf, there is something I must ask you."

"Well, out with it, lad. We have some heavy drinking to do."

"It is about your sister."

Grimly, Ulf put down his mug. "I hoped I was imagining things. Godwine, do not press me on this."

"Ulf, if I am to be an Earl, does that not make me worthy of her suit?"

The Jarl slapped his hand on the table. "Damn you, man, are you mad?"

Godwine's eyes flashed. "I have never been more serious in my life. I love her."

"Godwine, you are my friend. Else I would throttle you for your insolence. Mind your place. Earl or not, you are the son of a Thegn, and son of a Thegn you will remain. She is not for you."

Ulf did not seem to notice he had attracted an audience. But Godwine did, and pushed the mug back into Ulf's hand. "I understand you all too well, Ulf. I am good enough to be your friend, but not your brother-in-law."

"Now, do not take it that way. I am very fond of you, and wish you well. How does my sister take your suit?"

Frowning, Godwine did not answer.

"I thought so. Forget about her, lad. She is too proud, too

haughty. Why do you think I have not married her off yet? She has not found a man good enough for her."

Thinking the issue closed, Ulf ordered more ale. He was soon so immersed in conversation with the others, that he didn't notice Godwine slip out the door.

* * *

Jarl Ulf did not stay for more than a week before his fleet went looking for more adventure. He said he had much else to do, since Canute was already diminishing the size of the Danish fleet. Eirik was going with him, and Godwine was feeling quite alone already.

Ulf's parting with Godwine was cordial; neither mentioned the name of Gytha, though in Godwine's mind, at least, the thought was foremost. "You do me proud, lad," said the Jarl, taking his young friend into a crushing hug. "Serve Canute well, and your fortune is made."

For a moment, the Saxon was at a loss; Ulf was the last link to his past life. He knew that they might not meet again for a long time.

"Ulf..." He clasped the Dane's forearm, and the other returned the gesture. "I owe you much."

Underneath his boisterous exterior, the Jarl was a sentimentalist. He gave the youth a soft cuff on the head.

Then he was gone, and the ships were no more than a vision on the horizon.

* * *

Shortly after Ulf left, Canute called a Folkmoot; for as yet, he had not officially been sanctioned as King. The earls and lords of the land were called to London, and on the day of the Folkmoot the citizens of London were summoned by the tolling of the great bell to gather in the Roman amphitheater. This was an old Anglo-Saxon custom which Canute thought wise to follow.

Godwine was left to himself; no one saw fit to recognize him. As Canute stepped onto a raised platform, Godwine stood in the crowd, enjoying his anonymity. He raised his face to the sun, grateful for the gentle breeze that made this spring day seem fresh despite the thousands of bodies filling the ancient space.

"My Lords," began Canute, without preamble. "I summon Earl Eadric, Earl Eric, Earl Thorkill..." The list of names went on, but Godwine began to lose track of them; there were too many he did not know. Not exactly knowing what Canute had planned, the men whose names were called rose with more than a little trepidation. They came forward and knelt as a group, while Canute looked over their heads at the rest of the assembly.

"I call these men forth as witnesses to the Treaty of Olney. In the best interests of this country, all men should know that I, and I alone, have been given sovereignty over all lands hitherto belonging to Edmund Ironside..."

He motioned for a servant to bring him the treaty, signed on the very site where the agreement had been made. Unrolling the parchment, Canute held it up for all to see.

"It was agreed that either Edmund or I would inherit everything upon the other's death. This invalidates any possible claims that might have been made by Edmund's brothers or children. For, as no provisions were made for them during his life, so no provisions are made for them at his death.

"Is this not so, My Lords?" His voice, so often engaging, now possessed a quality like iron; he did not need to speak louder to make an impression. The question struck the assembly like thunder.

After a slight hesitation, Eadric Streona spoke first. "I swear that it is so," and he put a hand on his heart. Taking his lead, the other Earls followed, one after the other, swearing in voices so loud that they could be heard by almost everyone present.

Once this was done, Canute motioned for them to resume their original places. His face was a mask of indifference; after all this time, Godwine was still awed by his self-possession. It had been so easy, this triumph after much hard fighting. There was no cheering, no elation—just resignation. But Canute was not finished with his council.

"Hence, we shall no longer require our vast Danish fleet, and by next year I intend to dismiss all but 40 ships, which I will retain as the core of our national defense." He paused, watching the Earls nod to each other with agreement. "Nonetheless, like any other northern host they must be paid, and we need to start collecting the Danegeld at once."

A collective sigh was released. For the last 25 years, this burdensome tax had been a way of life, although every time it was collected, the amount was larger than before. If they had expected Canute to defer this tribute to the Northmen, the Saxon earls were destined to be sorely disappointed.

Stepping forward, Canute looked around again; this time he was more composed, less commanding. "I have come to a decision about taking a queen. It is my thought that she should be acceptable to both the Saxons and to my Danish countrymen. This is no easy choice, but I believe it would be a satisfactory move to recall Emma, the widow of Aethelred, from Normandy."

As he expected, the air was filled with rumbling. He paused, waiting for the noise to die down. The voices were surprised, but not really upset.

"There are several reasons for this. First, as you know, she is the sister of Richard, Duke of Normandy. Since his shore faces ours from across the channel, I would have him be my friend, so that no hostile force could use Normandy as a point from which to launch an invasion."

The murmurings were in agreement.

"Secondly, she is of Scandinavian stock, and therefore agreeable to our kinsmen in Northumbria. Also, since she has been queen in England already, I hope my Saxon subjects will see her as a link to their past, a promise of stability.

"What do you have to say on the subject, My Lords?"

For a moment, no one dared speak. But finally, Eadric came forward. "My liege, the most obvious question we all have is concerning her two sons by King Aethelred, Alfred and Edward. They could be considered rivals to your throne. Am I mistaken in my belief that they are already exiles in Normandy? Why would Richard consider your request, if he is providing them sanctuary?"

Godwine looked around as people on all sides spoke to each other, some nodding, some shaking their heads. For once, those present had to bestow Eadric grudging admiration for his outspokenness; only he dared give voice to such an objection.

Canute could not control a scowl. "It is true that those two are exiles. It is my intent to make it a condition that Emma's sons by a previous marriage be denied the right of succession. This should render them harmless. What difference will it make to Richard as long as one of his nephews becomes King, born or unborn?" The question was more of a challenge, and Eadric bowed, stepping back. Once again Godwine wondered if the little exchange was staged.

Later he found out that it was. When Godwine visited Canute that evening, the King was still chuckling. "Quite a display of showmanship, would you not say, Godwine?"

Godwine took some wine from him, a slow smile spreading across his face. "Then it was all pre-arranged between you and Eadric?"

"Of course. The man still has his uses, as you can see. Someday, I hope you and I can work together like that."

Godwine shivered. "Sire, please do not ask..."

"No, Godwine, I do not want another traitor on my hands. Merely a man who knows how to think like myself."

The smile gone, Godwine stared gloomily into his cup. "I

cannot fill his shoes."

"Never. I believe I can trust you."

It seemed that Canute had figured him out all too well. Godwine was not sure he was happy with himself...with the kind of man he was becoming. Pragmatism. Rationalization. Subterfuge. Words, all of them, but not very pleasant ones. And he knew he was capable of every one of them. Changing the subject, he said, "Then why the pretense at all? Why could you not just marry her and have done with it?"

"I must have the support of the Witan, or it would be hard going forward. I would govern England like an English King, not a conqueror." This was not the first time Canute had said this, and Godwine was beginning to believe he meant it. Odd, a Danish king and a Norseman, showing such preference to his subjects' needs.

A strange set of rules to follow, but ones that made sense, in the long run. Godwine nodded, mollified. Perhaps he would not need to be so dishonest with himself, after all.

* * *

There was still one more question to deal with: what to do about Edmund Ironside's two children, Edward and Eadmund, for whom no real provision had been made in the treaty at Olney. Although still babes, the heirs presented too real a threat, and had to be dealt with.

Even Canute balked at the thought of putting them to death in England. It had been Godwine who carefully suggested sending them out of the country. Grabbing at the solution, Canute had laughed, a little too heartily, and decided to send the boys to his half-brother Olaf, King of Sweden.

"Mayhap he will take my suggestion and lose these troublesome waifs," he said, calling for a quill and ink. "Either way, knowing Olaf, I can depend on not seeing them again."

Godwine didn't want to hear any more about it, and had moved out of earshot. But his curiosity got the better of him when a messenger from Normandy was ushered into the room.

Canute put his quill down, sitting back comfortably. "Good. I have been expecting an answer for a week now."

Godwine knew that the King had been on edge, ever since he sent his proposal to Emma. And yet now his face betrayed no uneasiness.

The envoy knelt, handing a scroll to Canute.

"Did she send any verbal message?"

"None, Sire."

"Then you may go. My steward will defray all your expenses."

Canute unrolled the scroll, looking sideways at Godwine. "I will read it to you. 'To Canute, King of England and Denmark. My Lord...'

"Sounds respectful enough, would you not say? 'My Lord, I received with great happiness your proposal of marriage. My brother Richard and I are in agreement, and I am pleased to accept your offer...with one condition.'"

Canute read on silently for a moment, then put the letter down. Godwine held his breath. "She wants me to exclude my children by Aelfgifu from the succession. How did she find out about them?"

Godwine wondered if Canute realized what he was saying. There was no secret about the King's long-term alliance with this lady from Northampton. Aelfgifu had borne him two sons, Harold Harefoot and Sweyn. Although no formal marriage had taken place, it was widely believed they were hand fasted. Regardless, the Danes did not bar illegitimate children from their inheritance.

"Emma is well known for her astuteness," he ventured. "Surely she would find out all she could about you."

After smoothing the letter and placing it safely on top of a pile of correspondence, Canute reached for a blank sheet. He dipped his quill into the ink. "Of course you are right, Godwine. Well, I do appreciate a good challenge. Perhaps I underestimated her because she married Aethelred." He laughed. "All right. I can live with it. It is only fair..."

He paused, still reluctant to commit himself to paper. "Then again, she seems to have fewer regrets than I have. I dare say, her own children may rot in Normandy for all she cares."

Emma had made no secret of her dislike for Aethelred's children. Perhaps it was because she didn't like the father, who she considered little more than a brute. Canute, on the other hand, was fond of his elder son Harold, but there was always Denmark. Or Sweden. Or Norway. To put his and Emma's unborn son on the English throne would satisfy the Saxons, and should help unite their people. He would worry about the other crowns later.

* * *

The King waited at Dover for his bride's ship. For a time, Godwine almost fancied he was acting the expectant groom, but Canute hastily disillusioned him. "For God's sake, Godwine," he said, "Emma is at least ten years older than myself. I don't know what kind of woman I am going to find; let us hope she is still of child-bearing years." Canute was nothing if not eloquent. Godwine smirked, offering his condolences to the man willing to make such a sacrifice for his kingdom.

But as the ship pulled to shore and the lady's men-at-arms jumped to the beach, Canute inadvertently grabbed his friend's arm. A slim, well-made woman was being carried to dry land, whose long brown braids did not show a hint of grey. As she was placed gently on the ground, Canute had already crossed the space between them, and had fallen to one knee, kissing the woman's hand.

Emma received his gesture with the refinement that comes to one accustomed to ruling. Her smile was elegant, her hands smooth and fine, her face, totally unwrinkled. Godwine hadn't realized what a beauty Aethelred's queen was.

As she spoke words of greeting, her voice was soft but efficient, much like Canute's. "I thank you, My Lord, for your welcome. I am pleased to be back in England once again."

The King rose; for once, his face was a mirror to his heart. It revealed satisfaction, delight, and most of all, relief.

8

It was nearing dark, and the servants were lighting the torches while Godwine played chess with the King. They sat in Canute's favorite room—perfect for entertaining the early arrivals of the Yuletide celebration. Already, Earl Eric of Northumbria was present, tasting some of the breads at the sideboard. Tovi was in his usual place behind the King speaking quietly with two other Danes, and a musician was in the corner, plucking on a harp.

The door opened and Godwine, whose back was to the newcomer, concluded who it was from Canute's grimace. The sleek voice of Eadric Streona confirmed his guess. "Good even', your grace. I hope you are well." All other voices in the room stopped.

Canute moved a piece, nodding an answer.

Two servants followed Eadric into the room, carrying a batch of firewood. For a moment, the sound of wood being stacked filled the silence. Then the servants left the room, bowing.

"And yourself, My Lord Eric?"

The Northumbrian Earl moved closer to the King, bending over the chess-board. "Considering the rare quiet within my earldom, I am content. And yourself, Eadric?"

Godwine heard the newcomer striding back and forth behind him. His concentration broken, the Saxon quickly turned around, watching Eadric rub his arms as though he needed more warmth. Godwine turned back to the board, but not before he noticed Eadric's mouth twitch.

"I could be better." Eadric's tone brought Canute's head up questioningly. Godwine straightened in his seat but Canute caught his eye, nodding at the board. Eadric took a stick and poked the fire.

Taking a closer look at the Earl, Godwine noticed that his hair was unbrushed, his fingernails were cracked, his clothing wrinkled. He began pacing again, adjusting his belt.

"How is that Christmas pie?" Canute asked Eric, holding out a hand for a taste. The Dane cut a piece for him, proffering it on the edge of his knife. Taking a long time to sample it, Canute leaned back, evidently enjoying the taste. He licked all five fingers and wiped his hand on his tunic, then reached for another chess piece. Eadric stopped pacing and faced Canute, his arms crossed over his chest.

"And what might be the problem?" The King's voice sounded appropriately concerned.

"My earldom is restive," he started slowly. "The populace has not yet recovered, the revenues are poor, and the people are hungry."

"That is a pity."

"More the pity that the King does not concern himself with their troubles."

"I see," said Canute, interested. "And what of the exemption I gave them from this year's taxes?"

Closing his eyes, the other gestured as if it were nothing.

"Eadric, this is not what is bothering you."

Stopping, the Earl glared at the King, unable to hide his antipathy. He came to the table, leaned over it. Godwine could smell alcohol on his breath.

"All right. I believe that I deserve better than this. You have given me the most devastated, the poorest earldom in the kingdom. You exclude me from your council. You treat me like a stranger. After all I have done for you."

"And what is it that you have done for me?"

Eadric straightened up, crossing his arms again. He took a deep breath. "You know damned well."

Intrigued, Canute gave Eadric his full attention. "I know damned well," he repeated softly.

The tension between them was so strong it felt as though there were only two people in the room. Everyone knew Canute was at his most dangerous when he was totally quiet. But Eadric seemed beyond caring.

"Ask Edmund Ironside, if you could."

Godwine gasped aloud, more in amazement at the man's blatant admission of the deed than its actuality. Even Canute had paled. Getting slowly to his feet, he faced Eadric so fiercely that the other stepped back.

"Then you shall get everything you deserve. You killed your own lord! My sworn brother! Your own mouth has pronounced you a traitor; let the blood be on your head.

"Eric, dispatch this man, lest he live to betray me as well."

The Earl of Northumbria was not loth to obey. Pulling an axe from his belt, the man moved purposefully toward his enemy, narrowed eyes reflecting his satisfaction with Canute's command.

For a moment, Eadric froze, unbelieving. Then his instinct for survival gained sway, and he pushed the table over, making a dash for the door.

But Godwine blocked the way—Godwine, this nonentity, who had barely rated his acknowledgment. The Saxon was standing with legs apart and drawn sword, opposing his exit.

Preferring to die under the blade of an equal, Eadric whirled, pulling his sword. But he was already too late. Eric's axe was making its deadly arc, and Eadric's blade came up uncertainly, not even delaying the impact of the edge as it cleanly severed his head from his body.

Canute had been watching from the fireplace. "Throw the wretch's carcass from the window, into the Thames."

Eric was glad to do so. He had hated the Earl, and saw this as a fitting end to a despicable career. Seizing one of the convulsing legs, he dragged the body across the floor, oblivious to the gushing blood. Stooping, he hoisted the corpse onto the sill and dumped it unceremoniously into the river.

Godwine stared at the disembodied face, as it gawked back at him. Then he grabbed the hair and came up behind Eric, flinging the head through the window and far out over the water.

As he listened for the inevitable splash, Godwine felt an eerie satisfaction; at least this once, he had done his part in wreaking revenge on the betrayer of Edmund Ironside, and possibly his own father way back in 1009.

Both bloodied Earls turned to Canute, who had observed the scene dispassionately. "Thank you. You have done me a great service."

Godwine controlled his trembling with an effort. "You drove him to it, didn't you?"

"You might say that. Although I was expecting his demands in a more rational form...and at a better time." He glanced at the horrified servants, who were huddled at the newly opened door. "Yes, come in, come in. As you can see, it is time we met the queen in the great hall and started our celebrations in earnest. Send for some water and buckets and take care of this mess.

"Oh, and come, my friends. Let me arrange for some clean tunics before you present yourselves."

9

By late summer of 1019, Canute felt well-enough established in England to make an expedition to his native Denmark; it was time he secured his hold on the country. And there had been a lot of trouble with the Wends, who threatened Denmark from the south.

Jarl Ulf was waiting for Canute when the King landed at the mouth of the Elbe with nine ships and a large Saxon contingent under the command of Earl Godwine.

"Well come, my liege," said Ulf, ceremoniously embracing the King. "And how is your son Harthacnut?"

"Talking already." Canute flushed with pride. "And you know, Ulf...if I didn't know any better, I'd say he took after you. You both share the same stubbornness."

The Jarl laughed, clapping his brother-in-law on the back. "And where is Godwine?"

"On board his own ship, with his own command. He has come a long way since you last saw him. I am sure he will be joining us soon."

Ulf led the King toward a tent which had been erected as a temporary shelter. "And will you be staying the winter?"

"Yes. I have a great desire to see my sister Estrid. How goes it in Denmark, otherwise?"

"Very well, very well..." The Jarl refused to look at the King. Canute detected a note of dissatisfaction in Ulf's tone, but decided to say nothing.

"Ah, there he is." Ulf dashed from the tent, clapping Godwine on the back and pretending to punch him in the chin as if he were still a boy. They embraced two or three times before returning, and Canute fancied that he saw Godwine wipe a tear from his eye. The King watched them silently, crossing his arms. His eyes were growing cold, and he knew his lips were tightening, against his will. Canute was glad they weren't looking at him; it was a hard thing to watch them together. And jealousy was not a very kingly attribute.

* * *

Earl Godwine stood at Canute's side, while they surveyed the enemy encampment from the summit of a large hill. The Wends were spread out nearly a half-mile away, but even from this distance it was easy to tell that there was no organization in their army.

A tribal race, the Slavs were more experienced at a hit-and-run style of warfare; they had no real commanders, only a handful of jealous chiefs temporarily joined in a common cause.

"I see no challenge here," said Canute, turning to Ulf.

The Jarl scratched his beard patiently. "Do not fool yourself, Sire. Though not used to fighting as a unit, they are fierce warriors, and do not seem to fear death."

Canute crossed his arms. "See you, Godwine, how they are scattered. Even their mounts are left to graze outside the encampment, though I dare say they are well guarded."

The Saxon nodded intently. This was his first command, and he was determined to make the most of it.

They turned back to camp, while Canute seemed deep in thought. "What is their favorite mode of fighting?" he asked Ulf.

"We haven't met them face-to-face. They excel with the knife. And they attack from behind. I lost many men who did not watch their back."

"I suggest we make good use of our bows, then, and kill as many as possible from a distance."

"Yet they are well armored, as you shall see. They boil their leather in wax, making it hard as iron."

"Then it shall be a challenge indeed," Canute said, more to himself. "But it is a shame to waste my men on such rabble."

Godwine was listening to this exchange in silence, but Canute gave him an idea. As soon as possible, he excused himself, and went looking for some of his men he could most trust.

The sun was going down when the Saxons met before Godwine's tent. Already the Earl of Kent's confident manner and quick wit had won over many a Saxon who originally scorned him as a Danish minion. Often and again, Godwine had stood up for one of his own vassals who had suffered from the inevitable hardships incurred by a new reign. It had soon become clear that Godwine was his own man; yet he managed to hold the King's ear.

He stood proudly before his sworn men, chin up, hands on hips, his lips parted in a half-smile that always served him well.

"Men," he said, "I have an idea."

"Make it a good one," someone called.

Smiling, the others chuckled.

"We have before us the opportunity to prove ourselves the most valiant fighters in Canute's army. Many of you still feel the shame of serving under a foreign king. Well, let me tell you: there is no disgrace in joining our arms with so formidable a force. And yet, we may yet prove to them the mettle of a Saxon warrior."

He bent forward, intent on his thoughts.

"These Wends have one large disadvantage that Canute seems to ignore: they are most vulnerable in their camp. I propose that we launch a night raid while they are sleeping, and dispose of the lot of them."

Straightening, Godwine watched as his companions talked among themselves.

One of them finally spoke aloud. "No one fights in the dark."

"Yes. How could we tell our enemies from our friends?" chimed in another.

"It is simple," Godwine said, knowing his argument was already won. "They will be the ones crawling out of their blankets."

Uncertain laughter followed that comment.

"But see, men, how this is to our advantage. It is not done. So they will not expect it. Nor will Canute. In the morning, when he finds that we have done his work for him, think how impressed he will be."

At first there was silence. Then a low murmur, rising to excited talking, gave the Earl his answer, as the others crowded around slapping him on the back. It was only a matter of informing the rest of his company, and establishing the appropriate signals.

As the evening passed the men carried on as usual, enjoying their secret and mixing with the Danes, until the moon had finally set and the Norsemen rolled themselves into their bedrolls. Godwine stared at the embers of his fire, listening to the sounds of camp die down. Finally, he raised his head, a glint of anticipation animating his features, and nodded to his few companions. In seconds they were gone.

Doffing his armor and strapping on his sword, Godwine felt an unaccustomed exhilaration. Before, he had faced his own countrymen across the field of battle. But now, with no such compunctions, the excitement was invigorating; he was beginning to understand the Danish lust for warfare.

Godwine met his men at the rope pen where the horses were tethered. At first he worried about trouble from the guards, for these were Ulf's animals. But a few well-phrased words explaining his purpose—and inviting them to join the expedition—were enough to gain the cooperation of these impulsive Northmen.

Before long, the Saxon force, four hundred strong, were quietly mounted; they moved well out of hearing before kicking the horses into a canter. As they covered the half-mile at a rapid pace, the Saxons spread out into a wide arc, many horses deep, with Godwine at their head. Seeing dying campfires directly before them, the Earl shouted "Now" and sank his heels into his horse. The steed leaped forward, with the others close behind.

Although surely the Wends must have heard the thundering hooves, they were not prepared for the ferocity of the attack. Running confusedly around the camp, many of them barely had the time to grab their weapons before the horsemen were among them, slashing and stabbing, running them down. The screams of the victims were drowned by shouts of triumph and the whinnies of horses.

Godwine spurred his mount toward what he thought was one of the chief's tents, and was nearly unhorsed by a brave youth who threw himself against his waist. Almost without thinking, the Saxon twisted in the saddle, bashed the pommel of his sword against the man's head, sending him spinning.

Lowering himself against the horse's neck, Godwine saw two of the leaders crouch before him, swords upraised. When he was only a few feet away from the pair, he jerked the horse into a rear, driving them apart.

One of the chiefs went down, struck by a flailing hoof. The other jumped clear and came back, intent on driving his blade into the beast's side. For a moment Godwine thought the man was going to succeed because he was clear-headed enough to stay out of reach. But suddenly another horse loomed behind the Wend, and the rider plunged an axe deep between the chief's shoulder-blades.

Godwine looked up, startled. "Eirik! How did you get here?"

"You didn't get away totally unobserved," the other grinned, wiping his face. "I thought you were up to something, and I didn't want to miss any action." Turning, they saw that the battle was over. Many of the Wends that hadn't been killed were scattering across the field, pursued by the Saxons. More than a few went down under their blades.

"Sound the recall," Godwine shouted. Turning to his companion, he added, "Once again you have saved my life. And I didn't even know you were with Ulf."

"You've grown too big for me, I'm afraid," began Eirik, but Godwine stopped him with a hand on his arm.

"What? Impossible. I've been lucky, that is all." He looked around. "As long as you're here, take that other chief prisoner for me, will you? He does not seem badly hurt."

As the horns were sounding, Eirik calmly dismounted, disarming the man who offered little resistance. Directing a place of confinement, Godwine went to survey the rest of the camp.

What he saw was a carnage. Men were lying in various unnatural positions, blood soaking the ground. Tents were strewn all over, belongings scattered, flames beginning to spread from untended fires. The wavering light cast an ominous glow across the scene.

Yet another glow was taking over, from the east. The sun was not far behind, and with it would come Canute.

* * *

Indeed, Godwine did not have long to wait. Before long he could hear the tramp of the Danish army, and after a while the horizon was darkened by an impressive array, spread wide to make it appear larger than it was.

Godwine turned to his men. "Let us face him head-on," he said. "I think the direct approach is the best. Only a dozen of you, I think, so he doesn't feel threatened. Eirik, will you come?"

The Dane hesitated only a moment before nodding his assent. Godwine felt comfortable with this man at his side; Eirik gave him confidence. Silently, the little troop rode out. A few furlongs away from the camp they stopped and waited. For a moment Godwine was tempted to turn back; it took a lot of courage to face such a formidable sight, looking for battle. What if Canute attacked without asking questions?

From the movements of Canute's army, it was apparent they didn't know what had happened. Finally, as they neared, a small group broke off under the leadership of Canute, and made its way forward. Godwine motioned for his men to do the same.

The Saxon had eyes for nothing but his King. Canute was seething with barely suppressed rage, and Godwine's throat momentarily tightened beneath the Dane's deadly stare. He was glad he hadn't turned against this unforgiving lord.

"So," Canute spoke icily when they had stopped, face to face. "You choose to desert me to the enemy. And you, too, Eirik. You disgrace yourselves."

"Why no, my liege," interrupted Godwine. "I merely wanted to spare you the trouble of an unnecessary battle."

"What?" The King stood in his stirrups, gazing over Godwine's head. "What mean you by this?"

"We took the camp during the night, destroying and scattering your enemies."

Godwine's companions audibly let out their breath as a smile broke over Canute's face. "You scoundrel. I was ready to thrash you!" Moving his horse forward, Canute embraced Godwine in front of everyone. "Come. Show me their encampment."

As the King moved away, his army broke into chaos, running forward, joking with the Saxons, looking for loot. Godwine brought Canute to the tent where a considerable number of hostages were kept at spear point. The chiefs were shoved forward. Meanwhile, feeling very much the Earl of Kent, he stepped back, leaving the fruits of victory to the King.

"Godwine!" he heard from the rear. "There you are. At least you could have asked me before you borrowed my horses."

The Saxon turned, seeing Ulf dismounting. "You might have spoiled my surprise," Godwine laughed, putting an arm around the Jarl.

"It might have gone better for you if I had," said Ulf in a lower voice. "I thought Canute was going to have your head. I never saw him so furious."

"But look at him now."

Ulf looked at the King, towering over his supplicating prisoners, hands on hips, and couldn't help shaking his head in wonder. "You are right, lad. If anything, he is the happier for all the relief he must feel. You take chances with him, for certes."

"I keep his life interesting. It is just a matter of knowing when I can get away with it."

* * *

The rest of the day, Canute wouldn't let Godwine out of his sight, treating him like a hero and laughing at the joke. They embarked on the King's ships and soon left the Elbe behind, heading for Roskilde ahead of Ulf, who still had to board his horses. At first, Godwine enjoyed the little voyage. The water seemed bluer than he remembered, and the little patches of water skirting the lowlands glistened in the sun. In the distance, the hills rose majestically on the verge of his sight. However, as they neared the settlement, Godwine became more and more uneasy. His nervousness was so obvious that Canute misinterpreted the reason.

"Be easy, Godwine," he said. "You gave me quite a turn, but I am content." He emphasized his words, putting a hand on Godwine's shoulder.

The other smiled, keeping silent. Canute did not need to know that he was not the reason for Godwine's uneasiness. It was Gytha's scornful face that kept intruding on Godwine's thoughts, and the more he tried to shrug off his stress, the worse it got. He had never mentioned the lady to Canute, but his secret wouldn't stay buried for long. By the time the ships sailed into the harbor at Roskilde, Godwine had broken into a sweat.

The people were streaming onto the beach as before, in welcome to their lord. This time at least, there would be no new widows. Canute made his way through them slowly, enjoying the ungrudging attention of his subjects, calling most by name.

At the gate of the settlement stood Estrid and Gytha, dressed in their best clothes; when the King approached, they bowed to the ground.

"Come, sister, that is no way to greet your brother," he called, striding up and raising Estrid by the shoulders. They embraced warmly, while Gytha remained in her uncomfortable pose.

"And you, sister-in-law."

Gracefully, Gytha straightened, allowing Canute to kiss her cheek. Godwine was breathless; she was even more beautiful than he dared remember.

Canute took each woman's arm, leading them inside. The Saxon followed reluctantly, feeling out of sorts. The lady had not even glanced at him. *What else had expected her to do?*

Ulf's great hall had been beautifully prepared for the King's welcome. Tapestries depicting heroic events of Canute's ancestors were hung on every wall, and the gold threads glistened to the dancing torch flames. Overlapping shields added even more color to the walls, and a wide carved throne overlooked the hall.

A great meal had been prepared for the King, and he sat at the head of the table, giving Godwine the place of honor at his side. Watching the King joke and laugh, Godwine envied his tranquility, for surely he felt none.

Trying not to watch Gytha, Godwine found himself too nervous to eat. At first, he was satisfied with furtive glances in her direction, until to his dismay Canute motioned for him to move over and make room for her between them. The pretense was finished.

Godwine could almost feel the air tingle as Gytha sat down. He tried to cover his anxiety by drinking a full horn of ale. Then, taking a deep breath, Godwine turned directly to Gytha, and found her looking at him. "Are you not going to greet me?" she asked.

He couldn't help but spit out a laugh. "I suppose I was waiting for you to say the first word."

"And why was that?"

Curse the woman for her taunting. She knew full well why that was. "I...was not sure of your welcome." He spoke in a low voice, so that she had to lean her head toward him. He caught another whiff of her musk.

"Ah."

Canute was speaking to her; Gytha turned and answered him, effortlessly sustaining two conversations at once.

"And did you know of Godwine's role in the battle?" the King said with a wink to his friend. "He stole upon the enemy camp without my even knowing of it, and scattered them without losing more than a score of men. I am so pleased with him, that I have decided to make him Earl of the West Saxons."

Godwine put down his knife, mouth open. He was totally unprepared for the honor. This earldom had never before been under any other jurisdiction than the King's. Even Gytha was forgotten in his excitement.

"Sire. I am overwhelmed."

Smirking, Canute pulled a piece of meat from the bone. "It is well deserved, Godwine. You have served me admirably as Earl of Kent."

"Earl of Kent?" asked Gytha, showing some interest.

"Just a part of the West Saxon earldom. Or Wessex, as it is commonly called. Of course, I'll do all the formalities within the law, so it won't be official for a month or so. But from now on, he will govern essentially all of England south of the Thames. My duties as King have not permitted me to give Wessex the attention it deserves. It is the most important of my earldoms, as well as the wealthiest."

"That is quite impressive, Godwine."

The Saxon turned a grateful look on the King.

"He has helped me with my Saxon subjects, who have looked to him as their spokesman," continued Canute, enjoying himself.

"This new position makes him the first subject in the kingdom." Godwine looked sideways at Gytha, hoping that she was paying attention. But she was in the process of getting up.

"Pardon me, Sire. I must attend the rest of our guests."

Canute graciously dismissed her, reaching for a game bird from the platter. "Will you share this with me, Godwine?"

The Saxon shook his head, moving closer to the King. "Sire, how can I thank you?"

Canute grinned. "For the earldom, or for telling you in front of Gytha?"

It was Godwine's turn to smile. "How did you know?"

"Aside from the fact that your face gives you away—and you really should work on that, Godwine, it only encourages her—there is little that escapes my notice. I know, for example, that you asked Ulf for her hand, and that he refused you."

Godwine sat back, astonished. "He told you."

"Of course not. But you must realize that, as a foreign King, I must have ears in every wall, eyes in every room. I do not relish the idea of being taken by surprise, with rare exceptions." He smiled, looking at Godwine sideways.

Godwine didn't know whether to be insulted or relieved; he had somehow thought himself too trusted to be spied upon. "Then I have suffered in silence for nothing."

"In my opinion, you should not suffer over a woman anyway. Though she is beautiful...but five years older than yourself, you know." He was eyeing a serving girl, who was pouring mead into his cup. "But if it makes you feel any better, I will do what I can to aid your suit."

"No, please. I would not like Ulf to resent me, thinking I curried favor with you to steal away his sister." He couldn't keep a note of bitterness from his voice. "Besides, I do not think she would have me."

"Whatever you want, Godwine." He grabbed at the wench, pulling her onto his lap. The Saxon thought it best to get some air.

He pushed away from the table, stopping here and there to talk before he reached the open door. The cool breeze felt good on his face, and Godwine stepped outside to look at the sky. It was fully dark by now; he watched the silhouettes of people walking through the settlement. Sitting on a bench before the longhouse, Godwine wondered how he was going to survive another maddening Danish winter.

As if in answer to his question, Gytha wandered outside. Without waiting for an invitation, she sat beside him, though she did not begin a conversation. Godwine decided to use her tactics against her. "I suppose you came out by accident."

She gave him a little half-smile. "Not really. I was not being fair to you, Godwine, and I wanted to apologize."

That was more like it. "Perhaps we were both a little uncomfortable."

"No." Her voice was flippant. "I just had so many things on my mind."

Godwine bit his lip. For once, he wanted to shout at her, compel her to admit to real feelings and stop this arrogant game-playing. But instead he said, "Then you will have a whole winter to be preoccupied with."

"And you may find me cruel. So let me apologize now for all the times I will be insensitive to you."

Godwine wondered if she was joking. Her face was inscrutable.

"Gytha," he ventured, leaning closer. "My status has changed considerably since the last time we spoke..."

She put a finger to his lips. "So soon? Let us not speak of this now."

And then she was gone, on another one of her duties. *So this is how it's going to be*, Godwine thought. *I must learn to forget her.*

* * *

Forgetting Gytha proved to be an impossibility. She was always near, always ready to talk to Godwine, as long as the conversation stayed away from the subject of love. Yet all the while, her movements were intentionally alluring – every stance a practiced pose. She wanted him to want her; he was sure of it. She seemed to take pleasure in his discomfiture.

Ulf returned in a couple of days, though his natural jollity was somewhat dampened by Canute's presence. The King affected not to notice, but Godwine was uncomfortable. At his first opportunity, he pulled the Jarl aside and asked him about it.

"It's nothing, lad. I just do not like the way Canute has been ignoring Denmark in favor of England these past couple of years. It is not good for our country. I can only do so much as regent, you understand, and I am not sure how to talk to him about it."

Godwine looked around. "It does not strike me that the people are suffering."

"Suffering? No. We can take care of ourselves." That was all he would say, shrugging off any further talk by assuring Godwine that his worries were for naught.

* * *

As the winter days reached their shortest, the hall resounded with laughter and excitement. The biggest oak Jul log was selected and brought inside so the ritual runes could be carved onto it, calling on the gods to protect one and all from ill-fortune. Outside, a live tree near the longhouse was ready for its annual decorating.

Svein grabbed Godwine by the hand and pulled him toward the door.

"Come," he called, laughing. "Help me with the ornaments."

The boy barely stopped wriggling as Gytha fastened the clasp of a heavy cloak around his shoulders. Godwine smiled at the domestic scene and picked up a box loaded with crackers, little carved statues, pieces of dried fruit, and even berries strung together.

"Come with us, Gytha," he said, holding out his free hand.

For a moment she hesitated, then with a smile, she grabbed her own wrap. The three of them joined the growing crowd outside who were already hanging small lanterns and candles from the tree. Godwine picked Svein up and held him high as the boy carefully fastened the little pieces to the branches. Gytha handed up her favorite choices as Svein clamored for more.

In the clearing, Ulf was putting a torch to a large bonfire and he called out the chorus to a solstice chant. Gytha joined in and Godwine looked at her profile against the flames, thinking that she looked like a magical fairy. Svein squirmed to be let down.

"Over there," he pointed. "I see a spot that needs a holly branch."

Many more decorations found a place on the tree before Svein tired of the task, and he pulled Godwine down to the bonfire. There was a mead vat nearby, and even the children were allowed a little drink for the holiday. Ulf grabbed his son and placed him on his shoulders.

"Now I am bigger than you," Svein called to Godwine. Ulf laughed and carried the boy away, leaving Godwine and Gytha together.

"Come," she invited him. "Let us sit before the bonfire." A circle of big logs were already placed around the fire and Godwine joined her after filling two flasks with mead.

"I don't exactly understand your celebrations," he said, "but I can't help but enjoy it!"

Gytha bent over to pet a white dog that was sniffing around their feet. "Ah, I forget your homeland is south of here and your days are longer. Jul begins just before the Solstice, bringing about the end of the darkness and the beginning of the light. For twelve days we celebrate, burning the Jul log to give power to the sun and bring warmth again to our shores."

Godwine raised the flagon to his lips. "I'll drink to that!"

Inside the great hall, lighting the Jul log was a happy and elaborate event. The carved log was sprinkled with mead and decorated with dry sprigs of pine and cones. As it was lit, musicians plucked the strings of their harps and started the singing. Soon the hall was echoing with laughter; Godwine and Gytha were squeezed together as the happy crowd surged around them.

The days started to blend together, but one night stood out from the others. This is when the children filled their shoes with straw, carrots and sugar lumps and set them out by the fire to feed Odin's flying eight-legged horse Sleipnir as the God led the Wild Hunt—the host of the restless dead—through the darkness. In return, Odin would leave the children small gifts and sweets as a reward.

Canute was relatively quiet during the festivities, and Godwine spent many hours by his side observing the drinking and dancing; the feasting was excellent and their seats overlooked everything. Most of the others kept their distance from the King, but Godwine felt no such compunction. Canute seemed to appreciate his company.

"I think this is the last time I will take part in the old celebrations," Canute said, running his finger along the carved dragon head on his chair arm. "It does not sit well with the Christian traditions." Nonetheless, the King allowed himself a sly smile. "Of course, perhaps we can introduce a few Norse traditions to the English, eh?" He rubbed his hands together. "But I yearn to go back. England feels more like home now, and I would see my wife and child."

* * *

The spring thaw came quickly this year, and even Gytha thawed a bit. Godwine fancied he was making progress with her, but before he was ready for it Canute was announcing their return to England. Ships were pulled down to the beach and inspected, caulked, and tarred. Boxes were packed, sails were patched, stores were readied.

Godwine busied himself with preparations, but finally the hour came to say goodbye to Gytha. He couldn't resist one more attempt to speak his mind, though he didn't really hope for much encouragement. He looked in the great hall and found Estrid instead, giving her a farewell kiss on the cheek. He strolled through the kitchen area and almost stumbled over Svein who was playing with some kittens. Ulf was on the beach disentangling a fishing net. He gave Godwine a big bear hug and promised to see him soon.

Finally, Godwine spotted Gytha in the garden, bending over the first spring flowers. She straightened as he approached, pushing back a wisp of hair.

"Wait," she said as he took her hand. "I know what you want to say, and I have not changed my mind."

Godwine cocked his head, discouraged from stepping any closer. "Can you really be so sure? Is parentage really so important to you? I can offer wealth, power, position. Is that so little?"

"Godwine, what makes you think I would want to move to England?"

He had never thought of that before. He blinked hard. "There is nothing for you here."

"Oh? I do not agree. Good-bye, Godwine. I shall miss you."

There was nothing more to say. With words of love unspoken, Godwine took his leave.

Canute was waiting for him before embarking. "Is the snowflake as frosty as ever?" he asked.

Godwine looked at the settlement. "I think she drives me mad. It is just as well that I am leaving this place."

10

One of the first things Godwine did on returning was to visit his parents. It had been more than three years since he left his home, a frightened boy with a brave face. For the time being he had been content to ignore his past, as though hard work would eliminate his unequal birth. But he was only fooling himself. His last words to Gytha proved that.

And so, he told himself, since he could never escape his background, it was time he dealt with it. Wiltshire was a part of his own earldom, now. His parents would be his subjects. How ironic that now, more than ever, he was unsure how to talk to them.

Godwine pulled rein at the very spot he had last turned to say farewell to his land. Ulf had been so right; he was a totally different person, now. This country where every tree, every bush was a landmark, all seemed so drear now, so alien.

Even Wulfnoth's farm showed a different front. At least his father had been putting the money he had sent to good use. The paddock area was twice its original size, filled with fat sheep and lowing cows.

As Godwine unsaddled his horse, Wulfnoth came around the corner, drawn by the noise. For a moment they stared at one another; then Wulfnoth straightened his back with an effort, trying to seem more vigorous than he looked. Godwine held his breath, taken aback by the way his father had aged. He had made sure that they did not suffer any hardships, but he had given little thought to their health.

"Father," he said, taking a step forward.

"My son." Wulfnoth met him, placing his hands on Godwine's shoulders. "You've changed."

So many unspoken thoughts went into those words. But Wulfnoth was not one to succumb to emotions. "Will you be staying long?"

"A few days. How is mother?"

"Not very well. She has missed you terribly."

Wulfnoth led the way to the house, walking in front of his son rather than beside him like the old days. He left Godwine inside an empty room, to await his mother's approach like any common guest. When she did appear, leaning on his father's arm, she showed nothing of Wulfnoth's restraint.

"Godwine!" she cried, throwing herself into his arms. He felt her bones through her garment, and was alarmed when she started sobbing and coughing. This wasn't what he expected.

"Now, Godgifu. Do you want to chase the boy away?" Wulfnoth chided.

Caressing his mother's hair, Godwine look up at his father. Wulfnoth had trouble meeting his eyes, but finally took a deep breath, holding his gaze.

"I owe my advancement to you," Godwine said softly. "Why didn't you tell me?"

Wulfnoth sighed heavily. "Son...I always meant to. But I was ashamed."

The two were hesitant as Godgifu sat down, wiping her eyes on her sleeve. It was clear she had nothing to say, and Godwine suspected that the conspiracy of silence had always been an issue between the two of them.

"Son," Wulfnoth started again, "I'm not sure what they told you..."

"The truth?" Godwine interrupted bitterly.

"Whose truth?" Wulfnoth snapped defensively. "What truth are you living in now?"

About to say something, Godwine stopped, closing his mouth. There was no point in pretending his innocence. They had both served the Danes; both had made enemies.

"Father," Godwine ventured, "how did it happen?"

Wulfnoth looked at Godgifu and she nodded, closing her

eyes. "Look," he said. "Anger, real anger will make a person do things they might regret later. I was in command of the royal fleet; I served the King well. Nonetheless, Brihtric Streona coveted my position, and when he told Aethelred that I had turned pirate, the King believed him at once. Without even listening to my defense. That was his way, you know," he added bitterly. "Aethelred stripped me of my command and I barely escaped with my skin. I fled the court with 20 ships, and lay waste to Brihtric's lands. When Brihtric came after me with my own fleet, he got caught in a storm and nearly all 80 ships were destroyed. The Royal fleet. My fleet. Just to finish him off, I set fire to the wreckage."

Godgifu got up and Godwine pursed his lips, watching her leave the room.

"It was said that I aided the Danes, Godwine, but my real aim was revenge. Once I started down that path, there was no turning back. Yes, I served with Swegn Forkbeard, to my great regret. But I never fought face-to-face against my own people." Those last words came out with more rancor than Godwine expected to hear.

Finished with the story, Wulfnoth got up and followed his wife from the room. Godwine sat a moment then walked to the door. His parents stood in the next chamber, arms around each other. They both turned and looked at him.

"That's why we lived so quietly," Godwine concluded. "You were in exile."

Wulfnoth shrugged. "Voluntary exile. The Saxons left me alone because they were afraid of the Danes. The Danes left me alone because they had no more use for me," he said.

And yet Canute remembered. Wulfnoth's shame led to Godwine's rise.

"All has changed now," Godwine said quietly. "You can come live with me."

Both parents shook their heads. "No, my son," his father said.

"We are finished with all that. I will never again leave this shire."

More uncomfortable silence. Godwine just stared at them. They were strangers now, and not part of his world. He hated to admit it to himself, but he was relieved at their decision. Why not just leave things as they were?

She started to cough again, and Wulfnoth supported Godgifu as he led her to bed.

Originally intending to stay for a couple of days, Godwine changed his mind. He wanted to be as far away from here as possible. When his father came back into the room, he could see they were in agreement.

"Son," Wulfnoth hesitated. "I think it would better if you did not come again. It upsets your mother too much." He turned away.

Godwine stared at his back for a moment, trying to think of something to say. Nothing came.

11

"Godwine, come look at this!"

Canute was bending over a low stone wall. He pulled some weeds out of the ground and pointed to the chiseled characters along its length. He ran his fingers over the letters, reading them aloud: "V-E-S-P-A-S-I... Yes, that is it! I knew it. This is the very spot that Vespasian had his camp. So this must be his palace."

He straightened up, looking at the ruins behind them. Although covered in places with mounds of dirt and sand, the foundations of a large structure were clearly in evidence. The building had been constructed well back from the shore, but it had the most splendid view of a deep inlet from the Chichester harbor. The Romans most obviously agreed that Bosham was a perfect port, for evidence of a long stay were everywhere. From the road to Winchester, they had passed the remains of an old amphitheater, and it was rumored that there was a Roman Bath somewhere around this town.

Godwine shaded his eyes, looking out over the wide tidal basin. He could see a short tree-line on the other side. The King took a deep breath. "Oh, how I love this spot, Godwine. It calls to me."

The other nodded. Not only was this a well-sheltered cove and perfectly configured to bring ships close in to shore, but the air was warm and the sun cast long shadows on the emerald-green seaweed at low tide. Three small boats leaned in the sand, as though waiting for the water to come in. Ducks were pecking for food, looking like patches of brown here and there as they moved across the beach. Canute's stone wall extended far to the left, apparently the remains of some ancient dyke, and a seagull sat on a projection, squawking at the world.

"This is it." Canute started up the hill toward the little stone church. "This is it, Godwine. I shall rebuild Vespasian's palace and make this my summer home. And since we are so close to the Isle of Wight we can rebuild the port so we can bring in materials for both our palaces, and attract plenty of trade as well."

"Both our palaces," Godwine breathed, catching up with Canute.

"Of course. But surely yours won't just be a summer home. Why not make this the center of your earldom? You have easy access to the sea, and a Roman road to Winchester. Look, I have the perfect spot in mind for you."

Godwine never saw Canute so animated. The Dane stopped before the heavy wood doors to the little stone church. "But first, come inside. Let me show you something."

They stepped into the building and had to pause a moment before their eyes adjusted to the poor light coming in from small windows near the roof. "Look." Canute pointed at an arch between the nave and the tower. "Look at the foundation of that arch. I am sure it is Roman."

Godwine was amazed. "I had no idea you were so interested in the Romans," he said. "How did this happen?"

Canute shrugged his shoulders. "Through my travels…I kept finding new things. You should see Fishbourne palace, right down the road." He sighed. "I will go there some day. To Rome, that is." They turned around when they heard a sound. Three monks were standing in surprise by the open door. Canute coughed.

"Do you tend to this church?" he asked quietly.

One of the monks stepped forward. "Yes, My Lord. There are five of us." He paused uncertainly. "May we offer you something?"

"No, no. Come, Godwine."

The others stepped aside, bowing as Canute passed.

"I doubt they know who we are," the King muttered. "But I need to repay a wrong…"

He strode forward and Godwine followed, shaking his head in wonder. This was quite a mystery.

Just a little to the north of the church, Canute beckoned to Godwine. "Here it is, you see. Another foundation. This would be a fine spot to build your house. The Romans have started it for you. We can still see the whole bay." He put his hands on his hips and nodded, looking to the east and west. "Very fine indeed. Don't you agree?"

"For certes. But how do you know this place?"

"Ah." Canute pursed his lips. "Well, I will tell you. Oh, there is Thurkill. He will remember." Canute waved to the Jarl, who had been exploring the other side of the point with a handful of his followers. Thurkill joined them and handed over a wineskin. "Tell Godwine what happened here," Canute said, wiping his mouth.

The other Dane grinned. "Let me see… I think that was just before your father became King in 1013. After old King Aethelred fled from the Isle of Wight, we explored the waters around Portsmouth. I remember coming up this harbor and finding Bosham. Young Canute wanted to stop here." He took back the wineskin and raised it to his lips. "And he was right… there was good plunder. I don't know what possessed us, but we had to have the great tenor bell in the tower." He gestured toward the church. "It took some time to get it down to the boats, but we eventually managed. We tied that bell to the cross-benches of the ship, good and tight. And after we left, the monks must have returned pretty quickly and started ringing the rest of the bells, to warn their neighbors, I suppose. Wouldn't you know, that big tenor bell made a huge bong in response, then crashed right through the keel of the boat!"

Canute nodded. "And fell to the bottom of the channel, taking the ship down with it. We lost many men that day. I take it as a sign of God's displeasure."

Thurkill made a dismissive gesture; he hadn't seen fit to

convert to Christianity.

"So you see, Godwine," Canute continued. "I intend to rebuild that church. It will be a fitting place to worship when I have done." He kicked a rock and watched it skitter over the ground. "But let us be on our way to Winchester. I would see the babe tomorrow night."

* * *

Winchester was one of the most important towns in England, and the walls built by Alfred the Great were still in good repair. As Canute led his little troop through the south-facing Kingsgate, his royal Housecarls joined him. They led the Danish King in state past the Minster to the Old Bishop's Palace, where Queen Emma was in residence. She was in the great hall when Canute entered, and smiled as the wolfhounds ran up to him, barking their greeting. The Thegns surrounding her bowed to the King.

The Queen had easily regained her figure after the birth of Harthacnut. As she turned toward Canute, her dress clung to her legs and draped prettily around her body. He tugged gently at a long braid as he kissed her on the cheek, lingering a moment to sniff her hair.

"Ah, Stigand," he said, raising his eye and giving Emma a quick squeeze on her arm. He approached the priest and put an arm around his shoulder. "And how goes our new Minster at Assandun?" he asked before moving out of earshot.

Godwine was behind Canute, and as the King moved away he found himself face-to-face with Emma. He bowed, not knowing what to say. Emma gave him one long appraising look then turned back to one of the men she had been talking to.

Taking a long sigh, Godwine went looking for some ale. She reminded him of Gytha, and he didn't want to dwell on the similarities.

* * *

Canute was as good as his word. Within a fortnight Godwine was back in Bosham directing the hordes of workers that showed up by boat bringing tools and supplies. A steady stream of wagons approached the town, loaded with timber and stones. Luckily, Godwine was very good at organization and he enjoyed the challenge. Of course, once the master mason and carpenter showed up Godwine knew his building days were over. He had already kept his petitioners waiting too long.

The building project started with Canute's palace, and at first the King made frequent visits to observe the progress. At the same time, the old port was revitalized and sea walls were strengthened. When the royal palace was well underway, Godwine started construction on his own house. But by then, his duties were growing and he had very little time to devote to their building project. It was just as well; the Queen was pregnant again and Canute spent most of his time in Winchester.

* * *

The Anglo-Saxon chroniclers were quiet in the early years of King Canute's reign. A great assembly was held in Oxford which was attended by all the chieftains in England. There it was decided to observe the laws held in Edgar the Peaceful's reign of two generations before. Both the Danes and the Saxons were content with the terms and all swore an oath to support the old ways. Canute continued to concentrate on religious issues and started building a new wing onto Bosham church.

It took two years to finish Vespasian's reconstructed palace, and Godwine's manor was not far behind. The little town grew quickly in importance, and many new buildings sprung up near the port. The old Roman mill-race was dug up and two new mills erected. Canute spent much time at his palace and the halls were beginning to look like Winchester, as men gathered to bring their disputes to the King and the resident Earl.

Even Canute's detractors began to agree that his rule was much better than the previous king. Prosperity was everywhere. Of course the Danish raids had stopped, even though Canute continued to demand a tax levy to pay for his remaining fleet. This was still preferable to the alternative.

* * *

March and April in 1021 were taken up with plans for Canute's royal progress into the North. Their ultimate destination was York, where Archbishop Wulfstan was busy compiling a set of laws that would codify for all time the testaments of the Oxford Assembly.

"We will call it the Winchester Code," Canute stated simply, wrapping up a clean set of vellum he was taking with them. "This will be more complete than the Oxford Code, and I intend for everyone to see my hand in it."

The packing was nearly finished; Canute put a beautifully embroidered cloth on top of the vellum and closed the wooden box. "The Archbishop is one of our most important allies," he said to Godwine. "We will present his laws to the people in a most convincing ceremony."

Canute had a way about him that convinced everybody that he meant business. Godwine bowed, and offered to carry the box himself. "I understand that we will be returning via Northampton?" he asked as they walked outside.

The King looked around to make sure that Emma was not in hearing. "We will spend a week there. I would visit my other children."

Godwine nodded. Canute's first wife, Aelfgifu, still held a place of honor among her own people, and Canute had no intention of putting her aside. Meanwhile Queen Emma was still recovering from the birth of their second child Gunhilda; she would be staying at Winchester. Godwine decided that the timing of this progress was not coincidental after all.

"I am looking forward to seeing all of them," Canute added, almost in a whisper. Godwine thought he saw a wistful smile cross the King's face. "Sweyn must be at least six years old by now, and Harold five. Oh, and we can't forget little Ingrid. She's the eldest, you know. We must bring them something very special to play with."

Canute's train was slightly smaller than a small army, and it was understood that none of his great lords could accommodate them all. They would pitch their tents along the way and make little camp cities, just like on campaign.

The King was in good spirits. At the head of his cavalcade, Canute turned back in satisfaction. "Imagine," he laughed. "It will be like the good old days without the raiding."

Tovi, riding on his other side, guffawed. "Without the women, too."

The riders matched their pace to the supply wagons which gave them time to actually enjoy the scenery. They stopped at every Saxon town so the populace could see their Danish King; it was a rare monarch who ventured this far north. Always a festive occasion, there was no shortage of people lining the streets and cheering at the gaily colored ranks. On occasion Canute would pause at a local church and leave a generous donation.

Aelfgifu lived in the timber palace that overlooked St. Peter's Church in Northampton. The main street, named after its patron saint, passed through the city gates and led to the palace itself. News of Canute's approach preceded them; Aelfgifu was waiting for him at the door of the palace with her three children, who were trying their best to hide behind her skirt. Canute dismounted and knelt on the bottom step. The little girl came forward first, curtsied to her father then ran into his arms.

"You're the very image of your mother," he said happily.

Canute stood, hugging the child then put her down. He turned the girl to face Godwine who had just come up behind them. "Ingrid, meet Earl Godwine, my good friend." Godwine bowed to the child; she put out a hand and he kissed it. The child tried to act dignified but broke into a grin and lowered her head, blushing.

By then, both Sweyn and Harold had come forward, pushed gently by their mother. Canute smiled at Aelfgifu then took each child by the hand, leading them through the door. Hesitating a moment, Aelfgifu turned to Godwine, smiling thinly.

"You are welcome, Earl Godwine. My men will show you to your lodging." She gestured to three men standing behind her then took Ingrid by the hand, giving her a little tug. Ingrid looked back before the door closed behind her.

The timber palace had a great room large enough to accommodate thirty of Canute's housecarls. Long trestle tables were loaded with breads and cheeses, and as the men picked their places on the benches the servants starting carrying out plates of meats. Canute and Aelfgifu sat on a little raised platform all by themselves, facing the other tables. He was relaxed while she sat quietly, taking very little food. Godwine noticed that the King watered his wine. Before the evening was over they slipped away, though by then very few of the revelers noticed.

The week passed quickly as Canute visited St. Peters and discussed ecclesiastical issues with the local bishops, walked by the river with Aelfgifu, and even took rides to neighboring villages. He mounted each child on a saddle in front of a warrior and brought them along. Harold and Swegn kept wanting to race, and at a sign from Canute the soldiers laughingly obliged. Ingrid insisted on riding with Godwine, and she kept up a lively chatter, introducing him to every flower and tree by name. Later that evening when her mother wasn't looking, she crawled into her father's lap. Canute smiled at Godwine over her head.

"I think we'll bring her back with us," he said. Ingrid looked up at him hopefully. "Would you like that?"

"Oh yes," the girl clapped enthusiastically, and he put her down.

"Then it's settled. You will stay in my new palace at Bosham by the sea." *Where Emma rarely went,* Godwine thought. "Go put together your favorite things," Canute added. "We leave the day after tomorrow." Patting her on the rump, he sent her off.

Canute looked at Aelfgifu across the room and leaned toward Godwine. "I noticed that she cares not for the child," he said quietly. Godwine had noticed too, but was reluctant to say anything.

* * *

Harold and Swegn weren't happy at the new arrangement, but Aelfgifu was indifferent as expected. "Why can't we come?" Harold pouted. "I want to go to the sea, too."

"And me, too," whined Swegn.

"Hush," their mother admonished them. "Remember that you are princes."

Harold hung his head. "I still want to go."

"It is not for you," Aelfgifu said gently. "I need you here. You must learn to rule one day."

If he could have, Godwine would have rolled his eyes. Canute pursed his lips. The boys were not happy but knew when to mind their mother. She herded them away with a backward look at Canute. It wasn't pretty, but the King pretended not to notice.

Godwine was glad to get away. It was a long journey but Ingrid never complained. Happy and curious, she liked an adventure, and was soon the favorite of all the King's companions. Canute decided that she would have her own little household at Bosham where she could get a royal upbringing without imposing on Emma. That should suit everybody just fine, especially Godwine. Before long little Ingrid was riding with him on his horse whenever he would let her, which was most of the time.

By the end of the summer they were home. By winter, it was as if they had never left.

12

The room was quiet as Canute and Godwine watched the Danish Thegn, Hakon of Strangeby, leave the room. Even the dogs didn't stir. Godwine could hear the patter of rain on the shutters and counted to ten before venturing to speak. "How did we ever manage to reach this pass?" he said quietly.

The King remained silent. Hakon's news was even worse than he expected. Of all the things Ulf was capable, he never expected the Jarl to abandon Roskilde and the island of Sjaelland, as well as Scania, leaving them open to King Olaf of Norway.

"It is well that the fleet is nearly ready," he finally said. "We must sail in a couple of days."

Godwine nodded. "And your son, Harthacnut?"

"Oh, he is still with Ulf. Of that there is no doubt. I have always regretted sending the child to Denmark, to represent the crown. And at Ulf's insistence! What a fool I was."

That was a full year ago, and Godwine remembered the comment Ulf had made to him so long ago implying that Canute was ignoring Denmark in preference to England. If only he had taken the Jarl's remark more seriously then, perhaps the present upheaval could have been avoided.

Once the boy was safely in his hands, Ulf had persuaded the other disgruntled Jarls to elect Harthacnut as King of Denmark, making himself, the Regent, virtual ruler. There was some report about a forged letter from Canute requesting the election, and even a rumor that Queen Emma was behind the whole plan. Whatever Canute thought about that possibility, he kept his feelings to himself.

When the King had first heard word about Ulf's stratagem, he slowly began putting together the largest fleet England had ever assembled. Initially, the incident did not seem to require a rash response, because he had eventually planned on making

Harthacnut king of Denmark anyway. Canute was willing to wait things out rather than move too soon.

Also, Ulf needed enough time to make a mess of things; so that when Canute finally did arrive, the other Jarls would abandon his cause. The Danes were ever an independent lot, and had to be handled carefully. What he hadn't counted on was the unexpected alliance between the kings of Sweden and Norway, whose traditional antagonism usually kept them at bay. But now, they had joined forces and invaded Denmark; and Ulf's disgruntled nobles were being bought off while the land was plundered mercilessly.

Only Hakon had alerted Canute in time.

In two days, the fleet was on its way, bound for Denmark. Canute was determined to deal with his recreant brother-in-law first. They sailed up the Limfjord to Aggersborg, on learning that Ulf resided in a palace there.

* * *

The King stood before his son, arms crossed, looking sternly down at him. Godwine could tell that Harthacnut desperately wanted to embrace his father, but knew better. Shifting his weight from foot to foot, the boy smiled, a little shamefaced, but not entirely sure what was happening. After an appropriately long wait, Canute's gaze softened, since it was impossible to hold a nine-year-old responsible for an insurrection. He bent, holding out his arms. Harthacnut responded without hesitation. Then, backing up, he thrust out his lower lip, remembering what he had been coached to say.

"My uncle Ulf requests that you take us into your forgiveness."

He dug into his pouch and brought out the royal seal. Bowing, he surrendered it to his father.

Canute nodded. "And where is your uncle Ulf?"

"Inside with my cousin Svein...father, did you bring Gunhild?"

"No, son, I had to leave your sister at home. Now take me to Ulf."

Considering himself back in his father's good graces, Harthacnut skipped up the walk, leading the way. He did not bother to look at Canute's expression, or he might well have trodden more carefully.

Ulf, on the other hand, felt no doubts as to the mood of his brother-in-law. As Canute entered the room, the Jarl and all his followers fell to their knees, bowing their heads. The King went directly to Ulf, looking down at him much the same way he had greeted his son.

"I do not want to hear any excuses, Ulf. Just gather all your ships and prepare to join me against Olaf."

Without waiting for a response, the King turned on his heel and left. Ulf's face, when he dared raise it, expressed a mixture of relief and hostility; the day of reckoning was yet to come.

Obedient to his liege lord's command, Ulf fell into place with forty of his own ships; the rest were to join the fleet en route. Godwine did not have a chance to speak to him. Canute continued through the fjord and south into the sound, cutting off Olaf's escape route to Norway. They spotted the enemy toward the southern end of Sweden and quickly gave chase, lowering their sails. The Norwegian King gathered his 120 vessels and dashed east to the far side of the Scania peninsula. He had a good head start, and Canute decided to wait for the rest of his fleet before challenging Olaf to battle.

In two days they were ready. The Danes sailed around the tip of Scania, very much on the offensive. But rather than finding the whole enemy fleet in battle formation, they were greeted with only a quarter of their reported number, and these at anchor along the shore just beyond Helge River.

"I cannot see any banners," Canute said.

Godwine was a stranger to the sea, but he sensed that something was wrong. "Why would they drop anchor there? Wouldn't it be safer in the harbor?"

"Quite right, Godwine. Perhaps, because there are so few of them, they preferred maneuverability. You see, that river is very short, and ends in a large lake. To retreat that way could prove dangerous. But I think we should take advantage of their gift, and move into the space they left us. It is too late for battle today."

"Putting us into the same predicament they attempted to avoid."

"Not exactly. Our fleet is larger than theirs, and I intend to leave Ulf's flotilla here."

But still Godwine was uneasy. "Did we not hear reports that Olaf had joined forces with the King of Sweden? Their flotilla should be much larger."

"And yet many of them were supposed to have already returned home, loaded with plunder from my lands." These lasts words came out with enough emphasis to alert Godwine that the discussion was over.

The Danes boldly sailed into the mouth of Helge River, which opened into a natural harbor. Finding no opposition from the enemy, Canute concluded that they were prepared to wait for the next day to begin hostilities. He gave permission for some of his men to disembark and set up camp on shore—with the exception of those on board his own ship.

Godwine wondered at his apparent carelessness, but did not venture any more arguments. As he had once told Ulf, he knew when the time wasn't right.

The night went without incident. But when the morning sun was nearly over the horizon, Godwine was startled out of his sleep by a fierce rumbling. He jumped to his feet along with the other crew members, and turned his head in the direction of the noise.

"God's blood...What goes on there?"

Canute came running across the deck. "Quick, to your oars! Get us out of here."

Used to instant submission, the men raced to their benches without too much confusion. It took a bit longer to get the oars out and ready. Godwine looked at the enemy warships; they were still silently waiting.

"What is it?" he asked Canute, who gripped the gunnel with white-knuckled hands.

"A flood," answered the King, his voice harsh, "and we shall not escape it."

Too soon, events proved him right. All eyes were on Helge River when with a roar, a mighty white-capped wave came roaring directly at them, gushing over the banks, submerging the shore and its dozens of screaming inhabitants. To make matters worse, huge logs tumbled in the swell, shooting toward the passive ships like giant spears.

Canute didn't waste his breath shouting at his men. They had their oars in the water, but could not manage the ship's bulk in such unruly conditions. Gripping the sides, Godwine waited for the impact.

The surge hit the ship with a smashing wrench, tipping it so dangerously that Godwine thought they would capsize for sure. But no, the vessel righted itself with the loss of several oars yet nothing more.

However, there was no time to take a breath of relief. In the crush, some of the smaller ships were battered to pieces by the logs, and others bashed against each other. Canute's ship was in danger of destruction by his own fleet. The rowers were hard put to avoid the wreckage and the logs, and didn't realize at first that the angry current was pushing them toward the waiting armada.

After the first great wave, the water continued to pour through the little conduit of the river, flooding the bank. There was no hope for the men stranded on the shore; Canute watched mutely while they drowned and were borne into the sea along with the rubble.

Then, as the surge lessened, the masts of Olaf's ships appeared, bearing down on Canute from the lake he had dammed.

"Confound that man. So we were facing the Swedes all night, while the Norwegians hid in the lake. Why didn't I listen to your advice, Godwine?" The King crossed to the other side, realizing their predicament. "We are heading for the enemy, with the enemy behind us. Can you pick up some speed, men?"

The rowers tried the best they could, finally managing to hit their rhythm. For a few strokes they surged forward, then began a wide turn. But it was clear that they were too close to the Swedes.

"I fear we must fight for it. Arm yourselves. The enemy is upon us."

The Vikings were not loth to obey. Putting up their oars, they snatched their shields from the sides as the first volley of missiles flew over their heads. Some of the warriors picked up bows, and began firing at the ships nearest them. Godwine ducked, taking firm hold of a shield strap. He drew his sword, looking for Canute.

He could see that despite their precarious position, the advantage was still Canute's; since his ship's sides were so much higher than the others', the enemy could not board without climbing ropes. His men tossed the grappling hooks overboard as soon as they caught.

But the Swedes knew whose ship this was, and they began converging upon it, threatening to overwhelm the King by sheer numbers. More and more boats pulled alongside. At first, due to the height of their sides, Canute's men were able to keep the enemy at bay, throwing rocks down onto their heads, using javelins and spears and slings to great advantage. Though finally the numbers broke through Danes' defenses.

Godwine stood back to back with Canute, slashing with his sword, blocking deadly cuts aimed for the King's head. Canute's Danes had thrown themselves into a defensive circle around him; pushing forward, finding themselves forced back, they slipped on the blood spreading across the deck.

It began to look like the situation was hopeless. Then suddenly, a roar sounding like the growling of hundreds of wolves drew Godwine's attention momentarily to the west.

Bearing down on them in a tight formation, Ulf came on with a score of ships, intending to shatter the enemy's grip. The predators found themselves in an uncompromising position, and abandoned the attack, flowing down the ropes and into their own boats. Breaking loose, they prepared to meet the new onslaught.

The ships rocked when they clashed, and the Danes leaped aboard the Swedish vessels, axes upraised, shouting curses. The Swedes were not entirely ready for them, and many of their number were knocked overboard in the first assault. Both sides were well trained for this warfare, but the rocking decks made for poor footing, and the benches tripped unwary defenders moving backwards.

From Canute's deck, where Godwine paused for breath, all he could see were heaving arms, flailing swords and axes, bodies splashing into the sea. It was almost impossible to distinguish friend from enemy. More and more ships joined the fray, and men began running from one deck to another, searching for new opponents, looking for more space to fight.

And then they were returning to Canute's ship, climbing the ropes again, for here was their target. Revived, Canute's house-carls leaped to the sides, hacking at attackers still clinging to the ropes. Godwine did not leave the King, but rarely did an enemy break the strong ring of the hardy warriors.

After a time, the call for retreat was sounded. Deciding that he had won as much as he could from the element of surprise, Olaf had abandoned the battle. Unsupported, the Swedes fought with the intent of getting away, pushing the Danes from their decks. Some of them couldn't succeed in disentangling their vessels, and were forced to leap into the water and swim for their lives.

The Danes were too disorganized to give chase. Ulf went back toward the mouth of the river, to pick up any survivors from the disaster. The others began throwing the dead enemies overboard. Canute bent over one of his retainers, helping him into a sitting position.

"Sire, what happened?" the man said weakly.

The King looked at the mouth of the river. "As best as I can tell, Olaf dammed up the lake with a mass of trees he cut down. When morning came, he unleashed the whole blockage upon us, catching us sleeping. It was truly a clever move, and I was a simpleton for not suspecting it."

"Do not blame yourself, Sire. It could have happened to anyone."

Canute straightened up as Godwine approached, wiping the blood off his sword. "Not anyone who wants to survive. Godwine, next time you feel uneasy about something, do not let me shut you up."

The Saxon smiled grimly, knowing that to be impossible. "Do you think they will be back?"

"No." Canute shook his head. "We still outnumber them. They will wait for us to leave so they can return home. Victorious."

Godwine knew what that meant to Canute. It was a small victory for the Norwegians; nonetheless, it was Canute's first real defeat.

"But I shall not let him pass." The threat in Canute's voice was unmistakable.

13

Leaving a portion of his fleet to guard the northern end of the sound, Canute and Godwine went back to Roskilde with Ulf. Many of the servants had already come out of hiding, and a ship had been sent to Aggersborg for the women and children.

The night after the battle, Ulf was pacing the room, trying to walk off the effects of a particularly good meal. They had cleared the tables, but many of the Danes were still drinking deeply, Ulf included, attempting to boost the spirits of the King. The Jarl was almost festive, which contrasted strongly with Canute's dangerous brooding.

Ulf was the only one who appeared merry. The rest were heavy with uneasiness; when Canute acted like this, someone usually got hurt. Everyone remembered the 200 mutilated hostages when the Saxons recalled Aethelred after Swegn Forkbeard's death. Even Godwine felt shut out, as Canute had not exchanged more than a few words with him all day.

Finally, Ulf came to a stop with a snap of his fingers. "I know, Sire. How about a game of chess? We used to spend many hours pursuing the art of warfare with ivory pieces."

Scowling, Canute shook his head. But as Ulf turned away disappointedly, he held out his hand. "All right. It is not such a bad idea after all."

Grinning, Ulf took the board from its special box, and laid out the pieces, black in front of the King. "As usual," he said, winking at Godwine.

At first, no one paid particular attention to the game, until Canute said, "Put my knight back, Ulf."

The Jarl pushed his stool violently back from the table.

"I want to make another move," the King said.

"No. Your move was finished and cannot be unmade."

"And I say you shall."

Clenching his fists then thinking better of it, the Jarl shoved the board from the table, scattering the pieces across the room. As he made for the door, Canute jeered after him, "Are you running away, Ulf the coward?"

The Jarl froze, his back to the room. When he finally turned, his expression was reckless. "You would have run, if you could, at Helge River. Then, you didn't call me Ulf the coward, when I saved you from the Swedes who were beating you like dogs."

In a room full of silence, the closing door sounded like a slam. Everyone stared at Canute, who stared at the place where the board had been.

Godwine got up and followed Ulf; he was probably the only one who dared. He found the Jarl at the shore, gazing out to sea. For a while the two stood in troubled silence, until Ulf spoke. "I have not learned, like yourself, to choose the right moment."

Godwine laughed shortly. "I doubt if you could have chosen a worse."

The Jarl shrugged. "What you say is true. I doubt whether things will ever be the same between us again."

"Ulf... what made you put Harthacnut..."

"On the Danish throne? That is easy. Without a king here, Denmark looked like a loaf of bread, ready to be carved up by the first hungry sovereign. At least Harthacnut would have been a figurehead."

"They came anyway."

"Only because my supporters turned their backs on me," he growled. "We Northmen are an independent and hardy lot, Godwine. Under the command of a strong leader, we are invincible. But when left leaderless for a long period of time, our chiefs take matters into their own hands. That is what happened. The other Jarls wouldn't accept me as the regent; I was an equal, not their King. Only Canute could have held them together."

Ulf's voice was resigned. He put an arm around Godwine's shoulders. "He let me down, Godwine. I suppose that is why I blundered tonight. Tell me. Do you think you can talk to him for me?"

"In a couple of days. When he has cooled off."

"Then you will have done me a great service. I do not think anyone is as close to him as you are."

How ironic, thought Godwine, watching Ulf walk slowly back to the buildings. *And I would not have been, but for you.*

When Godwine went back into the room, most of the men had left. Canute sat at the head of the table, silent and brooding, staring at his hands. He didn't look up when the door closed; nor did he acknowledge Godwine's presence as the Saxon sat by his side. Godwine swallowed the last of his ale, watched Canute for a long moment, and then went to bed without saying anything. It was probably the biggest mistake he ever made.

When he woke up the next morning, his first action was to see if the ship from Aggersborg arrived. It had come just before dawn and the women had already disembarked. Tarrying to help unload, Godwine was returning to Ulf's longhouse with one of Gytha's bags when a servant nearly knocked him over, running toward the shore.

"Slow down," said Godwine, as the boy bent to help him retrieve the bag. "What is the rush?"

"Oh, My Lord." The servant burst into tears. "My master has been killed."

The Saxon stopped, the sack forgotten. "Killed! What are you talking about?"

"By orders from the King. He was murdered in the church this morning, while at prayer."

Godwine crossed himself superstitiously. "Ulf, murdered? Are you certain?"

"I saw his body myself. It was done by Ivar White, a heathen who has no fear of God. Ulf knocked the altar down as he fell, spilling the sacrificial wine all over the floor and himself. He was on the ground face down. I need some help." The boy continued on his way, shouting for the other servants.

Not thinking about what he was doing, Godwine shoved the last of the things into the bag and swung it over his shoulder, stumbling into the stronghold. He ran through the settlement, taking no notice of the hushed voices and nervous stares, and burst through the door. Canute sat alone at the table, calmly eating a piece of bread and cheese. He did not look around when Godwine stopped at the threshold, breathing heavily.

When he had gained control of his voice, the Saxon moved slowly into the room, placing the bag on the table. "You could not have done it." Canute looked sideways at him, then tore off another piece of bread. "Sit down, Godwine."

"Why did you do it?" He couldn't control it after all; his voice had raised to the point of hysteria.

"I said, sit down!" Canute's tone forbid any argument. Godwine sat.

"Sire, he asked me to interpose for him." Shaken, Godwine put his head onto his arms, an unforgivable act in the presence of a king. But Canute did not object.

"Godwine. This was between Ulf and myself. There were many things at issue." He slammed his fist on the table. "Curse him for a traitor! Ulf should never have threatened me at Olney."

Olney. So long ago. But Canute had not forgotten.

Godwine raised his head.

"But..."

Holding up a hand, Canute stared at him unblinkingly.

"I offer you his sister in marriage. She is yours."

Gytha. The unapproachable Gytha. With a word from the King, she could never again say no. But at such a cost! Godwine stared back, dreading this man and what he himself had become under the King's influence. Canute offered him the only thing he had no power to refuse.

He knew it was a bribe. To silence him. To keep his support.

Bowing his head, he said, "I accept."

Canute nodded; Godwine could tell he was relieved.

"Go, Godwine. Make sure he gets a proper burial. Order the monks to open the church and go on with the mass."

Here was a chance to make his peace with Ulf. Godwine left the room as quickly as he could, and ran to the church, ignoring the several people who were trying to question him. As if his very life depended on it, he pounded at the church door: no response. Angered, as if the monks were deliberately keeping him from his friend, Godwine pulled his sword and banged with the hilt; it made a mournful, booming sound. After a while, a monk timidly opened the door.

"I have come for him," Godwine said to the other's relief. "Canute has ordered you to continue with the mass."

"This house has been violated," the little man said officiously. "We cannot celebrate the sacrament..."

"It is not wise to disobey the King," the Saxon interrupted, pushing his way inside. "If you observe his will, I am certain you will find him grateful."

The other bowed thoughtfully, before scurrying off.

Godwine strode forward, passing the monks who were busily scrubbing the floor. He saw the body of Ulf on the top step near the altar, hands carefully folded atop his chest, the blood still seeping through his fingers. *At least the servant boy had done his duty*, Godwine thought, feeling soiled and unworthy.

Then, falling to his knees, Godwine burst into tears. "Oh, my dear friend. I have let you down. It happened such a little time ago?"

He stared at Ulf, half-expecting him to answer. "Can you really be dead? Ulf, you were so full of life."

The Jarl's face was set, frowning, lines of strain about his mouth—not his usual expression at all.

"I know you cannot forgive me for what I am about to do. But I promise you, I will take care of your sister, whether she will or no."

Wiping his eyes, Godwine tore a piece from his tunic and stuffed it into the wound. Getting up, he saw that the monks were staring at him.

"What is the matter with you? Have you never seen a man grieve before?"

Embarrassed, the others went back to their tasks.

"Leave him here. I shall return with help."

Belatedly, Godwine remembered that he had left Gytha's bag on the table next to Canute. He slowly left the church, in a quandary as to whether he should retrieve it and risk having to face the King in his present state. His sense of duty won and he retraced his footsteps. This time, he opened the door slowly and was relieved to see that the King was gone. Luckily, the bag was untouched and he quickly gathered it up.

Approaching Gytha's sleeping area, Godwine's steps slowed. How was he going to approach her? One thing was for sure: Canute's offer would keep. There must be a way to get her used to the idea or he was lost. But first, he wasn't sure she even knew about Ulf's death.

Coming around the corner, Gytha seemed to be looking for him and he saw that she knew nothing. "Ah, there you are, Godwine. I wondered what happened to my belongings. You certainly took your time..." She stopped, warned by his expression. "Godwine?"

He was blinking back tears. It was all he could do to keep from sobbing.

"What is wrong?" Gytha looked through the doorway, finally noticing that people were hurrying toward the church. "Godwine?"

He rested her bag against a post. "Canute," he forced out. "Canute was unyielding. He couldn't forgive Ulf."

"What?" Gytha whirled around as Estrid cried out behind her. "What about Ulf?"

Both women were staring at him. "Ulf has been killed by the

King's orders."

Estrid staggered back, catching herself at a trestle table. She sat down hard on the bench. Gytha sat beside her, taking Estrid into her arms. Both started crying.

"My brother killed by your brother," Gytha whispered. "How could this possibly have happened?"

Estrid shook her head, wiping her eyes on her sleeve. ""I saw this trouble coming for many months," she said. "Ulf would not listen to me. He said he knew what to do with the King…he said Canute looked up to him. Oh, my husband."

Gytha glanced helplessly at Godwine, tears streaming down her face. Looking at her, he almost forgot his own misery but he knew she was unlikely to accept any comfort from him.

Eirik came into the room and started toward Godwine.

"There you are," he said. "I was looking for you. We need your help."

Awkwardly, Godwine sat for a moment by Estrid's other side. "I loved him like a father," he whispered in her ear. Still leaning her head against Gytha, she reached for his hand. Giving her fingers a squeeze, he patted her back and followed Eirik out the door. Secretly, he was relieved to get away.

* * *

Godwine knew very little of the burial customs of the Northmen; he was grateful for the prompt aid from the others of the settlement. First, they dug a shallow grave. Then they helped Godwine carry Ulf respectfully from the church. The body was lowered into the grave dressed in the clothes he died in; certain fruits were added, to hinder decomposition. A wooden board was placed over the body then covered with a layer of earth. It would take ten days, they told him, to prepare for the funeral.

Godwine worked with them every step of the way, avoiding the King as much as possible. They pulled Ulf's favorite warship onto the shore; four posts were sunk into the ground, and a wooden platform built between them, onto which they dragged the ship.

On the deck, the men constructed a wooden tent. A couch was put inside sewn with a rich brocaded fabric, and cushions added, similarly covered and tasseled.

When this was done, two days were left out of the ten, during which the Danes indulged in every sort of drinking and wenching, imbibing something called *nabid* that left them numb and senseless. Godwine avoided this part of the ritual. Canute still had business to finish, and had asked Godwine to help.

As a penance of sorts, the King had hardly moved from the room where everything had gone wrong. He was pale and haggard; his clothes were dirty, his hair unbrushed. Some of Canute's leading navigators were present, and he was bending over a parchment with them. He raised his head as Godwine came in, greeting him with a brief nod.

"The current runs here, Sire, and there," one of the men was saying, drawing lines with a piece of coal.

The Saxon came forward. "What is it?" he asked, sitting next to Canute.

"It is an outline of the Roskilde fjord. We are going to sink five ships at its narrowest point, here," Canute pointed. "This will hinder the Norwegians from ever penetrating as far as Roskilde again."

"Nor will we be able to pass through, ourselves."

"This is true. But a small price to pay. It is not far overland." The King turned to Godwine, his eyes thoughtful. Their camaraderie was so special, Godwine felt the antipathy he had nursed all week begin to fade.

Smiling briefly, Canute turned back to the map. "I intend to leave a small fleet blocking the sound. Olaf will have to either stay in Sweden, fight it out, or go back to Norway overland. I just want to secure a few of my settlements just in case."

Reaching under his bench, Canute pulled out a bag full of coins. "This is for the monks. Would you bring it to them for me, Godwine? Tell them I intend to give them regular endowments, and ask them to pray for Ulf." So that was what the King needed him for. His eyes misting, Godwine took the bag.

Two days later, the whole settlement attended the funeral. The body was disinterred, and redressed in trousers, boots, a silk tunic, and a fur hat. Ulf was carried to the ship and propped in a sitting position on the couch, surrounded by plants, fruit, meat, onions, and a variety of other necessities. His weapons were placed at his side. Two dogs, two horses, two chickens, and two cows were killed and cut to pieces, adding to his collection. Wood and kindling were stuffed under the platform.

When this was done, everyone picked up a stick from a pile; Canute came forward, carrying a burning torch which he used to light some of the other pieces. As the participants lit their neighbors' staves, Canute thrust his torch into the pile under the platform. The others moved forward as a group, adding their own sticks, until the flames flickered around the edge, growing in intensity.

A brisk wind fed the blaze, and everyone was forced to back away, watching in silence while the wood crackled and the ship took fire, sending a shower of sparks flying into the sky.

Godwine heard Gytha's voice at his ear, though he hadn't realized she was near him. "Is it not better to burn him in a moment, so he can enter Valhalla in an instant?"

When he looked at her, the blaze made her face glow with an unearthly light.

* * *

The next morning, Godwine received an early summons to Canute. For once, he wished he had something else to do; he had a good idea what was going to happen and didn't have the energy to face yet another crisis.

The servants were just finishing the morning chores and Canute dismissed them, gesturing for the last to close the door. "Scratch my back, will you, Godwine?" He turned around, stretching, while the other vigorously complied.

"Lower...there. Aaah, that is better. Something bit me last night...blasted straw. I'll be glad to be back home; it's just as well we are leaving tomorrow."

Godwine stopped scratching. "Tomorrow?"

"Well, of course. There is nothing else to do here, and much to do in England. Oh, by the way...I summoned Gytha; I'm going to tell her about my decision." He gave his friend a sidelong look, waiting for a reaction. He wasn't disappointed; Godwine was frantic.

"Is this not unseemly? She has not had time to mourn her brother."

Canute shrugged impatiently. "There is no choice. We cannot wait. Besides, I do not think Gytha would waste much time grieving for anyone."

There was a knock at the door, and Canute grunted. "Enter." Gytha opened the door and stood outside for a moment. Seeing her face as the sun fell upon it, Godwine was not sure he agreed with Canute. Taking a deep breath Gytha came slowly into the gloomy room and knelt, stiff, restrained.

"Gytha. I have decided to give you in marriage to Godwine."

She looked at Canute in disbelief; he returned her gaze impassively. "Surely you do not mean it, Sire."

Stung by her attitude, the King stepped forward, towering over her. "Do you dare deny me?"

Gytha faced him boldly, then seemed to think better of it. "I would not dare." She lowered her eyes, though her bearing did not indicate submission.

Ignoring her implication, Canute went on. "Then pack your things. We leave tomorrow."

Straightening, backing up, Gytha turned her face toward Godwine, a bit bewildered. There were tears in her eyes.

He hesitated, watching her pass through the door, then decided to follow. At his questioning glance, Canute carelessly gestured for him to go.

Godwine knew this was a mistake. He knew she would not wish to speak to him. But he couldn't just let their new life start this way.

Catching up with her, Godwine touched her elbow. "Gytha..."

She whirled around, her cheeks wet, lip trembling. "Well. It seems you finally got what you wanted."

"Gytha, it was Canute's idea."

"I am sure. And did you help kill my brother to accomplish this act of gratitude?"

Godwine stepped back as if she slapped him. Finding herself released, she took two steps forward. Then she stopped.

"I know that you did not," she said, her back to him. "But can't you see? Whether you did or no, you are stained with his blood."

"No. I loved him as you do."

"Loved?" She turned on him, surprised to see the tears on his face though she was too angry to care. "When he stood in your way? Do you expect me to believe that?"

"*You* stood in my way, not him."

"And yet you have me, since he is gone."

"What would you have me do? Refuse this marriage?"

"Yes!"

The word came out with too much vehemence. Godwine looked away from her. But when he faced around again, she saw that she had gone too far.

"No. You will find, Gytha, that being the wife of a mere Earl is not the end of the world. Perhaps it will teach you some humility."

He left her then, trembling at the bitterness in his voice. Gytha looked hopelessly around, feeling totally alone for the first time in her life.

* * *

Gytha traveled in state, accompanied by a horde of servants. Godwine personally escorted her to his own ship, but chose, himself, to make the journey in Canute's company. Perhaps the week spent alone would give her time get resigned to her new life.

At least she could have shown him a little gratitude for his consideration. But no...as expected, she permitted him to take her hand and walked silently by his side, not deigning even to glance in his direction. Godwine bowed to her when she was safely aboard, then retreated without expecting a response.

The fleet was ready to go, but Canute had not appeared as yet. Deciding to leave Harthacnut in Estrid's protection until he could appoint a suitable regent, the King was making his last arrangements. He had deferred discussing the matter with her until now; Estrid had not been entirely gracious toward him after Ulf's death. When he finally appeared, giving the instruction to raise anchor, Godwine noticed that he was unusually pale.

"Is she speaking to you yet?" he asked.

Canute sighed. "She is a tough woman, my sister. By the time she was finished with me, I must have yielded half of Sjaelland to her. And she is terribly upset about Gytha."

Godwine reddened.

"No, Godwine. It is not that she doesn't like you. She just feels very much alone. But I have something in mind that might ease her loneliness..." He stopped, looking thoughtful.

"Since Richard of Normandy died and his son Robert has become Duke, our relationship is a little strained...they call him 'The Devil', you know. I heard that he makes his vassals swear on two altars, a Christian and a pagan, to insure that they are bound by their oaths." He laughed shortly. "Considering the talents of those Normans for treachery, it is not a bad idea. Perhaps he would take Estrid as a wife."

"So that he does not suddenly choose to champion the cause of Emma's sons by Aethelred," Godwine finished.

The King smiled grimly. "You get better all the time. Yes. One never knows when an exile will turn into a threat. I dare say Edward and Alfred are merely awaiting their opportunity to cause trouble. Better to pull their fangs now, since their current Duke is young and healthy, and promises to live a long life."

Godwine sighed, watching the coast recede. "So much has happened, Sire. It seems so unreal. And now I have an unwilling bride, and I do not know what to do with her."

Canute did not answer, chewing his lip. Godwine frowned anxiously, hoping he did not give offense.

"I miss Ulf, too," he said finally, answering Godwine's silent thought. "But with my people, treachery like his cannot go unpunished, or it will breed more treachery. And yet, his death lies heavy on my heart. I wish it could have gone some other way."

So did Godwine. Gytha's accusation would forever come between them.

14

Closing the door to their bridal chamber, Godwine turned nervously, at a loss for words. He had certainly not been idle these many years, but never had he felt more than a passing interest for any woman who crossed his portal. Relationships had been lively, but meaningless.

But this time it mattered. It seemed like any word could erect impassable barriers between them, when he so desperately wanted to make things right. Gytha sat on the edge of the bed, her hands motionless at the neck of her gown, staring at him with eyes so wide he thought he would drown in them.

What did he detect in her expression? Search though he did, Godwine could not discover any hate, or scorn—nor tenderness, for that matter. Her face was inscrutable, yet there was a barely noticeable trembling to her fingers.

Deciding after all not to say anything, Godwine sat beside her, taking both hands in his own and kissing her fingers one at a time. Surprisingly, she did not attempt to pull away. Daring a glance at her face, he saw her expression unchanged, though the mouth had softened a bit. He opened her hands and kissed both palms, pausing with his eyes closed, as if to convey his desire through the sensitive skin.

Her arms trembled; he dare not yet reach further.

Concentrating on her right hand, Godwine slid his lips to her wrist, tickling the skin with his tongue. He clasped her other hand, entrapping it, bringing it to his face where he pressed her yielding fingers against his cheek.

Expecting to be repulsed, Godwine was astounded that his bride seemed to be compliant, if not willing. Encouraged, he reached around her waist and pulled her toward him, delighted to feel her whole body trembling in his arms.

For a moment her hands were against his chest to push him

away, but when his eager lips found hers, Gytha forgot her reticence and clasped him to her, opening her mouth, encouraging him to explore her. Her husband responded like a starved soul; indeed, he had hungered for her many long years.

What he didn't realize was that her yearning had been great as his—just smothered under a rational assessment of their inequality.

Releasing her, Godwine pulled back, studying Gytha's face for a hint of her thoughts. Still her expression was unreadable, but he no longer doubted that he would possess her body; only her mind was closed to him.

Carefully, watching him from beneath lowered lashes, Gytha began to unbraid her blonde hair, fluffing out the strands with long, deliberate sweeps of her hand. It seemed to glisten in the light of the room's little fire. Godwine plunged his hands into its fullness, grasping the back of her neck, and drew her toward him. This time, his kiss was tender, long, and sweet, his hands caressed her head, moving her hair forward and back.

He faced her around, unlacing the dress and sliding it down over her shoulders, kissing lightly on the nape of her neck. Gytha turned then, putting a hand to her sleeve and pulling, lowering the fabric below her nipple. She reached for his head and drew his lips to her white skin and arched her back, making the little pointy breast meet him halfway.

Godwine closed his eyes, experiencing a bliss he had never imagined. He pulled the other sleeve down, cupping her breasts in his hand; burying his face between them, he savored her scent with deep breaths.

Pushing Gytha back against the coverlets, Godwine slipped his hand underneath her skirts, marveling at the curves of her thighs, her hips. She strained against him and he found her buttocks, smooth, tight, round, and he felt her hands on him, tugging at his clothes.

An urgency washed over him, and Godwine knelt on the bed,

yanking his clothes off and throwing them, until he towered over her, naked and hard. Slowly, hesitantly, she reached up for him, grasping his manhood with the light touch of unfamiliarity.

Godwine pulled up her skirts, stroking the wet place between her thighs. He lowered his body between her unfolding legs, slowly, smoothly, finding himself slipping easily into her softness—only until he barely entered her.

She stiffened then, not knowing what to do, until he kissed her lips and neck, willing her to relax, to trust him. With a soft, rocking motion he found himself entering deeper, taking her for his own, possessing her in the way no man ever dared to, while she wrapped her arms around his back and pulled and pulled...

Discovering his rhythm, Gytha curled her legs around him, surrendering herself to his motions as his passion gained control and he thrust himself deeply. She gasped out loud and he held himself pulsing against her, as if to cleave her in two.

Gasping, Godwine eased off, feeling the sticky blood against her legs, stroked her thighs and kissed them. Her legs still spread, she pulled him back atop her and refused to let go. Then burying her face into his shoulder, she wept like a child.

Godwine didn't know what to do. He rolled on his back, nestling her head on his shoulder, and embraced her as comfortingly as he could. He suspected he knew why she was crying; even the strongest of wills could break under the stress she had to endure. He knew that Gytha loved Ulf; he knew how mortified she was, being traded off like chattel.

They couldn't have married under worse conditions. Only through patience would he win her affection; but at least this was a start, he thought, kissing her hair. If he could reach her through love-making, perhaps in time her heart would come to accept him.

When her tears subsided, Gytha rolled out of his arms, turning her back to him and practically hugging the edge of the bed. Reluctantly, he left her alone, and listened as her breathing deepened into a sound sleep.

Neither had spoken a word on their wedding night.

Shortly before dawn, Godwine finally dropped into a fitful sleep. He tossed and turned; laying an arm across the bed, he woke to discover himself alone. Godwine sat up abruptly, looked around the room. It was empty. He sighed, lowering himself against the pillows. So this was how it was going to be. She did not want to risk that intimacy which morning imparted to lovers.

* * *

But it was not Godwine's way to feel sorry for himself. He was soon up and washed, and as he entered the hall his steps slowed at the sight of Gytha.

She was not aware of his presence, seated at the window with her back to him; so he shouldn't have been surprised at the way she jumped when he kissed the back of her neck.

But he was surprised.

He could tell that Gytha recovered with an effort, though her voice was flat and expressionless.

"Is Winchester anything like London?"

Godwine sat beside her, following her gaze. It was hard to remember that she had never left Denmark before.

"Since it is the capital of Wessex, the city is nearly as large...though more placid. But it is very much aware of its importance."

"When do we leave?"

Godwine was surprised. He thought she would like to see a bit of London first. "Whenever you desire."

"At the soonest, if you would. My Lord." The last two words came out levelly, though Godwine suspected he read an undertone of sarcasm. Her eyes were averted.

"As you wish. I have some business to attend today, and we shall be on our way tomorrow."

"Good." She shivered, as though wanting to leave this hated place.

"Is it really so bad?" He bent forward, reaching for a hand, but she drew away.

"Godwine..." She hesitated, not knowing how far she could push him. He had already stood up impatiently. "Is it not proper for people of our rank to keep separate bedrooms?"

"For God's sake, woman." He spun on his heel. "In due time," was all she heard, as he strode away, kicking a bench from his path. If Godwine had bothered to turn at that moment, he would have been livid at the triumphant smile on her face.

Gytha was not prepared for the fierceness of their lovemaking that night. He had come in late smelling of ale and taken her without asking permission, or even considering her comfort. He pushed her back against the pillows and ripped open her expensive chemise, thrusting into her until she bit her lip in pain, for she was still tender from the night before.

But struggle how she would, he refused to acknowledge her resistance—not bothering with caressing or coaxing, but forcing his will upon her. And much to Gytha's chagrin, she liked his mastery, enjoyed his wrath, for it fed her own and gave her strength to fight him. As he climaxed with a groan, her legs were already wrapped around him; and she found herself pushing and pulling at the same time, drawing him into her by the very motions she made to repel him.

Then he was spent, panting, laying all his weight against her and she discovered that she still wanted him, still desired his presence inside of her. Yet he ignored her embrace and rolled away, leaving her throbbing and longing, and she couldn't bring herself to beg.

The next morning they were on their way as promised; her household items brought from Denmark loaded neatly onto mules. Gytha was carried in a litter as became her rank, and for two days she watched the countryside pass from behind the curtains. Godwine came by occasionally to check on her comfort, but she rarely favored him with more than the barest of answers.

As customary for his rank, Godwine had many residences throughout Wessex. Although Bosham was his favorite, he maintained a palace at Winchester so he could be near the King. As the cavalcade crossed over the river Itchen and through the East Gate, Gytha drew back the curtains, watching with interest. The people milled the high road, pushing past them as if seeing an Earl was a common occurrence. She didn't have the opportunity to observe very much, since they turned off the road almost immediately.

They covered an open, grassy space toward a solitary wooden building which rose majestically on a hill, two stories tall. Godwine came up beside her again, a welcome sight for once since she was pleased with her new home.

"It is called Wolvesey Palace," he said, pointing. "They call it that because King Eadgar, who died in 975, used to collect a tribute of 300 wolves' heads from the Prince of Wales every year. Rather gruesome, would you not say?"

Gytha nodded appreciatively. "It will take me a while to get used to such a palace, but I find it very agreeable."

Godwine smiled a bit nervously. "Do you now? I am pleased." Trusting himself no further, he spurred his horse forward.

Gytha led her servants into the palace, running her hand over the carved doorposts. They were done in the Norse manner, and immediately made her feel more at home. The great hall was built with a high roof, supported by many wooden beams painted with snakes and dragons, intertwined with leaves.

Godwine came up, carrying some of her bags. "If this is where you live, where does the King stay?" she asked.

"In the castle, the other side of town. We shall go there tomorrow, for it is the Queen's favorite residence and Canute says she is here now."

"Oh." Gytha's face fell; she was not looking forward to

meeting Canute's formidable wife.

"Follow me, Gytha. I will show you where we sleep."

She didn't miss his use of the word "we". Gytha followed reluctantly.

Godwine climbed a wooden staircase and pushed a door open with his foot, revealing a room as luxurious as it was oversized. Heavy tapestries hung the walls; fresh rushes were scattered deeply over the floor. The bed was hung with thick curtains.

Gytha gasped despite herself. It was quite a change from the sparse environment of Northern settlements.

"I do not know whether you realize it, but your husband is one of the wealthiest men in England," her husband stated, almost flatly.

Gytha looked around as she put her things on the bed. "And where do you sleep?"

"Why, here of course." Godwine's tone was much like Canute's could be; she pursed her lips, remembering the last time the King had spoken to her like that.

He shrugged impatiently. "I did not prepare a separate room for you. As you may remember, when I left here I wasn't aware I would be returning with a bride."

She cursed herself for her stupidity.

"Unless, of course, you do not believe me," he added bitterly. Going over to the door, he closed it, then turned to her with a new resolve.

"Gytha, even if I did know, it would not have mattered. Your place is with me." He strode forward, pulling her unwilling body against his. "You had better get used to being my wife."

He kissed her hard, drawing a reluctant response, then let go. "I can make your life happy, if you would only let me." Softening, he pushed a strand of hair from her face. "I am not your enemy."

Her eyes widening, she caught at the comfortable, familiar

challenge; it was the only way she knew how to deal with him. "Then why did you tear me from my home? Why did you force me into this marriage? Are these the actions of a friend?"

But somehow, his response was not what she expected. Rather than succumb as he used to, rather than allow her to intimidate him, Godwine's grasp on her arm tightened and his eye shot fire. For the first time, Gytha wondered if this was bottled up inside him all those years, waiting to explode.

"The matter is closed," he said. "You will join me at dinner."

Gytha did as she was told.

* * *

The food really was not that bad, she thought, spooning another ladle of thick venison stew on her trencher bread. She looked sideways at Godwine who shared a wide, throne-like bench with her. They were raised a step above the rest of the household, and she wondered again why these others treated a Thegn's son with so much respect.

Godwine must have felt her eyes upon him, for he glanced around, frowning. He was still angry with her—bewildered—and she felt strengthened by his hostility. It was a reaction she could identify with.

How else did he expect her to feel? Grateful? She wanted him to suffer as she did: victimized just as Ulf was. Humility was a lesson he needed to learn, too.

And yet, when he looked away, she couldn't help that tightening in her throat. His profile was as chiseled as stone, and as strong; she longed to reach out and touch him. Her mind involuntarily returned to their first night together and the excitement of his caresses. Jerking her head in denial, her hand knocked over a chalice of wine.

Before she knew it, Godwine pulled her onto his lap as the ruby liquid dripped over the edge. The servants hurried to sop up the mess and her husband went on talking with the fellow beside him, his arm about her waist in an amiable embrace. She found herself relaxing despite herself, leaning onto his chest, feeling his hand tightening ever so slowly through the layers of her dress.

Gytha wouldn't speak throughout the evening, but when Godwine chose to retire, she accompanied him to their chamber.

* * *

Godwine woke earlier than usual, to an empty bed. He sighed, rubbing his eyes. How could she be so receptive at night, and so restrained by day? He didn't fail to notice that the accord between them was like an enchantment that could easily be snapped by the first spoken word.

They could not carry on like that forever.

In the next room he found Gytha, dressed in a beautiful, ivory gown trimmed in pearls, and her servant was just pinning her hair at the base of her neck. She turned, unsmiling.

"Does my appearance please you?"

"Very much."

He saw how it was going to be: an uneasy truce by day—broken by occasional skirmishes—then silent, anxious nights, when their bodies spoke words denied their lips.

"Come, then. There is much I must say to the Queen. Canute will join us here in a fortnight."

The morning held a sharp edge of chill, adding color to Gytha's cheeks as a servant hoisted her into the saddle. Godwine stood for a moment adjusting his stirrup, while Gytha's maid ran back for a cloak.

He turned at Eirik's footsteps. Eirik had returned with him from Denmark—not merely as a friend, but as head of his household troops. He was honored by this man's loyalty. "I am your man, now," Eirik had said when Godwine protested that he was a friend, not a servant. "Ulf was my master, and Ulf is gone. I cannot go with Canute...But I must serve someone. Let that someone be my friend." And so it was agreed.

Eirik bowed to Gytha before addressing Godwine. "My Lord," he said, "we received a message this morning from the King." He held out a scroll with Canute's seal intact.

Godwine unrolled it with a sense of relief, hoping it was a summons. Instead, the King was alerting him to some trouble that had arisen in Kent during their absence. "As you see, my bride, I must prepare to leave you already." He would have said more, but was cut short by the look of satisfaction on her face.

"We leave tomorrow, Eirik," he said shortly, swinging into the saddle. He spurred his horse forward, not waiting for his wife to catch up. But Gytha was a fine rider and was soon at his side. Eirik and five men followed.

They turned onto Cyp Street, sometimes called High Street, heading directly for the West Gate. They passed the New Minster, where the bones of St. Swithun were interred, and rode silently by the market vendors who vied with each other to attract the attention of such a wealthy patron. Next to the West Gate, surrounded by a wall of its own, rose a stone fortress much more severe than Wolvesey Palace. They dismounted in the cobblestone courtyard, and Godwine preceded his wife through the heavy studded doors.

They were faced with a bevy of servants, who led them through a number of rooms, each opening into the next. Queen Emma was sitting in a chamber with high, small windows, and Godwine was grateful for the roaring fire that gave the only comfort to their surroundings. The room was austere as its inhabitant.

"Well come, Godwine," Emma said graciously, rising to her feet and holding out a small white hand. He bowed, marveling again at how beautiful her cold features could be. She was like a statue, perfectly featured but remote, eyes seeing but not warming, lips full but lifeless.

"And of course, you are Gytha," she said, embracing the other.

From the first moment, Godwine thought they were well suited. Indeed, Gytha seemed to be impressed, and returned the Queen's hug with more than her usual enthusiasm. Godwine had not stopped to think how lonely both of them might be.

"And how is my husband?" Emma asked, showing Gytha a seat. Godwine remained standing.

"He sends you his warmest regards, and asked me to tell you he will be here in a fortnight."

Emma acknowledged his words with a nod. "And Harthacnut?" Her eyes glittered; Godwine fancied he saw tears in them. The Queen had always been uncharacteristically fond of the child. "I was so worried that Canute would be too harsh with him, poor boy." She turned to Gytha for assurance.

Godwine frowned, knowing how much of the trouble was the Queen's own making. "The boy did not really understand the issue. His father forgave him."

Emma's relief was unmistakable. She really seemed to care.

"It was Ulf who paid the penalty." Godwine couldn't keep the bitterness from his voice. He did not look at Gytha. "He was executed by order of the King."

If Emma felt any guilt, she did not show it. "I had heard," was all she said. Then the Queen turned to Gytha. "I am sorry for you. It is a hard thing to be caught like this, between brother and king."

The other lowered her head, saying nothing.

"Will you leave us, Godwine?" the Queen asked.

He felt outnumbered, already. Godwine was so glad to go that he left the castle altogether, instructing Eirik to wait for his wife.

* * *

Godwine went to London after resolving his problems in Kent, and waited for the King so they could return to Winchester together. It was another week before Canute was ready, but that suited Godwine perfectly.

He paced the floor of the King's antechamber, waiting for Canute to finish his discussion with the ambassador from Normandy. Again, his mind returned to the stiff and formal leave-taking between himself and his wife; it grated on him, as she knew it would. The night before he left, they had coupled with such vehemence that they were reduced to sweating, panting exhaustion; but by morning she seemed anxious to get rid of him.

His thoughts were disturbed by the door opening. The Norman who was just leaving paused to look at Godwine; his chin automatically jutted forward in a stance of arrogance.

The Saxon could barely stop his hand from going to his sword. He shared the natural antipathy of his people toward their neighbors across the channel. Canute's marriage to Emma had rather heightened the friction than dampened it because the union seemed to open the door to further unwelcome contact with her kin. Suppressing his impulse, Godwine pushed past the ambassador with a curt nod. He understood Canute's policy, much though he didn't like it.

It seemed that the King had gotten what he wanted. As the door closed behind Godwine, he pushed his papers across the table. "It is done. The marriage contract is sealed between Duke Robert and Estrid."

Godwine looked at the parchment. It seemed that Estrid's dowry was substantial. "And what of her children?"

"I shall leave them with Harthacnut, and have decided to send Earl Thurkill as regent in Denmark. He is best suited as a ruler of northmen, and strains at the bit in East Anglia. His nephew Thored shall be his replacement there.

"You, Godwine, shall attend him to Denmark, along with

Leofric. Leofric has not yet served as my official representative since he succeeded his father as Earl of Mercia. I think Seward will go too, to represent my northern earldoms. From Denmark, you shall accompany my sister to Normandy, and attend the wedding."

Godwine squirmed uncomfortably. He had met this Leofric and did not much like him.

"It is a necessary evil," Canute added, reading his frown. "Do you think I like all the men I promote?"

The word *all* brought a reluctant smile to Godwine's face.

* * *

They were soon on their way to Winchester, a king eager to see his wife after a long absence, and a reluctant bridegroom. Godwine's homecoming proved to be worse than he anticipated.

As soon as he entered the great hall, Godwine knew that something was amiss. The servants scurried out of his way, looking worriedly over their shoulders. Silence settled over each room as he entered, until his footsteps jarred the stairs in anger, taking them two at a time. One of Gytha's maids stood on the landing, holding out a shaky hand as he advanced.

"My lady will not open the door," she warned, her voice barely more than a whisper.

"Is she sick, then?" he asked impatiently.

"Not exactly. She..."

Godwine did not wait for the rest of the answer. He tried the door, found it locked, and pounded with his fist.

"Open, Gytha. It is me." He hoped his voice sounded reasonable. There was no answer.

"I said open, woman. I lose patience with you." Those words at least were true. Godwine's early resolve had weakened under constant rejection.

After a few more minutes of pounding, she shouted at him to

leave her alone. It was too much. He was locked out of his own room. Godwine swung around to the servant, who stood cowering against a pillar. "How long has she been in there like that?"

"Three days. We do not know what the matter is."

Was the woman trying to starve herself to death? Godwine flew down the stairs, pulling an axe from the wall, and came back, his anger nearly boiling over.

"Gytha, will you open the door?"

Silence. He swung the axe against the wood with a crunching blow. The effort filled him with an intense satisfaction, and he brought the blade back again, smiting harder. After the first few chops, splinters started flying in all directions; Godwine kept hewing at the resisting door, spitting now and then to clear his mouth.

Finally, the door gave way and he stepped inside—and ducked, grateful for his years of training. A clay pot shattered against the wall behind him.

"Go away," she screamed.

Godwine straightened, ready to sidestep again, but her energy seemed to be spent in that single throw. Gytha lay slumped against the window, sobbing hysterically.

Forgetting his anger, Godwine ran to her side, trying to take her in his arms. But she eluded him with a push that nearly sent him sprawling.

"I hope you are happy," she sobbed, tears dripping from her chin. "At least you will get an heir."

Godwine stared, his mouth ajar. "*Already*?" screamed a voice in his head. He sat on the edge of his bed, fighting the disappointment. He had hoped to win her, first. Now all his plans seemed ruined.

"Are you certain?"

Even to him, the words seemed inane.

"What do you think?" she spat. "At least now, will you give

me a separate room?"

How could she continue to hurt him like this, stabbing him with words as sharp as knives? Godwine got up, shaking his head.

"Whatever you wish," he said, denying his own will. He looked at Gytha, expecting to see satisfaction on her face. But to his puzzlement, she broke into tears all over again.

15

In a week he was out of the country, and glad to be gone. He hadn't spent more than two days at his house before leaving without bidding farewell to his wife.

This time, he was the one who refused to see her, giving orders to replace the door and move his things from his own chamber. He had locked himself in the council room, heaping logs onto the fire and making arrangements with the steward concerning the household while he was gone.

Godwine knew that Gytha was up and about, resuming her usual tasks. Twice, he even recognized her footsteps outside his door, and his heart raced as he listened to her knock. But he wouldn't give her the satisfaction of taunting him again. Not before he succeeded in hardening his resolve.

* * *

At least, Eirik's presence on board ship gave him comfort; the Dane asserted in that pragmatic way of his that she was only a woman after all, and not worth such a fuss. Godwine wished heartily that he could convince himself of the truth of those words.

But it was Leofric who took his mind off of domestic troubles: this doughty Saxon whose natural stance—chest out, arms held apart from his sides—made up for his small stature. Leofric was all ears, darting black eyes, and decisive opinion.

Seward told Godwine privately that he didn't like their fellow Earl, but said that he respected him, nevertheless. Leofric was one of those men who was maddeningly efficient, making himself indispensable to his superiors, while not caring what his equals thought of him. Seward was his total opposite. Tall, burly, imposing, he had given up none of his Northern characteristics and looked every bit the Dane. He felt himself equal even to the King.

"Watch out for Leofric, Godwine. He could prove a lot of trouble if you make him an enemy."

"Then I suggest we be his friend," Godwine said, shrugging his shoulders.

Seward laughed. "Try it. See if you can stand him."

It was almost as if they had bet on it. Godwine spent the whole journey to Denmark trying to make conversation with Leofric. Each time he ended up searching for Seward, accepting a good-natured wineskin and shaking his head dubiously.

"He makes every conversation a challenge. It seems, Seward, that we are rivals already. Does he mean to rule East Anglia and Wessex as well as Mercia?"

Seward grunted, then shook his head. "I expect he would be satisfied making an even swap, for now. You must control more than double his revenues."

"Well, he will just have to be satisfied with what he has. But I think you are right, Seward. I must not make an enemy out of him."

They found Denmark in much the same state it was when Godwine left. The landing was at Skuldelev rather than Roskilde because of the five sunken ships in the fjord, but a wide new road had been built between the two towns, making traveling easy.

Estrid had been waiting for them, bags packed. She had very little to say to Thurkill, but her eyes glistened when she saw Godwine.

"How is Gytha?" she asked, kissing him on the cheek.

"She is with child," he said, wishing he could tell her all. "Though she is not too happy in England."

"I think I will soon know how she feels. At least she understands your language."

Godwine felt sorry for her. He would not relish the idea of living in Normandy. "They are only a couple of generations from their Northern ancestors. Perhaps they have retained some of the old tongue."

"Do you think so?" Estrid asked without much hope.

They were interrupted by the children who were gathered around Godwine, tugging for attention. He picked Beorn off the ground, lifting him high in the air. "You have grown, you little fox. You are going to be a mighty fighter."

The child squealed in delight. "Can I come to England with you, uncle Godwine?"

His simple question fell on the others like a wet blanket. Beorn's elder brother Svein, still a boy in Godwine's view, wiped his eyes. "Not yet, lad." Godwine put him on the ground, bending to embrace the others. "Thurkill will take care of you for a while. He is a fine warrior, just you wait and see."

Harthacnut edged his way forward. "Does my mother miss me?"

Godwine looked the boy over. He was filling out quickly, more deserving than ever of his name, which derived from Canute the Hardy. Even as a baby he had been plump and strong.

"Your mother misses you terribly. She told me so."

Estrid was herding them off to dinner. Godwine stood and found himself looking at Leofric. He didn't know how long the Earl had been lingering there, unnoticed.

"You are quite the favorite, I see," said the other.

Godwine realized that Leofric had not been introduced. "You know how children are."

"Impressionable."

Godwine watched him stomp off, sorry to have made such a mistake. It was destined not to be his last.

* * *

Estrid was married in a small but sumptuous ceremony, and the guests were given a hearty celebration then shipped off to

England at the soonest opportunity. No one was sorry to leave.

Godwine was back in Winchester before he knew it. Only a month had passed, not enough time to dull the pain. Although Gytha was fairly genial, Godwine made no especial attempt to seek her out and busied himself with meeting petitioners, collecting revenues, supervising his household militia, and a thousand other duties.

Shortly after Godwine's return, Canute decided to go on pilgrimage to Rome. Though he left the regency to Emma, many of the duties fell on Godwine's shoulders. This suited the Earl just fine, since more and more of the Saxons naturally came to see him as their leader.

Godwine often received guests in his home as well, entertaining them in the great hall. When all the food was cleared away and the trestle tables put up, their meetings went deep into the night.

Gytha, of course, was not invited to attend; but Godwine did not realize that she often stood in a dark corner, listening.

There was much that Godwine did not notice these days about his wife. He wasn't aware of how her eyes followed him about the room, or how her pulse quickened when he came through the door. He did not realize that her pride was no longer enough to sustain her and was giving way to an unfamiliar emotion, which she had not yet identified as love.

When Gytha found that she ached for his presence, and not merely for his body, at first she shrugged it off as confusion. Her husband was avoiding her and his attitude fed the anger she was comfortably familiar with. But somehow the wrath would turn into hurt, and she was forced to shut herself into her room so no one would discover the tears.

Before long she was reduced to finding comfort in his company, even when he did not know she was there—especially when he did not know when she was there. It was at times like this that she could observe his little mannerisms, suddenly so important to her. The way he carried himself around his vassals was a revelation, for in private his bearing was altogether different. She blamed her husband for his neglect; yet she knew the cause. Still, when Gytha's birthing time came, he did stay home, unwilling to admit how important the birth was to him but unable to keep away. As was usual in these cases, Godwine waited in another room, away from the inevitable commotion attending childbirth. Gytha was in labor through the night, but by dawn he was summoned into her room.

Godwine stood at the open door, leaning against the frame and trying to ignore the sickly smell of blood. Gytha turned her head to him weakly; the hardships of the night had wiped away all signs of her usual belligerence. He marveled at her beauty after such a strain and came to the bed, kissing her hand.

He could tell that she was fighting her exhaustion, summoning her habitual defiance. "Not now, my love," he spoke, as soothingly as possible. "It is not necessary."

Gytha pursed her lips. "Don't you even want to see your son?"

His son. Godwine stared at her in wonder, then turned as the midwife carried a child to him. The baby was crying, his wrinkled face screwed up into a righteous fury. He laughed, turning to his wife. "I think we should call him Swegn after our King's father."

"And my nephew, who so wanted to marry me," she said, laughing faintly. It was a hollow gesture, but Godwine thought it was a start. He took the baby and tried to put him into Gytha's arms. But to his surprise, she pushed him back.

"He is yours, Godwine. Your heir. Is that not what you wanted?"

Her eyes shot defiance. She had found the strength to deny him, after all.

Godwine looked at his little son, unable to stop a tear from escaping his eye. How unfortunate for this tiny thing, defenseless in a world where its father could not even capture the love of its mother. "Must you do this to us?" He met Gytha's eyes, begging.

She looked away. "I cannot control how I feel."

"You will not allow yourself to feel what I know is there!" He knew that he was raising his voice. Swegn began crying louder, waving tiny fists in the air. The midwife took the child away and ushered him, unresisting, from the room.

Godwine left home that very night, not trusting himself in the same house with his wife. He alternated between moments of desperate love and murderous anger, and knew that the day was coming when they would have it out, once and for all. But the time was not yet.

* * *

There was only one place he could go that would comfort him. Godwine turned his horse's head south to Bosham, riding ahead of his retainers who knew enough to keep a respectable distance. His little homestead had turned into quite an estate, housing a significant staff of servants and carpenters; he and the King had established a shipyard next to the harbor. Godwine's first ship of his very own was still under construction and he was anxious to see its progress. But first, he wanted to see little Ingrid.

By the time they reached Bosham, Godwine's natural equilibrium had reasserted itself. They neared the port as the setting sun was casting long shadows across the bay and the sky was turning a splendid shade of pink. He was happy to see Canute's daughter walking along the edge of the sand in the company of her tutor. Ingrid bent over to pick up a seashell then saw Godwine approaching on his horse. She let out a wild shout of delight and ran toward him. He was waiting for her.

"Well met!" he laughed, picking up the child and twirling her around. "I am so glad to see you."

"Come," she said breathlessly, pulling his hand as he put her down. "I want to show you my new favorite place." Laughing,

Godwine waved at his companions to relax and handed his mount to a servant. Ingrid had already run far ahead of him then came back, skipping. Her tutor picked up a light cloak the girl had dropped on the sand. He smiled at the Earl as Godwine reached for the cloak.

"She has been very good with her lessons," the tutor said. "I thought she deserved the afternoon off."

"Indeed. Why waste this beautiful evening?" They followed the girl to the top of a small sand dune. Ingrid stood tall and threw out her arms.

"I am queen of the hill," she called. "And you are my servant." Godwine bowed. He looked back at the church steeple, glowing in the last rays of the setting sun. Behind the church he could just see the timber walls of his palace.

He sighed. One day, perhaps he could bring Gytha to live here. But not yet. He would have no discord at his lovely home.

* * *

He was back to Winchester in two weeks, learning on his return that Gytha had found a wet-nurse for the child. It came as no surprise; it was not at all uncommon. But he knew why she chose to do so, rather than nurse the baby herself. She had already rejected her first-born.

Godwine was surprised when she made an appearance at dinner. As usual, the hall was crowded, and Gytha made her way slowly to head table, taking her place at his side. She smiled to him, all signs of conflict gone from her face.

They had not spoken a word since that terrible dawn. She still did not speak, as though ready to continue their familiar game of silent compliance, spoken discord.

But as her hand rested lightly on his leg, Godwine felt an odd disgust for the same old routine. It was no longer possible for him to pretend that everything was all right. He wanted her unconditionally or not at all.

Trying to seem unobtrusive, he moved away slightly. But he could not help glancing at her and found the shocked expression gratifying. Pretending not to notice Godwine gnawed on a bone, throwing it to the dogs.

After a while, she touched him again; again he pulled away. He fought the urge to respond, knowing that he would hate himself later. Gytha seemed to get the idea and let him be, but her expression when he left the table was nearly too much for his resolve. But Godwine was happy he resisted; for the first night in months he slept soundly.

The next few days were uncomfortable. Gytha harped on her servants; she refused to see the baby. Her absence at dinner was much commented on. But at the end of the week, as Godwine was mounting his horse, he was surprised to see her tugging at his stirrup.

"Where are you going, my husband?"

It was all he could do to keep his mouth from falling open. "I must attend the King as a witness for signing some new charters. He only returned from Rome a few weeks ago, as you know."

"Oh." She stepped back, letting him go.

Godwine thought she wanted to say more, but he was in too much of a hurry to wait for her. "I will be back in a week," he said, waving as he spurred his horse out of the gate. Though he tried to ignore it the look on her face lingered in his mind; it was the oddest mixture of hope and frustration.

That expression had its effect on him. What had started as a natural reaction to the situation, began to develop into a deliberate plan. Was his resistance cutting through her blockade? Was he finally getting to her?

16

From the moment his horse rode into the courtyard, Godwine systematically avoided his wife. He dined alone, closeted with a pile of papers. He hunted at dawn and came back after dark. When he did run across his wife Godwine put on his most distracted face, barely finding time to greet her.

Gytha was stumped. She had never been witness—like so many others—to the wiles of her husband in council, where his well-known guile had become notorious. She didn't know that he was so adept at changing peoples' minds that often an argument was won before his opposition even entered the room.

But he had never used his talent on her. His wife had always considered Godwine a guileless man, moldable to her will. Until now. Suddenly he was a different person: unforgiving, unsympathetic, and worst of all, unapproachable.

* * *

What else Gytha didn't know at first was the length of time he spent with the baby. Little Swegn was a squalling child; and no wonder, thought Godwine for the hundredth time, picking him up and walking about the room. With a father rarely home and an indifferent mother the boy found little comfort in this cold, drafty nursery.

Godwine bent over the cradle, putting the infant on his stomach. He murmured a few words, stroking the baby's head. Looking up, he was startled to see Gytha standing in the doorway. She was staring at him with a new look of respect in her eyes.

"So this is where you spend all of your time," she said softly.

He coughed, embarrassed. "Only some of it."

Gytha came in, looking at the child as if he was a stranger.

"The nurse said he is a fretful baby..."

"Perhaps he is lonely."

The rebuke was not lost on her. "Try how I will, I feel nothing for him." Her voice was defensive.

"The same way you feel about his father," he muttered. This was going nowhere. Godwine turned to leave.

"Wait."

Her hand was on his arm. Godwine stared at it, wishing it gone. "Perhaps that has changed," she said.

"Oh?" He was pleased with the rancor in his own voice.

"I have missed you these weeks."

He pulled carefully from her grasp. "Do you think it so easy, Gytha? You reject me, you reject my child. Then you think everything will be all right just because you miss me?"

Gytha turned from him, a hand before her mouth.

"Surely I am not the fool I once was," he added, unmoved. "You can stay or go however you will. I leave tomorrow for Norway with Canute. He campaigns against King Olaf."

Gytha put out her trembling hand to stop him, but he was gone without a pause. Godwine did not want her to see how difficult those words had been.

She turned, looking down at the child. Swegn coughed sleepily, and she bent to pick him up. At that moment the nurse walked into the room and Gytha straightened, relieved. Here was somebody else to comfort the child. She left the babe to the nurse, ignoring the woman's expression of surprise at her presence.

* * *

Gytha paced the floor of her bedchamber. A maddening sense of unreality overwhelmed her. What if Godwine died on campaign? What if she were never to see him again? Could she really leave their misunderstanding unresolved, perhaps forever?

No...*misunderstanding* was not exactly the right word. It would be better to call it deliberate injury. She had set out to hurt him as much as she could and had succeeded beyond her wildest imaginings.

But something had gone wrong with her plans.

She grabbed a brush, running it through her hair and tugging impatiently at the tangles. In hurting him she had injured herself; for somehow her bitterness had turned to love. Had she always felt affection—smothered, denied, yet enduring?

She turned at the sound of footsteps but they continued past her door. No, they weren't his. She slowly replaced her brush, holding her breath; then she ran to her bed, grabbing a cloak and pulling it around her shoulders. It had suddenly occurred to her he might leave during the night.

Breathing heavily, ignoring the cold floor beneath her bare feet, she ran as fast as she could to his room. Then, unsure of her welcome, Gytha paused before Godwine's chamber. What if there was another woman inside? What if he turned her out of the room? How could she stand the humiliation? There was light coming from beneath the door. Hesitating, a hand on the latch, she listened for voices; hearing none, she gave a soft push.

Staring at the bent back of her husband, Gytha realized with embarrassment that she had never bothered to see the inside of this room before. She was surprised at the austerity of the surroundings, more like a barracks than a bedchamber. A lone candle barely gave enough light for him to work.

Hearing the door close, Godwine whirled around in anger, ready to hurl abuse on the intruder. But the words froze on his lips at the apparition of his wife. He put down the quill and stood, formally, hands crossed behind him, chin uplifted.

Gytha summoned as much grace as she could and crossed the distance between them, putting her arms around his neck. He did not move, so she pursued her advantage and kissed him on the lips, long and passionately.

He could not restrain himself any longer. Involuntarily, his arms wrapped around her, his lips working their way down her throat. Then, coming to himself, Godwine put her at arm's length. "Gytha," he began, and she stopped him with a finger to his lips.

"No." Angrily, he pulled her hand away. "No, Gytha. You will not stop me. I can no longer love you in silence like shameful suitor. We are man and wife, though God alone knows we are more nearly perfect strangers."

She gasped, insulted by his audacity. But after a moment's reflection she knew he was right.

"If you cannot stand the thought of marriage to me, I will arrange an annulment," Godwine pursued. "If you truly have changed your mind, you must give yourself to me. No more separate beds, no more imposed silence. I must have all of you, or none. It can be no other way."

Gytha had never been spoken to like that. She positively gaped at her husband, admiring his commanding presence despite herself. He seemed so tall, so overwhelming. Is this what inspired such respect? Sure of himself, refusing to be intimidated by her, he exuded irresistible power. Never more would she be able to consider him of common stock.

"You have won me," she whispered, hoping he would take her in his arms.

Like a thunderstorm he scooped her from the floor, sinking with her onto the little bed. If Gytha had thought she knew what his lovemaking was like, she was soon undeceived. Set free, he filled her ears with endearments, touched her in ways that she might originally have denied him. When they climaxed in a fervid, shattering wave, she felt like it was the very first time.

17

The clattering of horse hooves in the courtyard signaled the return of Godwine's company. Before he was even dismounted, grooms were shouting and mixing with the riders and a half-dozen eager hands held his bridle, asking for news. Godwine answered as best as he could then smiled, seeing his wife on the doorstep. Her hands were folded over a belly so large he wondered how she could walk.

Gytha's greetings always brought him back to that first real welcome when he had returned from Norway, nervous and edgy. Their parting had been too cordial, too uncharacteristic; he had feared it wouldn't last. But the absence of two months had rather sharpened her appetite for him, and she had flown down the steps into his arms.

It was like a real marriage, when a man could bring news home to his wife and enjoy the comfortable domestic pleasure of sharing one's little accomplishments. "We did it," he remembered having said to her, as if they were already old friends, "Canute is now King of Norway as well as England."

Gytha had been truly interested. "And what of Olaf? I never liked that man."

"He never recovered his subjects' respect, that winter after Helge River when he was forced to abandon his ships and return home overland. The last couple of years, Canute has been buying the loyalty of his Thegns in Norway. When we finally appeared with our fleet the Norwegians came over to us and Olaf fled the country."

"Will he be back?" She put a hand over his.

"Probably. But he will find his welcome a little too hot."

It was the first time Gytha had really listened to him as one equal to another. But it certainly wasn't the last. Her unique point of view often gave him a new perspective. Godwine found that he usually preferred to include his wife in decision making, even when it concerned his earldom.

And now, as their eyes met, Godwine felt the happiest man on earth. Once it was safe to bring her to Bosham he had done so in state, with a bevy of servants and no expense spared. As he had hoped, Gytha fell in love with her new home on the instant and swore she would live nowhere else. She even took charge of Ingrid whenever she could, making the child part of their household.

This second pregnancy had been the opposite of the first; although she had never been able to view Swegn with more than indifference, she was determined to make up for it with the next child.

"How goes it with My Lord?" she asked when he came closer. He gathered her into a hug, kissing her unabashedly before the others.

"Well, Gytha. And you?"

"I think my time is very near," she spoke into his ear. "I have alerted the midwife to be ready for an instant summons."

Godwine put a hand on her belly. "At least you waited for me."

In two days Gytha's time had come. While Godwine was reviewing the household accounts, she looked up calmly and spoke his name. Godwine leaped to his feet, all business forgotten. The steward went in search of the midwife while the anxious husband got in everybody's way, trying to help his fragile wife upstairs.

Godwine paced the whole night before her door; no one could persuade him to get some sleep. "My wife isn't sleeping," he said. "Neither will I."

Time was forgotten while Godwine listened to every groan, every whisper emanating from the room. Finally, when Godwine thought he was coming to the end of his strength, a great cry came from behind the door. Forgetting all the restrictions he burst through, frantic.

Looking up the midwife frowned, scolding.

"No, please," Gytha said, holding out her hand. "Let him stay."

Godwine sat beside her on the bed, trying not to remember the last birthing. She put a nervous hand into his.

"What do you think of him?"

"I have decided to call him Harold," he told her, bending over the freshly cleaned infant. Gytha smiled.

"I am content. He will grow up just like you."

Godwine smiled back, saddened despite himself. The newborn was a fine looking boy but his heart still went out to that frail, unwanted child squalling alone in the nursery. Swegn was conceived and borne under the influence of their antagonism. Could any good come from a child exposed to such bad humors?

* * *

It just so happened that Godwine and Gytha were in London when Estrid came back. They were dining privately with Canute when a knock on the door announced yet another visitor. Canute gave Godwine a look of exasperation before saying, "Come in."

The King hadn't even bothered to look up, but Godwine's gasp brought his head about. Behind a guard stood his sister Estrid, bundled up in a heavy cloak.

Canute leaped to his feet, gesturing for her to take a place beside him. But instead she ran to Gytha, throwing both arms around her neck. The cloak slid to the floor, uncovering a body dangerously underweight.

"My God, sister. What has happened to you?"

Ignoring him, Estrid took Gytha's face between her hands, kissing her sweetly. "I thought I'd never see you again," she said.

Gytha shook her head, tears falling. "Has he hurt you, then?"

"Hurt? That would be putting it kindly." Estrid stood, picked up the cloak; she went over to Canute, kissing his cheek. "I would ask you one thing, dear brother. Next time you seek to better my situation, leave it be." Smiling bitterly, she poured herself some wine. "Your Robert really is a devil."

She emptied the cup in one long draught, then poured another. Godwine saw that her hand was shaking.

Looking deliberately at the same hand, she carefully put down the cup, turning to Canute. "See this?" she said, pulling her hair back from the right temple. A long scar ran from forehead to ear, barely healed. "Nearly killed me with that one. I won't bother to show you my most recent bruises; at least they aren't permanent."

Estrid was trying to be flippant, but she couldn't sustain it. Breaking into tears, she buried her face into Canute's shoulder. "I couldn't stand it any longer," she sobbed. "I tried to starve myself, but I had no heart for suicide."

She threw her head back, looking him in the eyes. "I was lucky he took a liking to that tanner's daughter. Gave her a bastard son, he did, and left me alone."

Still trying to retain his neutrality, Canute stroked her hair. "Does he know where you went?"

"Know? He sent me. And he gave me a message, too. He says that it is time you turned England over to the true heir: Edward Aethelredson."

"Damn him!" Canute knocked his plate off the table, Estrid's troubles forgotten. "I knew it." He threw an angry look at Godwine. "There is no cosseting that bastard."

"Cosseting!" Estrid began to laugh hysterically. "Why didn't you tell me I was supposed to cosset him?" The laughs turned into wails.

The men stared uncomfortably while Gytha helped her from the room, whispering soothing words into her ear. On the way out, Estrid shot them an accusing frown.

* * *

Gytha insisted on taking Estrid back to Winchester with her. In a few days, Canute's sister was ready to travel again, and the King was secretly relieved to see her off; the woman's reproaching looks were getting on his nerves. As the women rode away with their escorts, Canute turned to Godwine. "She will be good for Gytha... And the children," he said apologetically. He felt guilty about all of this.

Godwine nodded silently, though he was not so sure. Estrid had obviously been mistreated, and she clearly wasn't the same person he had escorted to Normandy. Perhaps rest and care would heal her.

Meanwhile, it was just as well that he needed to stay behind with the King. *Let Gytha handle this; she knew Estrid best.*

As it turned out, the day after Estrid's arrival official representatives appeared at court to emphasize Robert's demand. Canute was to give up his claim to the throne of England in favor of Edward Aethelredson. They were horrified when Canute laughed in their faces.

"Surely your master has lost his mind," said the Dane, his face changing rapidly. "He does not have the means to support this absurd claim."

"He has the means, and will pursue the matter," said the boldest emissary.

Canute stood, facing them down. His visage was fearful. "Get you from this court, before I skin you alive. If Robert dares set foot on this land, I will crush him for what he did to my sister."

He didn't need to say more. The ambassadors left the room as quickly as possible.

* * *

Godwine stayed in London a month more, preparing for

invasion. Messengers were sent to every corner of Wessex, alerting the inhabitants to the danger. But no invasion came. Robert sailed all right, announcing his nephew's claims to anyone who would listen. However, a gale sprang up in the channel and blew his fleet to Brittany. There, he decided to change tactics and pursue a campaign against his cousin, Duke Alain.

Providence, Robert said, stepped in and determined the fate of the Norman invasion of England. Eadward Aethelredson would just have to await a more opportune moment.

18

Godwine held Ingrid's hand as Canute approached his palace on horseback, though she was soon tugging to get away and he let her go. The King quickly dismounted and held out his arms to the child and she ran toward him, ignoring the other horses milling around the courtyard.

"What did you bring me?" she called, laughing. "Did you bring a pony?"

Canute was already giving instructions and greeting a handful of dignified churchmen that were every bit as anxious to see him as his child was. He put a hand on her head and pulled her against his waist.

"You are growing so fast," he said with a grin, before letting go. "I must tend to these visitors before you and I talk about what I brought you."

Ingrid was used to all the activity. She waved goodbye to her father and ran toward the town while Canute and Godwine escorted their petitioners up the steps. Godwine took one last look at her before he entered the building.

Canute was planning yet another one of his churches and they were soon bent over a set of drawings. The master architect was explaining the proportions of width to height and Canute took exception here and there, listening patiently as the stone masons gave an explanation. Half the day had passed thus when they were interrupted by handful of men at the door, subdued and nervous. None of them wanted to draw attention to himself. Godwine walked over to the little group as Eirik entered behind them; the others parted as the Dane moved forward.

"What is it?" Godwine asked in a low voice.

Eirik pursed his lips. "I think you had better come outside."

Canute had already turned back to the drawings. Godwine followed Eirik, closing the door.

There was a little wagon near the Roman wall; it was pulled by hand and the men were standing around it; two of them were wet. Eirik was already headed toward it and Godwine felt a sinking feeling in his stomach as he followed.

It was worse than he thought. A little hand was sticking out from under a blanket and a few drops of water fell from its fingers. Godwine slowly put his head to the side as he anxiously pulled the blanket off the bundle. Ingrid was staring at him, eyes glassy, her mouth partially open. Hand shaking, Godwine closed her eyelids.

"They found her at the bottom of the mill race," Eirik said. "No one saw her drown, though there were some loose rocks. She must have fallen in."

Godwine tried to straighten her body in the wagon and when he pulled his hand away he had blood on his fingers. "Look," he started, then had to clear his throat. "She must have struck a rock with the back of her head. There." He turned her head where the blood was still seeping out of the wound. "Oohhh, it must have happened so quickly." He looked around at the others but no one seemed able to face him. They were busying themselves trying to put things in order. He bent over the child. "My sweet, sweet girl. How am I going to tell your father?"

Wiping tears from his eyes, Godwine kissed Ingrid on the cheek and tucked the blanket around her. He took a deep breath. "Let us get a proper wagon," he started before noticing that the others were staring at something else. Without turning, he knew. Canute was coming. Godwine didn't move.

The King's hand gently touched Ingrid's soggy blonde curls. He reached into his tunic and pulled out a little wooden horse. "I was going to give this to her," he murmured, "as a promise. I hadn't found a gentle enough horse for her." Two tears ran down his face, quickly brushed off.

Gytha came running up, breathless, followed by some of the other women in the village. A few started wailing. Gytha took one look at Godwine then gently pushed her husband aside and directed Eirik to help move the wagon to the palace.

"She will know what to do," Canute said, putting a hand on Godwine's shoulder. "Take me to the church." Godwine put an arm around Canute's shoulders. No one else came near them as the two men slowly walked down the path.

Canute never seemed so weary before. His steps were heavy and so was his breathing. Godwine expected him to bellow, to curse, to find someone to blame. He almost wished Canute would do so rather than continue this terrible silence. They went into the church and Canute collapsed onto a bench. He put his head into his hands.

Godwine watched the King quietly as the setting sun cast a long red square onto the floor through the doorway. Canute raised his head, looking at the floor.

"There," he pointed. "We will bury her there. I killed Ulf in a church and now I will bury my daughter in a church. Maybe God will forgive me." He let out a gasp then straightened. "Come, Godwine. We have much to do."

By the time they returned to the palace, the child had been laid out on a table and the priests were gathered around her, intoning their funeral prayers in Latin. Godwine suspected their concern was mostly to impress Canute, but the King seemed to derive some comfort from their efforts. He knelt down on a little prayer bench and took a vigil that lasted through the night. He didn't seem to notice when Godwine and Gytha took their leave.

Although it was dark, they choose to walk back to their manor on the far side of the church. Their retainers walked ahead, lighting the way with torches. Gytha pointed at the stars.

"Do you see those four stars like a dipper, with three stars like a handle?" she asked, putting her other arm though her husband's. "In my world, we call that the *Hellewagen*, the wagon of the dead, which travels along the Helweg all the way to the underworld. I've heard that called the Milky Way. I think Ingrid is on the Hellewagen right now taking her last voyage. Goodbye, my child," she added, blowing a kiss to the sky. "I will see you in my own time."

It took a week to carve out the stone coffin and by then the local churchmen had broken a hole in the floor of Bosham church. After placing the body wrapped with fine linen into the coffin they packed it with flowers and herbs. Canute tucked in the little toy horse before they sealed the lid with wax. The King stood quietly at the back of the church as they lowered the box into its resting place, all signs of grief wiped from his face. But Godwine knew what he was hiding because he felt it himself.

The bells in the tower started their mournful peal when suddenly was heard an answering chime from the bay. Slowly and sonorously, the tone rang clearly in answer to its brothers in the tower. Even the local priests were startled as they turned around in wonder. Canute turned the latch and slowly opened the church door, cocking his head as the tenor bongs from under the water gave answer to his prayers. Maybe here was a sign of God's forgiveness, or at least he chose to believe it so. Never mind that the Danes were responsible for dropping the bell into the sea. It was his bell now.

* * *

Canute seemed reluctant to leave Bosham and preferred to bury himself in work. The longer he stayed the more petitioners showed up, filling his great hall and arguing amongst themselves until the King walked out among them, greeting one and all by name. The visitors bowed before him like a field of grain before the wind. Godwine followed Canute, pulling aside an occasional person they had already chosen to speak with.

This particular day, the King had arranged to meet with merchants who were setting up trade routes on the continent. Ever since Canute's visit to Rome in 1027 relationships had improved overall, especially since the King had negotiated that the Christian leaders reduce tolls for the pilgrims to the Holy City. Before long, Canute found himself besieged on all sides.

"Mighty King," one man said. "I beg you to intercede with the Lord of Lusignan, who is imposing crippling taxes on my sales of goods. I know you have great powers of persuasion."

"Dread Lord," another bowed. "I humbly request protection for my caravan to Chartres. I know the bishops fear your might and would open the roads before your representatives."

"Great King," cried a third, "who strikes fear in the hearts of the Counts of La Marche. Aid my suit as I know all will bow before you."

"You are master of everything you touch. Even the sea would do your bidding."

Others pushed forward, straining to be heard. Canute abruptly turned with a frown and all fell silent. He passed through the crowd, heading for the door. Somewhat daunted, the others followed him in a group, occasionally calling their praise. The King strode purposefully toward the shore then followed the beach, slowing his pace. A little surprised, the group of petitioners hesitated.

"Bring my throne," Canute bellowed, and three courtiers made haste to obey.

While they were waiting, Canute pulled Godwine close. "This is your town now," he said softly. "My lovely Bosham has ceased to please me. It will forever remind me of my poor child." Godwine bowed his head in acknowledgement. "Tomorrow, let us move our business back to Winchester," Canute finished as the men carried his throne forward.

The King pointed at the sand. "Put my throne there," he ordered, crossing his arms. As the courtiers obliged he looked at the rest of the small crowd, pausing his gaze at every face.

"See my might," he said in a low voice, then sat on the throne. His cloak touched the ground just inches from the surf. Canute pointed at the water. "You are part of my dominion, and the ground that I am seated upon is mine. Nor has anyone disobeyed my orders with impunity. Therefore, I order you not to rise onto my land, nor to wet the clothes or body of your Lord."

The courtiers looked at each other, not knowing what to do. They looked at Godwine for instruction but the Earl stood aside, waiting. A hush fell over them as they stood uncomfortably together, watching the little waves lap against the sand. It seemed like an interminable time passed as the tide rose slowly higher, wetting the cloak then the feet of Canute. Suddenly he leapt off the throne, walking back onto dry land.

"Let all men know how empty and worthless is the power of kings," he said purposely. "For there is none worthy of the name but God, whom heaven, earth and sea obey."

At that, he removed the crown from his head and handed it to Godwine. "Nevermore will I wear this trinket. We shall offer it to our savior in the Cathedral at Westminster."

Having made his point, Canute stomped back to the palace. None dared follow. Even Godwine was disconcerted as he gave orders to recover the throne. Canute was a changed man. He had become a true Christian King, and somewhere along the way he seemed to have shed much of his ferocity. Godwine wondered, and not for the first time, whether he missed the loss.

19

It was a cold November night in 1035 and Godwine had gotten out of bed to find an extra blanket when a retainer came forward with a message. For a moment the Earl stared at it uncomprehending, then shouted for his horse. He called for Eirik and a handful of others, only pausing as his wife came running after him.

"What is it, love?" she cried, holding his arm. "I have never seen you like this."

Godwine looked at her, his wide eyes brimming with tears. "It's the King. The note says he is dying."

"What? He was fine just last week."

Godwine swung into his saddle. "A fever." His voice cracked. "I'm off to Shaftesbury. Dear God I hope I am not too late."

For the first time he rode off without kissing her. As she watched him go she noticed Swegn and Harold clinging to her skirts, rubbing their eyes. Gytha put a hand on each boy's head. She often found comfort in her children, especially since Estrid's death—except for the eldest, whose mournful eyes reminded her of how things had once been.

With Godwine gone so often, she sometimes caught herself blaming the boy for her loneliness. After thirteen years of marriage and four children, she still trembled at the memory of those first terrible months. Even now, as she felt the stirring of another life in her belly, Gytha had to force herself to quit thinking about the bad times.

"Go inside, now. It is too cold out here." Gytha turned them around, emphasizing the words with a pat on their backs. Then she took one last look after her husband, wishing she had had the time to fetch his heavy cloak. The winter winds were all too unpredictable.

However, Godwine did not notice his discomfort even when

rain began to come down in a sharp, icy drizzle. He ignored the bent forms of his companions, thinking only about Canute and how important the King's life had been to his own.

It was more than just his position. As Earl of Wessex he was firmly established; it would take much to shake him from his post. No, it was Canute himself, who had come to confide in Godwine about every aspect of government and whose unswerving loyalty to his vassals was returned by fierce support. Canute was more than a chief; he was a dear friend, and Godwine couldn't imagine life without him.

But when he got to Shaftesbury, one look at the King's emaciated body was enough to undeceive any person in the sickroom. Godwine knelt at the bedside and Canute turned sunken eyes to him, blazing with denial.

"This can't be happening yet," the King whispered. "I have so much more to accomplish."

Godwine lowered his head, ashamed of his tears. Canute gripped him with a burning hand.

"Promise me you will do everything in your power to hold the throne for Harthacnut."

Both Canute and Godwine knew what he was asking. Harthacnut was occupied fighting for the throne of Denmark against the encroachments of Magnus, son of Olaf. Holding the English crown for a man in his absence was an unheard of feat.

But Harthacnut was also the son of his Lord. "I promise," said Godwine without hesitation.

"Then I have done the best I can," said the King, sinking into his pillows. Emma came out of the shadows, putting a damp cloth on his forehead.

"I am entrusting the royal treasury to my wife, to keep in Winchester," Canute continued, recovering his breath. "She will hold it for our son." He reached for her hand.

Formally clasping his hot fingers Emma looked at Godwine, her eyes piercing. Even through her grief she was coldly evaluating his trustworthiness.

"Then it shall be where I can best protect it," he said to both of them.

Canute smiled briefly. "Godwine, the kingdom is in your hands. I have made a worthy choice." He coughed then began to choke, bending over the side of the bed. The archbishop rushed everyone from the room so he could administer the last rites.

Godwine offered Emma his arm. She leaned heavily against him as the door closed behind them. The Earl looked down at the Queen whose sudden vulnerability took him by surprise. She had ever seemed a rock, unshakable and unyielding. He had always wondered if she had any love for Canute. For once, the pain in her face gave him an answer.

"What am I to do?" she whispered, more to herself than him. "Twice widowed and still too many years left to live. And what have I to live for?"

"To see Harthacnut on the throne," said Godwine softly, feeling an unaccustomed sympathy. Emma had always been too unapproachable before.

She looked at him quizzically, still unsure of his mettle. "And will you keep your promise to your King and put him there?"

"Madam, with all my heart."

Strengthened, Emma moved forward, letting him go. Her momentary weakness had passed and she had found reason to go on.

Godwine envied her that. What about himself? He had no fondness for any of Canute's children. His own life would never be the same; yet he, too, must go on. He had his own heirs to think about.

Canute died that very night and the death bells tolled throughout the land. His passing was mourned by everyone: some, because they knew and loved him, others because they had grown used to the peace and prosperity brought by his reign. To many, the death of Canute presaged a possible civil war because all knew there was more than one heir to the throne.

* * *

Godwine accompanied the funeral train to Winchester where Canute was to be buried. A magnificent monument would be carved for him at the New Minster; the ceremony was performed to the accompaniment of the great 400-piped organ which had to be operated by a whole troop of men. All did agree that the King's soul was spirited to heaven by the most awesome of vehicles.

Godwine and his wife walked back to Wolvesey Palace after the funeral, children in tow. Swegn was hand in hand with their new ward, Eadgifu, whose mother had died the previous year. Harold and Tostig were quarreling as usual, and Godwine shot them a warning look that momentarily curbed their tempers. Little Editha was holding Gytha's hand, trying to keep up with their slow pace.

"When is the Witenagemot to be held?" asked Gytha, pausing to pick up her daughter.

"At Christmas. It is to be held at Oxford," Godwine said. Then he turned to her anxiously. "Will you come, too, Gytha? You would be a great comfort to me, and to Emma as well."

Gytha looked back as Tostig's voice grew argumentative. "With pleasure."

* * *

Sitting on the raised dais next to Emma, Godwine looked worriedly around the room. He had already sounded a few of the Thegns and was not happy with their answers. As he had feared, there was strong support in the Danelaw for Harold Harefoot, the first son of Canute by Aelfgifu. Emma's reaction to this news was characteristically sarcastic.

"Leave it to that woman to profit from her licentiousness," she had said.

Godwine nodded. He remembered Harold, who was now waiting in London for the Witan's decision. Although physically impressive and a great runner, which led to the nick-name Harefoot, the man's dull eyes were easily animated by talk of riches and power. Godwine knew that Emma could well be correct: Aelfgifu had been grooming him for the throne all his life.

The Earl looked up as Seward entered the room. The Dane was a latecomer, and Godwine hadn't had the chance to ask his opinion. But Seward's behavior gave a clear enough answer. His fellow earl was avoiding his eyes; and what was worse, he took a seat with Leofric of Mercia.

Things were more desperate than he thought.

After Eadwulf, last of the expected nobles to arrive, Godwine called the meeting to order. "We might as well come right to the point," he said, standing and looking around. The council was large; every shire seemed to be represented. "We have assembled to choose a new king of the realm. It is my choice, and the will of Canute, that we elect Emma's son Harthacnut as king."

The outburst was so intense that he nearly sat down. For a time, no one voice could be singled out. Godwine knew that he had a long day ahead of him.

"Earl Leofric," he said wearily, knowing that the Earl of Mercia had already established a reputation as arbitrator between the North and South. "May I hear what you have to say?"

Leofric stood, amidst the supportive murmurs of his followers. "Those of us residing in the Danelaw have come to prefer a representative who has grown up among our hills and learned our ways.

"Harthacnut, although of royal birth..." He bowed to Emma who sat gripping the arms of her chair. "Harthacnut has been raised as a Dane. His primary throne is in Denmark, and we do not choose to be ruled from a foreign throne." Leofric had to raise his voice at the end, to be heard over the shouts of agreement. He waited smugly for the noise to die down.

"We choose a representative who is every bit the son of Canute. My choice is Harold Harefoot."

Godwine looked at all the faces who agreed with Leofric. Almost every one of them was from the north. Only Godwine's own vassals from Wessex stood behind him. "My Lords," he shouted, leaning forward. "Do you forget that Harthacnut was the heir, chosen by Canute on his deathbed?"

The voices faded uncertainly although Godwine knew that this factor was not decisive. The King's last wishes were merely a guideline, not a command. The best candidate would serve all of England, and the Witan made the final decision. He knew he had to respect this fact.

"Magnus Olafson threatens Denmark with invasion. Harthacnut cannot spare the time for us."

Godwine spun toward the owner of the new voice. It was Seward.

"Harold is here now. He is ready to reign," Seward went on, looking directly at Godwine. "I say we put forth our decisions."

Many of the others were on their feet, but Godwine saw none of them. His eyes were locked in a private quarrel with the speaker, berating him for his betrayal. Seward held his gaze, his mouth set.

"I select Harold," one man shouted.

"And I," said another.

"My voice is for Harold," said yet another.

"And mine."

"Myself as well."

"Wait!" shouted Godwine, slamming the table with his fist.

The hall fell silent. Godwine leaned on his knuckles, his voice commanding respect. "Harthacnut is the chosen heir. It was decreed long ago and cannot be changed now. Do you want to be responsible for civil war?" Many of his own Thegns stood, shouting their agreement.

Godwine was glad no one was close enough to observe the sweat on his forehead. He was fighting for more than the kingdom, now. If Harold gained power, he would remember that Godwine stood against him.

"Canute's housecarls serve me now, and Emma in Winchester." The subtle threat was not lost on the assembly. "Canute made me responsible for holding the throne for his son. It is a task I mean to accomplish." Godwine felt the Queen behind him, breathing on his neck. He looked at her then sat down, willing her to follow his example. No one dared yet speak.

Finally, Leofric took the responsibility. "Then I suggest you hold Wessex for Harthacnut and let Harold rule the rest of the Kingdom."

The words fell on the Witan like a blanket. It was a solution they remembered from before; almost all of them were old enough to remember Edmund Ironside. At least there was no Eadric to deal with this time. Godwine looked at Emma; she shook her head vehemently.

"We will serve no one else in the north," Leofric added, in answer to her gesture. "There is no question about the matter."

There was no question indeed. The tally was quickly taken, and the north unanimously chose Harold. Godwine had no choice but submit to their will.

* * *

However, Emma refused to see reason. At least she had enough sense to wait until they were alone before she let go her restraint.

"You gave him your word," she shouted at Godwine, as Gytha entered the room. "I was a witness."

Godwine threw himself into a chair, taking a mug of ale from his wife. "What did you want me to do, order the housecarls to cut them all to pieces?"

"Yes, if that's what it took."

He laughed at her scornfully. "I know you don't mean it. So do not act like a fool. At least we have saved part of the kingdom for him. The rest will follow, if Harold is the simpleton you say he is."

"He is. Do not doubt that." She reached a hand to Gytha who took it, sitting at her side. "How do you feel, my dear?"

Gytha sighed. "The morning sickness grows worse, but at least it does not continue all day like the last time."

"As you can see, children are a burden one carries even into their adulthood," Emma said bitterly. Gytha and Godwine exchanged glances.

But Emma wasn't through yet. "Harthacnut will not appreciate all this, when he hears of it," she said, changing tactics. "He is likely to invade England to get what is coming to him." Although Godwine felt she was talking nonsense, he cringed at the thought. Then another notion sprang into his head.

"There is one last chance," he murmured.

Emma pounced on his words. "What? What is it, Godwine?" Her eyes glinted with vengeance.

"A king must be crowned by the Archbishop of Canterbury; it is an integral part of the ceremony. Without the Archbishop's part, the king cannot be consecrated...he will not be truly king." He leaned back, giving it more thought. But Emma had already forged ahead.

"You know Archbishop Elnothus! He is your friend; persuade him to refuse his participation in the ceremony."

"Madam, the man does have a conscience!"

"Yes he does. And my husband committed Harthacnut to his trust. Why didn't I think of it before?"

Godwine considered this. "All right...I will go see him. He will not do anything against his judgment. But Emma, this might not work."

"Harold Harefoot dare not defy the church, as well."

Godwine was not so sure. But he was tired of arguing. "The worst is not over yet," he warned. "If Harthacnut does not return to claim his domain, I do not know how long I can hold it for him."

"Then I shall see that he complies," Emma declared.

* * *

Harold Harefoot trod into the Cathedral, not as reverent as his followers would have liked nor as humbled as they would have expected. The royal cavalcade hurried after him as though in the midst of some ludicrous race, scandalized by the man's disrespect for the coronation ceremony and its significance.

Even the citizens of London didn't know what was taking place. The few who happened to be walking the streets turned and watched curiously as Harold led his retinue through the streaming rain, dragging his gorgeous robe in the mud. Truly, Harold didn't want to advertise the event; already the church had made its objections known, and he was expecting some sort of trouble.

In this, he was not disappointed. Archbishop Elnothus stood sternly before the altar, his face a mask of disapproval, and behind him huddled the rest of the clergy in a protective cluster. As Harold approached, the Archbishop held out a commanding hand.

"Stop," he boomed, modulating his voice so it would echo in all the vaults. Despite himself, Harold halted.

"Come no further," Elnothus demanded. "I shall not consecrate any King as long as the Queen's true children live."

Harold lowered his head like a bull and continued forward. The Archbishop advanced another step.

"Do you persist in your wicked resolution?" Elnothus drew himself up, denying Harold with the force of his will. But he secretly knew that his powers were limited, as he was confronted by this man's determination.

Harold stopped again, taking the other's measure. "Your Grace," he said finally. "I am the King-elect by free choice of the Witan. You are obliged to submit to their will."

Elnothus hesitated, losing some of his audacity. Harold's argument was valid in the sense that the Witan alone chose the next king. But he still felt bound by his oath to Canute and the serious pressure applied by Godwine. He must find a way to shift the responsibility elsewhere.

"The scepter and crown I here lay down upon the altar," he finally submitted in a lower voice, nodding for a priest to bring them. "Neither do I deny nor deliver them unto you. But I forbid," he added, raising his voice again, "by the apostolic authority of all the bishops, that none of my brethren presume to give these symbols of kingship to you, or to consecrate you King." He swept his assembled clergy with a stern eye.

"As for yourself," he thundered at Harold, "if you dare, you may usurp that which I have committed unto God and his table."

Glaring for a moment at the King-elect, the Archbishop turned his back on him and swept away, beckoning for the bishops to follow.

Harold Harefoot watched them go, a triumphant smile on his face. Then, before anyone could say a word, he mounted the steps to the altar and took the crown in both hands. Turning, he gazed over his little audience, outstretching his arms.

"Behold the crown of England," he bellowed. "I take it unto myself as my rightful inheritance. Let no man gainsay my royalty."

With that, he placed the crown on his own head. Turning, he grabbed the scepter then faced the people, looking to the right and left for any objectors.

No one dared speak a word. Satisfied, King Harold I strode down the aisle past his silent supporters and out of the church.

20

Unfortunately, even Emma's most eloquent pleas could not budge Harthacnut from his unstable Danish throne. He remained unmoved when she complained that Harold had swooped unexpectedly on Winchester, confiscating Canute's royal treasure. He made his excuses when she wrote that Godwine's Thegns were slowly going over to Harold's camp.

Godwine kept a brave face in Emma's presence but at home he complained bitterly about his thankless role. He sat one night with Gytha, pouring out his frustrations while holding their new son Wulfnoth.

The other children played noisily at the far end of the room. Gyrth and Leofwine were combating with wooden soldiers while the others kept a puppy running back and forth, its nails skidding across the floor. Only Editha sat with her parents, practicing her stitches by the light of the fire.

"Confound the racket," Godwine complained, watching Harold and Tostig argue over the dog's ball. "Will those two ever get along?"

Gytha looked fondly at the boys. "They are at that age, you know. Harold wants to prove himself a man and Tostig wants to prove himself the stronger of the two."

"I never see Swegn bothering with such nonsense. Where is he, anyway?"

Gytha pursed her lips. He was always championing Swegn, no matter what the conversation. "I don't know. Last time I saw him, he and Eadgifu were playing." She paused, wiping the baby's face. "Godwine, I am beginning to worry about them. They spend way too much time together."

"Leave them be, wife. He is lonely enough."

There he goes with the old guilt, she sighed to herself. *Will he never stop throwing her neglect of Swegn back in her face? Hadn't she proved herself a good mother with the other eight children?*

"Well," she ventured, "he is only twelve. But she is an unsuitable mate for him." Gytha stopped, warned by her husband's look; it was a topic they usually chose to avoid. She was almost relieved when a knock on the door interrupted her. Eirik and a stranger blew in, bringing along a gust of dry leaves.

The newcomer knelt before Godwine. "There is a new threat, My Lord," he said, his head bowed. "I have been sent by Thegn Merewald. Alfred Aethelredson has landed in Kent."

Gytha held her breath. Her husband handed over the baby.

"Are you sure?"

"Yes. With 600 Norman supporters."

Godwine turned to his wife. "Too many for a social call."

The messenger cleared his throat. "That is the odd part. He claims he is on his way to visit his mother the Queen."

Gytha shivered. "Here," she said. "In Winchester."

"Then we must go and meet them. Eirik, put out a summons. I want three hundred men to meet me outside the city walls tonight. In two hours. We shall not threaten them," he added to his wife. "I would merely provide a suitable escort."

Eirik left; he did not need further instructions. He took the messenger with him.

Harold and Tostig had watched the exchange with interest. They came up to their father, standing expectantly before him.

"Can we come, father?" Harold ventured.

"Not this time, boys. It may be dangerous." He was not giving them his usual full attention.

"But father..."

"I need you here to protect your mother." Godwine looked at Gytha worriedly. "Emma does not give a thought for her sons by Aethelred. Why would he come to visit her?"

"And why isn't Edward with him?" Gytha added.

"Yes," said Godwine. He knew she was following his thought. "It makes sense for the younger to test the waters alone; his is the lesser threat. It is too dangerous for both of them...if that is their motive."

Harold edged his way closer to Godwine. "Are you going to tell the King?" he asked, trying to sound important.

"The Regent, you mean. He is not king here, yet."

Tostig made a face at his brother, pleased at Harold's embarrassment.

"But that is a good question, son. If I tell Harold Harefoot, then Alfred's life is not worth a farthing."

"And if you do not tell him," Gytha warned, "he might think you are scheming together."

"Pah. Imagine me in that company. With a mealy-mouthed son of a disgraceful king."

"And yet Harold knows you are against him."

Godwine stood, reaching for his sword. "I am also Earl of Wessex, and bound to keep peace the best way I know how. Fear not, Gytha. I will keep him and his friends under surveillance and escort them back to their ships when they have finished their visit. And I will make sure it is no more than a visit."

He bent to kiss her then he was gone as he always went: quickly and without a fuss. But this time, Gytha could not control a sense of foreboding which put a harsh edge to her voice as she sent her children unwillingly to bed.

* * *

Though Gytha did not know it, Godwine shared her apprehension. As they followed their guide, he was unusually silent. It was not until dawn, when they approached Merewald's shire, that he began to relax. So far there was no sign of disorder.

By late morning they came within sight of Eadhelmsbrigge, with tents spread out over the field. Merewald rode out to meet them. "Thank God you are here, Godwine. Alfred was getting impatient and was ready to move on without you. I could not hold him with my fifty men."

Godwine nodded, annoyed. *What did the exile hope to prove by his reckless behavior?* "Where is he lodging?"

"At my house, and a few of his men stayed in town. But most of them camped in their tents; we do not have enough room for all."

"Or my three hundred. I know. But we have ridden all night and must rest a few hours."

The Thegn led the way, shaking his head.

"Perhaps," added Godwine, thinking out loud, "we can make it to Guildford tonight. One of my lodgings is there and I believe the town is big enough to accommodate our guests."

The Thegn nodded vigorously. "A good idea. I will lend some of my people, if that will help."

"I do not think so. Listen. My men will rest here while Alfred's companions pack up their gear. Can you lend me a few horses?"

That settled, Godwine accompanied his Thegn to town, too tired to care what Alfred thought of his idea.

The exile rose with a weary pride as Godwine entered the room. Looking him up and down, Godwine smiled faintly. He had never seen King Aethelred but guessed that Alfred must have taken after him; he certainly bore no resemblance to Emma. Where the Queen had piercing black eyes, Alfred's were a limpid blue. His brown hair, flat against a round head, was a poor imitation of his mother's flowing tresses. Alfred's receding chin did not help his appearance any but he was saved by a broad forehead which gave his wide-spread eyes an appearance of intelligence.

Godwine wondered how intelligent he could possibly be, placing himself into such a dangerous position.

"Sit down, Earl Godwine," said the Aetheling calmly, "and let us understand each other. Am I your prisoner, or am I free to go?"

"Not so fast," the other answered patiently. "Surely you must understand that your unheralded appearance gives me pause."

"Of course. This is your earldom and you must keep the peace." He paused, leaning to the side as a companion whispered in his ear. "Nonetheless, I have come to visit my mother. Surely this is not a crime?"

"No. But did you require six hundred men for such a visit?"

"I feared for my safety, if you must know. Already we were attacked by pirates in the channel."

"Oh?" Godwine leaned forward, deliberately coming so close that Alfred had to pull back a little. "And do you expect us to have forgotten the little invasion Duke Robert planned not so many years ago? Your brother's designs for the throne are not exactly a secret."

They glared at each other for several moments before Godwine pretended to relax. He added, "I am sure you understand my desire to accompany you to your destination. I have a residence in Winchester, too, and I would make your stay as comfortable as possible."

A fleeting look of panic crossed Alfred's face, quickly suppressed. "That is kind of you but not necessary."

"I consider it very necessary."

Alfred closed his mouth then smiled. "Very well. When do we start?"

"My men must have rest; we rode through the night. I suggest we remove to my town of Guildford where I can comfortably house your friends."

Alfred had no choice but to agree.

The ride to Guildford lasted a couple of hours. Those men without horses followed on foot, escorted by several of Godwine's housecarls. Alfred was pleasant though guarded; Godwine found him too Normanized for his taste. He thought even less of his companions who bore themselves more arrogantly than became strangers in a foreign country.

When they reached Guildford, the sun was close to setting. Godwine prepared a chamber in his own house for Alfred and assigned housing throughout the town for the rest of the men. They had a pleasant dinner, entertained by one of Alfred's minstrels, and retired early after securing the town.

The day had been uneventful. But Godwine was exhausted; he had only rested a couple of hours, after all. This was probably why the commotion failed to immediately wake him.

A pounding on the outer door brought the Earl from his bed with a jolt. He heard shouting outside and grabbed his sword before running into the great hall in his bare feet. The door crashed open and several unknown warriors burst through. Godwine strode forward, shouting, "God's blood! What is going on here?" The man in charge whirled around.

"Ah, Earl Godwine. I have come to take your prisoners out of your care."

Godwine grabbed the man by his wrist. "On whose authority?"

"The King's, of course." The man looked at four of his companions who surround Godwine, disarming him. Some of Godwine's housecarls crowded through the doorway pulling their swords and shouting challenges. They flew at the strangers who eagerly charged back, swords upraised. The room rang with clangs of steel and cries of pain. "I suggest you call off your men before you are charged with interfering in the King's justice."

Godwine glared at him. "Who are you?"

"I am Thegn Osbert, if you must know. Now will you tell them to desist?" The last word was cut short as Osbert was knocked from his feet by a falling body.

"I am warning you, Godwine," he growled from the floor. One of Godwine's captors jabbed him with a sword.

"Men, halt," he commanded, none too gracefully. His housecarls paused, staring at him. Seeing his predicament they stepped back.

The Thegn got to his feet. “Get the Aetheling,” he said to someone. The man came back momentarily, still tying Alfred’s hands behind him.

The exile glared at Godwine. “Is this what you call hospitality?” he sneered, ignoring both Godwine’s difficulty and the bodies on the floor.

Thegn Osbert walked back and forth before his captive. They could all hear screams and sounds of fighting from the town.

“They are murdering my men in their beds,” Alfred said to the room. “I would have joined them but my window was too small.”

Osbert laughed. “Do not worry. You will see plenty of action. You must come to London and answer charges. Did you think you could escape our channel patrols without word of your invasion reaching the King?”

Alfred spat at him; the spittle clung to Osbert’s beard. “He is no King. He is the bastard son of a usurper.”

Osbert back-handed him then wiped his beard. Godwine looked away.

“Take him.” Osbert turned his back to the man and glared at Godwine. “I will be sure and tell King Harold about your activities here and your attempt to hide the Aetheling.” His lips curled back unpleasantly. “You may have your own charges to answer.”

21

Godwine was so exhausted he stumbled into the house without worrying about his mount. Gytha rose worriedly from her sewing, making him feel ashamed of himself and undeserving of all this comfort.

"I did not hear you...oh Godwine." She stopped short, seeing the disarray of his clothing. "What happened?"

Godwine fell rather than sat in a chair and allowed her to remove his boots. His hand strayed to her hair, lingering there for a moment. "It was a disaster. I must talk to Emma."

Gytha sat back on her heels. "Emma? I do not understand."

Godwine put his head in his hands. Gytha had never seen him so beaten.

"My husband..."

"Sometimes, I think my life ended with Canute. Now this..."

Little Editha ran into the room but Gytha waved her out. "Tell me," she said, shutting the door.

"Alfred...he is taken."

"Taken? By whom?"

"The King's men. It seems that Alfred encountered King Harold's patrol in the channel and managed to slip past them. He told me they were pirates, and like a fool I believed him."

"Why wouldn't you?"

"Because he came with six hundred men. I so wanted to believe his good intentions that I blinded myself to the danger. Now he is taken, his men murdered or sold into slavery, and I have been accused of hiding him and obstructing authority."

"That is ridiculous." She stood, her face flushed. "Surely they are not serious."

"King Harold has been searching for an excuse to be rid of me."

"Then you must go to him and clear yourself."

Godwine looked at her, taking courage from her anger. "Yes. I suppose I must. But first, I must see Emma. Will you come with me?"

* * *

Emma stood abruptly, staring at Godwine. "Do you mean to tell me he came here on a pretense of visiting me?" She looked aside, frowning. "Splendid. My own flesh and blood delivering me into the hands of an enemy."

Godwine rolled his eyes, at the end of his patience. "Madam, I do not believe that you are in the kind of danger he is. So you knew nothing of this?"

"Of course not. Do you think I wanted to lure him to his death? I do not despise him that much, though I always thought he had as little sense as his father. This proves it."

Emma gestured to one of her girls to finish pinning her hair. "At least Edward stayed in Normandy, where he belongs."

Godwine paced the room. "I heard a rumor that Edward landed in Southampton but quickly returned home."

She shook her head, causing the servant to drop some pins. "That sounds more like it," she said, suddenly tired. Her shoulders sagged for a moment.

For once, Godwine sympathized with her. But time was pressing. "I can't waste another minute going to King Harold. Gytha, I want you to stay with the Queen. I think you will be safer here."

"Yes, do," said Emma. "I suspect we have not heard the worst of this yet."

Gytha took her husband's hand. "You are going, then? I fear for your safety."

"I think I am too strong for that. And I intend to bring a contingent of housecarls."

* * *

Harold Harefoot lounged on his throne, looking at Godwine with a sideways tilt to his head. The Earl was on one knee before him and had been for some time; the King was enjoying the man's discomfiture.

"So tell me again, Godwine. You say you were escorting him?"

"Yes, to Winchester. It was my intent to guard him throughout the visit and return him personally to their ships."

"And then? Would he not be free to land elsewhere and continue the raid you interrupted?" Harold leaned purposefully forward, his whole attitude changed. "Or did you intend to sail with him to Normandy just to be sure he went back?"

Godwine watched the King clench both hands. Had he underestimated this man? He was Canute's son, after all, regardless of the slovenly way he ran the kingdom.

"I had hoped to fathom his intentions by then." Godwine spoke slowly and deliberately. "It is possible he was telling the truth."

"After that falsehood about pirates? I doubt it very much."

"I did not know it was a falsehood." Unbidden, Godwine stood. "He was in my earldom and I acted as I saw fit. That is why I rule there."

A slow smile broke over Harold's face. "Your earldom. That is the very question you are here to discuss."

Godwine gritted his teeth. So Harold had finally made his move. Remove the Earl of Wessex, remove Harthacnut. Most of his Thegns had been bought off already. "And what compromise do you want?" he asked, finally.

Harold motioned for Godwine to sit. "I had heard that you were reasonable. I merely wish you to be my man. It is only a technicality; I am already King of England in fact."

Godwine considered, frowning. He knew it was true. "And if

I become your man?"

"I drop the complaints against you. I was misinformed."

"And I carry the disgrace of Alfred's betrayal with me the rest of my life."

"I fear that can't be helped." Harold picked at his nails. "You see, Alfred Aetheling is dead. My men blinded him, to rid me of his threat. Unfortunately, they did a poor job of it and he didn't survive the night."

* * *

Godwine remembered little of the following days. He didn't know how he made it back to Winchester but once home he locked himself away from the world, refusing food and water.

But he wasn't destined to be left alone for long. Emma made her first visit ever to Wolvesey palace—and her last. When the Queen was ushered into his house, she was in the company of another strange group of guards. Godwine threw on a tunic and walked slowly into the room, aware that he was not presentable. Nor did he care.

Emma was hastily arrayed in traveling clothes, and threw her escort such a look of scorn that they backed away from her.

"Well, Godwine. I see you have fixed things up very prettily."

He raised heavy eyes to her face, too drained to react. "What is it you are saying?"

"Only that I am leaving the country. Now. This very minute. Harold has ejected me, and he told me that he has your support."

"Emma, I had no choice."

"Just like you had no choice with the Witan. Yes, I know how far that goes. Godwine, I thought you my friend but I see now that you are no better than the rest of them."

Gytha walked into the room, surveying the scene warily. She went to Emma, kissed her on the cheek. The Queen ignored her.

"So you see, I am going into exile. Perhaps Harthacnut will

help me come back. Then you had better find some real excuses."
She left the room in a huff with a swish of skirts and an angry backward look. Her escort followed her almost submissively.

Gytha stared after her. She turned at a groan from her husband.

"This is only the beginning," Godwine said.

22

"Raise your shield higher, Swegn." Godwine emphasized his warning with a resounding blow to the boy's helmet. It was only a glancing shot intended to jar rather than hurt him, but Swegn took a step backward, almost falling. Godwine looked away, grimacing. No matter how much he tried, he could not force his son to be a warrior. Although Swegn could be destructive enough in one of his tempers, his violence was random, undirected.

But Harold, on the other hand...

"Take a rest, Swegn. Harold, Tostig, let me see what you remember."

Godwine watched the boys circle. The pair of them were wildcats, especially when pitted against each other. Tostig's natural rivalry made him a powerhouse, but he always let his anger get the better of him in the end. Harold, on the other hand, was cool and calculating. He was on the verge of surpassing his father's lessons, which was no great feat except for the boy's age. Harold was only thirteen.

The two eyed each other over the edge of their shields. Finally they crossed blades, carefully at first, then with increasing vehemence.

It was always this way. Soon, he would have to step in and separate them before someone got hurt. If only Swegn could absorb some of their energies. Godwine turned, looking for his eldest son. He had to crane his neck completely around before he could spot the boy.

There he was, speaking earnestly with Eadgifu, not paying a bit of attention to his brothers. He had a hand on her arm, and she was beginning to let slip a pile of wet linens from her carelessly held basket.

"Eadgifu," he heard Gytha shout from the kitchen. Guiltily, the girl started, accomplishing the disaster. The basket's contents fell into the dust, and her cry of dismay even brought Harold and Tostig to a stop.

"Look at them go at it again," Tostig sneered. "Always getting into trouble."

"And what do you know about girls, anyway," prodded Harold, bracing himself for a fight. He was not disappointed. Dropping his sword and shield, Tostig lunged at his brother and they rolled in the dirt, weapons forgotten.

Godwine shook his head, starting toward Swegn who was helping the girl retrieve the laundry. Gytha met him halfway. She was furious. "This is the second time this week. Godwine, we have to do something."

Stunned, Swegn and Eadgifu looked up at them. The boy stood, shielding her from his parents. "It is not her fault. I was distracting her."

"And why were you doing that, Swegn?" Godwine asked. He was usually the one to discipline his son. "You were supposed to be watching your brothers fight."

Swegn nodded to them, making a face. "I see them fighting often enough."

Godwine shouted at Harold and Tostig to stop. They came reluctantly to their knees, glaring at each other.

"Clean up," Gytha told them. "We will be having dinner soon."

She turned to Swegn. "Eadgifu has enough trouble getting her work done without your interference. See that this does not happen again."

Ignoring his mother, Swegn turned to the girl. She was wiping her eyes. Gytha stomped off, exasperated.

"I would listen if I were you," Godwine said, not unkindly.

"Oh father. Why must she always treat my actions like they are crimes?" Swegn looked like he, too, was going to cry. "She is much more forgiving with Harold, and even Tostig. What have I done to deserve her hostility?"

"You are the oldest...it is often that way," Godwine said lamely. "Let us talk about it later."

"When?" Swegn stopped him from leaving. "You always say later, and later never comes."

Godwine looked at the girl. "When we are alone. Tonight." He pulled away, taking his eyes from the pair. He knew that someday Swegn would figure it all out, but somehow it always seemed easier to put off the ordeal.

But a confrontation was destined to happen much sooner than he wanted. Gytha was waiting for him and she pulled him into their bedroom, shutting the door.

"It is time we did something about that girl, Godwine."

"What do you mean?"

"You know what I mean. He is getting much too serious about her. I often find them off together, when they think I'm not looking. This has got to stop."

Godwine looked disconsolately out the window. Gytha could be so unyielding when she wanted to. Yet he loved her all the more for her spirit. "The boy is so lonely..." he began.

"All the more reason to separate them. Next thing you know he will want to marry her."

"Oh, come."

"I am dead serious. We cannot have our eldest son marrying beneath him."

Godwine bit his lip. *And why not,* he wanted to shout. But that argument was too personal to reopen, even after all these years.

"Godwine...we can place her in a nunnery. With a suitable dowry she will be well taken care of. She is at the right age, you know." Gytha was behind him, slipping her arms around his waist. "You know I am right." She kissed the back of his neck.

He turned, crushing her to him. When his wife used her body to win an argument, she made him so angry—and so passionate. He kissed her hard, making her gasp. Gytha put her arms around his neck, opening her mouth wide.

When they had finished making love, she ran her fingers through his chest hairs, kissing his cheek. "You will talk to him?"

He sighed, knowing he had lost. "Tonight."

No one remarked on their absence at dinner; it was a common enough occurrence. But Godwine was aware of Swegn's hungry gaze when he entered the hall, and he knew that he could not avoid him any longer. "Come with me, son," he said.

The night was clear and frosty, and Godwine pulled his cloak around his shoulder. He marveled once again that Swegn seemed impervious to the cold.

"There is something your mother and I have to say to you, son."

Swegn turned large eyes to his father, his face pale in the moon. "It is not about Eadgifu, I hope. I promise you, it will never happen again."

"Swegn, there are some things we must do in this world that are not pleasant. Letting go of her is one of them."

"Father..." Godwine could tell that he was struggling with the truth. "All right. Yes, I do care for her. I love her. Is that a crime?"

Godwine sighed. He had hoped Gytha was wrong. "A man of your position must not stoop..."

"Stoop? There is nothing wrong with her. She is pretty, intelligent. Father, she cares for me."

"Swegn..." Godwine faltered. His heart wasn't in this. "You have our family to consider. You are the eldest. You must marry a noble, and carry on the name."

"Of what nobility is our name?" Swegn gasped, clapping a hand over his mouth. The words had come out without his meaning to say them. "I am sorry."

"Do you not see?" Godwine cried, wounded. "Even you emphasize my point."

Swegn stared at the intensity of his father's voice.

"We have dragged ourselves from the most humble beginnings. You wonder why your mother is so hard on you. It is because she scorned me, and my issue, as commoners. Only time and perseverance won her over."

Godwine shivered. He had never admitted this to his son before. "We can never again associate with those of common birth, or we will become as they are and lose everything I fought so hard for. Do you think it has been easy to get here?" Godwine couldn't stop once he had started. "Did you think of what I had to give up?"

Swegn shook his head, overwhelmed. Godwine grabbed his arm.

"I'll tell you what. My self-respect. The love of my parents. The respect of the world, after what happened with Alfred two years ago. I must hold my head up and abide their remarks, or suffer the King's ill will. Or worse. Do you want to lose all we have? Swegn, you shall have an earldom in time. Do you want to make a commoner your countess?"

The boy turned his head, pulling away. Godwine let him go. Perhaps he had said more than he should. But he knew that he had made his point.

Eadgifu was sent off to a nunnery, near Hereford on the borderlands. She had accepted her lot with composure, more resignedly than Swegn. Perhaps she had expected their relationship to end this way, whereas he had managed to fool himself for some time.

Swegn moped around the house for weeks after her departure, speaking to no one. When he did finally speak, it was to tell his father he would never marry anyone.

23

In March, 1040, Godwine was summoned to Oxford with the same kind of urgency as that other time, which he dreaded to remember. At least now, he was not in a desperate hurry; he took the trouble to properly cloak himself against the wind and kiss his wife farewell. He bid Swegn attend him, since it was time the boy learned about the working of government.

"If King Harold dies how will it affect us?" Swegn asked as they rode at a leisurely pace.

Godwine looked proudly at his son. He was finally showing the proper interest in the family and in his role as the eldest.

"Well, at least I believe our position in Wessex is unassailable. Whoever the next king is, he will have need of experienced men in the government."

"Who do you think it will be?"

"There are several candidates. We have Harthacnut, who has finally patched things up with Magnus, and I hear he is currently in Bruges with Emma putting together an invasion fleet." He grunted shortly. "If we elect him, at least he can forget those plans."

"You expect him to succeed, then."

"Yes I do. But we must not forget Eadward Aetheling, son of Edmund Ironside. He is in Hungary at the court of King Stephen, and I think he is content there. Then there is Edward the Exile, waiting his turn in Normandy."

Swegn looked at his father. He knew that Edward was an unpleasant thought for Godwine, considering what happened to his brother Alfred. "You do not think it is his turn yet."

"No. But someday we may have to deal with him."

By the time they arrived in Oxford, King Harold had already died. Godwine was relieved. As they escorted Harold's body to Westminster, the mood of the funeral assembly was almost festive. The four years of his reign were fraught with injustices and favoritism, and everyone looked forward to reestablishing the observance of Canute's old laws.

* * *

The new Witan was set for Easter. Again, Godwine sat in the chairman's place.

This time, there was little argument. Everyone could see the value in Harthacnut's claim, especially considering his current invasion plans. A messenger was sent to Bruges formally inviting him to take the crown.

When the assembly was over, Godwine sought for Seward; they had not been in communication since the election of Harold. It was easy to locate him, since the Dane towered over most of the room. He turned at Godwine's approach, all smiles. "Congratulations on your marriage and your new earldom," Godwine said, grabbing him wrist to wrist. "You rule more than twice your old holdings, I hear."

"Yes. All of Deira. The northerners are a troublesome lot, but not nearly as quarrelsome as the Scots. Between the two I have my hands full; but I enjoy the challenge."

Seward pulled Godwine into a private corner, lowering his voice. "Now that we have elected Harthacnut, how do you think he will behave toward us, having resisted him the last time?"

"Speak for yourself, my friend. As you will remember, I held out for him."

"But gave way in the end. Do you think he will be grateful?"

Godwine smiled wryly. "No. You are right. But if he is angry with one of us, he will have to take all of us on. Surely he cannot expect to do so with ease?"

Seward let out his breath.

"By the way," Godwine added, "why is it I find you siding with Leofric? Have the two of you reached an understanding?"

"Not really. But he can threaten my border if he feels put out. It is something I think about."

Godwine frowned at him. "Let him have too much and he will threaten more than your border."

"It will never be so. I have you to balance his animosity, do I not?"

"And you give me leave to use you in the same way?"

Seward grinned. "What else are friends for?"

* * *

Harthacnut landed at Sandwich in June with his sixty-two ships and Emma proudly at his side. He was a regal-looking King and his subjects cheered him, full of hope. At this point, they were willing to give him any consideration.

He traveled to London and was again welcomed ceremoniously. Gytha watched the royal cavalcade pass under her window, more curious than affectionate; she remembered Harthacnut as a spoiled, willful child. In the old days, wanting to keep up appearances, her brother Ulf had always treated the boy like a king; this was not necessarily a good idea in every case. As she remembered, it led to Ulf's unfortunate demise at the hand of King Canute. And, though she was reluctant to admit it, her marriage to Godwine.

Harthacnut passed by without looking up. She was surprised at his great bulk, attesting to his famous eating habits; it was said he feasted his court four times a day. It took a huge horse to carry him comfortably.

In the King's train followed an individual who brought a glow of happiness to Gytha's face. As he neared, riding a sprightly horse, she called out "Beorn!" and the man shouted with glee, bringing his mount closer.

"Aunt Gytha. Still as beautiful as ever." He blew her a kiss. "Is Godwine with you?"

"Waiting for the King at Westminster. We are staying the week. Will you join us?"

"Gladly. Just as soon as my duties are over."

* * *

Godwine was delighted to see Beorn, who was his favorite out of Ulf's brood. He gave him an open invitation to serve in his household, but Beorn decided to stay with the King.

"I would be lying to say that I like him these days," Beorn laughed. "But he treats me well, and pays me even better. It seems that Harthacnut doesn't trust many people and regards me as incorruptible. I guess I am, at that."

Godwine nodded at Beorn, liking the man he had become. "How is his attitude toward me?"

Beorn's smile faded. "I can't honestly say. You see, he has become a stranger since his father died. He no longer talks to me as a cousin. All I know is that Queen Emma worked on him from the moment he met her at Bruges, which isn't a good sign. I think many of his actions will be dictated by her."

He tried to look reassuringly at Godwine. "He feels a stranger here, you know. Do your best to convince him that you are in charge of things, and everything should be all right. Harthacnut is a good one for letting the others do the work. He won't let personal feelings make his own job any more difficult."

"I hope so. He has summoned me to see him tomorrow."

* * *

Beorn did not know how unsettling his words were. Godwine went over them again and again, trying to dismiss a nagging foreboding as he dressed in his best silk tunic. Guessing that Harthacnut was going to take him to task for abandoning his cause, Godwine expected to face him alone. He was all the more surprised on entering the King's audience chamber to find others there before him. Aelfric, Archbishop of York was the most distinguished; Harthacnut's steward, captain of his guards, and many lesser nobles were also awaiting the King's pleasure.

It seemed that they were also waiting for Godwine, because Harthacnut entered soon after. The King stood for a long while, looking at each man in turn before sitting. His bulk filled the throne, making him seem even larger than on horseback. Beady eyes glinted from a hairy face; those eyes were strangers to kindness.

"So," he began, with a pause full of emphasis, "I am here at last, but only after much opposition. Not surprisingly, my half-brother Harold saw fit to usurp my throne..."

He looked directly at Godwine.

"...and no one was strong enough to withstand him. This is an affront I do not intend to stomach. Hence, I command you to disinter his unworthy corpse and throw it into the Thames."

After a startled gasp, the men looked at each other confusedly. Surely they must have heard him wrong.

"Tonight! This very minute. Now!"

They stared at their new King, taking in his clenched fists, his undisguised hatred. No one in the room suspected such violence in his mind. But the captain of his guards, used to obeying without question, started for the door. That broke the spell. He was followed by the collection of troubled, thoughtful men.

Harthacnut watched them go, not bothering to suppress a triumphant smile. He turned halfway in his throne, looking back over his shoulder at the heavy red drapery. The edges came apart and Emma stepped forth, putting a proud hand on her son's shoulder.

24

"I have never been party to such a shameful exhibition of bile." Godwine took a long draught of wine, his hand still trembling. Gytha peeled off his dripping cloak, saying nothing.

"We actually had to stand by while Harthacnut's men broke the tomb open and dragged the stinking body from its resting place. It was disgusting."

She helped pull off his ruined tunic. A maid gave Gytha a dry linen shift which she tugged down over his wet hair. Another servant was stoking the fire.

Godwine went on, unaware of his wife's careful administrations. "We went single-file down the narrow stairs to the river. By then it was pouring. It was so slippery that they dropped the body, and watched it roll down the rest of the steps. Laughing!" He shivered.

"When we got to the bottom, they grabbed Harold by his shroud and dragged him to the river. They left him there with his head in the water. Like a dog. And we had to watch, in silence. Then leave him like that, so we could report to the King."

Gytha rubbed his hair with a towel. He grabbed her arm gently.

"I feel so unclean."

She kissed him, sitting at his side. "Were you in a position to refuse?"

"No." He shook his head. "It was clear that Harthacnut wants to humble me. He is going to make me pay for submitting to Harold."

"At least you did not have to handle the corpse. Be grateful for that."

"Grateful. Yes, I suppose you are right." He pulled her toward him. "I think we will go back to Bosham as soon as possible. I want to spend some time with our growing family, and stay away from court."

* * *

Godwine didn't get to stay away as long as he would have liked; the incident with the body was only the beginning, and Harthacnut had big plans that required a heavy hand.

It had quickly become obvious that he had no intention of dismissing his fleet of 62 ships. A summons was received shortly after the Harold incident, and Godwine returned to London with heavy forebodings. He wasn't surprised to see all the chief earls, governors and sheriffs, called together to witness the King's pronouncements. Godwine edged over toward Earl Seward who turned his back to the room.

"A fine fix we got ourselves into," Seward said out the side of his mouth. "He seems to feel none too gracious toward us."

Godwine suppressed an angry response. If the northerners had not held out for Harold Harefoot, things would probably be different now. Or of course, maybe not. "One things is for sure," he growled. "No one feels like cheering this day."

In fact, when Harthacnut entered the room, the attendees barely bowed their acknowledgement. In response, the King barely deigned to notice. He lowered himself ponderously onto his throne. He was wearing a crown this time which looked a little too small for his head. A row of housecarls filed in and stood behind him.

Harthacnut had no interest in dragging things out. "I have an announcement to make," he started, gesturing for someone to give him a scroll. "We must raise 22,000 pounds to pay for the maintenance of my ships and men. The Danegeld required is eight marks per rowlock."

Silence. The witnesses were stunned.

"It is your duty to start the process," the King added. "I will be sending my housecarls to collect the taxes." There were gasps throughout the crowd. Housecarls were the closest thing a king or an earl had to a personal guard. But they had never been used for this purpose before.

Godwine stepped forward. "Sire," he began, looking behind him. A few of the others nodded their encouragement. "Sire. All of England has welcomed you to the throne. You have no need of these extra ships. All throughout your father and brother's reign, sixteen ships have sufficed."

Harthacnut shrugged his shoulders. "I see the need. We must have a standing fleet."

The hall broke out into clamors of disagreement. Someone in the back of the hall stepped forward. "We are not in a state of war!"

Someone else shouted, "We cannot justify such a burden on our people."

"Justify?" Harthacnut shouted, leaping from the throne with amazing agility. "I have no need to justify. The crews must be paid. That is all."

Godwine waited for the hubbub to die down and cleared his throat. "Sire," he ventured once again, "perhaps you are not aware of the huge gale we had right before you came. We are facing a crop failure this year."

"That is none of my concern," Harthacnut said scornfully, stepping down from the platform and leaning into Godwine's face. "By the way," he lowered his voice threateningly while the hall quieted down. "It is time you answered for the death of Alfred Aetheling. My brother. You are commanded to appear before the Witan and defend your role in this crime."

Godwine took a step back. It felt like he had taken a blow to the chest. For the moment he had nothing to say. As the King turned on his heels and left the room, he stood alone, dumbfounded. He clenched and unclenched his hands, then ran his fingers across his forehead. "I should have expected this," he murmured to himself.

But this was no time to falter. Taking a deep breath, he turned and faced his peers. Most were known to him. The room was unnervingly quiet, for all present knew that their turn could be next. One by one, Godwine looked at his fellow earls, trying to gauge their faces and how much support he could depend on. Seward, at his right, was looking thoughtfully at Godwine while he stroked his beard. Leofric was already leaving the room, but Godwine expected that.

Godwine heard a cough at his side and turned to see one of Harthacnut's emissaries holding the very same scroll he had seen in the King's hands. The man bowed.

"Earl Godwine," he said officiously, "The King is calling a Witenagemot a fortnight hence at his palace in London. He commands your presence. You have been accused of betraying, blinding and murdering Prince Alfred. Prepare your compurgation." He handed the scroll to Godwine.

"Who accuses me?" said the Earl of Wessex, straightening.

"The Archbishop Aelfric."

"Aaah." *Harthacnut's creature.* This man had already proven his worth. He was known to be grasping and greedy and had recently driven a rival from the Bishopric of Worcester so he could gather the revenues for himself.

By now, Seward had made a decision and approached Godwine's other side. "I will be an oath-helper," he said as they watched the emissary disappear. "We stand together." Godwine nodded to him appreciatively. He knew that Seward's recent elevation to Earl of all Northumbria was tainted; it was rumored that he had gained Harthacnut's favor by murdering the previous earl while the victim was under the King's protection. Seward asserted that he had the King's approval. Still, Harthacnut seemed to be notoriously fickle and who knew how long he would remember.

Seward moved on and others started to approach Godwine quietly, offering to testify in his behalf. As each new ally offered his support, Godwine began to get his old confidence back. Trial by Compurgation, more commonly known as the Wager of Law, required that the defendant produce eleven or twelve peers that would be willing to testify they believed the defendant's oath of innocence—even if they knew nothing about the crime. By the end of the day, Godwine had the sworn promises of more than twenty respectable men. Harthacnut had done himself more harm by this day's exhibition of bile than Harold Harefoot managed in his whole short reign. And Godwine discovered he had more support than he had dared hope.

* * *

Two weeks wasn't much time, but fortunately Godwine had already been hard at work building a ship for Harthacnut ever since the death of Harold Harefoot. A large gift from England's premier Earl was not unprecedented, nor even unexpected. But all along, Godwine had reckoned he needed to take measures to protect himself after the death of Alfred. Instead of being merely a gift, he was counting that the value of this ship would match the weregild if found guilty of the Aetheling's murder. Innocent or guilty, he would have to pay.

By now, it was clear that Godwine's need was most urgent. His shipbuilders worked morning, noon and night, and when the day of reckoning finally came he was pleased at the result.

All of nearby Portsmouth turned out to see the departure of Godwine and his family. Belying any worry, he stood proudly at the bow of the most glorious galley anyone had ever seen, with a gilded figure-head and eighty rowers. Each man wore golden arm bracelets weighing sixteen ounces, and was fully armed with a triple coat of mail, a gold-inlaid battle-axe, a gilded helmet, gilded shield, and gold-hilted sword. Never was there a more splendidly equipped crew.

They sailed through the harbor mouth amid the cheers of the

populace, and into the sea. Making their way around the southern coast and into the Thames, they rowed to London. Godwine sent an invitation to Harthacnut to meet him at the dock.

Filled with curiosity, the King came out to greet the Earl; even in disgrace, Godwine was still the first man in the kingdom. The King did his best to look imposing, surrounded by his advisors and dignitaries. But Harthacnut soon forgot all about ceremony; what he saw took his breath away.

Godwine disembarked with his wife and sons, arrayed in their finest. They bowed to the King, and Godwine indicated the ship with a wide sweep of his arm. The sun glinted off the figure-head.

"It is my gift to you, Sire. I hope you are pleased."

Harthacnut's eyes lit up greedily. He turned to Godwine. "Truly this is the most magnificent present a subject ever gave to a king." He even took Gytha's hand and kissed it, then stood back to admire the ship.

"My brother Ulf would have been proud this day," Gytha said quietly.

Both Godwine and Harthacnut stared at her in surprise. Ulf's name brought back painful memories and Godwine rarely spoke of him. But it was easy to see that Harthacnut was moved by the sudden reminder of their mutual ties from the past. For just a moment Godwine recognized the hopeful child who gave his father the royal seal of Denmark...just days before Ulf's death.

One of the King's followers leaned over and whispered in his ear, and Harthacnut nodded distractedly, turning back to Godwine. He cleared his throat. "The Witenagemot will be held at the third hour on the morrow," he said with a little less rancor than previously. "Please be prompt."

Godwine and party bowed again as the King reluctantly moved away, looking over his shoulder at his new gift. They didn't trust themselves to speak until he was well out of sight, but Godwine gave Gytha's hand a squeeze. She was truly his help-meet and she never ceased to amaze him.

"You are my most precious gift," he said, "and you may have saved the day for me."

* * *

Throughout the evening, visitors were announced and welcomed to partake of food and drink. Most of Godwine's supporters were already in London or had stayed the two weeks since the previous assembly. Many spent that night at his residence or stayed nearby in the local inns.

In the morning as they made their way on foot to the King's palace, Godwine was glad to see so many people heading in the same direction. As he entered the large courtyard before St. Paul's Cathedral, he stopped, holding his breath. Just for a moment, Godwine was carried back to that special day so many years ago, when Canute had entered London for the first time. The place was the same, but oh so many changes had torn the heart out of him. And now he was obliged to enter Canute's palace which once felt like a second home…so he could stand accused by the great King's son.

As though she was reading his mind, Gytha took Godwine by the hand. He blinked at her, grateful for her presence, while the crowd began to call his name. Taking Gytha's hand under his arm he stepped forward, nodding this way and that as a path opened before them. His young sons strode behind them in a rare show of solidarity. The oath-helpers fell in behind the family and the palace doors opened for them as if by magic.

Godwine and his advocates filed into the great hall. As usual, the room was dark with only a few windows near the roof. Torches along the wall cast long shaky shadows across the gloomy floor. The throne atop its raised platform was surrounded by tallow candles, drawing all eyes up as intended.

The hall filled quickly, and so many people had come that there wasn't sufficient room for all inside the building. Only the earls and Thegns and people of rank were permitted in the hall.

Naturally Harthacnut made sure to let everyone wait uncomfortably for his presence. The smoky hall was already stifling when the King entered with his housecarls and sat down without speaking to anyone. No one could tell from his face what kind of mood he was in. He beckoned Godwine forward; the Earl kneeled at the foot of the throne.

"Earl Godwine, you have been accused of betraying and murdering my brother, Alfred. How do you answer?"

Despite himself, Godwine had to suppress a shudder. He had never been on this side of a law court before, and he didn't like it. "I am innocent," he spoke, relieved that his voice sounded so clear and confident.

Harthacnut frowned. "Are you prepared to swear an oath to that effect?"

"I am." Godwine got to his feet and turned to the room. "I swear a most solemn oath that I had no culpability in the death of Alfred Aetheling. Upon his arrival in my earldom I met with Alfred and his followers, intending to accompany them to their declared destination. But they were forcibly removed by King Harold's soldiers and taken from my custody. I was not present when Alfred was blinded, nor was I privy to the King's orders. To this I do swear."

"And are you able to call Compurgators to uphold the validity of your oath?"

"Yes, they are present in this assembly."

"Then have them come forward."

Seward, the tallest and most formidable of all the Earls, stepped up to the throne. "Lord King," he said, bowing. "I will vouch for the good character of the defendant. I swear that I believe in his innocence, and I trust his oath."

Bowing again, he turned and took his place at Godwine's

back. Next to step forward was Tovi the Proud, retainer and faithful friend to King Canute since before the Danish conquest. Harthacnut knew Tovi since he himself was a child, for the proud Dane was ever in his father's retinue.

"I too swear to stand by the good character and innocence of Earl Godwine," he said. "I attest to the honesty and good faith of this man."

Thor of the Middle Angles stepped up next, followed by Roni of the Magesaetas. By then, Harthacnut was already starting to look bored. By the time Godwine had produced his twelfth oath-helper and looked ready to produce a dozen more, the King held up a hand.

"Enough," he said. "We are satisfied as to the Earl's innocence. This trial is finished, and the defendant is acquitted. Earl Godwine." The King raised his voice and stood. "Do you attest that the usurper King Harold ordered this terrible crime?"

Suddenly it was all starting to make sense. Godwine raised his head. "I do so attest."

"Then he deserved any and all sanctions against his miserable carcass. I declare Harold nithing and unworthy to wear the crown."

There. It was done. Harthacnut had arranged this whole trial to take attention away from his scandalous treatment of Harefoot's corpse. No one was fooled, but all were forewarned. The room was filled with murmurs, and the lesson was not lost. The King was like a force of nature, and they all felt like they had narrowly dodged a violent tempest.

* * *

The Witenagemot didn't hamper the King's efforts to collect the new Danegeld—or stern geld, as it was called. The King's tax-gatherers were already at work, accompanied by the King's housecarls who didn't to have any orders to spare the rod when needed. Indeed, some of them seemed to relish the work and took to terrorizing the surly ceorls and merchants with an enthusiasm their master would applaud.

At first Godwine wasn't directly involved in this unpleasant task. But as he made his annual progress across Wessex, he was frequently accosted by angry Thegns and shire-reeves. All complained remorselessly about the severe treatment they received at the hands of the King's servants. Godwine did the best he could to alleviate their problems, but he was unable to interfere.

Finally, one night late in May a messenger from the King found Godwine at his palace in Winchester. He was ushered into the feast hall as Godwine was just enjoying a last bite of stew. The Earl sat back in his chair and gestured for a servant to take away his food. "I think I just lost my appetite," he said to Gytha, who sat beside him.

The messenger was obviously exhausted and eyed the tables as he came forward to Godwine. But the Earl of Wessex was in no mood to coddle the lackey of Harthacnut.

"My Lord," the newcomer bowed. "The King commands you to gather a force and meet with the other great earls at Gloucester and put down this insurrection."

Godwine leaned forward wearily. "Insurrection? I have heard of no insurrection."

"Ahem. The townspeople of Worcester have risen up in rebellion and killed two of the King's guard. The housecarls took refuge in the minster tower but they were discovered, dragged forth and slain. The King demands that the town be put to the torch."

Godwine put his forehead into his hand while Gytha invited the messenger to take a place at the table. His task done, the man gratefully sat down and helped himself to a heaping portion of stew as a servant put a trencher before him. Gytha poured more ale into Godwine's cup as the room filled up with murmurs.

Many of those present were Godwine's retainers and knew they would be the first to be called up.

"As you know," Godwine announced to the room, "Worcester is in Mercia. I will consult with Earl Leofric before making any moves." Godwine had no interest in putting his men at risk for someone else's problem. But he knew that the King expected something from his great earls; so far, only a small portion of Harthacnut's great stern geld had been collected.

Godwine took his time responding to the King's demand, but he did send a message to Leofric the following day. A week later, he rode with a score of retainers to Gloucester. By then, some of Mercia's Thegns had already arrived and Seward was on his way.

On entering Leofric's great hall, Godwine saw that the King's messenger was standing by. Looking annoyed, Leofric invited Godwine to sit at an empty throne. Tired from his journey, Godwine accepted the seat and a goblet of wine.

"This King of ours is getting to be burdensome," Leofric began, but interrupted himself and stood at the entrance of his wife. "My wife, Godiva," Leofric stated, taking her hand and leading her to the throne on his other side.

Godwine stood as well and bowed. Godiva's beauty was well known, and her gentleness was said to curb her husband's ill temper. Her famous ride through Coventry clothed only in her long hair had reached legendary status; Godwine always doubted the veracity of the tale, but it was a fact that Coventry's taxes had been alleviated. "I am honored to meet you," he replied, meaning every word. She smiled, adjusting her skirt.

"My dear Earl," she said. "We welcome you under our roof. I abhor the necessity of this event, but appreciate the opportunity to meet such an influential man."

Leofric clasped his hands, putting his forefingers against his lips. Godwine almost laughed.

"My visit is long overdue," Godwine nodded, holding up his goblet in a gesture of acknowledgement. "I hope that between all of us, we can find a way out of this predicament. I would not cross the King again if I can help it. But I am loth to take such extreme measures."

"My thoughts exactly," Leofric spoke up with some heat. "I do not think Harthacnut has the measure of his Saxon subjects. We are not like sheep to submit without a murmur."

"Ah," Godwine sat back resignedly. "Submit we must. But let's see if we can delay the retribution until the King has cooled off."

And so it proved. Between them, the great Earls found repeated excuses not to raise an army to harry the people of Worcester. Six months passed, but after the last of the crops had been harvested, the King was demanding action. Reluctantly, Godwine called his fyrd and marched north into Mercia. But the earls had agreed among themselves to send warning to the people of Worcester that they were coming.

Five Earls were commanded to harry the district of Worcester; even so, their combined forces were only a couple of thousand. The leaders rode together in somber acquiescence; happily, due to their forewarning, very few people were sighted. Nonetheless, the soldiers were given free rein to plunder and burn the homesteads. They carried on thus for four days, traveling the length and breadth of the district. On the fifth day, they arrived at the city. The Earls breathed a sigh of relief to see that the vicinity was empty.

Leofric sent scouts to discover the whereabouts of the populace. The first of the scouts returned in a few hours. He knelt before the Earl.

"I have found them, your grace. The townspeople have retired to Bevere Island in the Severn River. They are ensconced in a fortified encampment."

Leofric turned to the others. "Attacking them could cost us men," he said, dismissing the scout. "And November is no sensible time to campaign. I say we tell the King they put up a good fight, and send him a wagon of plunder. Who is with me?"

For once, all the earls were in accord. So on the fifth day the city was burned and the army retired to their respective homes. The King received his booty, and the matter was closed.

* * *

Gytha was just tying a knot on her embroidery when Godwine found her; he was carrying a letter and had the most puzzled look on his face.

She laughed. "You look like you just discovered a new mystery and don't know what to do with it."

Her husband sat on the bench and kissed her ear. "Perceptive as usual," he said. "You might know better than I how to react to this one." He handed over the letter with a flourish.

Gytha took her time, then tapped it against her cheek speculatively.

"Well, this is a new turn. Since when has Queen Emma asked for your help for anything?"

Godwine grunted. "I usually have to force my advice down her throat." He couldn't help but be intrigued. "She is not specific about what she wants, but it doesn't sound like bad news. Still, will you come with me, Gytha? You always seem to have a steadying influence on her."

Gytha nodded enthusiastically. "I'd be happy to come. It's been a long winter and I'm glad it's over. I assume she is in Winchester?"

"Yes. This shouldn't take too long. Let us go, just the two of us..." And of course, his entourage led by the ever-present Eirik. Godwine never traveled alone.

Emma received Godwine and Gytha in her personal chamber. She was particularly gracious this time and kissed Gytha on both cheeks, complimenting her on keeping a slim figure after so many children. Godwine was bursting with curiosity but managed to keep his face expressionless. After the necessary greetings were over, Emma got straight to the point.

"Because of our long association, Godwine, my son Harthacnut has asked me to consult with you." She paused, while Godwine suppressed a snort. Gytha grabbed his hand.

"I am aware," the Queen went on, "that his popularity has...diminished. Never mind why. Here is my question: what do you suggest we do to improve his reputation?"

Godwine was momentary startled. This was totally unexpected.

"Come, Godwine. Your resourcefulness is well recognized by everyone."

He bowed his head, flattered despite himself. "Well, remitting the Danegeld would certainly help."

"Aside from the Danegeld. Harthacnut remains firm on that point."

Godwine pursed his lips. "Let me think on this," he said, and Gytha chose this moment to ask Emma some advice about an ecclesiastic appointment they were considering. As Emma warmed up to the subject, Godwine paced the room. He stood before the window admiring the view, when a solution came to him. He turned around and both women paused expectantly.

"Have him invite your son Edward to court."

Silence. Emma suppressed a frown, then looked thoughtful.

"Since Harthacnut hasn't married, our country needs an heir," Godwine pursued. "What better choice than someone from the ancient house of Cedric?" It was Gytha's turn to frown. She was thinking of her nephew Svein, grandson of Canute.

Emma cleared her throat. "Harthacnut has never met his brother," she started slowly. "But it could be the English would welcome my son." Never mind that he was mostly raised in Normandy. "Yes, Godwine, this might help regain his popularity after all."

For a moment, Godwine and Emma looked each other in the

eye. Much though she hated to admit it, Edward was a risk. There was no question that Emma always favored Canute's son over Aethelred's brood. She had practically abandoned her elder children and never seemed to give it a moment's thought. How would she face him now?

But first and foremost she was a practical woman. Godwine's suggestion was practical and useful and did help solve the question about the succession. Nodding, the Queen agreed to consult Harthacnut.

Gytha held her tongue until they were alone that night. But when Godwine reached out to her, she stopped him. "What have you done?" she asked bitterly.

Sighing, Godwine leaned back in the bed. He knew this was coming. "Gytha..."

"Svein is Canute's...come, he is my kin. How could you overlook him?"

"You think I don't remember?" A small smile came across his face. "And he is Ulf's son. Oh, how I would love to put him on the throne."

Ready to object further she paused, a little mollified.

"Gytha. I fear that England has had enough of Danish rule. You know, it is rumored that Harthacnut's Danegeld was mostly used to provide a fleet for Svein. His quarrel with King Magnus of Norway has nothing to do with us."

"I know, but..."

"Can you really expect that England will countenance more of the same?"

Gytha let out her breath. "I suppose not."

He put an arm around her and this time she obliged.

"Gytha, there is more." She raised her head from his shoulder. Godwine's eye glistened in the candle light.

"Perhaps, since it was my idea...perhaps Edward won't hold me responsible for Alfred's death. He is too important to ignore...forever. I hope to gain some of his favor, but it will not be easy. You see, my risk is as great as Emma's. He may hate the both of us."

He kissed her forehead then blew out the candle. "Or maybe he will see the advantage in forgiving us. If we have him in our debt."

* * *

Harthacnut was surprisingly eager to jump on Emma's suggestion. An invitation was immediately sent across the channel, and the Queen asked Godwine to meet Edward at Dover. Since he needed a visit to his coastal towns anyway, the Earl agreed. Bringing a small retinue and a few gifts from the King, Godwine gave himself enough time to prepare a worthy welcome.

Dover was a busy port town, and Godwine was inspecting import documents when the lookouts spotted the King's flag atop the mast of an approaching ship. Summoning his attendants, the Earl of Wessex positioned himself at the dock and awaited the landing.

He could see a tall man standing quietly at the gunnel, staring in his direction. When the boat was secured, someone addressed the newcomer respectfully and he seemed to pull himself together, allowing his companion to help him climb onto the dock. Godwine approached, bowing deeply.

Keeping his chin down as he straightened, he furtively studied the Aetheling and was not surprised to see a strong resemblance to Alfred. His hair was blond tending to white, and his pale skin made him seem fragile. Edward's beard was just beginning to fill out, his fingers were long, and he was slender overall. He was almost a handsome man, except for those eyes, full of distrust bordering on hostility.

It was pretty much as Godwine expected. He went through the usual ritual of greeting, presenting Prince Edward to the leading men of the town. Edward brought a small household, and introduced Godwine to the man who helped him from the boat.

"My sister's son, Ralph of Mantes." Edward turned to his nephew with an indulgent smile. "And this is Robert Champart, abbot of Jumieges." The abbot bowed in turn.

Nodding, the Earl of Wessex led the way toward the Prince's quarters. Not many words passed between them. Godwine was at a loss as how to break the ice; he wished Gytha had come along.

Edward's behavior was impeccably proper, and as they traveled to London the party paused in villages along the way to greet the citizenry. They stayed a couple of extra days at Canterbury, where they were entertained by the Archbishop. For the first time, Edward relaxed and he showed the most enthusiasm when they entered the minster. He stayed an extra hour to pray while his retinue waited for the Archbishop's meal to be served.

As they approached London, the King himself came out with great fanfare and embraced his half-brother with what looked like genuine affection. Even Edward was delicately receptive. Behind the King, Emma approached with a studied smile, and kissed her elder son before hugging him; she ventured a look at Godwine while her face was hidden from Edward and the Earl almost felt sorry for her.

Nonetheless, the crowd was pleased and cheered merrily as the royal entourage approached the Palace. Edward insisted they stop at St. Paul's and express thanksgiving for his safe journey. Grimacing briefly, Harthacnut obliged, then offered a generous donation to the local bishop. Edward was most impressed.

Godwine did not linger any longer than he had to; he took his leave of the King and Edward the following day. The Aetheling barely gave him a nod, and Godwine backed from the room, a little sick to his stomach. He called on Emma just before parting.

"Ah, my good Earl," she said, putting out her hand. "Or should I say, my good ally. I may need your services again one day soon." She let out a sigh as he kissed her hand. "I fear my son is not of a forgiving nature after all," she said quietly. "I will do my best to alleviate his bad humors."

Godwine heartily hoped she could find a way.

25

Harthacnut stood at the wedding feast of his good friend Tovi Prudan the Dane, drinking horn held high. He looked down at the bride who blushed furiously, plump and smiling. The room was filled with his family and friends, and the King was in a jovial mood.

"I propose a toast to this lovely couple, and wish them many happy..."

The guests looked at the King expectantly, waiting for him to finish. For a moment he stood immobile, then he dropped his horn, raising a hand to his throat.

Emma was the first to react. She leaped up, slapped the King on the back, then again. He was bent over, choking, his face turning red, then purple, eyes bulging. Finally, arms flailing, he fell forward across the table, scattering dishes in all directions.

Women were screaming, dogs leaped forward, fighting over the delicacies on the floor. Godwine was at Harthacnut's other side and Emma stepped back, giving him room. Grasping Harthacnut's shoulders, Godwine gave a heave. The King came up, eyes wild, gravy on his face. Emma made a move with a cloth, but she realized it didn't make any difference. He was already dead.

"No..." said Emma in a half whisper, then louder. "No! No! It cannot be true. My son!" Her voice rose hysterically.

Godwine tried to comfort her but she shoved him back with incredible strength. "Stay away from me! You always hated him. You all hated him." She threw herself on her son, wiping his face.

Glaring at Godwine, Edward stepped forward, putting an arm around his mother. To everyone's relief she submitted, and he drew her sobbing from the room.

As soon as they disappeared, the scene burst into confusion. People were babbling, some were congratulating each other, others shouted with laughter. For a moment, the body was forgotten, and the late King slumped sideways in his chair, staring at the guests.

Finally, Godwine shouted some order into the room. Servants were instructed to prepare a bed for the body, and it took six housecarls to carry the King away. Godwine turned to his hosts, offering his condolences at their spoiled wedding. Tovi looked shaken and Godwin put an arm around his shoulders.

"Do not worry, my friend," he said quietly. "He has been ailing for some time. I will make sure everyone knows he died from an excess of drink." He gave a sly smile. "It was the most appropriate death, wouldn't you say? For a man that feasts four times a day..."

Harthacnut, the last Danish king of England, was quietly buried in Winchester next to his father. No one but Emma mourned his passing. Two years of his reign had been more than enough.

* * *

Godwine and his family were anxious to get home to Bosham. As they were traveling, Godwine slowed his horse and rode side-by-side with his nephew.

"You are still welcome to join my household, Beorn." He smiled at the youth's relief. "I imagine that Harthacnut's death relieves you of your post, does it not?"

Beorn ran a hand through his beard. "I am sure it does. And yes, I would enjoy a spell with my family. You are pretty much all I have left these days, except for Svein. I don't think he will be coming here any time soon." He looked sideways at Godwine. "Or will he?"

Godwine frowned. "That is just the question I have been discussing with Gytha." He glanced over at his wife, who was riding on Beorn's other side. "Although Harthacnut treated

Edward Aetheling very honorably, he never officially declared him heir."

They rode for a moment in silence. "Svein does have a slight claim to the English crown although his descent from Swegn Forkbeard was on his mother's side." He cleared his throat. "On the other hand, King Harthacnut supported his claim to Denmark. It seems pretty clear he intended for Svein to stay over there." Godwine sounded lame even to himself. Gytha stayed silent, looking straight ahead.

"Edward Aethelredson is the only heir that is presently on English soil," he continued. "And he is the seventeenth descendant of the great Cedric, first King of West Saxons. That is a powerful natural right. But there is also Eadward Aetheling, who is still in Hungary. He is Edmund Ironside's son. And not hostile to our house. Still, he is of an unknown quality."

Despite himself, Godwine grimaced. "Both are descended from Aethelred the Redeless. We certainly don't want to go there again. At least Edmund Ironside fought for his people." He paused uncomfortably, recalling his own conflict of interest in those heady days. If he could do it again, would he have acted differently? He looked at Gytha who seemed like she was reading his mind again. "But the better man won," he added quietly.

* * *

Back at Bosham, the conversation continued.

"Although my authority has waned, my dear wife, the next King of England could make all the difference in the world. I need to back the right choice this time. And I might add that I still hold enough power to influence the Witan."

Gytha pursed her lips in thought. "Edward seems inclined toward his Norman friends. That could cause problems."

Godwine nodded. "People are grumbling already. There is no doubt that he needs to rally support. Yes, I would say that

Edward needs a champion. I think I could sway the southerners to follow me."

"Looks like you have made up your mind."

He sighed. "But the question remains, how much influence will I be able to wield over him? I think he still believes I killed Alfred."

"That was six years ago. Surely you can find ways to make him trust you."

"Trust." He said the word tenderly, as though savoring its very sound. "It is true: if I support Edward in this, he will have to accept that I couldn't have killed Alfred."

Godwine's chin had slipped into his hand, his thoughts turned inward. Editha poked her head into the room, and he beckoned her forward, patting the bench beside him. "You might as well listen too, my daughter. This could very much concern you."

He stopped to marvel at the beauty she had become. To him, Editha was still the precocious little girl, ever clamoring to be heard over the noise of her three elder brothers. But now she was fifteen, and old enough to be a bride.

"Father, this is all very interesting. But what could it possibly have to do with me?"

Smiling at last, her father turned a sparkling eye on her. "Why, I would make you queen of England, of course."

* * *

Swegn sat looking thoughtfully out the window, chewing on the end of his quill. He thought he was alone; letter-writing was a laborious task, and he would not willingly expose his inadequacy to anyone. As he bent once more over the parchment, his mind was so occupied that he never heard the stealthy footsteps enter the room.

"Dear Eadgifu?" came a deep voice behind him. "Isn't that the girl..."

Discovered, the writer spun around, his face crimson. Beorn seemed only mildly interested in his activity, but Swegn resented the interruption. Staring at his cousin, he deliberately crumpled the letter.

"Now, that wasn't necessary," said Beorn, detached.

"Neither is your presence."

"Ah, now that is another matter." Beorn sat down on a bench, spreading his arms across the back. "I am here, Swegn, and you might as well accept it. No one is attempting to supplant you. You are the eldest son. I am merely a cousin."

"Then why do you insist on being present at every family conference, sticking your nose where it doesn't belong?"

"Because I am still older than you." He leaned forward, elbows on knees. "And more experienced. It may come as a shock to you, but your father does respect my opinion."

"Only because of my mother."

"Oh? Do you think so?" He got up, walking aimlessly across the room. Suddenly he swooped down on the letter, picking it from the floor. He held it up like a prize. "Perhaps you are right. Aunt Gytha appreciates my good sense...something which you seem to lack." He threw the wad at Swegn.

Knocking the paper aside, Swegn stood threateningly. "Do not mention this letter to anyone. Do you understand? It is a very serious matter to me."

Grimacing in mock terror, Beorn backed up. Swegn followed him, grabbing his arm. "I am warning you. Stay out of my way."

Beorn attempted to slap his hand away, and failed. He wrenched his arm, loosing Swegn's hold, then pretended to step away; immediately he came back with a fist to his cousin's jaw. Swegn lurched back then dived for the other, catching him around the throat. They fell on the floor, knocking the table over, heedless of the ink splattering over their faces. Beorn punched Swegn in the nose, adding blood to the sticky mess.

Footsteps pounded into the room and the pair were dragged apart, none too gently. Swegn tried to pull away from his captor's grasp, but Harold held fast. Tostig, holding Beorn, laughed loudly, breaking the tension.

"Would you have believed it, Harold?" he roared. "You and I breaking up someone else's fight?"

Swegn tore loose, wiping his nose with his sleeve. "It was only a matter of time," he said bitterly. "He was getting too full of himself."

Beorn shrugged.

"Swegn," Harold said, "no one will respect you until you learn to control your temper."

Swegn glared at him, then stomped out of the room. The others looked at each other. Tostig broke the silence. "I just don't understand why he is our father's favorite?"

No one knew the answer.

* * *

Editha thought at first that her father was joking about making her queen; she did not realize that her hand was a bargaining point.

"I do not understand," she asked her mother. "Why is my father suddenly talking about marriage?"

Gytha's heart went out to the girl. Editha was at that uncertain age, when one discovers that life doesn't always cooperate with one's wishes. "It is the lot of noble women," she said, putting an arm around Editha's shoulders. "Daughters are often used as a means of insuring peace between countries, or of binding two families together. In your case, your marriage could very well mean that you will be the mother of a king. Does that not please you?"

"I suppose," Editha said slowly. "But don't I get a choice?"

"It's to be hoped that you will find love with your future

husband. Or at least contentment."

Editha frowned. "Contentment. Mother, I had always hoped I would find a man I wanted, like you did."

Gytha began to laugh, to her daughter's amazement. "What is so funny?" Editha asked, insulted.

"Do you think I married the man I chose? Of course not. I was commanded to do so by Canute."

Editha stared at her. "But you are so happy."

"Not at first. Oh, no. I resented being forced to marry. And you know, Editha, I nearly ruined everything. I would spare you this pain. My hostility did me no good; it merely made us both miserable. To think I came so close to rejecting such a fine man..."

She looked at her daughter. "So you see, it is all in the attitude."

* * *

Had Godwine heard Gytha say those words, he would have agreed wholeheartedly. He was staring at Edward Aethelredson, watching him get to his feet and pace the floor for the hundredth time that day—or so it seemed. Again Edward stopped, fists on hips, and stared at Godwine. He let out his breath in a heavy sigh.

"All right. What you say is true. There is no proof of your involvement. Perhaps you are telling me the truth. Perhaps I should let go of the past. But what makes you think I so want to be king?"

For a moment Godwine was stumped. This was a question he had not anticipated. "Because it is your duty," he said finally, hoping he sounded sincere. "Because yours is a destiny that very few share: to be the son of a king. It is not something that should be thrown away...or hidden inside of a monastery, tempting though that may seem to you."

Edward shook his head, began pacing again. "Yes. What you

say is true. God would not have made me an Aetheling if he did not want something from me." Spinning around with sudden decision, Edward said, "All right. I accept your reasoning. And choosing to support me, what do you want in return?"

"An earldom for my oldest son, Swegn."

"That is not unreasonable."

"And for you to marry my daughter Editha."

Edward's eyes widened. "Marry?" He started pacing again, looking doubtfully at Godwine. "I don't want to marry..." The rest of the sentence hung in the air between them: *I don't want to marry. Especially if I have to marry a daughter of yours*. "It is not an inclination of mine," he finished lamely.

Godwine took a deep breath, summoning his patience. This moment was too delicate to succumb to personal feelings. "You must have an heir, lest the kingdom fall prey to our neighbors after your death." He spoke as though to a child.

Edward sighed; he knew what was at stake. He knew how vital Godwine's support was. As though accepting a criminal's punishment, Edward mumbled, "Yes, Godwine, I shall marry your daughter...I hope she is pious."

"And well read, your Grace. She promises to be a great beauty."

Edward waved his hand. "That is no matter. As long as she is devout."

If Godwine had stopped to consider Edward's last words, he might have hesitated to commit his daughter to such a marriage. But no, his house was too close to the throne. Finally, he would have a king's confidence again; and this time he worked from a position of strength.

* * *

Godwine needed all his wits about him in the upcoming Witan. Like once before, the north held out for the Danish house, finding a champion in Svein Estridson. But this time, the resistance was not unanimous.

Godwine summoned his most convincing eloquence. He emphasized the need for unity in the country, pointing out how the last two reigns had nearly torn them apart. He supported bringing Saxon rule back to England. He praised Edward's good qualities, his piety and his wisdom.

Bit by bit, he won over the wavering votes. For once Leofric was the first to come over to Godwine's side, Seward soon followed suit, supporting Edward; Svein's claim was, after all, one generation removed.

It was enough. Edward Aethelredson was chosen King of England.

26

King Edward had declared that Gloucester seemed the perfect spot to hold his first Witenagemot. Located near the border of Wessex and Mercia and even Wales, the city seemed reasonably placed to keep an eye on his less-than-enthusiastic new subjects; his palace named Kingsholm was sufficiently large to house a good-sized assembly. Nonetheless Godwine was surprised Edward did not choose Winchester, but as his sway over the King was inconclusive, he stifled his curiosity and gathered his resources. Those resources included his sons.

Not surprisingly, he found two of them in the great hall; Swegn was sharpening his sword and Harold was finishing a late meal.

"Where is Tostig?" Godwine asked no one in particular.

Harold gestured toward the door. "Out hunting," he said. "As usual."

Godwine sat down at the table and reached across for some bread. "This time all of you need to attend the Witenagemot with me."

Swegn sat up straight; he had been waiting for this moment but had hoped it would be for him alone. He glanced jealously at Harold, but his younger brother didn't seem to notice.

"When do we leave?" Swegn breathed.

Godwine looked at him appraisingly. "In two days hence. Make sure you bring your best tunics. I believe Edward has something in store for us."

Gladdened, Swegn left the room. Harold took a full draught of ale. "An earldom?" he asked. Godwine nodded. "For my big brother. I hope he can hold it."

Godwine was about to answer when Tostig appeared at the door. "I just saw Swegn," he said lightly. "He didn't take a swipe at me."

Harold let out a grunt. "He's too busy thinking about his good fortune."

Tostig put his spear and bow against the wall before joining them. "I seem to have missed something. Are we talking about the King's meeting?"

Godwine stretched his back, playing for time.

"I thought so," said Tostig bitterly. "Swegn finally gets what's coming to him." He laughed briefly at his own joke. "Good. First him. Then you. Then me."

Their father shook his head. "Do you really think it's so easy?"

Harold and Tostig stopped, staring at him.

"Do you understand what we have to do, to retain our status?" Godwine sighed, surprised at his own disappointment. *What was he expecting from his boys?* So far, they had everything they wanted without having to work for it. "Look. Nothing is certain. Nothing at all. We must stick together as a family or we are finished."

His sons weren't sure what to say. They looked at each other then back at him.

"We cannot show any weakness. We have many enemies, my children. You must support each other. The world has to see the Godwines as England's first family. No matter how you feel about..."

"What?" Swegn had come up behind them, unnoticed.

"Each other," Godwine retorted, standing up. "I need no trouble, no arguments, no resentment. Swegn, you are their figurehead. You will need to act responsibly. All of you!"

With a sweep of his arm, Godwine left his three eldest, scratching their heads.

* * *

Nonetheless, when they rode with Godwine's entourage to Gloucester, his sons were on their best behavior. Riding straight and tall behind their father, Swegn, Harold and Tostig looked every bit the noble heirs. Occasionally Godwine looked behind him, proud of their bearing. Although they did not speak to each other, his sons seem to have understood the point of his little discussion.

The Witenagemot was well attended. Aside from the three great Earls, many Thegns and chieftains were present; all wanted to see how the new King was going to begin his reign. Edward took the trouble to mingle with the company for the full morning before calling the Witan together mid-afternoon. It was noted that many of his Norman associates followed close on his heels, but none deigned to address the Saxons.

As the assembly quieted down, Edward stood before his throne; his nephew Ralph stood behind it. "I am opening this Witan, this feast day of St. Martin of Tours, Year of Our Lord 1043. I thank you all for attending. I will begin this meeting by asking the governors to report on the condition of their lands. We will start with our Earl of Wessex."

Godwine was prepared and brought forward his steward, who read out the latest geld that had been collected to sustain the fleet. They also reported on the slow recovery from the recent famine and the harvest, which looked to be sustainable. Mercia and Northumbria reported next, and by the end of the afternoon many people had slipped from the room. Edward seemed content, and ended that day's session with one last announcement.

"I have decided to create Swegn Godwineson as Earl of Herefordshire. It will be his duty to guard the Marches and protect my good people against incursion from the Welsh borders. Come forward, Swegn."

Godwine bit his lip as his eldest son knelt before the King and bowed his head. As Edward lowered a chain of office over Swegn's head, Godwine marveled at how noble he looked at that moment; once again his hopes began to rise. Swegn was appropriately solemn and ignored the low murmuring about the hall.

Godwine could see that not everybody was happy with the King's action, and he noted the frowns on his other sons' faces. But at least Edward had kept his word. With luck he find would places for all of them, if he could see a way to build the King's confidence in his family.

The Witan went along without incident and on the last day Edward hosted a feast, inviting the three great Earls to share head table with him. Swegn was invited as well, and he couldn't disguise a sneer at his brothers as they found a place farther down the table. A brief glance at his father's cloudy face was enough to stop him in his tracks.

This was no Danish revel. Already Edward had gained a reputation as an abstemious eater, and today was no exception. The wine was well watered, but at least the guests were relieved to see platters heaping with game; Edward's passion for the hunt was equally well-known. But those at head table carefully followed the King's lead in not overfilling their trenchers.

Bishop Stigand, newly appointed to the See of Elmham, was seated between the King and Godwine, which suited the Earl of Wessex very well. He knew Stigand from Canute's days, and liked the bluff prelate who generally knew how to tiptoe around royal impulses. This day, however, the bishop seemed to be lacking his usual influence. At first, Edward was speaking softly into Stigand's ear, but the King's voice kept getting louder until everyone at the table was privy to the conversation.

"I know she is hoarding a great quantity of our treasure," Edward spoke harshly, wiping his hands on a cloth and handing it to a servant, who brought forth a clean one. "It seems my brother Harthacnut entrusted her with the royal coffers. Why hasn't she relinquished the funds that we require to run the affairs of this country?"

"Sire, I trust that..."

"You are her advisor, Stigand! Surely she will listen to you."

The bishop sat thinking a moment too long.

"Oh yes. I understand she is a generous benefactor to the Church. All the while neglecting her sons. As if it wasn't enough that she abandoned Alfred and myself to the tender mercies of my cousin Robert, Duke of Normandy." He took a deep breath. "And left us there without a sou. It seems my dear mother hasn't lost her taste for gold."

"Sire..."

"Or land. I understand she is the wealthiest woman in England. I think it is time we did something about it."

Godwine nearly coughed up his drink. Edward turned a baleful eye on him. "Yes, and my great Earls shall come with me, to make it official. Bring a small retinue and meet me on the morrow. All of you. We are going to pay a surprise visit to the Queen Mother in Winchester."

The morning dawned cloudy and cold. Godwine sat astride his favorite stallion frowning at his sons who were already grumbling about their change of plans.

"I had hoped to be on our way home by now," Swegn muttered.

"What do you care?" Tostig retorted. "You have a new home now. Or will have as soon as you pack your bags."

"Can't wait to get rid of me, can you!" Swegn put a hand on his sword hilt.

"Stop, you fools," Godwine growled, pushing his horse between the two of them who were glaring at each other. "Can't you restrain yourselves for another hour? Look at who is watching us!"

Abashed, Swegn glanced up and around. Earl Leofric sat his horse nearby, looking most disgusted. At the head of the party the King had turned around and pursed his lips thoughtfully.

"Don't make me do that again." Godwine pulled his rein and turned his back on the pair. He gestured to his retainers to fall in behind them and Harold rode up by his side, glad to be away from his brothers. The Royal company had already begun to move. Edward's Norman friends clustered protectively around him and the King didn't seem to mind any breach of protocol. In silent accord, Leofric, Seward, and Godwine fell in line behind Edward's housecarls.

Light rain was beginning to fall and the men pulled their cloaks around their heads. Godwine glanced at Seward who seemed unperturbed by the weather; this was nothing compared to Northumbria's blustery Novembers.

The Dane looked at him sideways. "It seems you are always on the wrong side of Queen Emma," he said. "What is her champion going to do now?"

Godwine grunted. "I was wondering the same thing. She will probably think we instigated this little performance."

"I suspect not. Edward has quite enough anger to come up with it, himself. I reckon he has been planning this for a long time."

Godwine nodded in agreement. He thought back to his last meeting with Emma. She had seemed almost resigned. But everyone knew how spirited she could be...and how spiteful when crossed.

"I don't look forward to this at all," he said to himself.

Seward nudged him with an elbow. "I would not want to be in your shoes. But be of good cheer; might is on our side!" He laughed briefly before covering up his own head. As if in answer, the rain came pouring down.

As the Royal cavalcade passed through the gates of Winchester, people streamed out of their shops and homes to gawk at their new King. Many had seen Edward before in Harthacnut's train, but few had bothered to take note. Edward raised a hand in greeting as he passed, but did not waver in his objective. He rode directly to Emma's palace and his retinue was forced to follow. It was clear that he didn't want to give Emma any opportunity to prepare for his visit.

Even though the rain had stopped the day before, the party was still damp and miserable. However, no one dared complain; as they got closer to the city, Edward's face grew more and more determined until even his closest allies gave him a wide berth. He dismounted before her palace and gestured for his Earls and chosen Thegns to follow him inside.

Pushing the doors open, Edward strode past the gaping servants. The rest followed and spilled into her chamber behind the King, though the room was too small for all to fit. Godwine dearly wished he could be standing outside, but Edward gave him such a look that he pushed to the front of the crowd. Emma sat at her embroidery, needle raised. Her face was such a look of surprise and panic that it was almost comic. But she was well acquainted with adversity and pulled herself together remarkably quickly. She stood gracefully.

"To what do I owe the honor of your visit?"

As the others stood as close to the wall as possible, the King began striding back and forth before his mother.

"I have come for the royal treasury."

Emma shook her head. "There is no royal treasury here."

"Oh come, mother. You have amassed quite a sum. Enough to pay a year's geld for the whole country, if it could be all counted."

She gasped. "That is not true."

"Not true." He stopped pacing and approached her closely. "Not any longer. I have come to relieve you of your burden which my brother so...unwisely entrusted to you. You will no longer need it to support your new estate."

"New estate? What are you talking about?"

"Dearest mother." He resumed his pacing. "You have no need of all my riches. Nor your vast lands, which I am returning to the crown."

Emma sat back down, stricken. The King smiled unpleasantly, satisfaction in his eyes. "Oh, don't worry. I will leave you enough to sustain your household for the rest of your life. Especially since you are commanded to restrict yourself to Winchester.

"Earl Seward, take my housecarls and discover the whereabouts of my coffers. I will put them in your safekeeping."

With a nod, Seward did the King's bidding. Edward barely noted his exit; he wasn't finished with the Queen.

"Mother, you have consistently put my welfare at risk. Never have you spoken out in favor of me..."

Emma glanced hard at Godwine, willing him to speak up in her defense. The Earl shook his head briefly at her.

"And now I hear that you sent letters to King Magnus encouraging him to claim the throne."

"Never!" she cried, hand to her chest.

"I have it on good authority. I cannot believe that even you would stoop to such a betrayal."

"That's not possible," she uttered, tears running down her face. "Earl Godwine, please, tell him so."

Edward turned all his malice on Godwine. "Well?"

This was unexpected. Godwine cleared his throat. "I know nothing of this, Sire."

He could see that Edward was considering a wicked retort but thought better of it. The King gave him a bitter look then started to leave the room. "You are fortunate, mother, that I do not send you into exile."

The crowd parted for the King then followed him from the room. Taking a deep breath, Godwine stepped toward Emma.

"Once again I see you among my enemies," she said, avoiding his eye.

Godwine kneeled. "Your son is not your enemy. You know that."

She looked away. "I don't know much of anything. I didn't see this coming."

"Nor did any of us." Godwine reached for her hand. "I promise you, I will do what I can to bring him around to reason."

"Oh, Godwine. What trust have I in your promises? Go, please. Leave me to my solitude."

Nothing loth, he rose. He had no particular interest in her company, nor was he comfortable with her accusation, deserved or not. How far should he go in defending her, anyway?

As he was leaving the building, his sons were helping Seward's men load heavy wooden boxes into wagons. The quantity of treasure was astonishing. Godwine wondered if the King was justified after all.

27

Editha looked at the flowers in her hand, grateful for any hint of beauty on this dismal day. It just didn't seem fair; she had done as she was told, hoping all the while for a reprieve, a reward from her parents for dutiful compliance. Instead, they seemed glad to be rid of her, congratulating themselves on a job well done.

There was some slight compensation in being Queen of England, she reasoned with herself. Now people would do as she said. And each time she stole a look at her father, Editha warmed to the glow on his face. He had been so unhappy lately.

King Edward stood beside her, listening reverently to the priest as the marriage vows droned on. She looked shyly up at her new husband, wishing for some sort of emotion. From the first, she had not been able to conquer a deadening apathy toward this man. No one would have cared, anyway; as her mother had said, it helped to make the best of it.

But what was she going to do on their wedding night? Everyone said that she was marrying a monk. If Edward couldn't show her what to do, she certainly didn't know herself.

* * *

Edward delayed the embarrassing procession to the wedding chamber as long as he could. Long after Editha had been ceremoniously taken away, he lingered at the table, talking to his bishops until he ran out of things to say. Everyone was staring at him expectantly, especially his father-in-law.

Clearing his throat, Edward stood, watching the rest of the room clamber unsteadily to their feet. For once, he wished he had imbibed the usual quantity of wine expected of a groom; but even in this extremity, he was repelled by the idea.

The thought of performing his dreaded duty was equally

disgusting. He was not sure why; the girl was pretty, even beautiful. She had done nothing to offend him...how could she, a girl of seventeen? Not for the first time, he wondered whether he resented his bride only because she was Godwine's daughter. That was an uncharitable thought. But somehow he couldn't help it.

When he closed the door on the celebration, Edward felt sorry for the girl. She was so tiny in that large bed, with the covers tucked under her chin as if for protection. It had never occurred to him that his bride would be less than willing to sleep with the King of England.

The thought brought a sly smile to his lips. Perhaps they could delay the inevitable.

Sitting on the edge of the bed, Edward looked at the girl, hands clasped in his lap. After a bit, her fright ebbed away. He didn't seem so threatening like this; without all of his formidable counselors, he was only a man. But there was no getting around his age. Edward was old enough to be her father.

"Are you frightened?" Edward asked.

Editha nodded.

"You mustn't be. I will not hurt you."

Taking a moment to find her voice, she said, "I know that. But I don't know what to do."

He laughed. "This is new to both of us. If you would like, Editha, we need do nothing but sleep." The relief on her face was insulting. Edward had to remind himself that he wanted the same thing. "I will even cut my finger so they will find the blood on the sheets."

Not understanding, her eyes opened wide. Edward sighed unhappily. He was going to have to teach her everything.

However, despite his best intentions, when he woke up in the middle of the night, Edward discovered an unbidden stiffening in his loins. The girl's warm body unconsciously pressed against his, gathering warmth. He reached a hand to her breast, enjoying the feel of her soft skin.

Why not, he thought to himself. *She belongs to me now.*

Editha awoke with a confused cry, crushed under a sudden weight. Edward shifted uncomfortably, grimacing in annoyance while she took a deep breath.

The girl was now wide awake. Realizing where she was—and what was happening—she tried to accommodate him. Opening her legs for his clumsy caresses, she turned her head, closing both eyes.

Edward didn't seem to notice. He was busy concentrating, trying to be gentle, but her gasp of pain made him lose his focus. Thinking to regain his ardor, he pushed against her dryness, sweating, panting, until he realized she was pressing her hands against his chest.

Edward's eyes flew open. He was horrified to see Editha clenching her teeth, eyes twisted shut. He rolled off, trying to ignore her groan of relief. "I'm sorry, child," he sighed, trying to take her into his arms. She flinched and he let go, rolling away from her.

* * *

As if to reward the family for his marital bliss, Edward awarded earldoms to Harold Godwineson and Beorn Estridson. Harold was made Earl of East Anglia, and Beorn, Earl of the Middle-Angles. This created an unwelcome stir in Leofric's camp, but Edward still needed Godwine too much to alienate him.

For many nights, Edward slept apart from his wife. But Editha knew her duty, and finally approached him, expressing her willingness. Edward wrinkled his nose in disgust; her breath smelled like alcohol. She had to get drunk before she could bring herself to sleep with him! But on second thought, Edward conceded her reasoning. Maybe she would be more relaxed.

This time, he succeeded. They both moaned with relief when

the task was done, and Editha even permitted herself to fall asleep in his arms. Edward sighed, wondering how he could continue to summon enough interest to perform his duty. He found the act distasteful, and the girl did nothing to encourage him.

Yes, it was all her fault. What did he expect from one of Godwine's brood?

28

Swegn could not help thinking, as the great Gruffydd ap Llewelyn sat beside him drinking ale, how pleased his father would be that day. The Prince of North Wales had come to him, as neighbor, to wage war on Gruffydd ap Rhydderch, Prince of South Wales for the murder of one hundred and forty of his nobles.

Swegn was proud of his status. He liked being an Earl, governor of a people who looked up to him for leadership. For the hundredth time, Swegn glanced proudly at the timber roof of his new great hall, which he had built from his own revenues. He had done everything without aid, and now he was to lead an army of his own vassals.

"How long will it take you to muster your troops?" the Prince asked.

"I can have a thousand in no more than a week." Swegn smiled. "Will that be enough?"

"That will do fine. We will make short work of him, I promise you." Gruffydd unconcernedly stuffed a piece of bread in his mouth. Swegn admired his self-assurance; this man already had a reputation as a fearless warrior.

As they marched into Wales a week later, Swegn gave Gruffydd authority over all the troops. He had never yet led a force into battle, and it was said these Welsh fought in the most uncivilized manner. Swegn was perfectly willing to relinquish such an inglorious command; he would watch and learn this time, and perhaps lead an army the next, when the spoils would be greater.

They marched for two days before engaging the enemy. Then the southern Prince burst upon them, leading a bristling rabble from the shelter of a forest. But Gruffydd ap Llewelyn had expected something of the sort. He ordered a counter attack, and the men leaped into the fray, aware that they outnumbered the enemy.

The battle was soon over, and Gruffydd ap Rhydderch lay dead on the ground. Leaderless, his army faded back into the trees, and the Prince of North Wales was content to let them go. Soon enough, he reasoned, they would be his own subjects.

Prince and Earl parted amiably, and Swegn led his triumphant army back home, stopping for the night near Leominster Abbey. Although there was a little grumbling about his choice as the men set up camp, he had a reason for being here: in this place lived his beloved Eadgifu.

Slipping away, Swegn rode alone to the Abbey. He knocked on the large wooden doors, his heart pounding. After what seemed a terribly long time, the doors creaked open an inch, and an eyeball carefully looked him up and down.

"Who are you?" asked a timorous voice.

"Has there been trouble here?"

"We heard that an army was passing through."

Swegn was beginning to feel exasperated. "Not every army wreaks havoc on an Abbey. I am Swegn Godwineson, your Earl. I am here to see Eadgifu." He heard an anxious rustling, then the door opened. He entered, among bowing nuns. One of them ushered him into a chamber and closed the door, leaving him alone.

Swegn looked about the darkened room. It was furnished with a table and chair and a shabby tapestry depicting a crucifixion. Evidently the Abbey wasn't blessed with any rich patrons. Well, maybe he could make up for that.

Minutes later, the door opened and a nun slipped in, locking it behind her. When she turned to face him, Swegn nearly gasped. It was Eadgifu, all right, but her face no longer reflected the youthful enthusiasm he had loved so well. Now, it was replaced by solemn composure, which barely covered a deeper resignation.

He stepped forward, holding out his hands. "My love..."

Eadgifu turned toward the window, a hand to her mouth. Swegn dropped his arms, embarrassed.

"Why did you never answer my letters?" he asked, trying to disguise the hurt.

"I am Abbess, now. There is much for me to do."

He moved to her side, trying not to touch her. "Surely that is not the reason. I had as much to do as you, yet I found the time."

Eadgifu spun toward him. "All right, Swegn. What was I supposed to do? I belong to God now, not you! You tempt me with your words of love, make me miserable in my prison. You remind me of what I cannot have." Her hand covered her eyes, and she wept. Swegn's lip quivered; before he knew it his arms were around her, pressing her face to his shoulder. She sobbed bitterly for a time, then he lifted her chin, kissing the tears away. His mouth covered her own, silencing her.

To both of their amazements, Eadgifu responded passionately, throwing her arms around his neck. Swegn pulled her tightly against his body, refusing to let go. When he relaxed his grip, they were gasping for breath. Eadgifu tried to pull away, but he brought her back, kissing her again before she could speak. Finally, he allowed her to break loose, knowing from her shaky laugh that she still loved him.

She took a step away and he was before her again, drawing her into his arms. "You belong to me, not God," he murmured, ignoring the other's gasp. Cupping her face in his hands, Swegn kissed her sweetly on both eyelids. She nodded, her objections silenced.

"I cannot fight you, my love. I have thought of you every day," she sighed. "I never thought you would come for me."

"It was all I could do to stay away. But you should not have come here in the first place. For nine long years I have tried to do the right thing. But I cannot live without you any longer."

He let Eadgifu slip from his arms, and watched her cross the room. She fingered the rosary hanging from her belt. When she turned, her mouth was set. "I feel that I have sinned all this time. I have never given my heart to God; it belongs to you."

Swegn held his breath; he hadn't dared hope she felt this way.

"Come away with me," he whispered.

"I cannot."

He moved toward her, pulling the veil from her head. Glistening brown hair tumbled to her shoulders. "You shouldn't hide such beauty from the world. My Eadgifu." He took a lock between his fingers. "It is your decision, my sweet. If you truly cannot leave, I will not force you."

Once again he drew her into his arms, kissing her like it was the last time. Then, releasing her, Swegn walked to the door. He paused with a hand on the frame.

Eadgifu was looking at the floor, refusing to meet his eyes. Taking that for a refusal, he lifted the latch.

"Wait."

Swegn froze. He didn't trust himself to move.

Eadgifu flew across the room, tearing his hand from the latch. She placed his fingers against her face, kissing his palm. "I will come."

"Then leave your things here, my love. Never again do I want to see you in that dreadful habit. We shall get you new clothes. Come...ride behind me on my horse."

He grabbed her hand and threw the door open, dragging her through. Many of the nuns were waiting uncertainly in the hallway; they fell back as he dashed outside, their Abbess with him. Thinking that he was abducting her they let out a wail, running after the pair. But Swegn jumped on his horse, lifting Eadgifu after him, and was gone before the nearest reached them.

They galloped off, kicking dust on the poor nuns who milled around, not knowing what to do. Her arms around Swegn's waist, Eadgifu let out a laugh though she immediately felt ashamed. They were only concerned with her welfare. "Perhaps I should have told them I was going," she said.

Swegn squeezed one of her hands. "Let them think I stole you away. It will be better for your reputation."

But Eadgifu didn't care about her reputation. All she knew was that she was with her love. *Let the world think what they would.*

The short ride to camp was probably the happiest time of her life. Eadgifu's head swam with images of herself as countess, lover, mother. She allowed herself to forget that she was unalterably pledged to God and unfit for such a role. She hugged Swegn hard around the waist, bringing forth a gay laugh from him which she joined, elated.

Too soon, they rode into camp. Eadgifu's face fell as Swegn's soldiers stared at her dusty habit. Some looked away; others frowned in such disgust that she shrunk against Swegn's back, trying to disappear.

"Never mind them, my love," he said. "I am their Earl. They will not give you any trouble. We'll get you some new clothes, and things will be all right."

Swegn couldn't have been more wrong. Word of his abduction spread like wildfire through his army, and men began deserting that very night. But what did he care? The campaign was over.

Swegn showed Eadgifu into his tent. "It's a little barren, but we'll be moving in the morning."

For a moment she stared, watching the flap close. The fabric's rustling, so final in her ears, was like a door shutting out her past life. Eadgifu swung around, clinging to him. "I don't care. I'm just grateful to get away from those staring eyes."

He held her, trying to be comforting. But a growing excitement kept getting in the way. "Here. Sit down on my blanket."

Ever obedient, she complied. Swegn was already on his knees, tugging at her habit. Eadgifu helped him take it off, but the first nagging doubts assailed her so suddenly that her hands shook.

Couldn't he just hold her for a while? Surely their love went beyond this physical craving.

Eadgifu remembered how she had never been able to say certain things to him; this was something she had gratefully forgotten over the years. In fact, she had forgotten most of his unpleasant traits, preferring to linger over the happy memories. After all, she never expected to see him again.

Just once, she wanted to cry *"stop and look at me"*; but the words stuck in her throat.

Unaware of her hesitation, Swegn threw the garment in a corner, then pressed her shoulders, lowering her to the ground. She put an arm around his neck. "I'm...unused to this," she said.

Swegn laughed. "I would expect so. Just relax, love. Trust me."

Eadgifu did her best to relax. She watched him run his hands up and down her body, pausing at her breasts. He caressed her nipples, put lips to her breasts, ran his tongue up to her neck.

Eadgifu started breathing heavily, stiffening. Her hands moved woodenly up his back and he groaned, covering her mouth with kisses. His fingers were all over her body, tickling, rubbing; she lay still, puffing, almost frightened. He had never been like this before.

Suddenly, the tent door parted, and Swegn's head shot up. "Get out!" he shouted, then his lips were on her again, his tongue slipping over her skin, making it wet. When he parted her legs, pressing his mouth between them, she recoiled.

"What is it?" he whispered, raising his face; suddenly, he was all solicitation. She relaxed, seeing the Swegn she remembered.

"It's just so fast...so sudden. You're scaring me."

He slid beside her, his arms soothing, drawing her close. Eadgifu felt comforted, until she felt his hardness pressuring her. It had happened before with him, when they were younger, but frightened of his manhood she had always managed to pull away.

But this time, without realizing it, he was holding her down with one arm, while he wrenched off his clothes with the other. Soon, he was naked, but she wasn't able to appreciate his body because he was on top of her, forcing her legs apart.

Again, he was that stranger, overwhelmed with lust, taking her for his own; she was certain he didn't even see her face or notice her fear. Eyes closed, Swegn was unreachable, his hardness finding an opening, nudging her gently at first then more insistently, pushing her backbone into the ground.

Eadgifu put her arms around him trying not to think about the pain until he thrust deep inside her, forcing a cry from her lips.

That seemed to make it worse but he soon stiffened, groaning. Slowly, he relaxed. His hands came up, stroking her face, and he kissed her sweetly.

Eadgifu didn't know what to think. *Is this what she had left the Abbey for?* It didn't seem worth it.

Kissing her, Swegn pulled up, leaning on an elbow. "Don't worry," he said softly. "Each time will get better, until you are as excited as myself. When you learn to relax, I will teach you things beyond your wildest dreams."

Eadgifu began to cry, knowing that her words would never come. Swegn didn't really want to know about her feelings; her troubles were her own. As it had always been, he wanted her to live only for himself, giving him what he needed regardless of her own wants. How had she forgotten this? Why did she think it would be different this time?

Her lover smiled sweetly, tucking her head under his chin. In his conceit, Swegn thought her tears were for him.

* * *

The next morning, Swegn stepped from his tent, grinning. But his face changed when he saw how many men had deserted. "What is going on?" he shouted, running through the camp. Men turned away from him, frowning. "All right, we leave at once."

He stomped back to the tent, recovering his composure before going in. Eadgifu didn't need to see him like that. Forcing a smile, he raised the tent flap; she was adjusting a new tunic over the belt. Looking up with a shy smile, Eadgifu's face made Swegn forgot how angry he was.

"I can't wait to get you home," he said, embracing her.

Once again, Eadgifu rode pillion with Swegn. She thought wistfully about the day before and how happy she had been. Somehow, she could no longer sustain the delusions; she knew how it was going to be. Swegn would try his best to protect her, but already his ineffective measures were apparent. No one was listening to his orders; discipline had totally broken down. Men treated her like a whore, and she was beginning to feel that she deserved it.

Swegn was aware of her unhappiness. When they made love that night he forced himself to be more careful. She was grateful, and tried her best to respond. It came a little easier this time, and the next, and before she knew it Eadgifu had forgotten many of her fears.

When they were safely ensconced at his estate, life quickly settled into a routine, and she began to find her own way of rationalizing her position. Swegn was teaching her how to enjoy his kind of love, and he scoffed at her shame. There was no shame, he said...only pleasure.

But by day, she wasn't so sure she believed him. No one would speak to her; she often caught the servants talking, pointing their fingers. Swegn tried to shrug it all off, but she could tell that he, too, was disturbed.

Eadgifu tried to deceive herself into believing they could go on like this forever, but reality trespassed on her delusions. With an odd sense that the waiting was over, Eadgifu watched from the window one day as Godwine showed up at the gate, accompanied by a bishop. She saw Swegn go out to greet him, smiling uneasily; his father did not smile back. Eadgifu waited until they entered the house, then sneaked into the next room, opening the door a crack.

Once inside, Godwine came right to the point. "My son, this good Father has informed me that you have committed a great sacrilege." He paused, watching Swegn bite his lip. "Just as I thought. Did you really abduct her?"

Swegn took a deep breath. "Yes. I love her. Father, I want to marry her."

"Impossible," Godwine said, nearly drowned out by the bishop's snort. "Don't you know what you have done? That woman was a consecrated virgin. She cannot marry. Ever."

Swegn's face grew red. "She should never have been forced into that nunnery in the first place."

"That is not the point." Feeling responsible, Godwine couldn't control his voice; it became louder and harsher. "You have violated an abbess. The good Sisters of Leominster sent to the Archbishop of Canterbury, telling him what you have done."

Godwine turned to the bishop. "Bishop Aelfwine brought the news to me rather than to the King, and for that I am grateful."

Swegn turned away, relieved. Then his earldom was not in jeopardy.

Godwine pursued the point. "He has also brought a writ of excommunication, unless you agree to renounce your shameless liaison and send her back to the Abbey."

Swegn gasped. But he wasn't the only one to react. Behind him stood Eadgifu, who had flung the door wide. The girl ran to the bishop, throwing herself at his feet. "No, don't do it to him."

Aelfwine put a hand on her head. "We are here to save you, child. You may come away, now...away from this house of sin."

Eadgifu burst into tears, pulling away from his comforting touch. She looked at Godwine, who refused to acknowledge her.

"I cannot go back there," she stated, coming to her feet.

All three looked at her in shock.

"I am with child."

Despite himself, Swegn smiled proudly. "Why didn't you tell me?"

"I wanted to be sure."

Godwine paced the room. "Well. A fine fix you got yourself into, son. Your whole earldom buzzes with rumors. I'm sure complaints will soon reach the King, though up to now, I have been able to delay any action. But I can help you no longer."

Swegn recovered some of his brashness. "I don't care. Let them complain. I am their Earl, and they must obey me."

His father looked at him sadly. "Haven't you learned anything? Your power can disappear overnight without the support of your subjects...and the King."

Godwine turned to Aelfwine with sudden decision. "I will take the girl back into my household, until the child is born. Then she will go back to Leominster. Swegn must leave the country until all this has blown over."

Swegn grabbed his father's arm. "No! I will not go."

"And I say you shall. You have no choice, Swegn. Better go now before the King gets wind of this scandal. You know how pious he is."

"Eadgifu and I will barricade ourselves in, if necessary. We stay!"

"I think otherwise, son. Look at her."

Swegn swung around. The girl was looking at the ground, arms limp. She raised miserable eyes to him, catching his gaze. "I will obey your father in all things," she said.

Godwine crossed his arms. He knew the argument was over.

Swegn spun from one to the other, looking for solace. He felt like a trapped animal. Never had his father treated him so. "Where shall I go?"

"I think we can find a place for you at the court of Flanders. Then, when your cousin Svein has overcome his difficulties with Magnus of Norway, you can go to him in Denmark. After that, I will let you know when it is safe for your return."

Swegn turned and left the room, defeated. Eadgifu looked hungrily after him, but he never glanced back at her.

29

Beorn leaned over toward Harold and Tostig as they waited for the Witenagemot to begin. "I heard that Swegn has gone on to Denmark without getting your father's permission," he said.

Tostig smirked. "And he is furious about it, I can tell you. He has sworn to let my brother sink himself."

"It's about time," Beorn answered. "He has caused Godwine more trouble than a pack of wolves."

He glanced across the room, where Godwine was deep in discussion with Earl Seward. The Danish Earl was nodding uncertainly. Just then the King entered, and the room quieted. Edward surveyed the assembly before he sat down next to Godwine.

"The first order of business," he said, "is to determine what to do with the vacant earldom, now that Swegn Godwineson has been banished." He could not forbear a triumphant glance at Godwine.

"After giving the matter much thought, I have divided it three ways. Herefordshire will come under the control of my cousin, Ralf de Mantes. Oxfordshire will henceforth be annexed to Earl Beorn's territory. And Gloucestershire will be given to Earl Harold."

Harold and Beorn exchanged smiling glances. Tostig bit his lips, turning a dark red; he had expected the earldom to go to himself.

But Godwine had only eyes for Leofric; his baleful stare promised trouble. The Earl of Mercia started to get up but thought better of it, balling his hands into fists. It was no secret that Leofric resented so much of England's rule going to the house of Godwine. From the river Humber in Yorkshire, south and west all around the coast of England, Godwine controlled the choicest ports, the largest cities. This left Leofric with a little chunk of land bordering the Welsh marches and the Midlands.

He saw this as no fair division and it was getting worse all the time. *Godwine still has four more sons; were there going to be earldoms for all them as well? What of my son Aelfgar?*

Knowing the consternation he was causing, Edward nevertheless pointedly ignored Leofric. *Nothing was permanent,* the King thought. *In time, Godwine will have enough rope to hang himself, and he will take his greedy sons with him.*

But Leofric knew nothing of the King's thoughts. All he could see was favoritism, and he promised himself—not for the first time—that he would do everything he could to frustrate Godwine's authority.

"The next matter is the Danish question. Earl Godwine will present his argument." The King leaned back, listening while some of his Norman friends whispered in his ear. Godwine stood.

"King Svein Estridson is presently in great need of our help. Magnus of Norway has been very successful with his incursions into Danish territory. Already he has overrun Jutland and Sjaelland, leaving Svein only Scania. I propose we send fifty ships to his aid, before Magnus has complete control over all of Denmark as well as Norway."

Leofric was the first to jump to his feet. "This is absurd! Why risk English blood over a foreign cause?" Many in the room voiced their agreement.

Godwine remained calm. "Who risked his ships and men to save us last year, when Magnus threatened to invade England? If it wasn't for Svein's intervention, we might this day be Norwegian subjects."

Edward frowned; the room was silent.

Godwine went on. "If Magnus gains undisputed control of Denmark, he will surely turn his attention back to us. This is not a foreign war, I say!" Godwine's voice filled the room without having to shout.

Leofric was still on his feet. "And I say that Godwine wants to expend our men and riches to secure the throne for his own nephew! We all know that his renegade son has joined Svein's cause. Do we really want to support such as him?"

The room resounded with shouts of agreement. Godwine sat down, deflated. His career—his influence—damaged by the reckless act of one son. He couldn't look at Edward; Godwine knew that the King would be savoring his humiliation.

Edward stood, hand out. "Then it is decided? We will not give aid to Svein? Who is in favor of this decision?"

Godwine had to try one more time. "Remember," he said. "If my predictions are true and Magnus does attack, we do not have the means to defend ourselves against him."

This time the murmurs were thoughtful. Godwine had struck at the heart of the problem, and they knew he was right. Magnus was a powerful force at sea, and his navy was more than triple what England possessed.

But when the vote came, it was overwhelmingly against Godwine's proposal. Leofric had carried the day. Even Seward went against Godwine.

* * *

During the feast afterward, it seemed that nearly everyone was in a bad mood. Godwine ate silently, scowling. Queen Editha felt sorry for her father; she knew what the Danish campaign meant to him. Tostig didn't eat at all, but filled his goblet again and again, emptying it each time in one draught. Seward was deep in thought, and Leofric found himself glaring at Godwine every couple of minutes.

Only Harold and Beorn were celebrating, and their good mood was shared by Edward, who was pleased with himself for winning the day against Godwine. Catching Harold's eye, the King gave him a toast.

"Here's to you, Harold, and may you ever continue in

prosperity."

Harold stood and bowed, enjoying himself. He didn't see Tostig jump unsteadily to his feet and lunge toward him, grabbing him by the hair.

"It's always Harold, isn't it?" Tostig roared, and pulled his hair viciously with both hands. Harold was off-balance, and couldn't right himself; he tumbled to the ground, Tostig after him. The pair rolled over each other, punching and kicking. Yet Harold's superior strength told in his favor, and he was soon towering over his brother, knees on both shoulders, and pummeling Tostig in the face.

The guests, already mostly drunk, cheered them on. But Edward was appalled that there was brawling in his presence. He pushed away from the table, staring at them while Godwine and Eirik leaped to their feet and went to break up the fight.

Tearing these two apart was no easy matter. Godwine used brute strength against Tostig, lifting him off the ground before he could pull him away.

"Everything goes to Harold," Tostig shouted. "You think you are so glorious, that men will die for you. Well, I tell you, Harold, you are nothing but a deceitful bastard!" Harold strained against Eirik, who had wrapped both arms around him.

"Enough!" Godwine shouted. "I am ashamed of you!"

Accustomed to obeying, even through the red haze of their tempers, Godwine's sons stood still, puffing and glaring at each other. Eirik let go of Harold, whose arms had relaxed.

The King looked at the offenders, his eyes clouding and vacant. They stared back, confused; no one knew what to do. "Beware of your quarrels, sons of Godwine," he said in a queer and unearthly voice. "For all of England will suffer for it. I see great misery for you, Tostig, because of your greed and jealousy. Be careful of your spite, lest it cause your death.

"And you, Harold," he turned, though his eyes looked over Harold's head, "for you I see great turmoil. I see the land in the clutch of the invader, lest you make your peace with Tostig. Do not let your covetousness overcome your brother's rights, or he will turn against you...to your own ruin, ruin, ruin." His voice shrilled, rising higher and higher.

Editha had run to Edward's side; she had seen him in the midst of his visions before, and she begged Godwine to hurry, help her. At his last words, Edward fell to the side, as if all his limbs failed him; Godwine was just in time to catch him before he hit the ground.

"Look what you have done," the Earl growled to his sons. "Go, leave this place before you cause any more trouble."

Editha showed her father where to carry the King, and they sat by his side until he awoke. The others crowded together, looking on; most had never seen Edward like this, and they crossed themselves, awed.

Edward woke with a start, looking around. For a moment he was disoriented, until Editha leaned over him, taking his hand. "It's all right, My Lord," she said. "You were taken with a vision."

Edward sighed. "What was it this time?"

"You spoke of terrible things, rising from Harold and Tostig's wrath."

"Did I?" He looked at Godwine. "Then keep a heavy hand on your sons," he said.

30

Within months, it looked like Godwine had correctly summed up the Danish situation. King Magnus defeated Svein in a huge naval battle, driving him into exile. England prepared as best as it could for the new threat.

But then fate stepped in. Magnus died almost as soon as he took the throne, and Svein was invited back to Denmark. The crown of Norway was passed on to Magnus's uncle, Harald Hardraada.

"So you see, Godwine," King Edward said to him in council. "We made the right decision."

Godwine looked around the room, noticing that he was the only Saxon present. "Your Grace," he ventured, "no one knows when a King is going to die. God saved us, not the Witan."

Edward scowled, beckoning for his cousin Ralph to bend an ear. They exchanged whispers.

Godwine frowned, watching. Things had not turned out like he expected; never had he felt so isolated. Rather than serve close to the King as son-in-law and foremost Earl, he often found himself on the outside, like now.

As the years passed, Edward had invited more and more Normans to his side, until the court began to resemble a foreign rather than an English one. French was spoken exclusively; courtiers dressed in the newest styles from the continent. All vacancies, both religious and secular, were filled by Normans.

Worse than that, the King usually followed their advice.

"I have here," Edward said, waving a rolled parchment, "another request from King Svein. He asks for fifty ships, so he can wage war against Harald Hardraada."

Despite himself, Godwine took a step forward. "Then we still have a chance to protect our interests."

"Oh, Godwine. Have you learned nothing? No one will

support you in this. I have decided to tell him no."

The Earl bit back his words of defiance. Instead, he said, "There is nothing left of the old navy. I suggest that we at least begin to rebuild your fleet, to protect our shores."

Again, he had to wait while Edward whispered to his friends. "I will consider it," the King said finally.

* * *

Godwine rode back to Bosham in a righteous rage. He was even unhappier when no one came to greet him on his return. The house was in an uproar.

"Where is Gytha?" he asked one of the servants.

The girl stopped, clutching an armful of linens. "Above, sir. Eadgifu is giving birth."

Godwine grimaced, letting her go. *That cursed girl, again.* Though she had tried to make herself useful, he hated the sight of her.

No one looked up as he opened the chamber door. Eadgifu was squeezing Gytha's hands, while his wife instructed her to take deep breaths and push. Despite himself, Godwine smiled. Gytha should know; she had borne nine children.

In between labor pains, Eadgifu opened her eyes; she gasped, seeing Godwine. Gytha turned.

"You know you aren't supposed to be here, my dear," she said kindly.

Frowning, Godwine turned to leave, but Eadgifu gasped, "Wait. Please, sir, I want to tell you something."

Sighing, Gytha nodded for him to come in.

Nearing the girl, Godwine felt a reluctant surge of pity for her. Like all of his sex, he viewed childbirth with a certain awe. Her hair was drenched with sweat, and those sunken eyes looked haunted in such a pale face.

"I wanted to tell you," she whispered, then gasped, arching

her back. For a moment she could only groan, while Gytha tried to comfort her. "Swegn... He did not abduct me. I went with him willingly."

Godwine turned away, reluctant to expose his pain. He had treated his son like a criminal, and had hated himself ever since. "Why did he say he did it, then?" he asked, his back to them.

"He wanted to protect my reputation. We didn't know it would turn out like this."

It was all he could stand to hear. Godwine dashed out of the room, slamming the door behind him.

* * *

Gytha found him later, clutching an ale-horn, his head sunk on an arm. She studied him thoughtfully. "Why do you torture yourself like this?"

He took so long to answer that she thought he was asleep. "I sent him away like an outcast, for something he didn't do." Godwine raised his head, glaring at her. "He loved her, Gytha."

She shrugged, exasperated. "Abduction or not, he violated an Abbess. Either way, it is a mortal sin."

"Doesn't it make any difference to you?" His voice was getting louder. "They belonged together, from the first. We are the guilty ones; we tore them apart, and brought this about ourselves."

Gytha sat by his side, taking the ale-horn in her hand. "I refuse to take the responsibility. He knew what he was doing."

"Wife, for once in your life, have pity on the boy! He has always been miserable, and it is our fault. No matter what I do for him, I can't make up for it."

Angry, she stood. "For God's sake, why don't you think about your other sons for a change? You have neglected them; you've given all your attention to Swegn. And for what? Has he ever shown any appreciation?"

He was about to defend himself, but she refused to let him.

"And even though you neglected them, they turned out all right. Can't you see? You can't blame yourself for everything. He is bad to the core, and it's about time you quit protecting him." She got up and strode to the door, then turned back to him. "Perhaps you can do better with his son."

The door slammed shut, leaving Godwine with his thoughts. A boy. The baby was a boy.

The next day, he made his apologies to Gytha, though neither of them believed the argument was finished. He went to see the baby.

"A nice healthy boy," he said to Eadgifu with a forced smile. "I have a fancy to call him Hakon."

* * *

As soon as she was able, the mother was sent back to Leominster, leaving her baby behind. But this wasn't the end of her troubles. When she went back, she found that the Abbey had been dissolved.

Godwine finally took pity on her. He made sure that she was allowed to live on the site, along with the nuns that chose to stay. The property had not been much, after all. A large donation to the church made them forget about its loss.

By then, the King had approved his suggestion for rebuilding a fleet. Godwine was relieved by the new distraction. There had been a new rash of Norsemen raids all along his coast; he wondered if they had anything to do with Edward's refusal to Svein Estridson.

The Earl was yet in Kent when his eldest son landed at Bosham with eight ships. Commanding his crew to stay aboard, Swegn went alone to the house.

The steward welcomed him uncomfortably, not daring to ask what he wanted. Swegn looked around, then asked where his father was.

"In Kent, My Lord, but I don't know exactly where. He could possibly be with the King at Sandwich."

"With the King." Swegn looked thoughtful. "Yes, that could suit my purposes quite well." He commandeered a horse, and told the steward to take care of his crew's needs. He was going to ride overland.

The man suggested nervously that he might do better to travel by ship. Swegn's laugh did not put him at ease. "I would not have anyone mistake me for one of those raiders," he said. "No. I will go as the penitent supplicant. And woe betide any who try to stop me!"

Once Swegn was safely gone, the steward mounted another horse and rode hard for Winchester, where he knew Harold was staying.

31

King Edward's head jerked around irritably as the stranger was introduced. For a moment, he didn't know the man. But as the other came closer, Edward recognized Godwine's hated features on the man's face. "Swegn Godwineson," the King gasped.

Indeed, it was no surprise that Edward didn't recognize him. There was little of the old Swegn left in this person. He had gained the leathery tan of a sailor; his chest had filled out, his eyes were more piercing. His face bore a new expression.

For a moment, Edward was overcome with rage at Swegn's audacity, appearing out of nowhere, unforgiven and uninvited. But, as ever, he remembered his wife, and the pledge had made to himself: to make up for his failure as a husband by ignoring his dislike for her family. He cleared his throat, though the noise sounded more like a choke. "It looks like you haven't suffered from your exile."

Swegn knelt at the King's feet, bowing his head.

"To what do I owe the honor of your visit?" Edward couldn't hide a note of sarcasm.

Swegn looked at him, perfectly composed. "I have come to ask your forgiveness."

Despite himself, Edward was dumbfounded. Of all the things he expected, this was not one of them. "It is not my forgiveness you need ask," he said more gently. "It is God's."

"Oh, I have been praying to him every day since my disgrace. I thought that if you were to bring me back into your favor, it would be His way of telling me I am forgiven." He bowed his head again.

Edward sat back, for once ignoring the fervid whispers of his counselors. He studied this man, whose face glowed with contrition; Swegn's every gesture was humble.

"I did everything that was required of me, Sire. I gave up the

Abbess, who was dearer to me than my very life. I left the country rather than bring disgrace to my father."

Swegn hoped Edward would forget the other things he did while in exile, like pirating. But his show of remorse seemed to be working. The Normans no longer prodded Edward with their objections. The King seemed on the verge of giving in.

"Here is what I will do," Edward said finally. "We are not far from Canterbury. I will send to the Archbishop, and if he feels that you may atone for your sin through penance, I will give you back your earldom."

Swegn ignored the gasps of disbelief. Kissing the King's hand, he let drop a tear. Then, bowing, he backed slowly from the room.

* * *

For two days Swegn played the penitent. He carefully listened to Edward's religious discussions, debated with Edward's Norman friends. The King was totally won over; even Editha noticed a change in him.

Yet finally, hearing the clatter of new arrivals, Swegn heaved an internal sigh of relief. The pressure had been nearly too much for him. He must hold out just a little longer, make peace with the Archbishop, and return home. He set his face, waiting for the august churchman.

But Swegn's composure was shattered by the entrance of Harold and Beorn, striding side by side into the room. They knelt at Edward's feet, though their bearing was far from humble.

"Sire," Harold said, "I fear you may be harboring a viper at your side."

Swegn jerked forward, but was restrained by the King's warning grasp.

"Surely you are not referring to your brother."

"I most certainly am."

Edward frowned. "I am of the opinion that Swegn repents the

wrongs he has done. We are awaiting the Archbishop of Canterbury's advice."

Harold considered this. "And if he is forgiven?"

"I intend to give back his earldom."

Both Earls jumped to their feet.

"I do not believe his people want him back," Harold said evenly.

Edward stood, glaring at them. "It is not for the populace to decide."

Beorn said, "But Sire, we have ruled well there. Do we deserve to have our lands taken from us?"

"I would have you remember that they are my lands, not yours." Edward's voice was icy.

Throwing a warning look at Beorn, Harold stepped forward. "I believe that Swegn has been leading the Danish raids on your shores."

"That is a lie!" Swegn cried, fists upraised.

"See, Sire, how quickly he returns to his old temperament."

Biting his lip, Swegn lowered his arms. "Brother, you push me too far."

Edward missed none of this. Shaken, he turned to Swegn. "Is there any truth in what he said?"

The other shook his head. "None, Sire. I came to England with eight ships, it is true, but I have led no raids."

"Why did you need eight ships?" Harold asked loudly.

Swegn glared at his brother. "Protection against pirates."

"Protection." Harold laughed. "Who will protect England against you?"

"That is enough!" Edward shouted, startling everyone. "You are forbidden to quarrel in my presence." He leaned back in his throne, exhausted. "Harold, Beorn, you refuse to give up Swegn's portion of your earldoms?"

The pair faced Edward squarely. "We refuse," Harold said for both of them.

The King shook his head. “Such strife,” he said. “I cannot have it. Swegn, the time has not yet come for your return. I give you four days to get your affairs in order, then you must leave again, and await my summons.”

Swegn’s glare shifted from Harold to Edward. “Sire, you do not mean this injustice!”

Edward’s face hardened. “I have decided. It is not for you to question my judgment.” Before his sentence was finished, Swegn strode from the room.

* * *

Swegn did not know where his father was, but he felt that only Godwine could help his cause now. He headed toward Dover first, thinking that was a good starting point. But he missed Godwine by half a day. His father had embarked with a small fleet and was sailing to Pevensey, which had been attacked by raiders.

Swegn rode hard on his trail. Arriving at Pevensey, he saw that Godwine was still present. There was no time to waste; Swegn leaped from his horse and ran to the great hall.

But he was too late. Beorn had already preceded him.

Swegn froze at the door, discovering Godwine in earnest conversation with his cousin. Despite himself, Swegn was overcome with that familiar surge of jealous rage, threatening to impair his badly needed judgment. Hoping for a happy reunion, he was greeted instead with a strained expression and a guarded smile.

“You are always welcome, son,” Godwine said, standing. “I hope you come in peace.”

“Father,” Swegn faltered, then glared at Beorn. “Will you leave us alone?”

“I think not,” Beorn retorted.

Godwine said nothing.

"Father, my brother and cousin seek to keep me from my earldom. Why do they need my lands, when they have their own?"

Godwine's expression softened. "Swegn..."

"As I was making my peace with Edward, they came charging in and refused to cooperate. They turned him against me by their selfish bickering."

Godwine swung on Beorn. "You did not tell me that. Is it true?"

"Partly. It would have happened anyway, in time."

"How do you know that?" Swegn snarled.

"Because I know what kind of man you are."

"Stop, both of you!" Godwine shook his head. "We are supposed to stick together. If our family is divided, our enemies will tear us to pieces."

Shamed, the others stopped.

"And you, Swegn. Are you so selfish you didn't take thought to ask about your son?"

Swegn's eyes widened. "My son?"

"Yes, for all you care. He is at Winchester with Gytha."

"What is his name?"

"Hakon."

"And...Eadgifu?"

"Back at Leominster. They are no longer an Abbey, thanks to you, but the sisters continue to care for the poor."

Swegn turned away to hide his feelings. Godwine swung on Beorn. "I am ashamed of you, and Harold, too. You should never have humiliated Swegn before the King. You have ruined all I worked for, these many months. I must start over again.

"What were you thinking of? Only your greed? If that's what was so important to you, I could have given you compensation out of my own earldom."

Beorn sighed. "Perhaps I can return to Edward, and change my position." Swegn's shoulders stiffened.

Godwine stared at Beorn, his eyes narrowing. "Do you mean that?"

"Yes, uncle. I would never willingly defy you."

Swegn turned, incredulous. "What about Harold?"

Godwine said, "He has already taken some of the ships and headed west, after the raiders. But I think I can talk him into agreeing, as well."

Swegn looked at Beorn. "You would do this for me?"

"I do it for your father."

Satisfied, Godwine did not see the hate flow between the two.

* * *

Rather than return directly to the King at Sandwich, Swegn convinced Beorn that it was better to return overland to his ships. "Some of my crew are mercenaries," he said. "I dare not leave them so long without a leader, or they may turn into pirates, in truth."

Beorn looked him up and down. "It is in the opposite direction."

"But then we can sail back to Sandwich, and make up for the lost time."

Nodding uncertainly, Beorn agreed.

Their trip to Bosham was conducted in silence. The only thing Swegn said was to insist that Beorn sail on the same ship he did. Reluctantly, his cousin agreed.

Leaving their horses at Godwine's estate, they had soon embarked on their way to Sandwich. The storms had passed to the west, and the sky was clear before them. Beorn stood at the bow of the ship, gazing forward, as if he could propel them faster toward their destination through sheer will. He heard rather than saw Swegn come up behind him.

"I suppose you think you have won," Beorn said finally, turning distastefully to his cousin.

Swegn gave him a frown. "I will not have won until I have rid my family of your unwanted presence."

Despite himself, Beorn was stung. "What makes you think your presence is so desirable?"

"I am the eldest. At least my father loves me."

"Pah. He feels guilty, that's all. Not that you deserve it."

At first, Beorn didn't realize the effect his words would have. But one look at Swegn told him he had gone too far.

His face flushed, Swegn was grabbing a knife from his belt. He snatched another from one of the crew and tossed it to his cousin.

"All right," he growled, "let's have it out once and for all."

Beorn was ready. He caught the handle and crouched, point out.

They circled, feinting with the knives, left hands held out to block. Already several men were watching curiously.

Swegn looked eager, almost too anxious, while Beorn set his mouth, searching for an opening. The Dane lunged all of a sudden, flicking the point across Swegn's face; then he smiled. A tiny line of red ran across the other's cheek.

Swegn slowly touched the cut then crouched even lower, eyes deadly. He suddenly reversed the knife in his grip, drawing the blade backward across Beorn's vision; the Dane threw up his arm for protection, taking a long slash across his forearm.

They had both drawn blood; both knew this was to the death. Swegn's cut settled him down; he eased into a steely control, losing that edgy nervousness. Beorn lashed out at him; he ducked easily, responding with a thrust to the side. He missed his mark, only tearing the other's tunic.

But Beorn was back again, feinting and striking, slashing again and again at his face. He was fast and effective, and Swegn had to step backwards, on the defensive; the blade cut into his right wrist, then slashed his other cheek.

Suddenly, Swegn switched the knife to his left hand, flying at his foe like a whirlwind. Caught off guard, Beorn tripped and fell, his knife flying. Somehow, Swegn couldn't stop his thrust; before Beorn even hit the deck, the blade was buried in his chest. Gasping, Swegn looked at the witnesses. "You saw," he said, wiping his bloody cheek. "It was a fair fight."

Mumbling, the others turned away.

For a time, Swegn stared at his cousin, who sprawled awkwardly on a pile of ropes. He felt no relief, no satisfaction from the deed. Rather, he felt overwhelmed with self-pity. Now look what happened. Why couldn't Beorn keep his mouth shut?

"Turn around," he ordered. "We cannot go to Edward now."

They proceeded west until Swegn decided what to do. By the time they reached Dartmouth, only two of the eight ships were with him; the rest had just sailed away. He put in at the town, so they could at least bury the body in the local church.

That done, the two ships sailed to Flanders.

* * *

Count Baldwin of Flanders had a reputation for offering sanctuary to whomever needed it. Hence, no one gave him much trouble, because a man never knew when it might be his own turn.

He wasn't surprised to see Swegn a second time. He welcomed the Saxon to his court, suspecting that something was amiss. Nonetheless, the Count prided himself on his open-mindedness.

This time, he found Swegn to be a much changed man. The Saxon's hand shook while he drank deeply from the welcoming cup. His face bore matching scars on each cheek, making him look more notorious than ever.

But his eyes were haunted.

Swegn had nowhere else to go. He stayed at Baldwin's court, his behavior subdued. After a couple of weeks, the story followed him across the channel. The tales of Swegn's new treachery had grown in the telling, and Swegn groaned aloud when he heard that the Witan declared him *nithing*, the worst censure of all. He was despicable to all.

In his defense, Swegn had little to add. Yes, it was true, he admitted, that they had fought. No, he did not murder his cousin; it was a fair fight. He said this last with little conviction, as if it was a phrase he had memorized. Baldwin did not ask any more questions.

Nevertheless, the Count of Flanders was glad to see the arrival of Bishop Ealdred some months later. Swegn was getting to be a bit much, feeling sorry for himself all the time. Baldwin ushered Ealdred into Swegn's room and disappeared.

Swegn looked up expectantly, but his face fell when he recognized the bishop. He was hoping his father would show up.

"I know, son," Ealdred said, sitting down without an invitation. "You are not looking forward to my presence. You fear that I will rant and rave, demanding some reparation. But I am not here for this reason."

Swegn glanced sideways at him, encouraged. "Did my father send you?"

"He gave me his blessing, and wishes for your speedy return."

"Alas, you break my heart. No one can wish it more than I."

Ealdred studied Swegn so intently that the latter squirmed uncomfortably. "It could be possible," he said finally, "if you were to show sincere remorse."

Without thinking, Swegn threw himself on his knees before the startled bishop. "I will do whatever you say. See here," he cried, ripping his tunic, "already I wear a hair shirt next to my skin."

Ealdred was impressed. This was more than he dared hope for. "My son..."

"I never meant to kill Beorn. He drove me into a frenzy with his taunting. He tried to take my place in the family. He said...he said my father didn't love me."

"My son..." Ealdred felt sorry for him. "If it makes you feel any better, King Edward has doubts that he did the right thing, in denying you the earldom."

Swegn's eyes shone through his tears. "Did he say that?"

"Not exactly. But he allowed me to come here and judge for myself. It was his way of making atonement."

Swegn kissed his hand. "You have made me a happy man. I was beginning to believe that even God had forsaken me."

"Never believe that, son. Never."

32

Gytha and Godwine glared at each other.

"You actually did this thing?" she spat. "You brought Swegn back and convinced Edward to reinstate him in his earldom?"

"And why not? He is our son, and deserves the best I can do for him."

"Deserves." She turned away, crossing her arms. "He deserves nothing."

Godwine was glad there was no one else in the room. "I tell you, he is repentant."

"I do not believe it. He always hated Beorn."

"But he never wanted him dead." Godwine moved to her, placing an arm around her waist. "He told me what started the fight. Beorn said I did not love him...that I merely acted from guilt. Gytha, even I don't know how true that is."

She sighed, leaning into his arms. "You are turning the country against you. They are incensed that Swegn is back."

Godwine stiffened. "How do you know?"

"People tell me things they don't dare tell you. You must be careful, my husband. Never has your support been so precarious." She turned, putting her arms around his neck. "Already Edward has elected that Norman, Robert of Jumieges, to be Archbishop of Canterbury, hasn't he? Just to spite you? Everyone knows how unsuitable he is for the position."

She kissed him, to take away the sting. "It is a reaction to Swegn's reinstatement. I'm sure it is. And I think it is only the beginning."

* * *

Godwine thought of Gytha's words as he waited for the Flemish ship to dock. Was he really so close to ruin? He hadn't wanted to admit how dangerous the new Archbishop was to his cause. But no sooner had Robert come to power, than the man started pouring poison into the King's ear.

Harold put a hand on Godwine's arm, pulling him from his reverie. "There's Tostig."

Godwine forced the worry from his face, trying for a smile. This was no time to spoil his son's wedding feast. Tostig waved enthusiastically from the deck, an arm around a smiling woman almost as tall as himself; he had never seen the boy look so happy.

Tostig was the first to leap ashore, reaching for his bride. As she landed on the ground, blushing and flustered, Tostig tugged playfully at a braid. "This is Judith, father. My sweeting...meet my father, and my brothers Harold, Leofwine, Gyrth, and little Wulfnoth. Where is Swegn?"

"On his way back from his earldom. He promised to come tonight. And how is Count Baldwin?"

"My father sends his greetings," Judith said, "and his invitation to visit to Flanders, as soon as you can arrange it."

"I hope it will be soon," Godwine laughed. "I would very much like to get away."

Godwine didn't realize just how soon his prophetic words would come to pass. Yet that very evening, while in the midst of wedding celebrations, a royal messenger demanded entrance into his hall. The happy noises came to a stop while the messenger, full of importance, strode up to head table. The man did not have to speak loudly to be heard throughout the silent room.

"King Edward of England summons Earl Godwine to appear before him at his palace of Gloucester, immediately."

Godwine stood up. "What is the purpose of this summons?"

"There has been a disturbance at Dover."

"What sort of disturbance?"

The man looked hungrily at the laden tables. "Count Eustace of Boulogne has been attacked by the townsmen, and driven thence."

A slow murmuring in the room increased in volume. "Eat," said Godwine, gesturing carelessly at the table. He left the room, wife and sons with him.

When they were alone, Godwine held up his hands. "I do not want to disturb the festivities. Go back; enjoy yourselves. I will deal with this matter, and return right away."

"Father," said Tostig, "we are already disturbed. Let us go with you."

"No." Godwine's voice was decisive. "He has summoned only myself. I do not want to blow things out of proportion."

"At least let me come." Still tired from his travels, Swegn stepped forward.

"No, son. Your presence might make things worse." Godwine's heart ached at Swegn's stricken expression, but he knew he was right. "Do not worry. How bad can this be?"

He was soon to find out.

* * *

The roomful of hostile faces in Edward's presence struck the first chords of unease in Godwine's heart. He knew Eustace of Boulogne, a cruel, arrogant Norman who shared his countrymen's scorn for the English. Now that he was Edward's brother-in-law, Eustace was all the more dangerous.

With a puffy eye and an arm in a sling, the Count of Boulogne sat next to the King, every bit the ill-treated guest. He dabbed at a cut with a handkerchief, while Edward played the champion for him.

"Do you see the condition my brother returned to me in?" said the King, already red in the face. "He wanted to go home, after visiting me in Gloucester, and your men of Dover attacked his people, killing nineteen of them. Is this how my friend and kinsman is treated?"

Godwine looked hard at Edward, trying to gauge the extent

of his anger. *Was this all pretense?*

"I will see to it that there is a thorough investigation of the matter," Godwine said, bowing. He started to back from the room.

"Who said anything about investigation?" the King barked. "I want you to punish them. I would have you show them what it means to insult the King's friends."

Godwine frowned uncertainly. "If they are found to be guilty," he said slowly, "I will surely punish the offenders."

Eustace turned a smug look on the King. "I told you so."

Edward stood, clenching his fists. "Do you dare defy me? I told you to chastise them. You will bring an army and burn the town to the ground. Is that clear enough?"

Godwine barely suppressed a gasp. Never before had Edward shown such tyranny. Again, the Earl looked around the room. Now, more than ever, the foreign threat had to be dealt with...or soon, the King's favorites would begin to treat the English like conquered subjects.

"Sire," he said, his voice even. "Perhaps Count Eustace does not realize that we have a law in this country to deal with wrong-doers. By our Law, no man can be denied justice. Just as I am given the power to govern and impose order in my earldom, so am I empowered to ensure that my subjects are protected from injury.

"If Count Eustace has been treated wrongly, the instigators will be called before a Witan and given a fair trial. If found guilty, they may well pay for the deed with their lives.

"I will deal with the situation immediately." Godwine bowed again, backing from the room without challenge.

King Edward sat in his throne, biting his lip. He knew the truth of Godwine's statement; even he did not dare violate this essence of Saxon law.

But when Godwine was gone, Eustace turned on him, barely controlling his rage. "How can you let your subjects defy you like that?"

Stung, Edward glared at him. "He is no ordinary subject. He is the most powerful man in England, next to myself."

"Or more than yourself?" The sneer was audible to everyone in the room.

"Things are different here, Eustace. The people have always had a voice in their own government."

"That sounds like something needing change, if you want to survive. How can a King be ruled by a peasant?"

Edward sat back, exhausted. "You simplify matters too much."

"And I say that if you allow even one man to dictate your terms, you have already acknowledged your weakness. Godwine must be reminded of his place."

Seeing that Edward was tiring of this discussion, Archbishop Robert leaned toward him, reviving his favorite theme. "Remember, you were never satisfied that he cleared himself of Alfred's murder."

That brought the King to himself. Edward turned and stared at Robert.

"Perhaps this is the time to give that question the attention it deserves," the Norman pursued.

Edward looked thoughtful. Robert signaled Eustace that enough had been said.

* * *

By the time Godwine returned home, representatives from Dover were waiting for him. Everyone else had heard their story, and Godwine was pulled into the house by his family, all talking at once.

"It is an insult," cried Tostig.

"They must be dealt with," said Harold.

"It's us against them," declared Swegn.

"Stop, stop, all of you. Give me a moment's rest."

Gytha pushed her way through them, giving him a mug of ale. Godwine gratefully accepted it, kissing her.

"Are you all right?" she whispered.

"Things are serious, like you warned me."

All signs of the feast had been cleared away. Godwine walked slowly into the room where six men near the fireplace turned in greeting. As one, they knelt before him.

"Up, all of you. Come, tell me in your own words what happened."

One of them, chosen as speaker, twisted his cap between nervous hands. "It's like this, My Lord. One of those Norman soldiers forced his way into my brother's house. Just knocked the door in, he did, and started shoving the children out of his way, and grabbed some food from the table as if he owned the place."

"Was he dressed like a soldier?" Godwine asked.

"Oh, yes sir. He was wearing his armor and all. He demanded that my brother put him up for the night, but my brother said no, it was his home, and no stranger was welcome in it without first asking leave. Then this Norman got mad, and slapped my brother across the face with the back of his hand, wearing his chain maille glove and all..." He looked at the others, who nodded their encouragement.

"Knocked him to the floor, he did, but my brother got right up and grabbed his axe off the wall and hit that Norman square in the chest with it. But sir, the Norman was only hurt, because his armor protected him."

Godwine nodded. "Go on."

"Well, the Norman got back up and pulled his sword, and stabbed my poor brother right through the stomach..." He turned away, shoulders heaving. One of the men comforted him, while another stood forward.

"His brother was killed, My Lord. But the rest of us heard what had been done, and we got together and faced the Normans as best as we could. Even so, we might not have done much, but Count Eustace rode up on his horse with some others, and rode that horse right into the house, trampling the wife and children underfoot like they was furniture. It was terrible, sir, them laughing and telling us the same thing would happen to us if we didn't cooperate…"

"It were too much," the first man said, stumbling back. "Our numbers were bigger than them, and we fought for our homes not caring if we died. Twenty of us died, too. But we killed nineteen of them before they ran away."

Their story told, the little group stood forlornly, staring at Godwine for help. The Earl turned to his family, who looked at him in much the same way.

"The King demanded military chastisement," he said.

The room filled with cries of outrage.

"I defied him."

His boys stopped objecting, their mouths open. Only Gytha realized the extent of the danger. "Godwine...that makes you a traitor."

Seeing his face, she was immediately sorry she said it. He looked like she had struck him.

"If it makes me a traitor, so be it. I must do what is right." The silence around him weighed heavily on Godwine's heart.

"I am with you, father," Swegn said finally, stepping forward.

The others stared, as if seeing him for the first time. "So am I," said Harold, and the others echoed his words.

Godwine looked at his family, tears in his eyes. "Then we are finally all together."

33

Godwine came out of the tent, wiping his forehead. He had not had enough sleep for days, and the pressure was wearing him down. The Earl had tried to take advantage of the time while waiting for Harold and Swegn to join him. But he was just too tired, too burdened for any kind of rest.

The town of Beverstone lay on the plain before him, surrounded by thousands of his own troops who had mustered with amazing enthusiasm. They were only twenty miles south of Gloucester, where the King sat unwarily, little realizing how serious his position was.

At least he was satisfied with the army. "Their hearts are with me," he said to Tostig, who had come up from behind. "Edward cannot ignore our cause now."

Tostig put a troubled hand on his arm; he had hoped to find his father sleeping. "Yet you seem uneasy about something else."

Godwine turned to him appraisingly. As of late, Tostig had shown more restraint than he expected. Perhaps he had learned something from Swegn's example. "You are right, son. I am very close to my home and would like to visit my parents."

Tostig was shocked. Never before had his father mentioned his family. "They are still alive?"

Godwine's face was strangely altered as he looked south. "I do not know, son."

It was rare that Godwine shared anything with Tostig. This new disclosure excited him, the more so because he alone was privy to the secret. "Then let us go. We still have a day or so before the others arrive." Tostig couldn't keep the enthusiasm from his voice.

Godwine shook his head uncertainly. "I doubt whether we will be welcome."

But Tostig was too curious about his grandparents to share his father's caution. "Come, let us go. I would like to meet your parents."

Looking at his son's eager face, Godwine's eyes cleared. He had never thought of it this way. "All right. They can only ask us to leave."

Tostig got the horses himself, unwilling to share this moment with anyone. They were soon off, Godwine leading the way, with many a backward look as though searching for an excuse not to go. Tostig was amazed by his father's uneasiness. Never had he seen Godwine so insecure.

They traveled most of the morning, crossing about fifteen miles before Godwine slowed his horse to a walk. He smiled self-consciously at Tostig.

"This is where I first met Jarl Ulf," he said, pointing to a clearing in the woods. "I was a shepherd then, and he was lost in the forest. I led the way back to his ships and he took me with him. That was the beginning of my career."

Tostig listened to his story, a little bit awed. He wondered why Godwine bothered to tell him now, after so many years of silence. But this was all his father said for the moment. Kicking his horse, Godwine trotted into the forest.

In time, they came upon a large farm. Tostig could tell from his father's face that this was his home.

They dismounted, seeing no one, and knocked on the door. After a time, an old man opened it and stared at the visitors in silence.

"Father," said Godwine.

Tostig looked curiously at the man, whose resemblance to Godwine was unmistakable. So far, his grandfather neglected to notice him.

"Thirty years," said Wulfnoth, "and not a single word."

"You told me not to come back," Godwine answered bitterly. "Have you forgotten?"

"Do you think I meant it?"

"Father, you always meant what you said."

They stared at each other, strong wills battling for dominance. Finally, Wulfnoth gave in first, changing his glance to Tostig.

Godwine cleared his throat. "This is your grandson, Tostig."

A series of emotions crossed the old man's face: hurt, astonishment, resentment, interest, followed by a smile. "A fine boy. Come inside, both of you."

Only Tostig heard Godwine's sigh of relief.

Wulfnoth busied himself trying to make his guests welcome. He poured them some ale, rummaged in the kitchen for food. When he returned with bread and cheese, Godwine put a hand on his arm.

"This is plenty. Sit, father. We came here to see you, not to eat."

Tostig knew that Wulfnoth had been trying to cover his nervousness. The old man nearly collapsed into a chair.

Godwine filled the silence. "Mother?"

"Dead these ten years. She ailed constantly at the end."

More silence.

"You have been alone?"

"Yes." Wulfnoth nervously rubbed his hands against his thighs. "Godwine...I was wrong for what I said. I have loved you all these years."

Trying to understand, Tostig watched his father cross the room, crouch at Wulfnoth's side. He thought they had forgotten his presence.

"Then why didn't you contact me?" Godwine asked. "You knew where I was."

"Son...I was just too proud. I was afraid you were ashamed of me."

Godwine looked around at Tostig. They hadn't forgotten him, after all. "I was ashamed...once. But no longer. I even named my last son after you."

It wasn't possible for Tostig to stay quiet any longer. "I'm not ashamed."

Wulfnoth looked at him, almost in awe. "You're such a fine young man, Tostig. What do you know of me?"

Tostig was at a loss for words. Godwine spoke up. "He knows nothing, father. I did not know what to tell them."

A tear found its way down Wulfnoth's cheek. "Them?"

"I have nine children. Tostig is the third."

"Then they do not know I am of common birth."

Godwine looked at Tostig. "I think they suspected."

Tostig knelt. "My brother Swegn told us." He heard Godwine's gasp of astonishment. "Grandfather...we always wanted to meet you. I am glad I had the chance."

Wulfnoth smiled. "I am glad, too. I have followed your father's career all these years. He has not shamed me, after all."

Godwine turned his head, unable to speak. In his arrogance—his selfish pride—he had endured the pain, mutely grieving, keeping his children from their own grandparents. And for what? Wulfnoth finally said what he had longed to hear, and he was so ashamed that the words gave him only pain.

"These years have aged you," he said finally, unable to express his true emotions. Too many words were unspoken; he didn't know where to begin.

"I have suffered for my pride, Godwine. I think I am close to death."

Tostig looked frantically at Godwine. "We should bring him back with us, father."

Wulfnoth shook his head. "No, son. Let us part amiably."

Tostig was about to argue, but Godwine spoke up. "Father, I am in trouble with the King. I will try to come back, but it may be a long time before you see me again."

Biting his lip, Tostig recalled their uncertain position. It was no time to drag Wulfnoth into their struggle.

"I understand, son. Even in the country we hear about the power of the Normans."

"Then you know what the trouble is about?"

"No." Wulfnoth shook his head. "But I know that you are the champion of our people. A confrontation was inevitable.

"Ironic, isn't it?" he continued as Godwine bowed his head. "I accused you of betraying us, and now you are our hero." He put his hand on Godwine's head. "Who would have thought? I guess I didn't give you a chance, son."

Tostig stared at them, astonished. He was beginning to understand. Later, as they were returning to Beverstone, he asked Godwine why Wulfnoth accused him of betrayal.

"I went with the Danes, abandoned my people," his father answered wearily. He paused for a moment, deep in thought, and Tostig had the sense not to interrupt. Finally, Godwine spoke again. "Loyalties seemed simpler then, though actually they were more complicated. At least now we know who our enemies are."

Tostig wondered whether he was right. "I don't know, father. Are our enemies the Normans, or the King?"

34

Harold rode back to camp, panting hard. "You were right, father," he gasped, before even dismounting. "Huge armies are arriving at Gloucester, led by Earls Leofric and Seward. It seems that all the north is against us."

Godwine rubbed a hand across his forehead. Why hadn't he foreseen this? What had started as a popular campaign against the Normans had twisted into a rebellion against the King. Rather than turn over Eustace of Boulogne for a proper trial by the Witan—which Godwine demanded—King Edward secretly summoned his northern earls in all haste.

The last thing Godwine wanted was a civil war. He had no choice but to wait for Edward's next move.

And the King was not long in moving; again he took Godwine by surprise. Edward sent a message to Godwine, offering to resolve their differences at a Witenagemot in London, on the feast of Michaelmas, 21 September.

Godwine agreed. He sent his son, Wulfnoth, and Swegn's son, Hakon, as hostages, and received hostages in return. His army marched to Southwark, where Godwine had his residence, and camped across the Thames from the northern earls.

By the time he arrived, the King and counsel were already engaged in a private discussion, to which the Earl of Wessex was not invited. Godwine was furious, but decided to wait them out. It was Seward who approached Godwine with the first decree of Edward's Witan. They met at Godwine's home, and Seward was invited inside, alone. Even the sons had to stay outside.

For a moment the two great Earls looked at one another. Seward had grown stouter with the years, although it all seemed to be in muscle rather than fat. His hair was long and silvery, his beard parted and braided.

Godwine, his friend noted, looked rather worn with worry.

His jaw was more angular than ever, his hawkish look harsher. "You are not as lucky as you used to be," Seward said.

Godwine laughed. "I used up all my good luck by the time Canute died." He offered a chair to his visitor.

"Ah, those were the days, Godwine. A man knew where he stood, and if he performed well, the King supported him." Seward looked hard at Godwine. "Just what were you up to this time?"

Godwine sighed. "Not rebellion. Edward wanted me to punish my subjects for standing up to Eustace's men. He wouldn't hear a word in their defense. I will not do it, Seward!"

The other nodded, bidding him to go on.

"I wanted a proper trial, that's all. I did not want to take the kingdom into my own hands."

Seward said, "I suspected it was something like that. I believe you, Godwine. That is why I tell you, in confidence, to get away from here, while there still is a chance."

Godwine stared at him. "Is it that bad?"

Seward nodded. "Edward's first decree was to declare Swegn an outlaw. You did yourself a disfavor by supporting him, you know."

"What would you have done in my case?" Godwine snapped.

The Dane shrugged. "Probably the same. I don't know."

Godwine gave Seward a long look. He trusted this man, who may have often taken sides against him, but who could be depended on to judge things fairly.

"I'm sorry, Seward. But how can the King outlaw him, when he already forgave him?"

"Kings do not need a reason. It is enough that he has the support of the Witan."

Godwine grumbled to himself, pacing the room.

"That is not all, my friend. As you may suppose, you and Harold are summoned to appear before the Witan, to answer the charges brought against you by Eustace of Boulogne…"

Godwine waved his arm in dismissal.

"And for the death of Alfred."

"What!"

The Dane frowned, expressing his distaste for the whole situation. "The Norman Archbishop Robert has not left the King's side these many weeks," said Seward in a lower voice.

"Then we are indeed lost."

After a pause, Seward said, "Godwine, even Leofric does not want to see you defeated. We all know that without you, the rest of us are nothing against the Normans. When we came south with our armies, it was to defend the King. Not to promote the Norman cause. We will not act in their favor."

Godwine stopped his pacing, and put a hand on Seward's shoulder. "Thank you. I am glad you said that." Then he began pacing again. "But if you honestly support me, why is your army prepared to pounce on mine, at the King's command?"

"Ah, Godwine, my private feelings do not always coincide with my duty. I will not let you start a civil war. Though perhaps..." Seward thought out loud, "perhaps we can manage the Witan yet, in your support. But not Swegn's cause, I'm afraid. That is already lost."

Godwine sat down, thinking. "Yes, one thing at a time. But I will not trust the King without a safe-conduct and more hostages."

"Of course. I will return to Edward with your request." Seward stood up, grasping Godwine's hand. "Good luck, my friend. I hope we can bring a quick end to this trouble."

* * *

Godwine did not conceal the danger from his sons. He called them in after Seward left, and studied their faces, one by one.

Swegn had undeniably changed after his reinstatement as Earl. His face had taken on a more serious expression, and he was much less prone to break out into a temper. Certainly during these last months, his support had been invaluable.

Next to him sat Harold, solid as bedrock, ever Godwine's support. As if seeing him for the first time, Godwine began to realize just how much he had always depended on Harold's strength, even his wisdom. If only he had been the first-born, so much would have been different.

And then there was Tostig, by far the most handsome of the bunch, with his long, curling blond hair and deep blue eyes. Ever since they visited Wulfnoth, Tostig's attitude toward himself had been more personal, actually, more intimate. He had never stopped to realize how much Tostig had needed his love.

Gyrth was the level-headed son, who worshipped Harold like a god and rarely left his side. His wisdom exceeded even Harold's, and Godwine felt sure that he would make a great governor in time, if Edward still gave them his countenance.

Leofwine was the quiet one who was a fine fighter when he wasn't buried in his books. Godwine thought he would have made a good monk, but since the boy showed little inclination for monastic life, he wasn't inclined to force him.

Once again, Gytha's words came back to Godwine. He really did neglect them when they were younger, in favor of Swegn. And now that he finally began to realize how wrong he had been, he was too busy fighting for his life, and theirs, to do anything about it.

Godwine sighed. "My sons...I am so proud of you all. Difficult times are upon us, and we need all our resources to stay out of trouble.

"Swegn..." Godwine's heart leaped at the trusting way his son looked at him. "I have some bad news for you. Edward reversed his decision, and declared you an outlaw again."

Swegn lowered his head into his hands. "I have done nothing wrong this time, father."

"I know, son. He is dragging up old grievances. Even I am to answer charges about the death of Alfred."

The others gasped, Swegn's plight forgotten.

"It cannot be," said Harold.

"What are you going to do?" asked Tostig.

"I do not know." Exhausted, Godwine sat in a chair. "The guilty are long dead, as are the innocent. I doubt that Emma would stand up in my defense." He grimaced at the thought. "I believe that Edward will go to any lengths to destroy our house. Perhaps he has been waiting all along for the right moment. He finally has his excuse with this Eustace thing, and he will not stop there."

"Father," said Harold, "we cannot give up without a fight."

Godwine looked up at him, relieved to share the burden. "Yes, Harold, I believe you are right. I have sent Seward back with a demand for a safe-conduct and hostages. We shall see what Edward does. In the meantime, think about it. There is the possibility we may have to flee the country."

The others jumped to their feet. "Never!" said Harold.

Godwine smiled; he was the only one sitting. "No, think about it, Harold. If we left in secret, think about how the others would feel. Abandoned, wouldn't you say? Without us, the Normans will be unchallenged, and will take over the King's council. Perhaps we should give them what they think they want...and more. Leofric wants to ruin us. But can he take my place? No. We have spoiled them, sheltered them from the Norman faction. Maybe it is time they saw what life in England would be like without us."

Gyrth was the one to understand first. "He is right. They will be begging us to come back before the year is out."

"There is another factor we haven't even discussed," Godwine added at the last. "Thinking our cause lost, our men have already begun to desert. Have you noticed that?"

Harold nodded glumly. "But once we give up our power, can we ever get it back?"

Godwine said, "I am certain we can. And more."

* * *

Bishop Stigand, Godwine's old friend, returned with the message from the King. Godwine invited him to dinner, in the company of his sons. He carefully avoided all references to the Witan. The bishop ate sparingly, confirming Godwine's opinion that he carried bad news.

When the dishes were cleared, Stigand turned to Godwine seriously. "You have ever been my friend," he said, "and I will continue to support you."

Godwine smiled at him, disguising his feelings. "Thank you. Your good regard has always been important to me."

Stigand took his hand. "Edward has assigned me a most unhappy task. He bids you present yourself to answer the charges already represented by Seward."

Godwine frowned. "Unjust though this is, your words are not a surprise."

"He has also denied your safe-conduct."

Godwine looked around at his sons before answering. "That is a surprise. How does he expect me to appear without a safe-conduct?"

"It is a royal command." Stigand spoke with no conviction.

"It sounds like a Norman command."

"Nevertheless, it comes from the King's lips." Stigand wiped a tear from his cheek.

Godwine pushed himself back from the table so quickly that his chair fell to the ground.

"Saddle our horses. We leave for Bosham now."

35

Godwine remembered little of the frantic ride. His mind was full of ideas, considered and rejected one by one. Still stinging, he seriously considered raising a true rebellion and showing Edward who really ran the country. Between himself and his sons, they controlled nearly half of England, and the most densely populated half at that. Their rule was more than popular; people were ecstatic in their cheering whenever a member of his family showed their face.

He had just seen how easily he could muster an army; thousands of men rallied to the Dragon of Wessex, and he hadn't even tried very hard.

But even in this most deadly mood, caution was Godwine's guiding force. Things had begun to change in England, and partly through his own doing. For the first time, the country was beginning to think of itself as a whole people, rather than separate kingdoms constantly at war. Wessex was an earldom, not a kingdom; Godwine was a governor, not a sovereign.

The events of the last week had gone far to convince him that the people respected the person of the King, over and above their private feelings for the man. Challenge Edward and he was challenging the whole country. As champion of the Saxons, this was something Godwine absolutely could not do.

Looking around, the Earl noticed that Harold and Tostig were arguing between themselves as to their next step. Harold felt the injustice most strongly, of course; he was losing an earldom. But already he was proposing the very action his father had just dismissed. He wanted to wage war on the King.

Godwine was surprised that Tostig contradicted him. If anything, he expected their positions to be reversed.

"Let us discuss this when we get home," Godwine shouted. "Pick up your pace, lest they catch up with us."

They made it to Bosham without incident, getting Gytha out of bed. She calmly listened to their discussion, then turned to Godwine. "What about Wulfnoth and Hakon?"

The others exchanged nervous glances. In their excitement, they had forgotten about the hostages.

Godwine cleared his throat. "I let Edward's hostages go. Surely he won't hurt them. They are only children."

"I suppose you are going to say he won't hurt Editha either, because she is his wife."

"Gytha...of course he won't hurt her."

"Godwine, do you think he loves her?"

He stared at her, surprised by the question. "I don't know. I never wondered."

She shook her head angrily. "Why is it that men never think about these things? Did you never wonder why they don't have children? Because they prefer not to sleep together, that's why. Edward bears Editha no love, probably because she is your daughter."

"And you think this puts her in danger?"

For the first time, Gytha showed her nervousness. "Oh, I don't know. I suppose even Edward is not capable of hurting his own wife. She hasn't given him any cause."

They gathered around the family table. Godwine took his wife's hand, pulling her next to him. "This concerns all of us. I say we trust Edward not to harm those who are already in his power. He bears me no love, but he is not a demon.

"Gytha, as I said to our sons, I believe we should get out of the country. Immediately. I suggest we all visit Count Baldwin, at least for the winter. We know we are welcome there."

Wearily, Gytha nodded, pinning up her hair. "What about our other two girls?"

Godwine sighed. "I hate to do it, but perhaps you should ask Emma to take care of them. She has nothing against them."

Harold had had enough. He stood up, leaning over the table.

"Are you just going to slink away, then? Like a dog that has been beaten? I cannot abide this!"

Godwine tried to stare him down, but failed. "Haven't you been listening, son? In time, we will get it all back through diplomacy, without shedding any blood."

"And I say that the time for diplomacy is at an end. We must drive the Norman invaders from our country, before it's too late. Let me go to Dublin, father, and raise a force there among the Irish Danes, who favor our cause."

Godwine sat deep in thought. There was some reason in what Harold said. With support from both sides of England, they could make a more effective return. And it was not a terrible idea to separate; if one of them was prevented from leaving the country, the other might remain free.

"On one condition, son. That you wait for my word before you come back. Stay the winter in Ireland. Gather support there. But do not return prematurely, lest you destroy any progress I might have made." Satisfied, Harold sat back down.

"I will go with you, Harold," Gyrth said eagerly.

"No," interrupted Godwine. "I need your counsel, Gyrth. Let Leofwine go with Harold, if he so desires."

Gyrth was flattered; rarely had his father expressed a need for him. He looked furtively at Harold, somewhat appeased.

Swegn stirred, as if shaking off an internal debate. "Harold, I have a ship ready at Bristol. Take it; it is yours."

The others stared at him. Swegn and Harold had always shared a mutual dislike, and nothing more. "I have no need of it where I am going," he added. No one gave his words much thought; but later, their import came back to Godwine with disturbing intensity.

"Why do you have a ship?" Harold asked suspiciously.

"To be honest, I never knew when Edward would reverse his sentence. I wanted to be ready to flee the country."

Godwine looked sadly at Swegn, while the others talked

excitedly.

"Then it is settled," Harold said definitely. "Leofwine and I will sail from Bristol to Ireland. We will leave after a good night's sleep. I think we will be safe until then, don't you, father?"

Godwine nodded distractedly. Edward always gave his outlawed subjects a few days to leave the country. He said, "Then the rest of us—myself, Gytha, Swegn, Tostig and Judith, and Gyrth—will go to Flanders. Yes, I think it is a good plan."

Before dawn, Godwine said farewell to Harold and Leofwine, sending them off with a tiny retinue. An hour later his housecarls were packing the remaining ships. Godwine's treasure had already been secured for easy access, and he was going to need every gold piece.

* * *

Edward could tell by the way Editha was glaring at him, that she had already heard the news. He sighed to himself, knowing how much harder this was all going to be now that she was prepared. Just where was she getting her information from?

The Queen dismissed her ladies curtly, making sure the door was closed firmly behind them. Then she turned to Edward, ready for a fight. "So," she said bitterly, "you think you have won this time."

Edward considered pretending ignorance, but abandoned the notion; Editha had grown shrewder as the years passed, until her guile exceeded his own. Indeed, this was no great feat, except that she was a woman, not a politician.

"Editha, sit down," he said calmly.

"I prefer to stand, thank you."

"As you wish. Do you really know exactly what happened?"

"I know what I need to know. That you refused to give my father fair treatment, after accepting hostages from him. That you declared him and my brothers outlawed this morning, taking away all their domains and leaving them penniless."

Edward tried to speak but she wouldn't let him interrupt. Her voice rose, grating on his nerves. "I know that you gave Harold's earldom to Leofric's son, and Swegn's earldom to your cousin Ralf. And that you gave some of Wessex to Odda, and held the rest for yourself, so you can keep my father's income.

"I know you think yourself free of my father's influence, and seek to be free of me as well!"

Daunted by her intensity, Edward was the one to sit down. He composed his face in a dignified mask, eyes hooded. Editha knew this expression by now; he assumed it whenever he was about to make an unpleasant demand.

"Surely you must see, Editha, that I cannot allow you near my side when I have outlawed the rest of your family…"

"And why not? I have done everything you asked. I have not caused a bit of trouble. Is this how you reward a faithful wife?"

"Editha…"

She closed in on him, like a wolf over its prey. "You have hated me all along, haven't you? Because you despise my father! Can't you see how unfair it all is? You have no reason to hate any of us, yet you persist in your unnatural malice despite everything we do for you."

Edward was aghast. Editha had never spoken to him like this. "And what has your father done for me?" he cried, defensively.

"He has put you on the throne, for one thing. Without his support, you would never have been crowned."

Edward shook his head vehemently. "Only after killing my brother Alfred."

"Oh, please. Not that old excuse!" She flung out her hands, eyes flashing. Edward winced, despite himself. "I saw him the day after it happened, Edward. He was nearly dead from the shock; he could barely move. No, my father had nothing to do with the murder of your brother. You do not really believe that yourself, anymore."

"That is a lie!" Edward had gone too far to retreat. "You forget your duty, wife, putting your father's interests before my own. I believe a stay in an abbey will put some sense back into your head. I am sending you to Wherwell, so that my sister the abbess can watch you. And because you dare defy me, your lands and personal goods shall revert to the crown. Perhaps after you have considered your own misfortunes, you might learn some humility."

Edward stood up, turning away to hide his triumph. He was surprised when she followed him to the door, grabbing a sleeve.

"Edward, please don't do this." Suddenly Editha was contrite, appealing to his sense of fairness.

But the King's need for freedom was stronger. "You are lucky I am not annulling you," was all he said before pulling away.

* * *

From Bosham, Godwine and his companions took a ship to Flanders. As they expected, Baldwin was on hand to greet them. The Count's face lit up as he grasped Godwine's hand. "I have been looking forward to meeting you, for a long time," he said. "You didn't have to wait until you were in trouble to come visit me. After all...we are related now." Saying those words, he took Judith into his arms. "Sweet sister." He kissed her on the forehead.

"I have wanted to come," Godwine smiled. "But didn't have the time to spare...until now."

Baldwin laughed heartily, kissing Gytha's hand. "And now you have more time than you want. Well, we shall see. I can't imagine they can do without you for long."

Godwine couldn't help but like this amiable Count. He watched as Baldwin shook his sons' hands, one by one, and made a flourish of leading them to his palace. "Come. There are a few people I want you to meet."

Baldwin's court was crowded with all types of men, but the Count made it a point to draw Godwine's attention toward a tall, well-built Norman. "That is Duke William," Baldwin whispered in the other's ear. "He is a man to watch out for. Bastard son of a tanner's daughter," he added with a grimace, "and wants to marry my daughter Matilda there, to whom he is talking."

"Son of Robert the Devil?" Godwine asked in surprise. "Estrid told us about him, before she died."

"Poor woman," Baldwin crossed himself. "Never deserved to be treated like that."

By then, they had reached the Duke. Baldwin made his introductions. "Before you leave, William, I want you to meet Godwine, Earl of Wessex."

They both bowed, and as they straightened the Duke held Godwine's eye. There was a fierce concentration in his look, as though he made it a point to memorize every detail of his surroundings.

Godwine returned his gaze steadily, trying to hide his uneasiness. He felt an intolerable threat from this man, though he didn't know why. Of course, he had heard something of William's ruthless reputation, but considering what the man had to deal with, it was no surprise. The Normans could only be ruled with an iron fist.

No, there was something else; the Duke's bearing commanded respect, even awe. But more than that, he exuded danger; menace seemed to ooze from his pores. Only when the Duke glanced away did Godwine feel released from this peril. He took an inward sigh of relief, then turned to look at what caught William's attention.

Tostig had come up beside him, grasping the Duke's hand in a hearty shake. He seemed perfectly composed in William's presence.

"Brother-in-law," he rumbled with a wolfish grin.

Godwine was astonished to see that Tostig took pleasure from

William's grimace. He was goading this man! Not for the first time, the Earl wondered at the audacity of his son—and felt a grudging admiration for Tostig's particular kind of courage.

Though he wasn't so sure this was a good idea.

36

Godwine pushed the Yule log deeper into the fireplace then straightened, brushing his hands together. He looked over at Tostig and Judith, engaged in a cheerful debate with her niece Matilda. Gyrth was listening to Baldwin discuss his collection of curious swords hanging from the wall.

And best of all, Gytha was approaching him, holding out a goblet full of Burgundy's red wine. As he reached out his hand, their eyes met, exchanging a look of love that neither time nor adversity could diminish.

"I hate to say this," he told her softly, "but I think this is one of the happiest moments of my life."

She drew him toward her, kissing him deeply. "I feel the same way. Do you know, this is the longest time we have ever spent together at one stretch?"

Godwine sighed. Gytha just reminded him how useless he had been feeling. "I got another letter today," he said, dismissing the thought. "This one was from Earl Seward, believe it or not. He told me that he disbanded his army and went home."

Gytha nodded, taking a sip from his goblet. "Then he intends to do nothing?"

"That is right. Edward's Norman friends are making enemies right and left; the King makes no move to curb their behavior. Seward has no stomach for Edward's new court, so he is going to sit back and let things develop."

"And Leofric?"

"I believe he is doing the same thing. You know, Gytha, I think my plan is working. We shall wait until all of England demands our return, then sweep the Normans out of our way."

Gytha laughed, putting a hand on Godwine's cheek. "Sometimes, I think you like being a hero."

He smiled sadly at her, with a little grunt. "Hero. Imagine

hearing you say that. How you've changed from that merciless woman who refused to have me."

"Oh, I don't remember being that bad. Perhaps you just needed to prove yourself to me."

They kissed again, but a scrambling at the door drew their attention. Swegn had just come in, and was shaking the rain from his cloak. He looked at Godwine. "Father," he said, "can you spare me a few moments?"

Exchanging confused glances with Gytha, Godwine approached him. He put an arm around his son's shoulders, moving into an alcove at the far end of the room. For a moment, they both looked out the window, watching fresh snow mix with the rain.

"You've been quiet these last few days, son."

Swegn was so deep in thought, for a minute he didn't answer.

"Is there something bothering you?"

Godwine's son turned to him, for once dropping his mask of detachment. All the pain, the grief, the remorse burned in his eyes, piercing Godwine's heart. "I am not coming back to England with you, father."

Overwhelmed with foreboding, Godwine stepped back, searching for a wall to lean against. "Son, we are all in this together."

Swegn shook his head, looking out the window again. "No. I am the cause of all your troubles. Because you stood by me, you have lost everything...even your good name."

Godwine pursed his lips. "That is not entirely true."

"It is true enough. Father, the death of Beorn and the wrongs I did to Eadgifu weigh heavily on my mind. The guilt I feel is almost unbearable. I have decided to atone for my sins by walking to Jerusalem."

Godwine's eyes widened. This sort of trip was usually fatal.

"You will not leave now! You will die of exposure on the way."

Swegn sighed. "What is the point of making a pilgrimage if I wait until it's convenient? Father, I cannot live with myself anymore; it no longer matters to me if I die. If God will receive my prayers of forgiveness, He will at least allow me to reach the Holy Sepulcher."

Godwine couldn't help himself. Before he knew it, his arms were around his son and he was sobbing like a child. Everyone in the room stopped and stared at them.

No one—not even Gytha—had seen Godwine cry before.

Swegn was overcome with emotion. He put his father at arm's length, tears running down his cheeks. "Thank you for your faith in me all these years," he said. "I will pray for you, too."

Godwine was not a religious man, but he had enough respect for Swegn not to argue further. He looked up to see that everyone else had moved closer. "Swegn is leaving on pilgrimage," he said, his voice breaking.

Nobody responded, but Godwine felt that something had to be said. "We shall all miss you, son."

Gytha turned away, ashamed. Like everyone else, she knew that this wasn't true. The only one who would miss Swegn was her husband.

* * *

Swegn Godwineson left that very night. All he took was a cloak and one change of clothing, enough food to last him a week, and a small bag of money that Godwine forced into his hand. For a long time the two stood outside together, while everyone watched from the window. Godwine seemed a bit dazed, and stared dumbly down the road long after Swegn disappeared.

"Tostig," Gytha said harshly, "go out and get him. He's soaking wet."

Grabbing a dry cloak, Tostig obeyed, though he had to argue to get his father inside. Finally, Godwine took the cloak and allowed Tostig to pull him through the door. Gytha led her husband to the fire, pushing some mulled wine into his hand and wiping his hair with a cloth. He refused to look at anyone.

"Did you think he would come back just because you were standing there?" she finally said, exasperated. Godwine shook his head, saying nothing.

"It was his decision," she pursued. "Once he returns to England, things will go much easier for him."

Those words brought him around. Godwine turned and stared at her so accusingly that she flushed, lowering her eyes. "He is not coming back." His voice was dismally final. "Couldn't you at least have given him a little love at the very end? Something? For God's sake, Gytha, he is going to die somewhere out there, and you sent him off like some mangy beast. He is your son! Have you forgotten that?"

Gytha threw the towel on the floor and stomped away. She knew he was right, and yet she was angry with him for shouting at her.

Oh, why did Swegn have to ruin the good feelings between his father and her? Especially on this night.

Standing across the room with Baldwin and Judith, Tostig shook his head. "I'm sorry you had to see that," he said. "This has been going on ever since I can remember. It is the only thing they ever fight about." He sighed. "Maybe now that he is gone, things will settle down between them. Swegn has always been causing some sort of trouble. I say good riddance to him."

Baldwin looked appraisingly at his son-in-law. Swegn had spent enough time in Flanders for him to know the man's faults; but he didn't seem all that bad. Not for the first time, he wondered if Tostig wasn't speaking from jealousy. "Surely you are being a bit hard on him," he said.

Rather than erupt in anger like Baldwin expected, Tostig grinned maliciously. "Oh, I don't know. Perhaps he is paying for all those times he was never punished. God works in mysterious ways, you know."

Baldwin nodded, thinking to himself. "He most certainly does."

* * *

Gytha thought that this argument would blow over like all the others. When she went to bed that night, Godwine refused to come with her, but she didn't worry too much about it. However, when she woke up to an empty bed, Gytha began to fret. Never had they slept apart when he was home. She quickly dressed and came downstairs, looking for him.

Godwine was sitting in the same chair as the night before. He was sleeping.

"Godwine." She knelt, shaking him. His eyes flew open, glaring at her. The anger had not passed.

"I am sorry," she murmured uncomfortably.

"Are you, Gytha? Are you really sorry? I don't think so. I think you were glad he went away, so you no longer have to face your guilt."

She bit her lip, afraid to speak. If she said the wrong thing, she might find her husband most unforgiving.

"No, Gytha. Don't even try. There really isn't anything you can say, is there?"

She stared at him, breathing hard. He was right. There wasn't. "I am sorry I feel the way I do. I have always been sorry. But it is how I feel, that's all."

"Yes, that is all," he said, turning away from her.

* * *

Sadly, things did not improve. Godwine showed little interest in anything for a long time afterward; it was as if he had started mourning Swegn's death the day his son left. He was soon on speaking terms again with his wife, although they had lost something along the way. Godwine was unfailingly civil, but she sometimes caught him looking at her in a way that made her cringe. Gytha wondered how long they could go on this way. Would Swegn have to come back before they lived once again as man and wife?

She was relieved, one morning in March, when Tostig finally talked his father into riding out for the hunt. They went with Baldwin and a large gathering of courtiers, and Godwine turned to her before mounting his horse. His face was flushed, the first color she had seen all winter.

"I feel good, Gytha," he said. "I never thought I would again."

She watched them ride off, biting her lip so hard she tasted blood.

* * *

When they returned to the castle, flushed and cheerful, Gytha came out to greet them, pleased that Godwine was still smiling. He even kissed her on the mouth. "I have a surprise for you," she said. "You have some visitors."

"Oh? From England?"

"Yes, come on, come on."

Interested despite himself, Godwine followed. When they entered Baldwin's great hall, six men stood up respectfully. They were Thegns of his from Wessex.

"Earl Godwine," said one, putting out a hand. "I have no doubt that we are only the first to come and offer our lives in your cause. We have decided amongst ourselves..." the man nodded, including his companions, "that we would rather share your exile than live another minute in the land from which you were banished."

Godwine looked at them in wonder. These heartfelt words began to thaw that hard place in his breast. The six of them knelt before him, pledging themselves as his men. Godwine went to them one by one, taking each man's hand and raising him from the floor.

Gytha watched them in silence, a hand before her mouth and tears in her eyes.

"What is happening, my friends?" Godwine asked, bidding them to sit again.

"All winter," the first speaker said, "we have been suffering the hardships of an oppressed people. The Normans raid our lands, taking what they want, killing and burning what they don't want. At court, the King is totally under their control. He listens to no one but his Norman counselors."

One of the others said, "Gruffydd ap Llewelyn feels no respect for the lands of Earl Ralf; they are not friends. The Welsh raid daily across the border into Gloucestershire and Herefordshire, plundering our lands, and the Earl makes no attempt to stop him."

"We bear the messages of our people," another one said. "They say come back home, and you will be joined by every true-blooded Saxon. They only need a leader they can trust."

Godwine looked at his wife, who nodded in silent affirmation.

"You are a God-send," he said to the Thegns. "I can't tell you what your support means to me."

The newcomers beamed at one another, basking in his approval.

Almost immediately, Baldwin's house erupted with activity: comings and goings at all hours of the night, men drilling for war, messengers crossing paths in and out. Godwine began sending petitions to King Edward, attempting reconciliation. He didn't expect much in response; but, as he told Tostig, a friendly gesture now could tell in his favor later.

Edward, of course, was covetous of his new unlimited power; he was not about to relinquish the reins of government to his father-in-law. His answers were either curt and dismissive, or else he neglected to answer at all. Even Baldwin sent a petition to Edward, along with the King of France. But still their appeals had no effect.

Godwine was soon receiving letters daily, urging him to take arms against Edward. His family watched him come back to life, grateful for any conflict that would give him something to fight for. What they couldn't understand was why they were still in Flanders. Surely the time had come?

37

Godwine was already in bed, watching his wife brush her hair. She still seemed as lovely to him as when he married her, thirty years ago. *Well,* Godwine smiled as he thought to himself, *nine children did add a tiny bit of girth to her slim waist, and her hair was colored with streaks of grey.* But Gytha's attitude was still young, and he supposed he depended on that outlook more than he realized.

She put the brush down and turned to him, enjoying his admiration. "Godwine..." she ventured.

He pulled the covers aside, patting the bed.

"What is it, love?"

"I would have us as we were...happy, close."

His face began to harden, and she hurried through her words. "I am sorrier than you know that Swegn is gone, but he did what he had to do. No one could have stopped him. Please don't go on blaming yourself. Or me."

She lay her head on his chest, playing with the little hairs.

"I thought your new enterprise in England would take your mind off our troubles. Are you afraid to go back there?"

Godwine surrendered with a sigh. "I just want to make sure I have enough support." He felt her stiffen for a second, distressed by his insecurity. Yes, it was something he was unused to, as well. Was there anything left of the old Godwine? Years ago, he would never have let his doubts assail him so; now he was nearly immobilized by them.

"I'm trying, Gytha. I do want to let Swegn go...It's just not all that easy."

"But you are aging before my eyes. Look at yourself." She got up, went for a piece of polished tin, then held it silently before his face.

Godwine looked, studying his own reflection like it belonged to a stranger. "Is that really me?" he asked, not especially concerned. The eyes that stared at him were nearly lifeless. "I didn't realize how many wrinkles I had."

"Or your grey hairs. Last year, there were none."

He pushed the mirror away. "Does it matter, Gytha?"

"It matters to me."

He nearly gave her a rude answer, but stopped himself. She was trying to make amends. He was the one who was difficult. "Come here." Holding out his arms, Godwine was surprised by how eagerly she slipped into them. She was like a puppy, unaware of why she was being punished.

Had he broken her proud spirit? In his own misery, he hadn't given her feelings any thought. There was no denying that she had hurt Swegn. But now he was hurting her. What was the point?

He kissed her forehead. "I will try to forget. For you."

Then she started to cry, making him feel guilty. This was not what he wanted. Perhaps they had both suffered enough.

* * *

By June, Godwine decided that the time had come. He sent a message to Harold in Dublin, telling him it was all right to move. Godwine planned to leave Flanders with a small fleet, as soon as word came that Harold had sailed. He had no intention of engaging Edward in battle; he wanted to raise support. With luck, he could arouse the hesitant to action.

The Earl of Wessex called his family together for a conference. Tostig was the first to appear, face glowing with excitement. Godwine looked at him blankly, saying nothing, until the rest came into the room.

"I want you all to listen closely," he said softly. "What I am planning is not a family outing. We are all declared outlaws—all of us—entitled to the worst punishment if we are captured and brought before the King. It is for this reason that I intend to leave you here."

Tostig and Gyrth looked dumbly at each other.

"It is enough that I am involving Harold and Leofwine in this enterprise. I will not endanger my whole family."

Just as he expected, his sons were on their feet, both shouting at once. Only Gytha sat impassively, nodding her head. "Your father is right," she said evenly. "If he is taken, who will be left to rescue him? Me?"

They both stopped talking, stared at her. Once again, Godwine was grateful that she understood him so well. "There is no glory in this expedition," he confirmed. "Most likely, I will be forced to compel some people into cooperating. It is not an easy thing to do, to wage war on one's own countrymen. I would spare you the pain."

"But we don't want you to do this alone," Gyrth said, less confidently.

Godwine laughed. "I don't think I will be alone. All those who came from England are going with me."

"All but us," Tostig said bitterly.

But Godwine would not tolerate any argument. He had decided, and his sons were forced to watch him sail away without them.

Though he wasn't gone for long. Before the week was out, a great gale blew up, driving his little fleet back to Flanders.

* * *

Godwine burst into Baldwin's great hall, in a much more festive mood than everyone anticipated. The servants were scurrying in with casks of ale for the travelers, and his crowd of Saxons thronged the room, shaking their wet cloaks.

Godwine found his wife, greeting her with a smacking kiss. His face was flushed, eyes sparkling with their old enthusiasm.

She smiled, overcome with relief. "Does this all mean that your invasion was a success, and you're coming back to get us?"

He laughed. "Not quite. But this gale came at the right time." He turned, rubbing a wolfhound that jumped on his chest for attention. "I had hoped Harold and Leofwine would have managed to draw Edward's attention away from us. According to plan, they sailed up the Bristol Channel with nine ships, landing at Porlock. But the local levies had already been raised against them, and gave our sons one hell of a fight."

He drank, then wiped his eyes. "Earls Ralf and Odda were still waiting for me, however. They came against us at the Isle of Wight, and things might have gone badly if it weren't for that thick mist. We couldn't see a thing, then the gale blew up and sent us back here."

"What about our sons?"

"Oh, they got the goods they needed at Porlock."

Godwine sobered, betraying his worry. "They were on their way to meet us when the storm blew up. At least the same storm pushed Edward's ships back up the channel toward Sandwich." He smiled encouragingly at his wife. "If I know Edward, that will be the end of his fleet. He will have a hard time keeping it together now.

"But I must return as soon as possible, and find Harold."

38

Godwine was amazed at the resistance from the locals when he landed on his own coast for supplies. He ordered his men to take only what they needed, and saw the fear in the defenders' eyes as they fought half-heartedly before abandoning their towns to the exiles. But he couldn't tell whether they were afraid of him or of Edward.

Fortunately, the resistance was scattered. Other towns welcomed them as if they were saviors, offering as much food and water as they wanted.

Godwine sailed for the Isle of Wight, which still held out for Ralf and Odda. Losing his patience, he plundered the island before settling in, using it as a base. The next step was to search for Harold.

Father and sons finally met up at Portland. Harold jumped down to embrace his father, then pulled away, looking hard at him. "You don't look well."

Godwine tried to smile. "Swegn left us at Christmas. He went on a pilgrimage to Jerusalem."

One of Harold's eyebrows went up; Godwine noted bitterly that he didn't look very upset. "He should have reached his goal by now, if he isn't dead," he added quietly.

"Don't say that. Swegn won't give up so easily."

"I don't know, son." Godwine sighed. "Either way, I have to go on. But it hasn't been easy."

Leofwine joined them. "All will go better now, that we are back together. Where are Tostig and Gyrth?"

"In Flanders."

Their expressions made Godwine feel defensive. "I can't risk all of you. They can join us later." He knew that his sons were taking his reticence as weakness. Perhaps they were right; but by now, Godwine didn't care. He had found out what it was like to lose a son. He didn't think he could stand losing another.

They sailed back along the coast, and this time, there was no more resistance. Word of Odda and Ralf's failure to capture Godwine had spread throughout Wessex. What's more, the King blamed them openly. No one else had risen to take their place, so the people reverted back to their natural preference to the Earl they had known for thirty years.

Not only was Godwine given free passage, but others joined him now, adding fully manned ships to his fleet. Their cry of challenge was taken up far and wide: "We will live and die with Earl Godwine!"

* * *

By the time they passed the Isle of Sheppey, every boat along the Wessex coast had joined Godwine's fleet. Hundreds strong they sailed to London, and Godwine could not restrain a smile of triumph as he looked back at his followers. The river was thick with ships, the decks packed with men ready to fight for his restoration.

"Ah, Harold," he said, putting an arm around his son. "This is a sight I never dared hoped for. Our house has not yet lost its ascendancy."

"Father," the other murmured thoughtfully, "what do we do next?"

"I don't think we have much to worry about. Even Edward cannot gainsay so many of his subjects."

As they neared Southwark, the very place from which they fled the year before, the fleet was forced to drop anchor and wait for the tide to come in.

"Harold," Godwine said, "it is not yet time for me to show myself. We shall send messages to the burghers of London and determine their mood."

Harold picked out the messengers, while Godwine stared

glumly at the north shore of the Thames. If he was wrong, by tomorrow he would be fleeing back to Flanders; he doubted whether he could ever find the resources to return. He felt his old depression creeping back.

As the hours passed, Godwine remained motionless, leaning against the gunnel; no one dared disturb him. A dense fog rolled in, as if to hide the fleet from unfriendly eyes. Shipmen went about their business quietly as possible, and a hush settled over the deck.

As the sky began to lighten with dawn, Godwine turned to find Leofwine at his side, silently supportive. He didn't know how long his son had been there. Putting a hand on Leofwine's arm, he said, "I had hoped for an earldom for every one of you."

Just then, they heard pounding hoof beats, and everyone rushed to the side, searching the mist. Bursting upon them, a messenger nearly dashed into the river. He reined in so suddenly, the animal ended up on its haunches.

"Earl Godwine," he shouted. "They are with us!"

The air was filled with deafening cheers. Godwine smiled at Leofwine, his heart swelling. London's support was the most decisive factor in this whole campaign; without it, he would never approach Edward.

But with it...

"Raise anchor," he shouted. "The tide and all of London is with us!"

He did not need to speak twice. With Harold and Leofwine at his side, Godwine was ready to face the world, and his people rushed to do his bidding.

They sailed smoothly up the Thames, coming within sight of London Bridge. At first, Godwine's throat tightened at the mob which lined the bridge and every inch of the shore. He thought that Edward had gained control after all, and they would have to fight.

But as they came closer, he could clearly hear the shouting. It was his name coming from those lips: Godwine they wanted, Godwine they would die for.

The drawbridge went up and they sailed under the bridge. The great Earl held up his hands in welcome. Recognizing him, the Londoners shouted to each other, throwing flowers into his ship as he passed. Not a hostile face was seen; they waved and laughed as though all was a festival.

However, once past the bridge, heading toward Westminster, the aspect of the crowd changed. Where Godwine had just seen the hearty faces of the citizens, now they were confronted with the grim visages of royal housecarls. Rank upon rank they stood, ready for action.

The Earl was studying them, when Harold put a hand on his shoulder. "Look," he said, pointing south.

Squinting through the breaking fog, Godwine followed his gaze, astounded to see an army gathering on the other shore, as though sprung from the very air itself. "Are we surrounded, then?" he said out loud.

"No, father, for they are shouting your name. Here are gathered your men of Wessex, come to fight for our cause."

And so it was. Even without a leader, Godwine's subjects came after him. They faced the royal army from across the river, sustaining their courage with conviction. Every man among them knew they defied the King; yet they were eager to fight, as were the shipmen. Godwine needed all his eloquence to hold them back.

"We do not want to start a civil war," he spoke to those who came to him with an argument. "The King's men yonder do not want to fight. They have no heart for it." He turned to Harold. "I say we send one more time to King Edward, and demand that he restore our rights and properties."

Everyone within hearing shouted their agreement.

Another messenger was dispatched. Edward's answer was to send ships to block Godwine's passage. The Earl quickly brought his leading vessels up, and surrounded the tiny royal fleet with very little trouble. The fog was lifting, and so was Godwine's mood as he leaned on the gunnel and surveyed the situation. There was no movement on Edward's ships; it seemed that they were waiting on events. The King's housecarls were only bolstered by a handful of northern levies; it was evident that Leofric and Seward were neutral this time around.

The advantage was with the exiles and they knew it. They dared to bring their ships to the north shore and drop anchor near Westminster.

"Now, we wait," said Godwine.

* * *

Even in his angriest moments, Edward could not inspire fear in the most timid of his subjects. Now, while he was standing with his fists clenched and eyes bulging in rage, he merely impressed those around him with his own impotence. Some of the men turned their backs on his raving; others looked almost bored, waiting for the storm to blow over.

Only the Normans agreed with him vociferously; but it was no secret that Edward was fighting their battle. What he most feared was that Godwine would deprive him of his foreign friends, and leave him isolated in an unfriendly court.

"He wants me to restore his rank and privileges? Never, I tell you! That man is an outlaw, and all of his family with him."

Bishop Stigand calmly stepped forward, speaking in a soothing voice. "Sire, not only has he surrounded your fleet, but the people are with him. Can you hear the cheering?" He stopped, listening, as did everyone else. The roar of the crowd outside the palace was as constant as the sea, rising and falling but never stopping.

"If you go against popular opinion this time," Stigand continued, "I do not believe you will find any support."

"Nonsense!" Edward snapped. "We have already called out the northern levies..."

"And they still haven't come. Sire, they do not support your cause."

"Is there no one to obey my command?" Edward blurted, in almost a whine.

"Sire," Stigand counseled, his words coaxing, "I counsel you to consider. Godwine's voice has always brought a balance to this court, which is sorely lacking now. He represents the Saxon interest, and that interest is making itself well known at this very moment."

His pointed comment against the Norman faction was duly noted and resented by Edward's advisors, who promptly crowded the King, whispering in his ears.

Bishop Stigand was undaunted. "Thirty years of uninterrupted service must bear some weight with the Witan. Let them decide."

A low murmur of agreement rose throughout the room, drowning the objections of the Normans. Edward looked helplessly at his foreign friends, who had banded together, pulling away from him. He could no longer protect them from the angry mob, and they knew it.

* * *

Every single minute seemed an eternity, as the grumbling along the south shore grew louder. Edward's men had more sense than to challenge the ships, so the antagonists faced each other warily, waiting for someone to make a decisive move.

The tension was broken by the appearance of Bishop Stigand, ceremoniously accompanied by a whole swarm of priests. The crowd parted before him and he paused now and then, blessing a kneeling supplicant. Godwine let out his breath in an explosive laugh. "Let down a plank for the good bishop," he cried, striding across the deck.

Conscious of his dignity, Stigand waited while a board was laid for him, then climbed up, grabbing outstretched hands for support. Puffing a bit, he faced Godwine, and the Earl detected a glint of triumph in his eye.

"I am so glad you are well," said Godwine, clasping his hand. Stigand drew him into an embrace. "All will be well," he whispered into the other's ear.

Pulling back, Godwine cocked his head. "Is Edward ready to concede my demands?"

Laughing, Stigand shook his head. "You are an impetuous man, Godwine. One step at a time. The King has to get used to the idea, you know."

"You mean he is stalling...buying time." Disappointed, Godwine began pacing the deck.

"I mean no such thing. Already he has agreed to a truce, until all are gathered at a Witenagemot on the morrow. You are free for now to return to Southwark."

Listening, Godwine's men began to talk excitedly.

"There will be no trouble?" the Earl persisted, dubious.

"Do you trust me, Godwine? There is more happening than I am free to disclose." He stared hard at the Earl, nodding very slowly. Satisfied, Godwine agreed. He embraced Stigand again, then walked him to the side of the ship. He smiled as the house-carls opened a path for the bishop.

Harold moved forward. "Father, there is something I would do," he said. Godwine nodded, listening, though he still watched the bishop's progress.

"I will set foot on the north bank, and judge for myself the disposition of these people."

Startled, Godwine jerked his head around; he felt a momentary panic. "Don't, please."

Harold set his mouth. "We must be sure there is no danger; it could be another trick. I will be less threatened than you."

His voice held the firm timbre of command. Godwine knew it; he had often used the same tone himself. He looked long at Harold, feeling his son's strength—and his own frailty. There was no denying it: Godwine felt old and worn, and he needed Harold to lean on.

Yet it was a good feeling to depend on a son.

"Yes, go, Harold. But be careful."

Harold gave him a quick second look before climbing down, alone. The noise of the crowd lessened considerably. Betraying no wariness, Harold walked among Edward's troops, exchanging words with those he knew. Head up, shoulders back, footsteps firm, Harold exuded a warm confidence, as though already their leader.

At first, the housecarls were confused, unsure of their loyalties. They stared at him silently, giving way before him, glancing uncertainly at each other. Few were willing to answer his pleasantries. But before they knew it, Harold's magnetism won them over, and they found themselves surrounding him, cheering and waving their spears, thumping him on the back.

There was absolutely no question about it; Godwine had won a bloodless battle.

But watching the scene from the deck of his ship, Godwine felt very little triumph, though it would have been hard for him to describe what he did feel. For the very first time, he saw a son of his win the hearts of his people, his own vassals. He watched with a sense of fatality, of seeing his own authority—his power—pass on to the next generation.

Harold influenced the crowd in a way he never had. With Godwine they had always shown respect—almost reverence. But to Harold, they gave their hearts; could this be a stronger and more lasting kind of loyalty?

Godwine felt proud of his son, and a little envious. It was a hard thing to witness one's own mortality. How could he have missed all this before?

39

Edward held out his arms to the Normans, pleading with them. "Do not worry. We shall find a way out of this."

He ignored the few cowards who were already running from the room, crying out that all was lost. Mustering his most forceful manner, the King drew himself up, facing the rest. "We must stand together against these rebels," he declared.

"Sire," ventured Archbishop Robert, who probably had the most to lose from Godwine's restoration, "it is over, at least for now. Let us go while we still have a chance." He looked longingly over his shoulder.

"No!" Edward shouted. "You can't leave me alone with them!"

The Norman gave him a look of scorn before withdrawing from the room; he tried not to hurry, attempting a show of dignity. After a moment's hesitation, the rest followed, pushing each other out of the way.

Edward moved to the window, watching the inglorious exit of the Normans; much of it happened right before him. The lucky ones managed to grab horses out of the hands of inattentive grooms. They leaped bareback on their mounts and bent low over the horses' necks, kicking them into a gallop. Men and women scattered, fleeing from the flying hooves of frantic beasts. The rest of them streamed into the streets, swords drawn, hacking and shoving their way through the crowd, searching for the quickest route to the city gates. The King gave a sly smile as he noted that the Archbishop dragged his hostages with him; that, at least, gave him some semblance of gratification.

At first, the Londoners gave way before the Normans, unaware of their intent. But soon they grasped the new situation and gave chase, howling in glee. Each Norman found a pack of vengeful Saxons at his heels, eager to tear him limb from limb, if only he would falter.

Godwine would have appreciated the commotion, if he had known what was happening. But as yet, he was watching Harold make friends with the King's men, and the exciting race was moving in the opposite direction.

But he would be informed of events soon enough.

* * *

The next morning, Godwine was on his way to the palace, already leading a horde of Londoners. There would be no tricks; Godwine was so well protected that Edward would not dare imprison him. But it soon became evident that treachery was the last thing Godwine needed to fear. He was totally unprepared for the Edward he met, sitting alone in a large room. The King was on his throne, elbows resting on the chair-arms, hands hanging lifelessly. He looked at the Earl without emotion.

"Sire." Godwine strode to Edward, knelt before him. "I am glad to be back in your service."

Godwine noticed a bitter smile flickering at the corner of Edward's mouth. "It seems that my subjects demand it," the King said.

Ignoring the comment, Godwine stood, beckoning his sons. "Would you give Harold and Leofwine your blessing?"

Edward cocked his head, looking at Harold. "You have turned into a fine man," he said, extending a hand. "And Leofwine, you have grown much since the last time I saw you."

When Harold knelt, Edward cupped his chin, studying him. "If you serve me well," he said softly, "you will go far toward healing the hurt between our houses. You see, Harold, my old advisors are all gone, and I need new ones by my side. You have your father's wisdom and courage, without the ill-will he and I feel toward each other. I am ready to open my heart toward you." He looked at Godwine. "I, too am getting old. It's too late to start over again."

Godwine tried his best to compose his face. He was astounded at the sudden favor Edward was showing Harold; he was stunned by the King's open reference to their animosity. Up until Godwine's exile, Edward had always pretended friendship, while nursing a healthy antipathy inside his heart. Perhaps now that he admitted his feelings, it would be easier for both of them to communicate.

But once again, he thought bitterly, Harold had won what he had unsuccessfully struggled for. It had been so effortless for the boy...so natural. The door was closed between Edward and Godwine; but Harold had all the advantages of position without those awful stains on his past.

Wasn't this what he had striven for? So why was he jealous of his own son?

But then again, he considered, perhaps Edward favored the son to hurt the father. Of course, once the King realized Harold's good qualities, he wouldn't be able to part with him. Clearing his throat, Godwine asked, "May I see the Queen?"

Edward looked embarrassed. "I sent for her this morning. She has been staying with my sister at Wherwell Abbey."

The Earl's eyes widened. He didn't realize that Editha had been sent away in disgrace.

"She is all right," Edward said defensively. "It was just too awkward to have her around."

"Awkward," Godwine murmured. "May I see my son and grandson then?"

Edward frowned, unable to meet Godwine's eyes. "They have gone to Normandy, as hostages to Duke William."

Leofwine grabbed his father's arm warningly. Godwine was holding his breath, his face turning red.

"Hostages?" Harold interjected calmly.

"Why yes, to ensure your father's good behavior."

Godwine's breath came out in a long audible heave. Ironically, if he had known that his boys were in the clutches of the fleeing Archbishop that very moment, he would not have been so resigned. He bowed, not trusting himself to speech.

Satisfied—even invigorated—by having won this last little battle, Edward stepped down from the dais, taking Harold's arm. "Come," the King said. "The Witan is waiting for us."

* * *

There was no place in the city large enough to accommodate all the people in attendance, so the great Mickel Gemot of September, 1052 was held outside the walls of London. The populace of England showed up to give judgment side by side with the King.

At the third hour of the day, Earl Godwine and his sons preceded King Edward in a slow parade to the platform built for the occasion. A single tall throne, surmounted by a crown and shaded with a silk canopy, indicated the place of honor.

It was seen by all that the King, as well as Godwine and his sons, were well armed; though this served only a ceremonial purpose.

Godwine began the occasion by laying his axe at the foot of Edward's throne, begging the King's indulgence in hearing his defense. Then, turning to the assembled, Earl Godwine spoke out loudly and clearly, his voice carrying a great distance.

"My Lords, my countrymen, I come to you, humbled, respectful, asking leave to resume my rightful place beside your King. Of the many accusations raised against my house, I can ask you truly: from whence came these slanderous reports? From those very men who fled at the sight of my ship masts, shamed by the deceit practiced on our sovereign.

"For four reigns I have served England. From the time of Canute, of glorious memory, I have worked hard to rid our country of its enemies, and rule my earldom as justice demands.

In this have I failed?" He paused, hoping for the right response. Fortunately, he was not disappointed. The listeners, already in favor of Godwine, cheered their support.

"And so I request, Sire," he said, turning to the King, "that you grant me and mine the positions of authority we occupied before the damaging reports. And more importantly, you find it in your heart to be reconciled with those who put your welfare and affection—nay, the very welfare of England—before our own needs and desires."

The acclamation of the people cleared Godwine of all charges. Seeing that he had no choice, Edward assumed an air of forgiveness. Picking up the axe, he gave it back to the Earl, thus demonstrating his restored favor.

The next point of business was to declare the wicked Normans outlawed, even though none were present to receive their sentences. Then it was proclaimed that England would return to the "good old laws", just as in the days when Godwine was Edward's chief advisor.

Godwine was satisfied. He knelt before the King, kissing his ring. Only Edward seemed unhappy, but no one particularly cared. For once, the Saxons reigned supreme; the dreaded Norman threat was over.

40

Godwine tried to tell himself he had much to be grateful for. He was back in his beloved Bosham, his wife and family had returned safely to England, and his popularity had reached heights he never dared hope for.

But this Yule brought back memories of his bereavement in the last. No matter how he tried, he couldn't summon up his old holiday cheer. His unease turned into alarm when on a particularly gusty night, Godwine heard a commotion in the courtyard; he had not been expecting anyone. He frowned when Eirik came in alone, betraying bad news by his expression. Godwine grasped the arms of his chair and told him to bring in the visitor, whoever it was.

He didn't recognize the man who entered, bowing. The fellow was dressed in dirty traveling clothes, and seemed exhausted from his ride. Godwine gestured for a servant to give the man a cup of mulled wine, then sent another servant for Gytha.

"Drink," he said, watching the man's every move, as if he wanted to retain this moment. He knew something significant was about to happen. The man obeyed nervously, obviously wishing himself elsewhere.

Gytha rushed in, sweeping the room with an all-encompassing gaze. "Something is wrong," she said out loud.

"Dear, this man has ridden hard to give me some news. I wanted you to hear it."

Embarrassed, the visitor concentrated on his wine. Finally, he put down the empty cup and looked directly at Godwine. "This isn't easy to tell you," he said sadly. "This sort of thing never is. But the truth of the matter goes like this: I was traveling through Constantinople, when I met your son Swegn."

The man paused, watching Godwine grab Gytha's arm; he could tell that the grip gave her pain, but the strong woman repressed a cry.

He cleared his throat. "He was on his way back from Jerusalem, My Lord, rest assured about that. Swegn did his penance all right; he looked content, like they all do when the see the Holy Sepulcher. I don't much recall ever seeing a man look so content..."

He trailed off, alarmed by Godwine's expression. The Earl's lips were drawn back tightly, making his face look like a skeleton.

"Go on," groaned Godwine, his voice a mockery of itself.

"He was very sick-like when I found him. Sick from exposure, I think. He had no shoes, no clothes, and his skin hung on his bones like there was no meat on him. But he was happy. He told me so...

"Anyway," the man rushed on, "he couldn't walk any more, so I took him in and fed him, as much as he would eat. But he died right in my arms, making me promise to come and tell you that God forgave him. That's about all." He took a deep breath, relieved to get it all out. He couldn't bring himself to look at the Earl.

Godwine was lucky the man had no more to say, because he had already fainted. Gytha remembered to pay the man handsomely before she helped the servants carry her husband upstairs to bed. The visitor didn't move for a very long time.

* * *

Godwine tossed and turned all night, and by morning he was feverish. Gytha sat by his side, replacing wet cloths on his forehead. Sleep was forgotten; nor did she allow anyone to take her place.

Surgeon after surgeon gave their assessments, came and went, but none of them knew what to do. There really wasn't a cure for an ailment such as this; Godwine suffered from grief. It was an illness that could kill its victim. But Gytha had never believed he would yield; this was the first time she had ever known him to be sick. How could such a strong man succumb to his emotions?

She talked incessantly to her husband, chiding him for weakness, begging him to answer, promising anything for just a single response. After a week, he finally opened his eyes, and Gytha was surprised to discover that she was crying.

"I am so sorry," she sobbed. "It was always my fault that I couldn't love him. I should have tried harder for your sake."

Godwine smiled weakly, though his eyes were clear. "It does me good to hear you say that." He spoke with little conviction, as if it didn't matter to him anymore. And when she encouraged him to sit in bed, he didn't see any reason to cooperate.

This went on for days. Godwine would lay in bed, staring at the walls, showing no interest in what was happening around him. Harold would come and talk to him about his earldom, and Godwine listened, nodding occasionally, but he didn't volunteer any opinion.

Finally, Harold got exasperated. "Father, are you still sick? What exactly is the matter? You can't mourn Swegn forever."

This brought some animation out of Godwine. "Someone has to," he growled, his eyes shooting fire. But still he wouldn't sit up.

"Father, we all know how much you loved him. But what about the rest of us? We need you, too."

"Do you, Harold? Do you really? No son, Swegn was the only one who ever needed me. Just look at you." Godwine struggled to his elbows. "You are bursting with good health. You have a hand-fasted wife at home who has always loved you. Your people— my own people—worship you, and you haven't any enemies. The whole world is unfolding before you, and you have nothing to regret. I envy you, son. My life is over, and yours is just beginning."

He fell back, exhausted. "No, you don't have any need for me. Look at how you handled Edward's housecarls, as though you were their King. Already you have surpassed my best efforts."

Despite himself, tears began to run down Godwine's face. "What a misery for me, though. I have wasted my life on the wrong son."

Harold stared at him, dumbfounded.

"Yes, Harold, I am well aware of it. I spent all my energy, risked everything, for the son who could never benefit from it. It should all have been for you. All for you. And if it had, just think of where we would be today."

Godwine's voice was growing weaker; Harold had to bend over to hear him. "We would be on the way to the throne, rather than struggling to maintain a hold on our position. It's up to you now." Godwine was whispering. "You must shepherd our King carefully. He has great need of your skills. And with luck, you can still find a way to succeed him."

Slurring the last few syllables, Godwine fell asleep. Harold straightened up, gazing at him thoughtfully. These words had never been spoken aloud. And yet, his father had been pondering them all along. And all along, he had kept the thoughts to himself.

Was it possible? Was it possible that a man without a drop of royal blood—of common ancestry, at that—could succeed to the throne of England? Harold wiped the sweat from his face. It was a heady thought, and dangerous. No, surely his father was still delirious. He was better off forgetting the whole thing.

* * *

After a few weeks, Godwine was back on his feet, taking control of his own earldom. But he no longer ruled with the same vigor; he tired quickly, found himself out of breath for no reason. Again and again he turned to Harold for help. Harold had a solution to every problem, and a strong arm to lean on. He took his son on every progress he made through Wessex, and Harold never complained, even though he had his own earldom to rule.

They never spoke of the throne of England again.

41

Not much was said between King and the Earl of Wessex these days. There was an unspoken truce between them, and Godwine wanted to keep it that way; he deferred to Harold whenever a potential conflict reared its ugly head.

Edward outwardly seemed to accept his old status, relying more and more on his earls to run the government. He had a new passion to occupy himself, anyway: the construction of an abbey at Westminster, intended to be England's foremost monument to God's greatness. This Easter Witenagemot would be concerned mostly with raising funds for this expensive project.

This year, out of consideration for Godwine's poor health, King Edward decided to hold the Easter Witan in Winchester. The royal castle was cleaned out and aired; it had been out of use since Emma's death the year before. A great feast was prepared, and the King and Queen came in state, happily reconciled after her return from Wherwell.

Godwine shared head table with Edward, smiling and peaceful, saying little. Harold and Tostig sat on either side of him, while Gytha sat at the women's table.

This was Edward's most sumptuous feast yet. Hundreds of platters flowed past the tables, loaded with every imaginable kind of bird, delicate eels brought from the east, elaborately decorated entremets, designed to tempt the eye as well as the palate.

The King's cup-bearer was moving to pour more wine, when one foot slipped from under him. He almost fell, but caught himself at the last moment, staggering but managing to keep the wine from spilling.

Godwine watched him, laughing. "And so one brother helps the other," he said amiably, cutting a slice of meat.

Everyone was shocked when Edward slammed down his

chalice. "And so my brother Alfred would have helped me, but for the treason of Godwine."

The smiled faded from the Earl's face. He put a hand on Harold's arm to steady himself. "Sire," he said slowly, "I do not know what brought about your comment. But so help me God, if I had anything to do with the murder of Alfred, let me choke on this morsel of bread."

His hands shaking, Godwine tore a piece from the loaf, and shoved it into his mouth. No one in the room spoke, as he chewed determinedly for a minute, staring at Edward.

Suddenly, his jaw froze and his eyes bulged. For a moment, it seemed that the Earl was joking. Then Godwine rose, spitting the bread all over himself, and fell back in his chair, chest heaving and mouth working. Harold and Tostig pulled him from the chair, pounding his back. But no more food came forth, nor could they hear the sound of choking.

Gytha ran to their side, pulling open his mouth; but there was no more food inside. Godwine's eyes rolled back in his head, and his two sons picked him off the ground and ran from the room. "Did you see that?" they could hear Edward say triumphantly to the room. "God has shown the world the truth of my brother's death. Alfred is finally avenged."

Edward sat triumphantly in his throne, expecting a confirmation from the assembly. Instead, they all glared at him, forcing his eyes into his lap. No one agreed with the King; no one shared his antipathy for Godwine. Editha stood, shunning his company. "How could you gloat at a time like this?" she cried, then ran from the room.

The King shrugged his shoulders. There were too many years of frustrated vengeance behind him. No one had mourned for Alfred when he died.

* * *

For five days they sat at Godwine's bedside, waiting for a last word. The surgeons declared that the Earl had had a stroke; no one expected him to live.

It looked like Edward was not going to set foot in the room, which suited the family just fine. But at the end he appeared in the doorway, haggard from sleeplessness. At first, everyone ignored him, despite the strict etiquette required of all his subjects. He leaned against the door frame, too spent to express any annoyance.

"I feel that I have committed a great sin," he said to the room, "in judging Godwine for myself. Do you think he will forgive me?"

They looked at the King in astonishment, then down at the pitiful body. All were shocked to see Godwine's eyes open.

"Husband," Gytha cried, throwing herself on her knees. She took Godwine's hands, but felt no response. He did not look at her; his eyes were only for Edward.

The King was drawn to the bedside, mesmerized by Godwine's eyes. He bent his ear toward the Earl's mouth; but he rose again, confused, and looked at the surgeon. "I think he is dead."

The family gathered around the bed, forgetting the King. They looked at the surgeon, who closed Godwine's eyes. Then everyone turned accusingly at Edward, who squirmed uncomfortably. *Where was their respect?* This thought reminded him of who he was, and Edward took off Godwine's dragon ring, holding it over Harold's finger.

"It is a heavy burden, but I think you can bear it," he said, trying to look stern. "As second Earl of Wessex, you will be my chief support in the Kingdom. Are you willing to take on the responsibility?"

Harold looked down at his father, so shrunken and pathetic. But, strange to say, his father's face looked more content than he had ever seen it.

He thought that he never hated Edward more than at this moment. But his father's words kept coming back. *Shepherd him carefully. Find a way to succeed Edward.* In a thousand years, could he ever think of a more fitting kind of justice?

"I will do it," he said, finally, controlling his emotions.

Smiling grimly, Edward shoved the ring onto his finger.

End of Part One

Footnotes

1. Ottarr Svarti's stanza
2. From *The Words of the High (or the Words of Odin),* translation by W. H. Auden and P. B. Taylor

Bibliography

Barlow, Frank, *Edward the Confessor*, Univ. of California Press, 1970

Barlow, Frank, *The Feudal Kingdom of England, 1042-1216*, Logmans, Green & Co., 1955

Barlow, Frank, *The Godwins*: *The Rise and Fall of a Noble Dynasty*, Pearson Education Ltd, London, 2002

Campbell, Miles W., *Queen Emma and Aelfgifu of Northampton: Canute the Great's Women*, from MEDIEVAL SCANDINAVIA, Vol. 4, 1971, Odense Univ. Press

Chambers, R.W., *England Before the Norman Conquest*, Logmans, Green, & Co., 1926

Florence of Worcester, *Chronicle*, Henry G. Bohn, London, 1854

Freeman, Edward A., *The History of the Norman Conquest of England*, Oxford at the Clarendon Press, 1870

Garmonsway, G.N., *Canute and his Empire*, Published for Univ. of London by H.K. Lewis & Co. Ltd. London, 1963

Green, John Richard, *The Conquest of England*, MacMillan & Co., London, 1883

Hall, Mrs. Matthew, *Lives of the Queens of England before the Norman Conquest*, Blanchard and Lea, Philadelphia, 1859

Henry of Huntingdon, *Chronicle*, Henry G. Bohn, London, 1853

Hill, Paul, *The Road to Hastings: The Politics of Power in Anglo-Saxon England,* Tempus Publishing LTD, Gloucestershire, 2005

Holinshed, Raphael, *Chronicles of England, Scotland and Ireland*, Henry G. Bohn, London, 1807

Hume, David, *The History of England*, Little, Brown & Co., Boston, 1863

Jones, Gwyn, *A History of the Vikings*, Oxford University Press, 1984

Larson, Laurence Marcellus, *Canute the Great*, G.P. Putnam's Sons, 1912

Lawson, M.K., *Cnut: The Danes in England in the Early Eleventh Century,* Longman Publishing, London & New York, 1993
Mason, Emma, *The House of Godwine: The History of a Dynasty,* Hambledon and London, 2004
Oman, Charles, *England Before the Norman Conquest,* G.P. Putnam's Sons, New York, 1910
Stenton, F.M., *Anglo-Saxon England,* Oxford at the Clarendon Press, 1971
Sturluson, Snorri, *The Stories of the Kings of Norway (Heimskringla),* Trans. By William Morris, Bernard Quaritch, London, 1894
Turner, Sharon, *History of the Anglo-Saxons,* Logman, Brown, Green, Logmans, 1852
Wernick, Robert, *The Vikings,* Time-Life Books, Alexandria, Virginia, 1979
William of Malmesbury, *Chronicle,* Henry G. Bohn, London, 1847

Historical fiction that lives.

We publish fiction that captures the contrasts, the achievements, the optimism and the radicalism of ordinary and extraordinary times across the world.

We're open to all time periods and we strive to go beyond the narrow, foggy slums of Victorian London. Where are the tales of the people of fifteenth century Australasia? The stories of eighth century India? The voices from Africa, Arabia, cities and forests, deserts and towns? Our books thrill, excite, delight and inspire.

The genres will be broad but clear. Whether we're publishing romance, thrillers, crime, or something else entirely, the unifying themes are timescale and enthusiasm. These books will be a celebration of the chaotic power of the human spirit in difficult times. The reader, when they finish, will snap the book closed with a satisfied smile.